W9-BLK-632

SEP 1997

SECOND LIVES

SECOND LIVES

A Novel of the Gilded Age

....

Richard S. Wheeler

A TOM DOHERTY ASSOCIATES BOOK

NEW YORK

SECOND LIVES: A NOVEL OF THE GILDED AGE

Copyright © 1997 by Richard S. Wheeler

This book is printed on acid-free paper.

A Forge Book
Published by Tom Doherty Associates, Inc.
175 Fifth Avenue
New York, NY 10010

Forge® is a registered trademark of Tom Doherty Associates, Inc.

Library of Congress Cataloging-in-Publication Data

Wheeler, Richard S.
    Second lives : a novel of the gilded age / Richard S. Wheeler. —
1st ed.
        p.   cm.
    A Tom Doherty Associates book.
    ISBN 0-312-86333-0
    1. City and town life—Colorado—Denver—History—19th century—
Fiction.   2. Tabor, Horace Austin Warner, 1830–1899—Fiction.
3. Baby Doe, d. 1935—Fiction.   I. Title.
PS3573.H4345S43   1997
813'.54—DC21   96-53275
                                                               CIP

First Edition: May 1997

Printed in the United States of America

0 9 8 7 6 5 4 3 2 1

To my treasured friends
Alston and Diana Chase

It matters not how strait the gate,
  How charged with punishments the scroll,
I am the master of my fate:
  I am the captain of my soul.

—W. E. Henley
Invictus

My soul is a dark ploughed field
  In the cold rain;
My soul is a broken field
  Ploughed by pain.

—Sara Teasdale
The Broken Field

SECOND LIVES

CHAPTER 1

. . . .

Lorenzo Carthage, better known to readers of the *Rocky Mountain News* as Lorenzo the Magnificent, stepped from the parlor car into the waiting arms of Denver. He flipped a silver dollar to the porter, and wished he hadn't. Old habits died hard.

He drew his velvet-trimmed black cape around him against the autumnal chill and hiked through steam, past the chuffing *Breckenridge,* a Mason double-truck locomotive of the Denver, South Park and Pacific, and into Union Station. He passed through its cavernous confines unobserved, unlike several former occasions when reporters, gossips, and pests mobbed him, and emerged at the hack stand beyond. A line of cabriolets awaited, but he chose to walk, the weather be damned.

He proceeded down Seventeenth Street past the grim barns of the horse-drawn street railroad, crossed Holladay Street, which exuded the aroma of sin, and continued another block to Larrimer, where he turned southwest to Sixteenth, and reached his destination, the elegant new Tabor Block. He entered that gaudy mercantile palace, glad to escape the bite of the wind, and pulled off his black silk top hat, which protected his bald head. He was thirty-three, and had been bald as an egg since his twenty-eighth birthday.

On the fifth floor he paused before a door of pebbled ground glass that announced the firm of Zagreb and Zagreb, dealers in precious metals, gemstones, jewelry, and curios. He had been there before, but only to buy. He entered, and was immediately greeted by Zagreb Senior, whose first name Lorenzo could never master.

"Ah, Mr. Carthage! In from Leadville, I see. Now, what may we do for you? A little Christmas gift for . . .'' He judiciously did not complete the sentence.

Lorenzo the Magnificent was in no mood for banter. He pulled a two-and-a-half-carat headlight diamond stickpin from his paisley cravat and placed it in the soft white palm of Zagreb. "How much can I get for that?" he asked.

Zagreb examined the stone, turning it this way and that under his magnifying lens. Then he sighed. "Two hundred dollars," he said softly.

"Two hundred dollars! I paid fifteen hundred for it."

"Unfortunately, not to me," Zagreb said. "It is a formidable stone, yes? But inferior in several respects. See that yellow tint? See its dullness? See the odd cut, which conceals a flaw in the plane hidden from sight?" He shrugged. "I would not keep it, myself. I'd auction it in a bulk sale, and hope to get three hundred for my trouble." He handed the pin back to Carthage.

"Let me see some good stones under your glass," Carthage said.

Zagreb obliged him. The better diamonds dazzled white or blue, shattering light. The headlight diamond glinted yellow and seemed to suck light into it.

"All right, two hundred," Carthage said tightly. What more blows could befall him?

"Well, ah, I'm not sure I want it. But since you've been a good customer, I'll buy it for a hundred sixty. You could try other dealers, of course. I can recommend—"

"Take it."

Zagreb nodded, extracted eight double eagles from a black cashbox, and put the headlight diamond on a tray. "Do you want a receipt?"

Carthage shook his head and stalked out wordlessly. He descended flights of stairs, which mimicked the downward spiral of his fortunes, and emerged into the chill of Larimer Street at a loss for a future. He had expected a thousand dollars, cash enough to do some trading in mining stocks at the Exchange and so restore his fortunes. No one knew the mines better than he.

He had intended to stay at the Windsor Hotel, the posh palace down the street, but now he couldn't. He could choose the American House, but it wouldn't save him much. The sad truth was that he would have to check into some dollar-a-day fleabag. He didn't even know where to find one.

He debated what to do, and found himself walking down Larimer to the Windsor. It might be wise just to be seen there, hobnobbing with powerful men. Appearances counted. He could imbibe a whiskey and branch and think things over. Maybe he would spot a friend or meet a future business associate. Most of those he met in the Windsor would not know of his misfortune.

The gilt and marble of the Windsor comforted him as he trod the red plush lobby toward the walnut-paneled hotel saloon. The elegant Windsor was his kind of place, the luxury as familiar to him as his own body. But somehow it seemed different this time, as if its doormen were waiting to pitch him into the street if he neglected to pay his tab.

He found himself the sole customer in the saloon, which reminded him it was only ten in the morning. But he ordered a rye anyway, and settled into a plush leather banquette seat to sort things out. This morning's encounter with Zagreb had been the final blow, the murderer of hope. He sipped the rye and found it to his liking, well served with ice in a large tumbler.

A year ago he was one of the richest mining magnates in Colorado, half owner of a fabulous Leadville mine, the Pandora. He had discovered it himself, boring twenty feet into the fabled ridge that had made Horace Tabor rich, uncovering rich carbonate ore in awesome quantities. To capitalize his discovery he had sold a half interest to a Boston syndicate, and within months the Pandora was yielding a clear profit of a thousand dollars a day for the partnership, his share being five hundred. He had been pocketing fifteen thousand each month, and he was not yet thirty years old. He had plunged into his new life exuberantly, investing in surrounding mines, building himself a manse, entertaining lavishly—he had hosted virtually every mining king, politician, demimondaine, and investment banker in the West, and these caviar affairs had won him his reputation in the sensational press as Lorenzo the Magnificent. He didn't really mind the sobriquet.

But his opulent life and fabulous mine had not gone unnoticed. The owners of adjoining claims filed apex suits, alleging that the vein of carbonate ore being mined at the Pandora actually apexed on their own claim, and therefore the ore belonged to one or another of those neighboring mines. That was an ancient ploy, and Carthage hired a battery of attorneys to take care of the matter, mostly by filing countersuits alleging that the neighboring mines were extracting ore from a vein that apexed on the Pandora. Carthage continued to bank a fortune, somewhat diminished now that he was paying for a posse of lawyers and a gaggle of expert witnesses.

Still, being a prudent man, he began investing widely in new mining ventures in the Leadville district, looking for another bonanza just in case the present one should be stolen from him by greedy neighbors.

Here his luck went sour, and he found himself a part owner of a dozen barren diggings. He envied that Leadville legend Horace Tabor, whose extravagant investing simply multiplied his fortune. One by one, the mines in which Carthage had bought an interest failed.

Then the price of silver declined, putting pressure on his profits, and while that was worrying him his Boston partners brought suit against him for alleged mismanagement, the result of which was a settlement giving the capitalists 75 percent of the now-diminished profits of the besieged Pandora. The end came when the Pandora lost the most crucial of the apex suits and was obliged to repay the neighboring Fanny Mine the entire value of ores removed, and to surrender remaining underground reserves. The Pandora failed. Its lawyers sued Carthage for unpaid services totaling a hundred twenty thousand dollars, and cleaned him out just ahead of the Boston syndicate, which sued him two hundred thousand for fraud and mismanagement. The sheriff took away his red brick manse, his vintage wines, his sterling silver and Haviland china, his furniture, his blooded drays and carriages, and his shares in worthless holes in the ground—one of which, the Morning Glory, proved to be a new bonanza when the new owners had recently pushed the shaft three feet deeper and hit carbonate ore worth three hundred seventeen dollars a ton. That blow, in particular, plunged him into a melancholia mixed with moments of rage.

Thus did Lorenzo Carthage fall from the pinnacle of life and a net worth of half a million to oblivion in a few breathless months. Now, in November of 1882, he sat in the Windsor's saloon, nursing his rye and rage, and resisting self-pity as best he could. There were lawyers he would gladly roast on a spit, and mine operators he would cheerfully hang from a gallows. But it did no good to think about them and their perfidies. His sole option was to start over. He had a few gold coins in his pockets, fifty thousand of debts—if indeed he actually owed anything, which he doubted—and a little clothing in a trunk at the Express office.

He nursed his bleak memories in the hotel awhile more, and then trudged up Fifteenth against a vicious north wind, heading for the Mining Exchange, the Denver stock market. He intended to establish some sort of living ere this day was over. The exchange, located in a ramshackle brick structure off Arapahoe, turned out to be quieter than he had expected. Men with blackboards posted bids and offers for mining shares, and the business proceeded in a soft drone. Inquiry directed him to the president of the exchange, a man with a pugilist's broken nose named Beall. There Carthage learned he could buy a seat for a thousand dollars and do his own trading; or he could work as a commission salesman if he were well connected and had lots of prospects; or he could work in the sweaty pit as a hired trader for a small commission against a weekly draw.

"But you'd need experience for that," Beall said, eyeing Carthage's luxurious clothing. "No trading firm would hire a . . . dilettante."

"Well, I know the mining companies—I've bought dozens—and a man must start some place—"

Beall shrugged. "Go ahead. Talk to anyone. No one minds. Maybe you'll find whatever you're looking for."

Carthage did, inquiring wherever he could, careful not to interrupt trades. No one recognized him, but he didn't expect them to: the Pandora had been a private partnership, not a public stock corporation. It all came to nothing. He wasn't a trader, and no one could use him unless he had connections.

He plunged into a bleak afternoon, knowing the clock was ticking and soon he would be out of cash. He took a room at the American House, not quite ready to give up a modicum of comfort, and had his trunk shipped from the Express office. It irked him to room in the second-best hotel.

The next days he sought clerical jobs, but skeptical managers examined his velvet-lined cloak, shiny shoes, silk hat, and paisley cravat and turned him down. One afternoon he took the five-cent horse tram out to the smelters northwest of town and tried his luck at the Argo, the Omaha and Grant, and Globe Smelting and Refining. In each case he told the hiring boss he knew mining and metals, but those rough men eyed his clothing, his soft hands, and turned him down.

He ran through his double eagles in a hurry. The American House wasn't much cheaper than the posh Windsor. Each evening, after another feckless search, he repaired to the saloon at the Windsor, hoping to make some sort of connection, find an owner who needed an experienced manager, find a broker who would train a new salesman.

One evening he did run into a mining man he knew, Jerome Wallheimer, operator of two successful, if small, carbonate mines outside of Leadville.

"Well, Jerome," Carthage said after they had downed a drink and exchanged some gossip, "I was wondering whether you could use an experienced mine manager."

"I'm always on the lookout, Carthage."

"I'm looking for a position."

"I don't think so. Not you."

"The Pandora was the most productive mine in the district, and I had a hand in that. It made a fine profit until the apex litigation cut into it. I'd be there still if we hadn't lost the apex suits. You can't fault me for the failure of the lawyers."

Wallheimer stared amiably at the bald younger man. "On the contrary, Carthage. Protecting a valuable mining asset from apex suits is the most important task a manager faces. *Nothing* is more important. If you lose, you lose the mine—as you and your unfortunate partners found out."

Carthage nodded unhappily. He had not paid enough attention to the ongoing lawsuits, nor had he ever opened negotiations with his rivals to deal his way out of trouble.

Wallheimer slapped him on the back. "Stay out of trouble, old boy," he said, and drifted off.

That was a bad moment, but Carthage persisted in his quest at the Windsor's saloon. He told his entire riches-to-rags story to a few whose boots rested on the brass rail beside him, but it wasn't the thing to do. No one wanted to hire a failure who had lost a fortune for himself and his partners. All he accomplished was to consume more rye than he could afford and make himself a pariah.

In desperation, Carthage bought ready-made work clothing from the Toiler's Friend clothing store, trousers of jeancloth, a scratchy woolen shirt, a knitted cap. Then he tried again, and this time won himself a job as a wheelbarrow man for two dollars a day at the Argo smelter.

"You don't look like you've done a lick of stoop labor," the boss at the Argo said, "but I'll put you on for two or three days and we'll see. I doubt that you can take it, but I need a working man."

"I've toiled, sir. I was a prospector for two years and developed a successful mine at Leadville."

The boss grunted, obviously not believing a word.

Lorenzo the Magnificent checked out of the American House with six dollars to spare and no place to go. He didn't know where or how to live on a two-dollar daily wage, but he knew he would be learning some hard lessons.

CHAPTER 2

. . . .

That first day at the smelter proved to be the longest in Lorenzo Carthage's life. His task was to shovel hot slag removed from a small furnace used to process refractory gold ores, and wheelbarrow it to a slag pile outside. They gave him a canvas apron and heavy gloves, but these didn't suffice to keep him from suffering burns on his face and ankles and forearms. Smoke from the slag scorched his lungs as he shoveled, and popping sparks made his task miserable. A dozen times he thought of quitting on the spot. Why on earth was he doing this grim work for two dollars a day? He knew why: it put food in him and a roof over him.

He persevered, trying to conserve energy, but the shift had scarcely run two hours before he wearied. Stubbornly he kept at it, and worked especially hard when the hiring man wandered by for a long squint. There were three others in the furnace crew, but Carthage barely got to meet them. He lacked funds for a lunchpail but had invested in some bread and cheese, which he devoured during the break. When the twelve-hour shift ended, he gratefully hung up his apron and headed into a raw overcast twilight.

He hiked back to the boardinghouse he had found north of the South Platte River in a grim district filled with other boardinghouses, corner saloons, and a few modest cottages. This place offered a narrow room with a cot for five dollars a week. It had a wash stand at the end of the dark hall, and a privy out back. No heat reached the rooms except through open transoms, so the denizens mostly left their doors ajar, the contents of their rooms vulnerable. It was a living, but just barely.

Carthage at first considered it a stopping-place on the road of life; he would find a better way to live as soon as possible. That's what he had told himself when he engaged the room and had draymen deliver his trunk. Except for a barkeep, all the men in the boardinghouse worked in the smelters to the north.

Carthage collapsed into the bunk that first evening, too weary to wash or eat. He had made two dollars, an amount he had casually tossed to serving people in his previous life. He would make twelve dollars in the week, pay five to his landlord, spend sixty cents on tram fare to the smelter, and most of the rest on food. He didn't know how he would replace his clothes, which soon would be ruined by sparks. He would need a little for a weekly bath at any of the local tonsorial parlors, and a little for a haircut. There might be enough for him to have a few ten-cent mugs of sour pilsener at the corner saloon on a Saturday night—which would constitute his entire social life.

He intended to dress up each evening and hike over to the Windsor, where he would mingle with the powerful and affluent, meet the right people and repair his fortunes. He was, after all, an experienced mine manager. But the first day on the job disillusioned him. He didn't even eat supper, and was asleep in moments although his aching body kept wakening him in the night. Then, a week into the job, all his glad rags vanished from his trunk, and he no longer possessed the clothing to walk through the front door of the Windsor Hotel, much less mix with the gentlemen there.

So, he thought, he lived among thieves. And yet they were not really criminals; just men so close to the edge of starvation that they took what they could. Back in that other life he had paid his miners three and a half dollars a day, and now he couldn't imagine how they supported their families with so little. No wonder they highgraded a little ore and their wives took in sewing or laundry.

The loss of his gentleman's attire hit him hard. He stared at the empty, perfidious trunk, knowing that a wall had risen between him and his previous life, between him and the classes of men and women he had enjoyed as a successful mining mogul. He could suspect any or none of those silent, surly men in the cubicles around him, men as weary as he.

With his first pay envelope he bought another week's rent and re-paired to the Home Saloon on the corner to suck a mug of suds. Here, at last, he found a shred or two of pleasure. Saturday nights offered working men a brief respite from their toil: a pocket full of pay, a chance to sleep late the next day, and some society, if only with other males. None of the corner saloons had any women in them, and Carthage wondered where a man could even meet one.

Until that first Saturday evening, he had barely had a chance to think. He had toiled, eaten starchy vittles, and fallen like a drunk into his bunk, only to begin the routine again before dawn. But this first payday he bought a bath ticket at the barbershop, scrubbed himself in some lukewarm gray water, had himself tonsured, and then headed for the corner saloon. It all seemed a wild luxury, even to a man who had devoured tins of caviar and cases of champagne.

Now, while sipping the sour beer, and surrounded by cheerful men with Slavic, or Bohemian, or Italian names, he again pondered his fate.

One thing seemed plain: it had nothing to do with justice or injustice. He was not being punished for a vicious nature or for maltreating other persons. He had paid his miners the prevailing wage, made sure of their safety with adequate timbering and air, contributed to Leadville's crying needs, including the volunteer firemen and an infirmary, kept a few sick or injured men on wages for long periods, and had handed out quarter-eagles to beggars.

Neither could he discover any grave defects of character: he had always worked hard, kept himself from excess. He was neither a drunk nor a voluptuary. But these assets had not kept his world from collapsing over him. No, justice had no part in it. Courts of law, the ploys of lawyers, the influence of some busy, busy politicians and scoundrels, envy, the greed of neighboring mining men—things like that had settled his fate.

And now he saw no way out.

"Well, Carthage, how do ya like the real life?" asked the hulking man next to him. Carthage recognized his neighbor at the boarding-house, a smelting furnace man named Vinovich.

"Real life?"

"Yeah, working-stiff life. Two dollars a day life. Not like the life of Lorenzo the Magnificent, eh?"

"The Magnificent?"

"Yeah, Carthage. You're the one wot was always in the papers, you and your big parties, the soirees, as the Frenchies call 'em. We all spotted that when you come in. Hard times for the Magnificent, no?"

"Temporary."

Vinovich laughed. "Temporary," he said. "You gave bigger tips than you get in a day of hard work at the Argo. Temporary is permanent. You know why? Because you never get ahead. You're always behind. Always owing. All of us, we stole your fancies in the trunk and sold 'em for a few dollars. So arrest us, heh? We done you a favor. As long as you got them fancy rags, you think you're better'n us. Now you don't, Lorenzo the Magnificent."

That riled up Carthage. "There are ways out for anyone who wants to make a better life. That's what the West is for. That's how people get ahead in this country. I'm here until I can figure out better."

Vinovich chuckled. "I like you, Magnificent. Lemme buy you a mug. You're looking parched."

"No, let me buy you one, Vinovich."

"There you go, back to your old ways, charity for the tradesmen."

"No, ordinary friendship."

"Okay, Magnificent. How you gonna bust out? You tell us. We'll bust out with you. Show us this here ladder to the hoity-toity life, and we'll foller you right up it."

Vinovich hollered at the keep and pointed at the empty mug. Moments later a full one, leaking foam, slid down the bar and halted miraculously before Carthage.

"Thank you, Mr. Vinovich."

"It's Janos. Janos Vinovich. So how are we going to get us a fancy living, Magnificent? Rob groceries?"

"I started as a prospector."

"Yeah, so where do I get a mule and all the rest? And how do I feed myself? And what do I do when I can't find ore? It's all over. You know what it's down to now? The Celestials. The Chinee are working the tailings for two cents an hour. You know what a prospector is nowadays? He's a bindlestiff with a shovel."

"Either one of us could file a homestead claim and farm."

"Farm! Where do I get plow, mule, harness and seed and some eats while I wait for them beans to grow? Magnificent, you gotta do better than that."

"You could put a little aside and speculate with it."

"Speculate! I buy me some numbers every payday, like now, and never win nothing."

Carthage sipped and pondered it. "You have to find your own way. I have to find mine. I only know that down-and-out people, working people like us, they find a way, and nothing stops them but themselves."

"Magnificent, I like you. You're a sentimentalist."

That was a pretty good description, Carthage thought. His own grip on this new reality was slippery.

Several weeks later on a cold winter day of 1883 Carthage wheeled some hot slag out the timber trestle to the pile. His barrow wheel hit a rock, the slag slid out of the barrow and started a fire on the trestle, which burned for twenty minutes before a foreman and some furnacemen chopped it out.

An hour later the foreman sent Carthage down to the front office, where he was given a brown pay envelope containing six dollars and a pink slip.

"I was right," the hiring boss told him gruffly. "Now get out."

· ·

ose Edenderry wept again. Every time she sat before the little altar she had fashioned on her bedside table, the tears welled up anew, as if she had never cried before. She buried her face in her hands and felt the hot tears on her cheeks.

She missed Andre so, but he was gone and would never return. He had died of consumption two weeks earlier, after a long, slow, miserable decline, weeks of coughing up blood, spasming on his sheets, gasping for air, swallowing Dover's powder and finally drinking a tincture of morphia to numb the maddening pain.

After she had buried him in his best black suit, there wasn't much left. The final decline had consumed his faro bank faster than it had consumed his lungs. Now she had only her little altar, a tintype of him taken a decade ago in New Orleans, even then a pale wisp of a man with a somber countenance, as if the knowledge of his early death were in his eyes.

The tintype was embraced by an ornate silver frame, tarnished now. And she had woven sprigs of balsam, which she supposed was the aromatic Balm of Gilead, about the frame to make a fragrance. And before the tintype she had placed his gold cuff links and his silver pocket watch, upon which were engraved the mysterious letters *A. V. et V. V.*—Andre Villard, and . . . a wife, perhaps.

He looked so handsome, so mournful and slight, in his silver frame, not like the skeletal consumptive she had tried to feed and wash and comfort at the end. They had met in Leadville three years earlier, in a glittering Harrison Street saloon and pleasure palace. She was a serving girl, he a tinhorn. She hated that word. Andre was a gentleman. His table was shrouded in peace, even amidst the roar of the saloon.

Even then the consumption ate him, and he bloodied one handkerchief after another, a dozen in an evening, furtively concealing the carmine stains from the players. But she saw it whenever she served the table. She yearned to heal him. She had that instinct in her, to mend every broken wing of every frail bird. It wasn't long before she had her chance, moving in with him, cooking greens and herbs for him, and comforting him in all the ways a woman could.

But Andre, really, was the stronger. He had saved her life, or at least had given her three good years. Before she moved into his little flat at the age of twenty-five, she had been rushing toward her doom and didn't know how to stop herself. She had been a serving girl in mining camp saloons for as long as she was old enough to be inside of them. She didn't know how to do anything else. She hated the thought of marriage, when there were so many bright nights ahead, so much banter and fun, so many men to enjoy, and so many big tips to tuck into her pocket. She knew she was wild, but she loved to soar to the skies and paid no attention to the darker side of life, such as when she was hauled into a pokey as a drunk, or when men propositioned her and wouldn't take no for an answer.

She had loved to sip a little whiskey as she worked, getting giddier as the evenings progressed. She had sampled other things, too, the powders derived from the poppy, and had sailed into the heavens each time, filled with an ephemeral joy that made her heart overflow. She loved male company, and loved moments of intimacy, but took care never to become a "bride of the multitude," as certain women were called. She swore by all the saints she wouldn't do that.

But that didn't mean she would never comfort a man, especially one who came to her shyly, asked her to share a cup of tea, and told her all about his lonely life far from his sweetheart in the East. Men like that she sometimes comforted in her arms, liking to watch their faces soften and their manner become tender and gentle after her comforting. Sometimes they tried to leave coins with her, but she let them know she would never comfort a man for cash, but only because she liked him, and liked the moment. All the saints in heaven knew that Rose Edenderry would never comfort for money. But the men sometimes gave her a gift, some fruit, or a bottle of wine, and she liked that.

But such a life wasn't without pain and danger. Wherever she drifted, she would end up with a reputation for being easy, and then she would have to fend off men who wanted to party, and sometimes have trouble with sheriffs or constables. Then she would drift somewhere else—until she got to Leadville, and fell into Andre's arms.

He had a strange ability to stop her spirals up or down. A soft word from him was all it took. It was as if he had an extra eye, always upon her, and when she had sipped too much, sometimes early in an evening, he would ring his brass bell to summon her, and simply say, "It's time, Rose."

And Rose would turn over her trade to other girls and go home. She always did. She never defied him. When he slipped into their flat later in the night, she had returned to quiet sobriety, and they had an hour or two to enjoy each other before sleep. In all their months and years together, she had never again gotten really drunk, had never sampled opiates, and had never comforted anyone but Andre. And during the whole time, she had never worried about sliding into the gutter, or ending up a Bride of the Multitudes, or being fined as a common drunk. Andre had been the ultimate comfort.

They had two and a half good years in Leadville, but his consumption worsened steadily, and finally he couldn't breathe in that nine-thousand-foot altitude, or keep his frail body warm during the long, brutal winters. They said that Leadville had ten months of winter and two months of late fall. Rose begged Andre to go to Denver where it was warmer and lower, but he wouldn't, and then it was too late. Andre Villard sank steadily.

She cared for him in their little flat in an alley off Harrison, rubbed balm upon him, bought herbs from a mumbling old woman and made fragrant steams with them, but Andre sank. Often he stared at her from fevered eyes, tears forming in them, his lips shaped into gratitude and despair. They didn't need to talk; there wasn't much to say now. He had shown her where he kept his dwindling faro bank, and she had paid the rent and bought stove-wood and food with it.

And then Andre died while she held his gasping frail body in her arms. And entering the tomb with him was that strange commanding force that kept the wild winds at bay in the soul of Rose Edenderry. His death saddened her, but it also frightened her. No quiet voice with iron in it would ever protect her from her own appetites again. It was only a matter of hours or days before that wild spirit would flap its wings in her cage, and cry to the skies to be let loose. She could even say when: the day she ran out of cash and started serving again.

Nothing anchored her to any place or thing. Her mother, dead five years, was an Englishwoman. Her father, an ungovernable Irish romantic, had been hanged for sedition against the Crown in 1872. She thought she took after her cheery, reckless father because she couldn't govern herself, and also because she loved the whole world so much. Sometimes, in her loneliest moments, a vision of her parents flooded into her mind, and with it an acute delight in their shepherding, and their cheerful hearth, and the two living sisters and dead brother she had left in County Offaly. She had loved Andre madly, and his mildest compliment had sent her into transports of joy. His gentlest request won her instant accession. Where had her own will hidden in all this?

Now, in her grief, she was tugged this way and that, wanting to soar to the wild aeries, yet wanting to be governed so that she would stay out of trouble. Andre's cash shrank alarmingly, and finally stark necessity forced her out of her mourning and into the streets of Leadville. Most saloons opened their doors to men only, but she knew she could find something. Women were scarce in mining towns. She would do better in Leadville or Gunnison, or even Pueblo, which wasn't a mining town at all but one of the wildest places in Colorado.

She found employment at a saloon and dancehall in the heart of the sporting district. She had never been a dancehall girl, but she thought it might be a good change. The girls got half of the two-bits for each dance, plus tips. She wasn't very pretty, a little thick with a shapeless nose, but she had a winning smile, a great softness, a womanly bosom, and—her real glory—a crown of chestnut hair that she washed until it glowed.

"Come in at four and work to midnight," said her new employer, whom she knew only as Jacob. "Most of the dollies wear full skirts they can stomp around in, and a white blouse. You'll get the hang of it. You try to push drinks, see? Get the galoots to sit with you and buy you one. Then you order two, and you get colored water—tea—and he gets the varnish."

"But what if I want a drink, too?"

"Then you gotta pay extra." He glared at her. "I don't want drunken dollies. You make trouble and you're outa here."

"If I get tea and the bozo pays for booze, don't I make something?"

"Nope, and don't try. You get one-bit a dance and tips. Some girls make a lot that way. You're grown up; you can figure how to get big tips. Other dollies make a little extra. That's their business, not mine." He squinted. "I don't like trouble. Keep the coppers off my back. Don't cheat the customers."

She nodded. Some dancehall girls were bad. She didn't intend to be one of those.

She showed up early so she could talk to some of the girls beforehand, and learn what to do. She discovered that most of them were just off the boats and spoke little English. Dancing was one thing they could do in the new world without knowing the tongue. But one called Irma promised to show her how.

At five the "perfesser" settled himself at an upright piano and began banging out waltzes and schottisches, but it wasn't until nine or so that Rose finally got her first dance. An unshaven miner whose body was rank handed her a dance ticket and spun her around to a polka while she smiled brightly and tried to glide to his awkward rhythms.

"How about a drink, honey?" she said. "I think you're good company."

"Yeah, sure, dolly."

"I'm—Aggie, call me Aggie."

"Sure, Aggie. Let's have us some of that turpentine they call booze."

"It's a dollar for two."

He shoveled some coins out of his pocket, and she headed for the bar. "Gimme two. Gimme a real one, too," she said.

"That's four-bits out of your take, sweetheart."

"Yeah, I know, but a girl gets thirsty," she said.

CHAPTER 4

he shiver of the lobby door drew Homer Peabody, Esquire, away from *Ben Hur*. Hastily he hid Lew Wallace's novel on top of a file cabinet, adjusted his frayed cravat, and opened the frosted glass door to the small waiting room. There, to his astonishment, he beheld the most striking young lady he had ever seen; certainly the fairest ever to walk into his humble chambers. His swift inventory revealed a costly green suit and a diamond solitaire big enough to obscure her ring finger, and an unearthly, chiseled, oval face framed by a riot of silky hair.

"Ah, what may I do for you, madam?"

"Consult with me."

"Very well, give me just a tad. Some things to wind up."

She smiled, and light filled the gloomy room. "Thank you. I'll read the *News* while I wait."

"I'll be with you directly."

He closed the door, amazed by the apparition beyond it. Hastily he dug into his file cabinet and extracted folders, briefs, a stack of correspondence, and scattered these across the naked black walnut table. He opened his rolltop desk and laid on the blotter an unfinished letter inviting a law student to clerk for him.

He pulled a small looking glass from a drawer in the rolltop desk and examined himself, worrying about spinach on his teeth, unruly hair, grimy collar, and dandruff on the shoulders of his thick black suit. The face in the mirror disappointed him. It always did. How could a fifty-five-year-old man with serious prostate trouble look like a boy? In spite of silvery hair and jowls and bags under his bright blue eyes, he somehow managed to look about seventeen, a phenomenon he couldn't explain.

At last, dissatisfied with himself, he let her in and marveled at this creature who settled herself in one of his battered swivel chairs across the table.

"Welcome, madam," he said effusively. "Let me tell you that never in a long life have I met such a fair and gracious example of the gentle sex."

"Yes," she said.

"Peabody here, and whom do I have the honor of addressing?"

"Cornelia Kimbrough. Mrs. Walter Kimbrough."

He knew the name. "Ah, indeed, you're the younger Mrs. Kimbrough."

"Walter's trophy."

"Ah, yes, trophy. Now how may a counselor be of service?"

"I want a divorce."

"A divorce. From your husband, I presume."

She eyed him as if he were crack-brained, and he regretted his unruly tongue that embarrassed him whenever he was rattled. Women did that to him, especially stunning women.

"Well, not from my Irish setter," she said, finding humor in it.

They laughed, enjoying rapport. "May I ask how you found your way to my door—who recommended me?"

"No one did. I hunted up the most obscure attorney in Denver. The Kimbroughs own all the rest of them—and all the judges too." She smiled. "Don't take me literally. It's just that the Kimbroughs are, well, prominent, and connected with just about everyone, and I need someone like—you."

"You've put it most graciously, Mrs. Kimbrough. I find that if one avoids connections and influence, one can practice law with a certain independence and fidelity to the highest standards."

She laughed, but not unkindly. "Mr. Peabody, when you wish to divorce a Kimbrough, you face certain realities. Such as banking, finance, railroads, gold and silver mines, the Denver street traction company, the waterworks, the electrical power company, city real estate— probably this building—the Denver country club on Cherry Creek, the Republican political machine, the judges, and—"

"The judges? Surely, madam, the Kimbroughs don't influence judges."

"Well, they play poker with judges, lose games to judges, tell the governors who to appoint—"

"You are a very knowledgeable and sophisticated young woman," he said. "You've chosen to engage independent counsel. Well, I won't disappoint you. I've practiced since the age of twenty-one, first in Crawfordsville—that's in Montgomery County, Indiana—and then here since eighteen and seventy-eight."

"Do you win regularly?"

"Well, ah, no."

"That settles it. Every attorney known to the Kimbroughs wins regularly. There isn't one who confesses to a lost case."

He sighed. It would have been better to tell a small white lie. All his life he'd been cursed with an honest tongue. Now, surely, she would rise, shake hands, and depart.

"Perhaps you should look for other counsel—"

"No, that's a good answer. I trust you more than all those ambitious sharpers around Walter Kimbrough. How do I get a divorce?"

He gazed at her, stricken by her smooth face, glossy chestnut hair, merry eyes, svelte figure, and perfect ease. She was one woman who'd been around men.

"We bring an action. He responds. There are three grounds—cruelty, desertion, and, ah, adultery. I presume that one or another of these little difficulties fills the bill?"

"Mr. Peabody, Walter is a rat. He makes me miserable by ignoring me, and enjoys doing it. The trouble is, he's never struck me or locked me in the closet, he's home most nights, and as far as I know he's never even looked at another woman. He's not the type. I have no proof of any misconduct."

"I can't imagine why any mortal male would not be at your side, devoted to your happiness, alert to your every need, Mrs. Kimbrough."

"He prefers his dog."

"Have you children?"

She wasn't quick with an answer. "Two little babies were stillborn," she said softly. "After that . . . we'll discuss that later."

"Divorce is painful. You'll need to steel yourself. Most of all, we need to make a case. The world frowns on divorce. Some states forbid it entirely, except for adultery. But Colorado's very permissive. Perhaps it would be best if you'd think back through your marriage—how long has it been, five or seven years? You must be about twenty-five—and make a note of every time he disappointed you. We must collect every fact. He'll have everything going for him in court, I'm sure."

"Are you sure you can do this? What are my chances?"

"Life is full of frustrations, madam. I could tell you our chances are

slim if you lack grounds, but that would be a most unfortunate view-
point. We must be courageous and bold. I must have facts, witnesses,
evidence, times, places. Together, we can triumph. Faint heart never
won a lawsuit.''

"I thought the saying is, faint heart never won a fair maiden.''

"Well, I was paraphrasing.''

"Are you married?''

"No, no—''

"Were you?''

That did it. He didn't want the case. "Ah, Mrs. Kimbrough, perhaps
you'd better find an attorney closer to your preconceptions.''

She waited, her lips lifted wryly.

"Somehow, Mrs. Kimbrough, the blessed estate of matrimony passed
me by. It is my deepest sorrow, the yearning that torments me in the
small hours of the night. The years of hope passed by, turned to decades, and now I fear the joy that is the ordinary portion of life for
other men shall never be mine.''

"Were you ever engaged? I'm being brazen, I suppose.''

"Oh, when I was twenty and enrolled at Wabash College, I was smitten by a sweet girl named Emily. I asked her for her lovely soft hand,
and she said no.''

"Did she say why?''

"Yes, she did.''

"Well, why?''

"I don't know that I can say. Perhaps I'm the wrong attorney for
you.''

Cornelia waited, that wry smile lifting her lips again.

"It was because—she said I lacked passion. She said that if I'd shown
less respect—ah, I phrased that wrong; this is most difficult. If I'd
crushed her to me and kissed her madly and let her know I was mad
for her, she'd have kissed me back and said yes. That's what she said.
But you see, I respect womanhood. Emily wanted me to be, ah, almost
improper. I would never do that—be improper. One must respect and
protect the gentler sex. It was very hard to let go. I was so fond of her.''

"Fond of her!''

"I mean, I loved her deeply, and truly, heart and soul, put her on
a pedestal; she was the fairest example of womanly virtue and gracious
conduct I had ever met, the flower of your sex.''

"Take it from a woman, Mr. Peabody—may I call you Homer? Most
women don't like to be put on pedestals. That's where I am. Take it

from me. When you think of a woman, don't think of saints. You weren't born of the Virgin Mary, Homer."

"Ah! This is improper." He glared at her, not caring what she thought. "Now, Mrs. Kimbrough, tell me about your marriage, what you want by way of settlement, and what grounds you think we can develop."

"I'll make some notes and come back tomorrow, Mr. Peabody. I should've prepared better, but I didn't really know what was needed. I don't care about the settlement. All I want is my liberty. I think the ground will be desertion, if you can make that case about a man whose body still lives in the same house with me, even when his thoughts are off on the West Slope or Antarctica. And we haven't discussed fees." She stared at him. "Say, are you listening?"

"I am most certainly listening to every word. The fee will vary with the amount of work. I charge three dollars an hour."

"I can afford it, I think," she said.

"I can't guarantee results, but I always give my best to each treasured client."

"I like you," she said. "Even if you don't know anything about women."

CHAPTER 5

The blank paper rebuked Cornelia Kimbrough. She had sat with pen in hand for over an hour, trying to come up with the incidents, times, places, witnesses, and recollections that would give Mr. Peabody his case and win her freedom. And yet, each time she pursued some tenuous thread of memory, it all dissolved into nothing. Years of wedlock should have yielded plenty of material, but in fact the whole time seemed more like a featureless plain without landmarks.

A good image, she thought. She had met Walter Kimbrough at her own coming-out party, thrown by her suddenly affluent parents. Her father, Davis Montfort, had made a killing speculating in real estate along both sides of Cherry Creek, and had emerged as a leading light in early Denver. She could scarcely remember a time when she lacked comfort and luxury, although she was nine or ten at the time the Mont-forts could move from a white cottage to a spacious brick home just a few blocks from Capitol Hill.

She was flattered that Walter Kimbrough came. The Kimbroughs dominated Denver, set its tone, directed its hectic growth, and funneled the awesome gold and silver of the mountain hinterlands into the bold city on the plains. She had reached maturity surrounded by suitors. She didn't really believe she was pretty, but the whole world insisted she was. In her own mind she was really a young woman who made use of her assets, with a smile that displayed even teeth, rowdy eyes given to bold stares, and reckless hair that defeated her efforts to subdue it, giving her a faint air of disorder.

One awful boy told her she had a bedroom look. She didn't quite know what that was, but she redoubled her efforts to defeat her unruly features. Her father had insisted on a public schooling, and she had dutifully attended classes and graduated at seventeen, high in her class, a Latin scholar. After that the matchmaking began. Finding a proper husband was the thing for a socially prominent young lady to do, and she plunged in with her usual gusto.

Walter Kimbrough didn't appeal to her, although he had the virtue of being an adult among half-baked callow youths. He had inherited his family's business acumen and had already plunged into a world of fi-nance and enterprise while the rest of her beaux had barely decided what to do with their lives. He seemed rather uninterested in her, and never asked her questions or turned the conversation to her own life or that of her family. Instead, he would talk of mining shares, or raising capital to extend the tramway to a new subdivision.

Still, he seemed to enjoy her company, and took her out to dinner, and seemed especially pleased when one or another Denver financier complimented her—and even more pleased when they complimented him for having her on his arm. He was always decorous, and never embarrassed her or took the slightest liberty. She rather wished he would; she tired of being a china doll and would have liked to experi-ment with some kissing as long as they were a steady twosome.

She liked his father and mother more than she liked him. They weren't a bit stuffy and welcomed an acceptable young lady into their home. When at last his expected proposal came—after a lovely dinner—she said yes, as she expected she would. She wasn't exactly in love, but Walter Kimbrough had a maturity the other young men lacked. Her parents were openly promoting the match, but of course they were thinking of his family's wealth and prominence. She accepted, shed a few tears of doubt, and was married on Christmas Day, 1877, in the Kimbrough mansion.

During her honeymoon she realized it had been a mistake and she should have heeded her doubts. He was as warm as an iceberg, as intimate as a stockholder's meeting. The simple, stark reality was that Walter wasn't interested in her other than to have a desirable woman on his arm at social occasions. He was bored soon after the honeymoon trip and found ways to dodge her and surround himself with business cronies.

His lovemaking had been perfunctory and had left her empty, lonely, unfulfilled, hurt, and insecure. She had dreamed of warmth and tenderness and ecstasy. She had encouraged friendship and intimacy. But she had gotten none of those things; only a young stranger who came less and less to her bedroom and dinner table and parlor, and spent more and more time at his club or in the fashionable saloons with business colleagues, or off on one trip or another to the mining camps burgeoning all over the mountain hinterlands.

She finally managed to get pregnant, more or less by seducing him, but that ended miserably five months later in a miscarriage and a long despondency. She managed pregnancy one more time, this one going nearly full-term and ending with a stillborn girl. She was too desolated even to cry. After that, she stopped trying to woo him and settled into a bleak isolation, yearning for a real husband, yearning for love and attention and kisses, yearning for ordinary friendship.

She wasn't wholly isolated: on occasion, he used her. That was how she saw it. He took her to balls, or great parties, as if she were some porcelain object, a Ming vase to show off before envious colleagues; his trophy. This stranger of a husband always turned warm for the few hours they shared Thanksgiving with the senior Kimbroughs and Walter's brothers and sisters each year, only to slide into his indifference afterward.

It wasn't a life. She ached for more. As far as she knew, he wasn't unfaithful to her, except in the most terrible sense of all. She meant nothing to him. Neither was he cruel except in the most terrible sense. She meant nothing to him. And neither had he deserted her except in the most terrible sense of being utterly apart. He wasn't present in the marriage.

She stared at that blank paper, wondering what on earth she could come up with as grounds for a divorce. She supposed many women would be thrilled to be married to Walter and would enjoy having all the money they wanted, all the luxury, access to all the most interesting people. Such women would be amazed that Cornelia was unhappy. More than unhappy. She lacked even the consolation of children.

Some women would enjoy a husband's indifference and would build a life of their own, virtually unencumbered by marriage, traveling through Europe, or going from spa to spa, or getting involved with charities. But Cornelia wasn't like that. She designed no secret life for herself, no backdoor romances, no illicit lover, no violation of a sacred vow. Nor would she ever become the sort of cynical woman who gathered others of like mind around her, belittling her husband and rejoicing in his absence.

She stared at the blank paper, feeling defeat. She could not remember one thing in those several years of wedlock that amounted to desertion, cruelty, or adultery, the grounds available to her. Somehow, some way, she had to make them work—or suffer an agony. Ruefully, she set aside her pen, gathered her purse and a parasol against the fierce summer sun, and set out across town to consult with Mr. Peabody again. Maybe he could find a way.

He greeted her in exactly the same way, making her wait a few minutes while he pretended to be busy. She didn't mind. She rather enjoyed the courtly, genteel old attorney, and thought he might be effectual this time, even if he usually wasn't.

"Ah, Mrs. Kimbrough," he said, waving her in. "Now we can begin. I trust you've written a bill of goods."

"No, I haven't."

"Surely some notes, some incidents, some witnesses?"

"No."

Nonplussed, the attorney settled back in his chair and waited attentively. She liked that. Carefully she described a life as a neglected wife, a woman trotted out on certain occasions to show off, and then turned back into her own lonely domain. She talked about the stillbirths, about having so little to do because maids and a cook did all the chores, about his long trips, the brief happier moments with his family on holidays, her efforts to find something useful and meaningful to do to fill the aching hours, the abuse, such as it was, of being isolated and ignored, kept out of her husband's male business world.

He took no notes at all. "Ah, Mrs. Kimbrough, you can think of absolutely no episode you could describe as cruelty? Did he ever shout at you, or hit you, or embarrass you before others, or demean you, or imprison you, or . . ." He shrugged.

"No."

"And he's never abandoned you for extensive periods or failed to provide for you?"

"Never."

"And you believe he has always been true to you?"

"He's not the type to wander."

"Ah, forgive me, but has he been a husband? Has he performed his marital duties?"

She smiled at the old bachelor's way of expressing it. "Walter is a perfectly capable male," she replied. "He just isn't very interested in any of that."

"Was this always so? This seems the best material we have to work with."

"I had a pleasant honeymoon," she said. "He was trying to be attentive. But later I had to, um, encourage him."

"You have separate chambers?"

"Don't most people?"

He didn't answer. "Has he come to you for, ah, the marital bliss, regularly?"

She enjoyed this. The topic was making Mr. Peabody distinctly itchy. "We haven't been together—we haven't made love in three years, if that's what you want to know."

"I see. Is this your wish?"

She laughed for an answer, and he fidgeted.

"I take it then that he's derelict in his duties."

She laughed again, not able to help herself. "If he considers it a duty, Mr. Peabody, I would not want him in my arms."

"I see. You've ah, never discouraged him?"

She smiled wryly. "I've walked into his chambers wearing little more than a smile, carrying a bottle of champagne and two glasses, and found him preferring the company of his dog."

The attorney sighed softly. "We'll have to build our case on this, Mrs. Kimbrough. Now, of course, this is going to be embarrassing for you. It's a public court, and the press is going to cover a divorce of Denver's most prominent young couple."

"I would rather enjoy telling the whole world about it."

"You would?" He looked as if he could barely swallow the idea.

"I would enjoy the headline in the *Rocky Mountain News*. 'Kimbrough Spurns Advances of Beautiful Wife.' "

Homer Peabody swallowed and peered at some spot on the floor near her feet. "Your husband doesn't know what he's . . . It says somewhere in the Bible that one mustn't throw pearls before swine."

"Mr. Peabody, you're one of a kind."

"I'm going to try to make a case on that. I think we'll be hard put for precedent, but I'll know better after some research. But we could perhaps call it desertion, or maybe even cruelty. And it nicely leaves a presumption of infidelity, though we won't pursue it."

"You think I can win a divorce?"

"With the right judge, the right precedent, and some corroboration. And if he doesn't contest it. Or maybe we can work out a separation or an agreement to divorce and present it to a judge. Now, if you can find some way to corroborate this, so it's not simply your word against his."

"I don't want a separation. What good would it do me? I'm already separated! And I have no way to corroborate it. These things happen in the privacy of our second floor."

"Well, you have a maid, I take it?"

"Two."

"And they do the linens and laundry?"

"No, we send them out to the Chinaman."

"Are your maids on duty at night?"

"They don't live in the house, no."

"Tell me about the stillborn children, if you would."

"Well . . ." For once she felt helpless. "I was with child the first time soon after we were married. I miscarried at five months. And the next time . . . long ago."

"You know, he'll use that to rebut you. He may say that after the second loss, you, ah, closed your door to him."

"But it's not true!"

"It's something to think about. You must put on your thinking cap. Ransack your memory." He sighed, as if saddened by some memory. "Some men have treasures lovelier than the *Mona Lisa* and don't even appreciate them."

She couldn't quite say why that moved her, but it did. Maybe it was the first real appreciation she'd heard in years.

"There, there," he said, handing her a fresh handkerchief. "I'm sorry to upset you."

"Mr. Peabody, if you knew me better, you'd know I'm not upset," she said, dabbing at her cheek.

"We'll win your freedom for you," he said. "I'll file as soon as I can."

CHAPTER 6

. . . .

Homer Peabody saw Mrs. Kimbrough to the door, retreated to his swivel chair, turned down the lamp wick until the flame blued out, and buried his head in his hands in the dusk. Her visits had stirred an ancient sadness in him, and he needed a few minutes to cope with an old, old sorrow.

He wished he could shed a few tears, but he was a fifty-five-year-old man and tears were beyond him. His walk upon the earth hadn't turned out very well, and now he was getting along, suffering from an enlarged prostate that was gradually shutting off his water and would kill him some day after a final agony. The future would be as bleak as the past.

Self-pity wasn't fruitful and he didn't intend to indulge in it. He would live out the rest of his months and years as best he could, with the same external cheer and courtly manner. He would give his few clients the same undivided attention, and tip his hat to the ladies in the same gentlemanly way. He would practice the best law he could, earn a sufficiency—if only that—to survive, and avoid the poor farm. He would conceal his psychic pain from public view, and when the physical pain became intense he would conceal that, too, perhaps with opiates if necessary.

He would lie in a lonely grave, the end of a line of Peabodys. He would leave behind no wife or children, only an older sister back in Crawfordsville who might not survive him. No one would miss him. No children or grandchildren would visit his last resting place. No beloved wife would lie beside him for eternity. There would be nothing on his headstone but a name and dates, because he had accomplished so little and would not be remembered for any great achievement.

He could not say with any certitude how his life took a wrong turn. But the failure to live well had started very early, surely in his youth when his parents still governed his life and established its moral and spiritual tone. He knew only that he suffered from an excess of virtue, an oversized conscience, a plenitude of shyness which worked to inhibit him, dampen his natural male spirit, and render him indecisive in law and a hopeless wallflower socially.

He suffered most in his relationship to women, and could not explain how that came about. Mrs. Kimbrough had stirred all that anguish once again, and she would every time they met. Somehow, in the space of a minute or two, she had gotten out of him things that he had never told anyone all these years. And she would no doubt guess the rest: that he was an elderly virgin, had never lived intimately with a woman and could not ever do so, having long since fallen into bachelor ways. He was a biological dead end, giving nothing to the future of the human race. Her grace stirred something in him, made him ache to be young again and find a bride. But that was all an absurdity now. No woman would want some jowly, balding old fogy who had to go to the water closet about once an hour and dribble for three minutes.

For a few more minutes he hid in darkness, flashing scenes from his life upon his mind like stereopticon slides: now his slim nervous mother and then his phlegmatic merchant father, then his sister Marcia, then his first law trials when he wore his hair slicked down with goose grease and tried to impress the owlish judge with his erudition. And then the years when he learned he wasn't much of a litigator because he wasn't as relentless as other attorneys, was too polite, too conciliatory, too inclined to look at rights and wrongs instead of doing whatever it took to win. He sighed. A whole life. There wasn't much to be proud of.

He lit his lamp again. He would need to research the case law, finding out whether sheer neglect could be interpreted as desertion or cruelty or some other valid defect in a marriage. He wanted desperately to win for her, to give her the freedom she yearned for. Maybe, with luck, he would stumble on something that would win the day. But he knew the odds, even if she didn't. She had come to him full of hope, little knowing what sort of attorney she had selected.

He was as futile at law as he was with women. He cursed the excesses of virtue and conscience he had been born with. In Crawfordsville, practicing at the Montgomery County courthouse, he had been a joke. No one willingly came to Homer Peabody, such was his reputation as a loser. He survived mostly as a court-appointed attorney for impoverished men accused of crimes, and more than one of them had laughed in his face and said that his appointment doomed them.

That hurt, because he had a penchant for thorough research and an ability to see the weaknesses of the other side and exploit them. But let a defendant privately confess to him that he was guilty, and Homer Peabody would talk the man into pleading guilty. Peabody could not imagine justice any other way.

Late in life he removed to Denver, hoping to begin anew in a robust, barely christened state where reputations didn't sink a man and one could try a new approach to life. But things went even worse in Colorado than in Indiana. Here Peabody met more than his match in lawyers less scrupulous and less civil than in old, settled Indiana. The law of tooth and fang ruled here, and a genteel, courtly old man didn't stand a chance. He became a joke again. His practice was soon reduced to drawing up wills and business agreements because litigation stumped him. And in Denver his loneliness and isolation tormented him worse than ever. At least he had roots and childhood friends and family ties in Crawfordsville. In Denver he became a sad and lonely atom of mankind.

He set to work reading law, wanting to please Mrs. Kimbrough. He hadn't felt such a need in years. The young woman seemed like some holy vision bestowed upon a forgotten, suffering man. He remembered everything about her: the nuances of voice, the things she found amusing, the grace and ease, the unconscious self-possession that told the world of her status in life. He built a little altar around her in his heart. He could never have the affection of a woman like her, but by some miracle she had come to his shabby office and had engaged him, and had even taken an interest in him, old flabby Homer Peabody with the soft white jowls and falling hair.

He ransacked his law books, wanting precedents, strategies, ways around judges who interpreted common law strictly, and especially cases in which neglect itself was grounds enough to grant a divorce. It turned out to be a bootless quest. Mere neglect wasn't much of a ground to sever the sacred bonds. What's more, Cornelia was rich and privileged, and her husband had not cut her off from funds or neglected her comforts. He was simply an oaf with a heart of stone and the obsessions of the robber barons who seemed to infect commerce and enterprise these days.

Walter Kimbrough was a blind man before Venus, a deaf man confronting a Beethoven symphony. But one thing he wasn't: if the facts were as she presented them, he wasn't vulnerable to divorce.

Peabody felt a sort of impotent rage rise in him. How could this rich lout of a man ignore a woman like Cornelia? Especially in a universe in which love didn't come to all mortals, and some, like himself, were impoverished beggars in the blossomfields of bliss. He dreaded what he would be obliged to tell her. He would say that she had no case. It was not in him to fudge, or to say things not quite true. He had never done that. It was his best opinion that she would waste time and substance pursuing the hopeless case. And that would be that. He would charge her ten or fifteen dollars and never see her again.

He made one final search of the case law at the prestigious firm of Denver lawyers Dilworth and Atcheson, who occasionally extended him the courtesy of their library. He said nothing of his case, of course, nor did they ask him. Every man in the firm was connected in multiple ways to the Kimbrough interests. He always chatted with them a moment or two, absorbing their cheerful and slightly condescending banter, knowing full well their tone would be very different if he were a formidable adversary.

He found nothing helpful there, either, and then, employing a messenger boy, summoned Mrs. Kimbrough to hear his counsel.

She came at once, and the sight of her renewed Homer Peabody's sense of his own futility.

"Well, Mr. Peabody?"

"I've searched the case law. There's little of it in Colorado—it's still a rather new state. I've searched American and British common law. I'm sorry to report that ordinary neglect of a spouse, while a most reprehensible habit, is scarcely a ground for divorce. It can't be construed as desertion or cruelty."

"Oh. But surely there's some way—"

"There really isn't a way. But there are some judges who enjoy novelty and don't feel quite so oath-bound to uphold law. I'll pursue some novel avenues, if you insist, but don't count on success."

She eyed him. "You know, Mr. Peabody, my husband's lawyer friends say there's always a way around anything."

"There is, Mrs. Kimbrough. But I believe that justice is sacred and not to be tampered with or bent or twisted."

"Uh, where in all this idealism is your wish to win a case? Especially my case?"

"It's very powerful, madam, and never more so than in yours. You are not only abused by an uncaring man, but a gift of God to whomever you chose for a mate, a woman divinely purposed for wifehood, for comforting a man, for raising fine, sweet children, for—"

"Oh, Homer!" She was laughing at him. He didn't really mind so much. The only moments in his life when he became oratorical and poetical and sublime involved women. Give him an hour in court, and he could turn women into saints, into patient mothers, loyal sweethearts, envoys of peace and goodwill, bosom friends, with sacred natures and pure, holy bodies. He loved to expound on women, and sometimes did so in court, where he had a captive audience.

"I mean every word," he said.

"Mr. Peabody, you just take this case anyway. You go tell the judge everything I've told you about my marriage, such as it is. Don't appeal to precedent if there is none; just appeal to his common sense, to his gallantry."

"I'll do that, Mrs. Kimbrough, but I won't promise results. There is, in law, something called equity, which is simply justice on its merits, rather than on precedent or even on statute. I can proceed along those lines, but it would be sheer novelty in a divorce case. May I ask why you continue with me? You could employ dozens of attorneys more suited to achieve your purpose."

"I like your integrity," she said.

"By any chance, Mrs. Kimbrough, do you privately wish to lose? Is this divorce action intended merely as a threat to your husband to awaken him to your discontents?"

"No, I'm dead serious. Almost every other lawyer in town's beholden to the Kimbroughs. There'd be conflicts of interest. But I would still have choices. Plenty of lawyers in Golden and Boulder and Central City. There's something in you that appeals to me. You've a dignified and honorable way about you."

Homer Peabody blinked back the feelings he could never display to her.

But then she brought him back to earth. "Mr. Peabody, you have a strange perception of women. You turn us into saints. Beautiful little mothers ruling our little domestic kingdoms with some sort of God-given virtue. What sentiment! We're not like that. We're mean and selfish sometimes, and I'm sure we enjoy things that would dismay you.

"Chew on that for a while. I think if you would investigate us, you might find out that we're not what you think and we don't belong on pedestals. It's a way of denying our nature, you know, putting us up on pedestals while you men run around and do as you please. When you put us up there, you're really saying we're the weaker sex."

"I—hadn't thought of that," he said. "Thank you for illumining my thoughts, Mrs. Kimbrough. You inspire me. We all must grow, lift our vision to the horizon. I wish the world were filled with lovely women like you, brimming with grace and courage and virtue. Women like you could change the human race for the better."

She smiled, wryly. "That's what I like about you, Mr. Peabody," she said.

CHAPTER 7

. . . .

The prospect of imminent starvation had a wondrous effect on the energies of Lorenzo Carthage. He caught a tram back to central Denver but did not stop at his boarding-house, where his rent would come due Saturday. He meandered the shopping streets, looking for help wanted signs in the windows and finding none. Every day, newcomers flooded in from the East, all of them with visions of a new life in a new state. Jobs were scarce.

A better idea would be to find temporary employment among the rich. They were always looking for a man to perform some sort of humble task. So he hiked toward Capitol Hill and the formidable homes of the city's most prominent citizens. And there he beheld the rococo mansion of his old Leadville friend and colleague, Horace Tabor, and his acerbic wife Augusta. Why yes! Tabor had bought that place and was busily transforming Denver with his Tabor Block and opera house and other vast construction projects.

Carthage decided to visit his friend and ask for a job. No, no, he would do better: he'd ask Tabor for a grubstake. He'd start over, locate a new claim. Hadn't Tabor given hundreds of out-of-luck miners a grubstake? And hadn't a few of those grubstakes made Tabor the richest man in the West?

Carthage fairly danced toward the mansion, his body and soul alive to new possibilities. He was greeted by Augusta herself, who looked him up and down with distaste.

"Is Hod Tabor present?"

"And who are you?"

"Lorenzo Carthage from Leadville. I once owned a mine—"

"Oh, you want a grubstake. A handout. You all do. Well, you know how to get one. I never saw a man so ready to throw away money."

"Mrs. Tabor, we've met many times socially—"

"I don't recall it."

"May I speak to him?"

She peered at him from half glasses perched on a long nose. "I suppose you're the only mortal in Colorado who is unaware that I've divorced Mr. Tabor," she said. "Horace is not present."

"Divorced?" It didn't surprise him. All of Colorado had been absorbed in Tabor's marital problems for months. But Carthage had scarcely paid attention in the midst of his own travails. "Perhaps you could tell me—"

"The Windsor Hotel. With his concubine." She closed the door abruptly.

With Baby Doe. Openly now. So much had happened since Carthage had been embroiled in his struggles. He hiked toward the Windsor, wondering if he could get through the lobby without being stopped, and just how he would find the Leadville silver king there. Still, it was a bright hope. Inspired by the thought of a grubstake, he purchased a large manila envelope at a stationers and proceeded to the grand hotel, marveling at its twenty-foot ceilings and opulent style.

Boldly he approached the desk clerk. "Please direct me to Mr. Tabor," he said.

"We'll deliver that," the clerk replied. "I doubt that he's in, this time of day."

"No, sir, I must deliver this myself."

The clerk shrugged. "Top floor. The Denver Suite."

An Otis electric elevator run by a flunky lifted Carthage to the top and deposited him there.

The woman who opened to him had been a legend in Leadville, and now was one all the more. Baby Doe, Elizabeth McCourt, peered up at him with frank curiosity. He was smitten by her once again. She had never been a raving beauty, but had something else, a bold bright blue-eyed gaze, porcelain complexion, coppery brass hair, a winsome innocence and sultriness. There was something wildly sensual about her, too.

She didn't recognize him, even though they had socialized in Leadville many times.

"Is Hod Tabor here?" he asked.

"I don't know who you're talking about," she replied.

"Horace."

"I'm afraid I don't know—"

"Elizabeth, I'm Lorenzo Carthage. Forgive the work clothes."

"Oh," she said. She looked embarrassed. He understood. For three years she had been the veiled lady, the mysterious blonde sometimes seen with H. A. W. Tabor, almost never with her face exposed to public view because the silver king had been married to Augusta for many years, and Augusta was a respected pioneer and helpmeet.

This time her bold eyes lit with recognition. "Oh, dear, I'm sorry, Lorenzo," she said. "I have to—you know."

He knew.

"Horace has a suite at the American House," she said. "He's a prominent man and he's going to be a senator and we . . ." Her sultry voice trailed off. "I think he's downstairs in one of the saloons. He owns this place, you know. He's in with a British consortium."

"I didn't know."

"If you want you can leave that envelope here."

"No, no, Baby. I'll deliver it. It's good to see you. It's been a year or two."

"I guess so," she said. "We're going to get married. We already did in St. Louis—a judge did it, but I mean, a Catholic wedding. I keep asking him to."

"Baby, you'll both be happy."

"It's all I want. Just to be married to Hod. And be Elizabeth again. Hod and me, we want to have a girl."

She seemed lonely and was hanging on to the moment, but he needed to find Tabor.

"Baby, I've got to go. Tell Hod I'm looking for him."

"Oh, all right," she said. Disappointment filled her voice.

He retreated, finding himself somehow discomfited by that strange, powerful will behind the blue eyes. He located Tabor in a corner banquette of the saloon, surrounded as usual by half a dozen parasites.

Unlike Baby Doe, Hod Tabor recognized him instantly, gritty clothes, stubble on the chin, and all.

"Why, it's old Carthage out of Leadville, Lorenzo the Magnificent. How I envied you that one. No one ever called me Horace the Magnificent. Sit down and let me buy you a bottle, Lorenzo."

"Could I speak to you privately, Horace?"

"Ah, there's nothing said here that'll travel ten yards. Meet my colleagues," he said, introducing two state senators and several other politicians and a couple of businessmen, one of them the legendary Walter Kimbrough. "We're fixing to send me to Washington. Now, man, what's happened to you? Last I knew, you—"

"Yes, I'm out. The Pandora was stolen—apex suits."

"By God, Carthage, I have a whole platoon of lawyers fighting off the apex suits. If the bloodsuckers don't get me, the litigation will. By God, if you need anything from old Hod, you just speak up."

That was the Tabor he remembered, the man who flooded out his generosity as if it were the Mississippi River.

"I'd like a grubstake."

"Consider it done!"

"I know silver ores. I'd like to head out to the San Juans and look over those silver districts. I think I could start over. I got my break by picking up a claim a fellow thought was worthless. You're in for whatever you say if you'd stake me.''

"Why, there's no better man when it comes to silver ores. You should be a millionaire twice over now. Bad luck. How about five hundred, Lorenzo? A thousand? Against a quarter of your claim? That's how I started, and every time I turn around some other grubstake of mine pays me another million.''

"Yes, sir,'' Carthage said, half choked. "A thousand would be enough to buy a claim. Or prospect for a few months.''

"Shake on 'er,'' Tabor said, extending a big soft paw.

Carthage shook vigorously, and then Tabor peeled off ten hundreds from a fat roll, and handed over the greenbacks.

"Now see here, Lorenzo, I always get my due, and my due is, you got to be a Republican now.''

Men laughed.

"Horace, I am the truest bluest Republican in Colorado.''

"Lorenzo, son, now if you run through that pile, you come back to the well. I got so much I don't know what to do with it. You hit borrasca first time around, you come back and see old Hod and we'll go another round. Them bloodsuckers, stealing good mines, why, it makes a man's blood boil. And them was some mighty nice parties you used to throw out there. Me and—Augusta had a fine time.''

Carthage felt uncomfortable around the generous old bear and his smoothshaven cronies. He retreated. A big grubstake. Tabor's usual tap was a hundred dollars. Dizzily, Carthage hurried to a tonsorial parlor, got himself shaved and shorn and witch hazeled, took a bath, headed for a ready-made clothing store, bought a plain black suit and white shirt with a spare collar and cuffs, and two pairs of hickory pants and flannel shirts. He was going to be outside doing some prospecting, just as he had when he was a young man.

He checked out of the boardinghouse, remembering the cynical Vinovich who was certain a man couldn't fight his way up. At that moment Vinovich was working in the smelter, a prisoner of his own lack of vision. Carthage arranged for a drayman to take his trunk to Union Station, and then walked across town, feeling more and more alive and young.

He caught the four-thirty passenger train to Durango on the narrow-gauge Rio Grande and Western. It would follow a tortuous route all night and deposit him there early the next morning. There he would connect with a mixed passenger and freight train on the new rails to

Silverton. And once he reached that general area, he would study the mining claims in a vast caldera, the core of an extinct volcano that was laden especially with silver ores, but with gold and other metals as well. It had been pawed over by prospectors for several years, but Carthage had discovered that the average prospector knew almost nothing of mineralogy and even less about geology, and a man with some scientific background could step in—just as he had done in Leadville, long after the major strikes had occurred there.

Lorenzo the Magnificent was on his way up again.

CHAPTER 8

Rose Edenderry danced and drank until they pitched her out of the dancehall.

"I knew you'd hit the bottle," said the owner, Jacob. "I could see that the day you walked in. I run a proper place, so don't come back."

"I don't like your lousy dancehall anyway," she said. "It's dull. Why don't you get a good musician?"

"Out."

She stumbled out into a cold night. Every sporting joint on Harrison radiated light and warmth and laughter. She'd become a serving girl again. To hell with dancehalls, and getting her toes stepped on, and holding some smelly galoot in her arms, and fetching watered tonsil varnish, and pretending each man who gave her a dance ticket was just the dandiest fellow in the whole world even when he was pawing her as they took a whirl. To hell with that life. Half the girls weren't nice and made money on the side. The other half, like Rose, were simply the world's dumb doras, smiling and dancing because that's all they could do. In the few weeks she'd been there, she'd seen it all.

Well, tough luck. She owed her landlord money for the room, and he was always getting mad because she kept promising to pay him and didn't. Then he wanted more than money, and she got mad and told him to get out of her room. Oh, if only Andre was around. Everything would be all right.

But he wasn't, and she was standing on the street in the shank of the night, with a few tips in her pocket and too many drinks in her belly. Men passed, eyed her, and sometimes approached.

"I'm not one of those!" she snapped at one galoot.

But she would be if she didn't get ahold of herself. The cold air brought her back to reality, and the giddiness passed away. She'd better start looking for a job as a serving girl and right now. Next door was the Palace, a large, long saloon with a stage in it for shows, and a lot of gambling tables.

She plowed into its bright, smoky confines, discovering noisy crowds, almost all male, drinking whiskey or beer, playing keno or faro or poker or monte, or joking with pretty girls who wore skimpy blouses and very short skirts, almost up to the knee. Well, she could do that. She'd wear short skirts and low blouses and get lots of tips. Rose Edenderry would survive, one way or another.

She knew how to do all this. She corralled a barkeep and asked for the boss. He thumbed her toward a rear table, where an ancient gentleman in an old-fashioned frock coat sat watching his world, a cigarillo dangling from his wrinkled, discolored lips.

"You the boss?"

He nodded.

"I'm a serving girl, lots of experience. You take me on?"

He studied her as if she were a hanging beef. "You drink too much," he said.

"I'll be good."

"You'll be a problem."

"I'm experienced, I really am."

He shrugged. "That's what I don't like. All right. You make tips. Tell the bozo at the bar I said okay. Don't sample the merchandise."

"Just tips?"

"In this joint, sweetheart, it can be ten dollars a night."

"Oh!"

She found the barman again and told him. He shrugged and handed her a tray. "Pick up dead soldiers and take orders," he said. "Don't let one customer go dry, or out you go."

She maneuvered through the throng, picking up empty glasses and dead bottles, eyeing the tables. She ran into another serving girl and asked if they worked areas or certain tables.

"Nah, when they ring the dingdong, whoever gets there takes the order. You're the sixth on shift tonight. You gotta be fast, honey."

"Thanks. I'm Rose. We'll talk later, eh?"

The other one shrugged.

A tinhorn rang his bell, and she hurried to his table.

"New heah? Very well, Ah'm buying whiskeys foah these illustrious gents who wish to break mah bank." He coughed spastically, set down his cigar, and reached for a handkerchief, discreetly covering his mouth. Swiftly he tucked it away.

It amazed her how much he reminded her of Andre. Of course Andre had been almost wispy, and this man was solid and compact and had a square face framed by dark hair. But this one's soft southern slur, his gentlemanly manner, and especially his consumption, all evoked a sudden warmth in Rose. The tinhorn looked so lost and needful, just like Andre. Maybe she could take care of him.

Hastily she ordered the whiskeys and served them at the table, collecting some dead glasses as she did.

"Put it on mah tab, honey," the tinhorn said.

She waited for a name, but he seemed not to notice. He was busy pulling the soda from the faro deck. He coughed again, and turned to her.

"John Holliday."

"Oh, thank you."

"You won't thank me when you see the size of my tip."

She hurried away, aware that coincidences don't mean anything. She didn't think she would like this man Holliday.

She waited on his table half a dozen times that night. Holliday looked more and more feverish as the crowds thinned, but he hung on. She watched him furtively, familiar with the cough, the bloodied handkerchiefs, the black hollows under the eyes, and the testy nature. Andre's pain had made him cross and sometimes mean. This man's pain was written upon everything he did or said.

She waited him out. She had gotten over three dollars just in the half-evening, and had spent only a little on the sauce. Holliday didn't put away his cards and cover his table until two in the morning, and then she stood in his path as he threaded his way out.

"What do you want?"

"My tip."

"I'll give you the flat of mah hand."

She didn't budge.

He smiled suddenly and pressed a silver dollar into her hand. She let him pass and he coughed his way into the night.

The next morning her landlord booted her out. She was eleven dollars in arrears. She packed her clothing into three carpetbags and headed for the Palace. She parked her bags in a rear storage room and then sat on a stool in the sour-smelling gloomy cavern. The harsh light of day erased the magical glow of the night, when yellow light spilled from its chandeliers and a throb of life filled the place.

"How can I find Mr. Holliday?" she asked the barkeep, a stocky fellow whose hair had been cleaved down the center of his skull.

"Whosat?"

"I guess you wouldn't know him, being the day man."

At noon, when another barman came in, she tried again.

"Holliday? In the Wertham House, two blocks thataway. What do you want with that killer?"

"Oh . . . nothing."

She headed into the bright glare of a winter afternoon and headed for Wertham House, a shabby rooming lodge. The six interior quarters weren't marked. She gathered her courage and knocked. No response came from four, and on the fifth Holliday opened. He wore gray longjohns and trousers.

"Give one tip and you're stuck for life," he said. "Feed a stray cat and you own it for life. You want some java? That's all I manufacture here. It'll float a horseshoe. Help yourself. I just got up."

"Yes," she said, pushing in.

The room was as anonymous as Holliday. He had not personalized it. Not even a tintype stood on a table. She pulled the pot off the little woodstove and poured a cup of thick dark southern coffee with chicory in it.

"You want me to finish dressing or start undressing?" he asked. "I'm always curious about the purpose of these visits."

"Maybe I'd better go. I thought maybe I could—oh, I don't know."

"Stray cat. You look homeless. Yoah looking for a little heat and a roof over yoah head."

"Yes." The rest came in a rush. "I used to live with a gambler, Andre—"

"Oh, Villard, friend of mine, almost shot him once in a friendly game. Funny I never met you. I know half the sports in town."

"He died. I took care of him."

"And now you want another Andre to leach upon."

"I just was curious about you. I'll go. You're like Andre."

"Ah devoutly hope not."

"But cards are your profession, Mr. Holliday."

"No, strictly a sideline. My profession is dying. I'm getting good at it. A croaker."

"You and Andre both have consumption. You're both gentlemen. You're both gamblers, and you're both from the South."

"How bright you are," Holliday said. "Now do Ah put on a shirt or do you want to see my consumption?"

"You aren't a gentleman."

Holliday coughed. A bloodstained cloth appeared in his hand, and he hacked into it. After he quieted his body, he smiled. "Villard and I differed in the most important respect. He never killed anyone."

She sat silently, absorbing that, and decided to ignore it. "If you'd let me stay here I'd look after you. I know some herbs that help. I just like to comfort a man."

"When you're sober."

She stared.

"It's written all over you, sweetheart. You like the sauce. And you've fooled with a few extracts of the coca leaf and poppy fruit. You probably gypped your landlady or snitched her cooking sherry. Sure, move in, comfort me, wash my bloody kerchiefs. Get drunk. Make love."

"That's what you need," she said. "You're just lonely, like Andre. He was always afraid of dying alone."

John Holliday laughed until a fit of coughing stopped him.

CHAPTER 9

Yves Poulenc wished that the English syndicate that had announced its intention to build a spa and call it Glenwood Springs would get on with it. He despised the sprawl of crude log cabins that had mushroomed on the site of the huge hot springs that rose there and drained into the nearby Colorado River.

The place had become a mecca for lungers, people dying of consumption—like himself. The pellucid air and the sulphurous fumes of the hot water boiling from the bowels of the earth were said to hold the disease at bay, and even cure it. That had made the long trip from Denver worthwhile, even though it took days of bouncing along a sad excuse for a road that often negotiated fearsome canyons and threatened to slide into the river.

If a man were going to die at a young age, let him at least expire in comfort, if not luxury. He was twenty-seven, and knew he would not last more than a few more months unless this isolated place hard by the Ute Reservation performed some sort of magic upon his frail and feverish body. He had devoted all his adult life and much of his childhood to the business of expiring, and had thought about it at great length.

He felt himself to be the victim of injustice, some perversity of nature or God. What a cruel fate, to suffer this mysterious wasting disease just at the moment when he was entering life. He yearned to become somebody, master some field of scholarship. If he was a little vague about all that, it was because he understood himself in the past tense. Only when he examined his wasted body, which he did minutely several times a day, did he consider himself to be among the quick.

He did write tragic poetry in both English and French, and had become a master of the form. The omnipresence of death had inspired verse after verse as his fevered mind roamed through tragedy, scything sorrow as a peasant scythed a field of wheat. He loved especially to compose lines about loss. Loss of life, loss of friends and love, loss of hope, loss of faith in God, loss of a future, loss of joy, loss of love, loss of children, loss of a chance to become someone memorable.

On other occasions he wrote about cemeteries, and the lives that ended in those graves, and the sorrows of those who came to visit their lost loved ones. He wrote of epitaphs, and proud and humble tombstones, and children who laid daisies on the graves of their mothers. He wrote tender verses about orphans, and lost brides, and young da Vincis or Mozarts whose promise was extinguished at the very beginnings of their lives. He wrote of proud marble monuments that stood over corrupt rich men's remains, and unmarked graves where holy saints and unknown martyrs lay buried. He had a whole trunk full of these mournful verses, and when he died they would be published in an illuminated volume and make his name sacred in the world of belles lettres. So much genius in him, and so little time.

His hero was John Keats, the immortal English poet who had died of consumption at the age of twenty-five. In one brief burst, Keats had blessed the world with some of the finest and most lyrical poems ever written. Yves' favorite was "La Belle Dame Sans Merci."

> I see a lily on thy brow
>   With anguish moist and fever dew;
> And on thy cheek a fading rose
>   Fast withereth too.

Ah, to die an immortal poet like that, at almost the same age as Keats! If Yves Poulenc could not have the fullest portion of life, then let him become a famous dead poet. That was all he could ask, but it meant everything.

On this autumnal day, as he had on each of the preceding days for months, he hastened to the pool in his robe and bathing drawers, and there he breathed in the sulphurous steam, as much as his fragile lungs would permit. He could never get enough breath. But he fancied that the acrid sulphur fumes were slowly triumphing over the disease. A medical tract penned by the excellent Dr. Pierce had informed him that consumption arose from any of several exciting causes, including dyspepsia, catarrh, whooping cough, smallpox, pleurisy, prolonged exposure to cold, masturbation, excessive venery, wastes from intensive mental activity, and impure air. Whatever the source, it had destroyed his body, seared his lungs, reduced his voice to a hollow rumble, and subjected him to violent spasms of coughing.

He breathed the steam for a while and then stepped into a little pool, where the 123 degree water flowing from the earth had cooled down to bearable levels. There, in the company of three other silent lungers, he wallowed in the heat until he could no longer stand his racing pulse. No one talked. No one wished to enflame abscessed throats or force their ruined lungs to perform unwonted labor. Then he dizzily clambered out, let his pulse settle, and headed for his bunk for more boring hours of absolute rest or composing some new stanzas of tragic verse. He performed this ritual thrice daily, on a schedule as regular as a clock's pendulum.

He might read this afternoon, and again he might not. He was working through the five volumes of Louis Agassiz's *Recherches sur les poissons fossiles.* But what good did it do to decorate the mind of one who was about to depart into the mists of the unknown? Had he not been a frail, aching, fevered, 110-pound walking cadaver, he might have enjoyed educating himself. He had always wished to be a scholar, and he would have been, had it not been for the misery of an evil fate.

Yes, it would help if the English came and built their spa. Thousands and thousands of lungers came to Colorado to be healed by the crystalline air, dry climate, and excellent altitude. A third of the population of Colorado had consumption. The English syndicate would get rich. He would be their first patron. Money was not a consideration. His parents had migrated to Boston during the Civil War to market Brussels lace and other rare European fabrics and dry goods to the voracious new American markets. They had immediately prospered, selling acres of lace and tulle to Boston and New York clothiers. If the Poulencs weren't rich, they were most certainly affluent, and Yves need never worry about getting a living. That only wounded him the more. The one thing money could not buy was health. Here he had a competence awaiting him—the chance to devote a life to the purest pursuit of truth and beauty—and fate had robbed him of the chance to enjoy it. Every miserable beggar who could look ahead to another twenty years had the advantage of him.

As swiftly as consumptives gathered at this isolated place on the west slope, once called Defiance but now Glenwood in deference to the British consortium, entrepreneurs founded small businesses to serve them, including restaurants, porters, a Chinese laundry, an apothecary shop, and a mortician. The weakest of the unfortunates could arrange to be fed and washed in their rustic cabins. Poulenc had made such arrangements, even though he was still quite capable of wending his breathless way to the log restaurant.

That evening he attended a lecture in the board and batten funeral parlor of Andrew Perkins, who also ran the general store and the cemetery. Poulenc enjoyed that austere whitewashed place, and had come many times to bury other lungers there. As sure as the clock ticked, it soon would be his turn to receive his farewells and prayers within that hall. But no one would be buried this evening. Instead, Mr. Perkins had arranged for several colleagues from Denver to discuss dignified dying and discreetly offer their wares. The topic could scarcely interest Poulenc more. He had given much thought to all of that, but this was the first opportunity to make concrete plans for his demise.

Lanterns in wall sconces illuminated the hall with buttery light as he found his way to a pew and sat down. At the front, on sawhorses, rested half a dozen coffins ranging from plain dark boxes to handsome walnut or mahogany caskets with nickelplate furniture and ornate scrollwork. Pinned to a display board were fine engravings of twenty or thirty headstones and monuments, ranging from a small plain marker to obelisks and above-ground crypts. These dazzled Poulenc, and made him feel he was back in civilization again instead of languishing in this despicable wilderness hard by murderous Ute savages.

The event drew the whole lunger congregation, which settled into the pews, hacked, spat blood, and panted. When all had assembled, Mr. Perkins, wearing his finest black suit and freshly starched white shirt and somberest expression, rose to introduce the two similarly attired gents beside him.

"I know that the manner of your passing is foremost in the minds of all of you," he began. "That you may depart with dignity and grace, and leave an appropriate remembrance of yourselves is your most important remaining business before you are taken up to heaven. Therefore I've invited two Denver colleagues to assist you in your passage, make necessary arrangements if you wish to be laid to rest elsewhere, and offer you a variety of dignified items suited to your tastes and needs. Now then, let me introduce Mr. Garth V. A. P. O'Higgins, director of the beauteous Riverside Cemetery in Denver, and Mr. Wilhelm Kaltbrenner, of the Denver firm of Kaltbrenner and Odom, monument makers. We'll hear Mr. O'Higgins first."

Mr. O'Higgins turned out to be a man of comforting gravity. He surveyed his quiet audience slowly, his watery eyes taking in each and every consumptive before he spoke.

"Eternity is a long time," he began mellifluously. "We who are about to abandon our mortal coil hope it will be eternal peace and comfort and repose. We're here tonight to help you plan your passage to a better world. Mr. Kaltbrenner will help you select headstones and monuments that will endure as long as the mountains, and bear witness to your passage on earth before God took you up. He has suitable inscriptions, or he will help you devise something memorable about your own life, the thing you want to convey to those who, with bowed head and reverent demeanor, pause at your resting place. I will make myself available to those wishing to discuss caskets and plots at beautiful Riverside Cemetery in Denver, where you may gaze forever upon the purple mountain majesties across the fruited plain, or those who may wish to be transported to other places.

"Now some of you have thought of nothing else while you seek the cures that, God willing, you may find here in these medicinal waters and crystalline air, but others have wisely and naturally desired to put off these matters to the last, feeling that to make such arrangements is to surrender hope and courage, and surrender to despair. We understand both views, and will talk with you privately in the tenderest manner we can summon. Your wishes are our concern; your sorrows are our own, for we, too, must enter that dread habitat where all is still. Now, of course, we have brought these caskets a long distance, and any of you who wish may purchase them at a ten percent discount to save us the cost of carrying them back to Denver. . . ."

Poulenc listened alertly, his soul agreeing with these austere gentlemen who would paddle him across the River Styx. Truly the time had come to prepare for the passage. After the two addresses, the Denver gentlemen invited the guests forward to receive the prices and terms, almost like calling up sinners at a revival meeting. Poulenc hastened forward, studied the brochures, decided at once on the costly nickel-plated casket of burnished teak, with a blue silk lining and a soft pillow for the head, for only three hundred fifty, minus the ten percent.

"I'll take it," he told O'Higgins, "if you'll deliver it to my cabin a few yards distant. And of course I'll want your best plot at Riverside, just for me alone because I was cut off from the living, from wife and family, at the age of eleven. You can't imagine how it feels to be buried alone."

"Very well, sir; we'll proceed at once," said Mr. O'Higgins. He spread out a plat of the Denver cemetery and suggested a hillside lot on a slope facing the mountains, where a man's spirit could gaze forever upon the Front Range. The price was only a hundred twenty dollars, plus another hundred for the burying when the time came.

Happily, Yves Poulenc agreed, filled in the blanks in the printed contract, wrote a draft on the First National Bank of Denver, and received his receipts.

"We'll deliver the casket directly," O'Higgins said. "With a shawl over it, it makes a fine casual table in any home, and the nickel doesn't tarnish the way silver does. You'll be proud to lie in such comfort and elegance, and I suggest you try it just to get the feel of it. You'll like the pillow. We put a lot of thought into making it comfortable. There's no lock and you can't be trapped."

"Thank you, sir. I'm truly honored," Poulenc said, and then coughed violently.

He studied the fine engraved images of monuments, beautiful and bewildering in their array, and finally arranged with Mr. Kaltbrenner for a twenty-two-foot obelisk of noble red granite on a six-foot-square pedestal. But he couldn't imagine what he wished to be engraved on it. Surely he would need to go through his sheafs of poetry and select the verse most searing, most soul-wrenching, most profound, so that all the world would know that Yves Poulenc had triumphed over misfortune in his brief life to become the most famous poet of all.

An hour later, Messrs. Kaltbrenner and O'Higgins appeared at his door, hefted the elegant and somber casket into his quarters, and doffed their silk top hats.

"You're a farsighted gentleman," O'Higgins said. "To sleep in Denver is to sleep in Paradise."

CHAPTER 10

. . . .

Silverton had a way of making Lorenzo Carthage feel lonely. It huddled in a vast red-rock mountain wilderness, leagues from anything, so alone that whole civilizations could rise and fall without word ever reaching town. Its log and plank buildings huddled together, as if its eight hundred residents needed proximity to ward off the fearsome wilds. And even though the San Juans offered mild winters and lots of sun, there was something so mysterious, silent, and impersonal in them that Carthage felt cold every time he peered at the majestic distant peaks lying in all directions.

He had eight hundred fifty dollars left with which to start over. He could not waste a minute. He found a raw, new boardinghouse that supplied a narrow room, breakfast, and supper for ten dollars a week. That would do. He rented a saddle horse from a bewhiskered one-armed complainer named Folger, and began at once to examine the terrain, noting every claim he could find, mineral outcrops, working mines, glory holes, and trails that vanished into long gulches. There had been a lot of exploration, and now a dozen mines were lifting silver ore from high slopes that weren't easy to reach. Nothing in Silverton was easy to reach.

At the log courthouse he studied the four thousand claims, selected the most likely prospects, drew a rough map, and recorded the names of the claimants. Some claims had already changed hands ten or twelve times. From the local newspaper editor, Albert Battle, he got a running commentary about the town's riches, the best mines, the legal wrangles, the slopes that seemed least likely to produce, and a little gossip about the prospectors. In the saloons he picked up information about the quality of various ores, known reserves at various mines, who was hiring and who was laying off men.

The two assayers in town were good sources, gabby about ores, values, seams, depths, owners, prospects, and profits. From one he learned that over three hundred prospectors were still roaming the San Juans looking for more bonanzas, even though the district was a dozen years old. Many had brought their ores to him for assay.

Carthage discovered that he wasn't the only one looking for an overlooked bonanza in an abandoned or low-grade claim. A local madam had acquired two hundred claims more or less through horizontal prospecting. Two bankers were acquiring them as fast as they could; tinhorns collected them as gambling debts. One faro dealer named Earp over in Gunnison owned a dozen. Successful mining entrepreneurs steadily bought every available claim around their mines, in part to lessen the possibility of apex suits, and in part to control mineral land near their own.

It was all helpful in a way, but none of it pointed anywhere in particular. Two weeks of intensive exploration had not opened any avenues to a new fortune, although he had a better knowledge of what not to do. He would not prospect out in the crags and gulches, even though that was what Tabor had expected him to do. This district was showing all the signs of age. The best chance—perhaps the only chance—was to buy into a proven mine that needed development capital, or offer the owners of such a mine his expertise as a manager. Whatever arrangement he made, he would still owe Horace Tabor a quarter of his profits. If he could bird-dog a good mine for Tabor, he would probably do better than locating a claim.

He headed one wintry day for the red stone San Juan County Bank for a talk with its sole owner, L. E. Baumgartner, known to be the most knowledgeable man about the financing of San Juan mines. This day he wore his cheap black suit, hoping the banker wouldn't look too closely at it. He would present himself not only as the manager of the Pandora, in Leadville, but as an agent of the legendary Horace Tabor. That would stretch the truth only slightly; he and Tabor did have a grubstake deal, and he knew Horace would plunge if a good prospect showed up.

Baumgartner had the presence of a patent medicine salesman, alert and shrewd and not above bending realities for his purposes. They understood each other.

"Tabor's man, eh? Well, yes, I suppose he would be scouting for more. It's a little late here, though. Leadville's a baby compared to Silverton. What's your argument, did you say?"

"We're looking for proven properties that need development capital," Carthage said. "I'm a silver man, have been for years. The mine I developed, the Pandora, is one of the great successes of the Leadville district."

"They all are," Baumgartner replied. "Well, yes, there's a few around here looking for capital. But the owners are skinflints, some of them so crazy with fear they'll lose a nickel to some sharper that they won't deal. There's one in particular comes to mind, pretty good ore, assays a hundred twenty a ton, high up and hard to get at, hanging right on a steep slope like a spider on a wall. They've got ore and need capital—nothing but a burro can get up there right now—and they're likely to shoot anyone showing up on the premises, even to offer cash for part of the mine."

"I'll go. That's what Mr. Tabor's looking for."

"It is, is it? Seems to me a man with millions to pitch into opera houses and mistresses could find a better deal. What'd you say your name is again?"

"Lorenzo Carthage."

"Dangdest name I ever heard. What is that, Swahili?"

"My parents were enthused about Italian Renaissance artists. Mr. Baumgartner, where's this place? Who owns it?"

"I'll draw you a map and she'll probably come storming in here and move the account over to First Colorado."

"She?"

"You'd better think in he-terms. She's the biggest blond amazon in Colorado, and could likely bust your arm or mash your toe in ten seconds. And she's a good shot. Bill Cody tried to hire her for his show."

"Well, what's her name?"

"Not only that, but she don't think much of moneymen. You climb up there and make an offer, and she's likely to throw you off the ledge."

"Well, I'll take the chance. What did you say—"

"They was a sight. That pint-sized man of hers, and she a head taller and a foot broader, coming in to buy supplies every couple of weeks. She ran him around like a hired man, getting groceries, trading a few bags of good ore for credit at Ike's store."

"Bags of ore wouldn't be worth much at a hundred twenty a ton, Mr. Baumgartner."

"Well, you got a head on you after all. I thought I saw another mountebank in that chair. I run mountebanks through here faster than I do fifty-dollar bills. Actually, they got a thin vein of highgrade argentite running about thirty percent silver surrounded by a ten-foot seam of the hundred twenty ounces a ton. They dig up the good stuff and trade it for supplies. She does, anyway. He died a few months ago. She claims she threw him over the cliff and let the bears clean up the carcass."

"Yes, but what's her name and where is this place?"

"Her name's Dixie, and I'll draw you a map because words fail me trying to describe the way to an eagle's nest."

Carthage rented a good saddle mule, not trusting a horse on a trail like that, and headed north, toward Ouray. Following instructions, he turned west and headed up a huge delta fan and into a canyon, climbing all the while. By mid-afternoon he found himself on a trail along the ledge of a major fault, with a precipice on one side and a vaulting wall on the other. He marveled at the view, the disorderly San Juans forming a maze to the north and east.

Eventually he came to a log cabin in a small side canyon, found no one home, and continued another hundred yards to the mine. Scarcely three yards separated the horizontal shaft from the precipice. He dismounted, grateful for the steadiness of the big saddle mule.

"Hello," he bawled into the gloomy shaft, which had been driven into what was obviously mineralized rock that outcropped there.

"What do you want?" asked a woman behind him.

He turned and found himself facing a large young woman in men's rough clothing, but the small-bore shotgun aimed at him was what drew his attention.

"I'm looking for Dixie."

"What do you want with me?" she asked.

"Well, I thought I'd propose marriage."

She smiled at that, lighting up a square wind-chapped face framed by whipping dishwater hair. He liked her smile. This woman could not have reached thirty. She stood at least six feet tall, had broad shoulders, full hips, a richly sculpted bosom, and a direct gaze. "I think I like you, temporarily. You're after the mine. They all are." The bore of the shotgun didn't waver.

"If you marry me, I'll manage the mine and you. I'm an experienced manager. In fact, I'll manage it even if you don't marry me."

"They all say that. I pitched my last husband over the cliff and fed him to the wolves. I guess you want to be the next. I'm straight off the farm. I've butchered beef and wrung the neck of chickens, so don't tempt me."

The conversation was getting out of hand. The muzzle of the shotgun didn't move an iota.

"Mr. Baumgartner at the bank said you've a need for capital to put this operation on a profitable basis."

"If you brought some, put it on the ground in front of you and back away from it." Amusement lit her eyes.

"Not until you marry me," he said.

"Well, you're harmless. I'll follow you down to the cabin and you can worry whether I'll make tea or shoot you in the back."

He could think of no reply to that, so he took up the reins of the mule and led it down the alarming ledge, heading for the cabin. She let him in and he found himself in a bright, well-lit room with peeled log walls glistening under shellac, homemade furniture, and a few dashes of bold color in the cushions and curtains.

She busied herself at the stove, stuffing kindling into it, and setting a pot to boil.

"My husband Army—his name's really Armand—died of pneumonia a few months ago. I took him down to Doc Webb, but it was too late. His lungs had filled up and he sort of drowned. He's buried down there. But I tell people I threw him off the cliff. You'd be amazed at the pests that come up here. Maybe you're one, but after this steeps a little, you can tell me what you want and I'll decide."

"What's your last name? Everyone seems to use first names around here."

"Cotton."

"Dixie Cotton. I think you're inventing things."

"No, Army's name was Cotton. I don't believe you've told me yours."

"Lorenzo Carthage."

"Are you Lorenzo the Magnificent of Leadville?"

"Ah . . ." Carthage didn't know whether to lie or not. He decided against it. "Yes. Now associated with Senator Tabor."

"Lorenzo the Magnificent! I've been to your parties."

"Ah—"

"You wouldn't remember me. I was working for the Clarendon Hotel, serving pastries in a black uniform with white collar and cuffs. You sure threw corkers. That was before they stole your mine."

Lorenzo the Magnificent liked the sound of that, and liked the look in her eye when she handed him a mug of tea.

"I don't know how I missed you," he said. "I must have been blind."

"No, just tipsy," she said.

CHAPTER 11

he hot tea tasted just fine after that cold ascent.

"All right, Carthage, lay your cards on the table," Dixie said after some small talk.

"I will, but it'd be best if you tell me what you want."

"I'll tell you exactly what I want. I want to head for Silverton. Living on a mountaintop and chopping ore out of a twenty-foot shaft on a cold mountaintop doesn't tickle my funnybone. I'm a farmgirl by breeding and instinct, and I'm not cut out for this."

"That means you're looking for a way out."

"Just because I'm looking doesn't mean that I'll surrender easily." She laughed. "Galoots wander up here and offer bum deals. Most want two-thirds. Some want three-quarters. Others want to buy the mine for two thousand dollars. But I'm asking two-thirds and control. This female's going to keep a majority share and operate the mine from Silverton. I know what I've got here. The partner with the capital gets a third of the profits. What's your proposition, Carthage?"

"Let's go see what you've got up there."

"I'll show you the assay reports. I've a dozen of them."

She set a sheaf of papers before him, and he studied them. The values were impressive, but he would have to verify them with his own assays. This silver ore had significant traces of gold, and some base metals. The ore was not refractory; it could be reduced easily.

"Let's go look," he said. "I'll want some samples."

She nodded.

They bundled up against the bitter wind and hiked the ledge to the mine. She lit a lamp and they plunged in. He saw no timbering, and eyed the rock above him nervously.

"Army never got to it. He said it's good rock, not rotten, and it wouldn't fall down."

He grunted. The shaft ascended slightly. A small drift opened on the left.

"That follows the good vein," she said. He could see it, a foot or so of glistening dark ore high up. He measured. The seam was thirteen inches at the rear of the drift, eleven inches at its junction with shaft. Good news. The highgrade was expanding.

He chipped some samples from both sides of the shaft every six feet to the rear face. In the main shaft he chipped more samples. The shallow workings had no rails or ore cars, and was still a wheelbarrow operation.

He took more measurements. The main ore body was thicker than the six-foot-high shaft, and did not pinch down at the face, twenty feet in. More good news.

"I'm a millionaire," she said.

He grunted. The realities rarely matched the dreams. Out in the blustering air of the ledge, he peered downward. The mine stood about eight hundred or a thousand feet above the floor of a valley that no doubt opened into the Silverton area.

"Army said the only way to work this is to chute the ore down there," she said. "Otherwise it has to be hauled by wagon down five miles of grade. Chutes cost money."

"He's right—they're costly. Did you or he file a claim on the valley floor?"

"No."

"Was this his claim?"

"Yes. He located it."

Carthage hiked the ledge beyond the shaft, finding the massive ore outcrop ran another fifty yards before it was swallowed by a fault.

"Where are your corners?" he asked.

"He filed on the direction of the outcrop. Seven hundred fifty feet each way from the shaft. Six hundred feet into the mountain."

More good news. The claim covered the entire outcrop on the cliff-side, making apex litigation less likely or profitable. But he could not climb up that wall of rock to see if the ascending seam of ore out-cropped somewhere on top. That was the only weakness he could see in the whole deal.

"How do I get up there?"

"There's no outcrop up there. Army looked. It takes ropes to crawl around up there."

"That's the one weakness. That seam ascends, and it could outcrop a mile from here."

"So do I look for another capitalist?"

"You have more tea?" he asked.

They fled the wind. The warmth of the glowing cabin delighted him. His mind whirled with possibilities, but he thought it might be best just to find out what she wanted.

"You want two-thirds of the profit and majority ownership. Is there anything else?"

"Action," she said. "I want to get out of here and into Silverton."

"Why haven't others accepted your terms?"

"The cost of the chute. The cost of getting mining timbers up here. And water. I have to carry every drop from a spring a mile away. They all said they want at least half the profits if they do all that."

"Did they estimate the cost?"

"Seventy-five to a hundred thousand."

"Did any propose a lift rather than a chute? Cable or cog?"

"No. What would you want a lift for?"

"To bring timber, men, and water from that valley floor, and take ore down. Save time and four or five miles of trail. Put the buildings down there."

"You're the first person to make any sense of it, Carthage."

"That's my business," he replied. "If my samples assay the same as yours, I'll take this whole deal to Hod Tabor. He'll go for it if I say so. I'm fairly sure of it. You'll own it, Tabor will supply the capital, and I'll manage it for a good wage and a small percent that you and Tabor agree on."

"I'm keeping my two-thirds. No percent from me. But you can run it. Only this time keep the pirates and their lawsuits out of here."

"That would be my highest priority, as important as making a profit. Tabor has a platoon of mining lawyers."

She seemed doubtful. "I don't know," she said. "I'm not a miner and I'm not a businesswoman. I just want to find someone I can trust, who'd care about my interests."

"I hope that I can do that."

"Carthage, you're famous for parties and good wine and dance orchestras. Tabor's famous for being lucky. No one ever said he's very smart."

"I developed a mine from nothing but a claim, and did a good job."

"And you lost it. I don't know about this."

"What can I say?"

"Oh, don't take it personally. I have to be careful. This is my one chance in life and I'm likely to make a mistake if I don't watch out, because there's no one else watching out for me." She gazed ruefully at him. "I'm not so good at picking men. Every time I trust one, I get ruined again. I fall for every line ever told, I guess."

He could see the bluster and bravado ebbing in her, and thought that maybe now they could get beyond banter and come to some sort of agreement. "Talk about what you want, Dixie. You have a dream, I'm sure."

A softness filled her face. "I grew up with a mess of brothers," she said. "But it don't help me when it comes to men. A slick-talking drummer got me out of the farm, and bad as he was I don't mind what happened, because it meant a better life than just being a maid for my pa and my brothers all my life.

"I won't go into all that. I done a lot of things, like waiting tables for the Clarendon Hotel in Leadville. That didn't have much future either, though I could've married a miner. I got a few proposals and propositions. I drifted over here, met Armand, and we got thick. He already had this mine going and was working it while he figured out what to do.

"You know what this means to some farmgirl like me? This is a fairy tale. Striking it rich. I wish Army was here with me to enjoy it. I get took real easily. So I'll think about it, and if I don't like this deal, I'll just keep on digging a little ore out until I get a deal I like."

"What don't you like about it?"

"Well, Mr. Carthage, while you were partying and carrying on, you left the back door open and the wolves came in and ate up your mine."

"It won't happen again."

"This is my only chance to strike it rich. I can't make even one mistake." She glared. "How'm I supposed to know what's on the level and what don't cut the mustard?"

"You're dealing with men you know, Dixie. You know Tabor's good for the money, and you know two things about me. I turned the Pandora into one of the richest producers in Leadville, and I didn't pay enough attention to the pirates. I've learned from that mistake. One thing we can do is file claims clear around this one to keep the pirates at bay. As for the rest, you'll get an experienced silver mine manager, a known capitalist, and the terms you ask. You and Horace can decide what to pay me, and whether to give me a cut."

She grinned. "All right, Magnificent, you've suckered me into it."

He didn't know how to reply to that.

"Shake on it," she said.

He did. "I've a lot to do," he said. "I'll need to go to Denver. I'll need these samples, a notarized copy of Cotton's claim, copies of the assay reports, and an agreement with your initials on it."

"I'd go with you and meet old Hod Tabor, but I got to keep the crooks outa here. There's some in Silverton that'd come up here and chip out that highgrade if I wasn't around or even jump this place."

It took another day to put things in order, and then Carthage caught the narrow-gauge back to Denver. A thousand things could go wrong. Tabor might not go for it. He might be traveling. He might want different terms. Any of his sycophants might try to talk him out of it. Or he might delay interminably until the deal was lost.

Carthage spent his hours in the rattling coach rehearsing his arguments, and when he reached Union Station he felt fairly confident he could talk Horace Tabor into it.

But when he did catch up with the silver king, at the American House, it turned out to be a lark.

"Why, Lorenzo, this is just what I'm looking for. I was born under a four-leaf clover. We'll git some papers cobbled up today, and you git started with development. I'll go out there one of these days and have me a look. Now, what do you want for a salary?"

"Well, sir, I was thinking a thousand a month during development, and two thousand a month when production starts, and some sort of bonuses based on profits. How about five percent of net profits? The more net profits I wring out of it, the more I get and the more you and Mrs. Cotton get."

"That seems fair enough. Now, Carthage, you got all the ends tied down this time?"

"Yes, sir. I'm filing claims on all sides of this claim. With those claims in the bag, and your own mining lawyers to fight off suits, we have it licked."

"All right. Just so's we don't get into the same hole that cost you the Pandora. Maybe this'll be another Matchless. That little old pit makes me another million every time I turn around. All right, let 'er roll, Magnificent," said Tabor.

CHAPTER 12

omer Peabody filed a complaint alleging desertion and cruelty, petitioning the restitution of Cornelia's maiden name, and seeking a hundred-thousand-dollar lump-sum settlement. Without children, she didn't want to retain the Kimbrough name, and she wanted a clean break rather than alimony.

Within days, Kimbrough's counsel, Roderick and Hamilton, filed a response contesting the divorce and a cross-complaint alleging the same ground, cruelty, by Cornelia.

Peabody had expected it. The Kimbroughs never did anything halfway, and Walter would rather throw away tens of thousands of dollars on litigation than surrender property—which is how he viewed his wife. Peabody had a sense of foreboding, as if some giant force had been unleashed, a boulder rolling down a mountain that would flatten him and Mrs. Kimbrough.

He sent a messenger boy to summon her, and she showed up an hour later.

"I didn't expect a response so soon," she said.

"It's a way of showing combativeness."

He handed her the document, which she perused carefully. He watched her cheeks redden. "Cruelty? Me?"

"It's a standard tactic in contested divorces," he said. "If they can prove it, then the judge will usually throw out the divorce and let the marriage stand. A divorce requires a victim, and when both sides claim to be victimized, it's a wash."

"But I've never been cruel to Walter. Not once in my life. And I've never even been unkind, not one day."

"A determined spouse can usually conjure up grounds," Peabody said.

"I can't bear this!"

"You could try reconciliation, and stop the entire litigation. Marriage is a sacred thing, and maybe you and your spouse could, with an intermediary's help, restore the old tenderness, the gentle moments, the caring—"

She laughed. "That did it, Homer. We'll fight the swine."

Homer Peabody reddened. It was the first time in all his years he had heard such coarse language from the mouth of a privileged gentlewoman and lady. Once, when he had been a court-appointed attorney defending a harridan who had stuck a butcher knife into her husband's leg in Indiana, he had heard such things. "Mrs. Kimbrough, perhaps you'd like to compose yourself while I wander down the hall."

"I love you, Homer," she said. "You're a gem."

Puzzled, he cleared his throat. "We've things to discuss. I've ransacked the case law, and here and there are some oddities, some precedents. Since you're now a defendant, we'll need to probe into these matters."

"That's Walter for you. Now I'm a defendant."

"Yes, and I warned you of it. We'll proceed. Have you ever nagged Walter, especially in public?"

"Never."

"Did he ever nag you?"

"Sometimes he doesn't like the way I dress."

"Has he criticized you before others?"

"No."

"Has he ever told you he doesn't love you, or have you ever said that to him?"

"He doesn't talk at all about love. He mumbled something or other about it during our engagement, but he's not the sort to demonstrate. He's the silent type. I've never told him I don't love him, but I think it's time he found out."

"Ah, ah, just mind your tongue for a few weeks more. Now, Mrs. Kimbrough—"

"Cornelia, Homer. You're too proper."

"Yes, yes, it's the way I am. Have you ever failed to perform your household duties?"

"Me? With two maids and a cook? I fail to perform my household duties every day of our marriage." She laughed.

"Has he ever told you he loves another, or have you ever told him that?"

"Never."

"Now, ah—"

"Say it, Homer. I'm all grown up."

"Has he ever demanded, shall we say, repellent acts from you?"

"I wish he had."

"Oh. Well, I see." He summoned his courage. "Did you ever demand such things from him?"

"No, never."

"That's a mercy. I'd hate to think he could bring that ground into court." She was smiling at him like a Cheshire cat, which seemed entirely unsuitable. "Did he ever tell you he was unhappy, or miserable, because of something in your conduct? Or did you ever tell him that?"

"He never cared enough to tell me anything. And yes, I've told him I'm miserable in this nonmarriage. I've even told him I wish he'd be a little amorous now and then. A lady gets to feeling left out."

"Were there witnesses?"

"No, but next time I have the opportunity—"

"Ah, ah, ah, patience, Mrs. Kimbrough. During litigation, silence is golden. Now, are you or he addicted to spirits or drugs?"

"No, but there are times I wish I were."

"And what about him?"

"He's no drunk. I wish he would get plastered, just once. Maybe he wouldn't be such a cold fish. If Walter would just get crocked once, I think he could be redeemed."

"That's it, I take it. He's a cold fish."

"That's the whole thing."

"Do you have friends who think he's a cold fish and have said so?"

"I wish I did. They all think I'm the luckiest woman in Denver."

He frowned. "Cornelia, we haven't much to go on, I'm afraid. And you may be shocked when witnesses testify that you've been cruel to him one way or another. Since you were the first to file on these grounds, you have the benefit of a certain presumption. That is, the court will probably assume that the cross-complaint has less merit."

"Just get me out of it. Just free me, Homer. I want to start over. If it means ditching the lump settlement, ditch it."

"Yes, as you wish," he said, handing her his handkerchief. "We probably have a case. Not in his indifference—hard to establish without a lot of witnesses—but in his refusal to engage in, ah, eh, blessed and holy marital relations for several years. You'll have to gather your courage and say it. I'll lead you through it. It's our ace card. It's our only card. But it'll be your word against his."

She had such a peculiar look on her face that it gave him pause. "My dear Mrs. Kimbrough, I fear I've done something to offend . . ."

Her pensive look transformed itself into a smile. "I think I can manage," she said cheerfully.

The meeting ended on that note, except for one strange and disturbing event. She kissed him good-bye at the door. She actually put an arm about him, and bussed his left cheek and smiled. He reacted so spastically that she started laughing.

"See you in court," she said, and vanished in a haze of scented English soap and the music of heavenly choirs.

He rubbed his cheek, savoring the miracle of her lips upon it. Then guilt swarmed him like a hive of bees, and he knew he had come precariously close to actually thinking adulterous thoughts. Still, as he sat there in his shabby office, her smiles still filled his mind and the kiss lingered on his cheek. What did it mean? Did she see something in him? Had she looked beyond the man who had stumbled over himself all his long life, and seen the other man, still yearning to be born? If she got her divorce, would she welcome his attentions?

He permitted himself a small dream, as fragile as a butterfly's wing, of love and domesticity. She was thirty years his junior, and probably had never heard of a prostate gland, much less an enlarged one. But maybe—if God was making up for Homer Peabody's thwarted dreams, or recognizing Homer Peabody's sterling character and integrity—maybe a miracle would happen and that lovely young woman might find a few years of bliss in the arms of her counselor-at-law and new husband. No woman would be more loved or cherished or nurtured.

It was a silly dream, of course, but still, strange things happened in this world. Energetically, he turned to his divorce case, virtually the only business sustaining him at the moment, and began to draft an outline of his oral argument. It wasn't likely that the desertion ground would go far, but he intended to argue that Walter Kimbrough's sheer neglect of his spirited and beautiful young wife was a species of desertion; that one could be physically present and yet abandon the marriage and the neglected spouse. A novel argument in common and Colorado law, but one worth trying.

But the other ground, cruelty, was the one in which he placed his confidence. Neglect was cruel, and Kimbrough had neglected his wife, wounded her tender heart, and had scorned her outreached arms. *There* was the case. Let him ask the right questions. Let her tell it, in anguish and sorrow, and soon the whole courtroom would be awash in tears. Yes indeed, a husband's indifference to a wife's yearning arms would be the ground that would work.

As he labored in the lamplight, he grew aware that this would be the defining case of his life. Winning it would make his entire life worthwhile. A victory for Cornelia Kimbrough would win him the collegial respect he pined for, swiftly expand his earnings, give meaning to his move to Denver, supply him with a certain prowess and reputation among lawyers as well as the public—for every nuance of this trial would be recorded in the *Rocky Mountain News* and other journals. He might enter the courtroom as an obscure attorney, but with a victory his name would be known throughout Denver. All the years of failure would be cleaned off the slate.

All he had to do was win.

CHAPTER 13

he jar of the office door spurred Homer Peabody out of his reverie. With practiced skill, he scattered file folders and casebooks across his work table, pleased by the instant chaos.

He opened his frosted glass inner door to two men he recognized instantly, gray-haired Sterling Hamilton and dandruff-laden Fisher Roderick, counsel for Walter Kimbrough.

"Gentlemen?"

"Have a few moments, Homer?" Hamilton asked.

"Why, I'll make time if necessary." Peabody ushered them into his sanctum. "Let me just put a marker in this book."

"Nice little suite you have here, Peabody. I don't believe I've ever been here," Roderick said.

"Tastefully done," Hamilton added, taking a seat in one of the hard wooden chairs. "Nice frosted glass."

"It serves," Peabody said. "I presume you're here about the Kimbrough matter."

"Well, just to talk a little. Sometimes a powwow can get things straightened away without a lot of fuss and bother," Hamilton said.

"You've been instructed to negotiate."

"Well, no, but Walter asked us to talk a little to see if we can just put this little matter to rest. He regards it as a minor tantrum on the part of Mrs. Kimbrough, and sees no reason why the whole thing can't be buried. He thinks a few differences need airing, and then it can all be dropped. He'd be happy to take care of your time and expense, of course."

"Mrs. Kimbrough's quite serious."

"Well, Homer, serious about what? She lives in luxury."

"Serious about a divorce. Serious about cruelty and desertion as the grounds."

"Well, what has she in mind? It's hard to imagine a man like Walter being cruel to an ant, much less the most attractive lady in Denver."

"We'll make that case in court. She wishes to be free."

"It's money. This is about money," Roderick said.

"That's part of it. But it's about cruelty."

"Would you mind telling us where and how she thinks Walter's cruel?" Hamilton asked. "You realize, of course, that all this'll be blown up in the papers. The Kimbroughs aren't obscure."

"Well, gentlemen, you've filed a cross-complaint alleging cruelty on Mrs. Kimbrough's part. You can start by telling me what Walter's complaint will be."

The two counselors glanced at each other. "No, Homer," said Hamilton. "This matter's a great embarrassment to Walter. He doesn't want his good name dragged through the press for days on end. He also has no intention of agreeing to a divorce. He prizes her."

"That's exactly what she says. Walter prizes her. He prizes his terrier, too, and the Denver Traction Company."

"There aren't grounds," Roderick said, an edge in his voice. "Her complaint'll be denied. This goes before old Judge Plowman, a traditionalist when it comes to the sacred hearth of the family. Why not just handle this privately? We'll make certain concessions. We're authorized to offer Mrs. Kimbrough a separate life—not separate maintenance or anything on the record—but an apartment of her own, and no questions asked about her associates. All Walter wants is for her to appear on his arm a few times a year. At balls, parties, that sort of thing."

"Is that so? My goodness, that helps make Mrs. Kimbrough's case. I'm delighted you brought it up."

"Now, look, Homer, the thing that concerns Walter is that this case is going to open the door to their bedroom and the whole world'll look upon them. Now, you know how divorces are. No one believes any of the testimony; it's all put on the record for effect."

Peabody shook his head. "No, I won't lead Mrs. Kimbrough down that path. I won't ask her to perjure herself. Neither would she do it. Whatever she testifies, you may be sure it is just as accurate as she can make it and as I can elicit it, and it'll stand up to your examination."

Hamilton frowned. "If she's going to engage in that sort of accusation, we'll counter. She won't like it. Walter's prepared to testify that she's denied him his marital rights and hasn't welcomed him in her chambers since her second miscarriage. We'll put several witnesses on the stand. Walter confided his unhappiness to several close friends over the years."

Homer sat quietly, absorbing that. "Then perhaps Walter should be the one filing for divorce," he said. "How strange that she's the one filing, and he's the one who's allegedly being denied his conjugal rights."

"No, no, no, he's not interested in divorce, not in the slightest," Roderick said. "He's rather fond of her I should say. Yes, quite. He dotes on her beauty—"

Hamilton interrupted. "Look, Homer. Walter's concerned that she may testify that she's been denied her marital rights. The thought of that sort of public disclosure embarrasses him. Even if it's just divorce testimony, which no one believes, it's still grist for the gossips. He's authorized us to make an offer. If she remains silent on the subject of conjugal rights and visits, he'll make some accommodations. He won't say just what at the moment. Meanwhile she can do what she wants."

"I see. And does he intend to testify that she denied him his marital rights?"

"If you force him to."

"I see. Good day, gentlemen. I won't even take a proposition like that to her. You can propose it to her yourselves, or Walter can, but I won't be your messenger. I won't be a party to deceiving the court. If Walter wishes to perjure himself, don't count on my cooperation."

Sterling Hamilton smiled tightly. "You may wish to reconsider, Homer, for Mrs. Kimbrough's sake. Walter's given her an out. In a few years, while she's still in her thirties, he may accommodate her wishes, and meanwhile—"

"Good afternoon, gentlemen," Peabody interrupted.

The pair retreated under Peabody's glare.

He slumped into his hard wooden swivel chair, his mind racing. Kimbrough was trying to silence her. Buy her off. Deceive the court. It took them a long time to get around to it, but that's what they were after. They offered one thing after another, each larger, but it boiled down to two things. Walter didn't want a divorce, and he didn't want the world to discover that he no longer came to the bed of his beautiful wife. Plainly, he dreaded the public exposure of his private life.

The next day, during his final pretrial meeting with Cornelia, he brought up the visit by Walter's counsel.

"They made several offers, including one that I won't convey because it involves collusion to deceive the court," he said.

"I know. Walter proposed it last night. And all the rest."

"Well, what do you think?" he asked. She looked ravishing this wintry day. The cold had nipped her cheeks. The closer they came to the trial, the more animated she had become, and now she fairly glowed.

"I don't want to wait all those years for some vague accommodation, as they delicately call it. I've suffered neglect long enough," she said. "And I'm not staying silent about anything. And I'm not interested in a separation. I want to be free to make a new life and remarry. What good is a separation? Would I be able to have a good life, or a family?"

He nodded. "Cornelia, he's going to testify that you denied him his, ah, marital rights, and you're going to testify that he denied you your marital rights. What's a judge going to make of that?"

She shook her head, grinning slightly.

"Is there the slightest truth in Walter's accusation?"

She turned very quiet for a moment. "After I lost my babies I just didn't want him—you know."

"Yes, of course. How long did these periods last?"

"Two or three months."

"Well, that's nothing. It's not a ground. It's natural."

"I guess you'd know, Homer." She laughed.

That hurt, but he smiled. "My dear Cornelia, it always struck me as strange that a defense against a divorce complaint is to prove that the spouse seeking a divorce was also abusive. Then the court says both spouses are at fault, and therefore the marriage must continue because the state has an overriding interest in preserving the union. An odd doctrine. If both parties are victims, all the more reason to grant a divorce. You realize that Walter's going to do his best to prove you've been cruel—in order to stay married."

She nodded.

"Is there anything else I should know? Surprises in court are very bad."

"Oh, God, I don't know. How can anyone know?"

"Very well, then. We'll soon be in court. I want you to know that I believe in this case. Sometimes lawyers handle cases that offend their private beliefs or ideals. I believe in it not only because your happiness and liberty depend on the outcome, but also because I believe in marriage. That's the whole thing, you see. You're not really married to Walter, except in the most formal and legalistic sense. I've come to despise the travesty of this nonmarriage, and my every impulse is to free you so that you can enter into a true and beautiful marriage. I want you to know I've never tackled a case with as much conviction inspiring me. . . ."

She was smiling at him.

"I'm going to be presenting some novel avenues. I'm going to extend certain arguments and precedents into new realms. My purpose isn't to attack poor Walter, hollow and unloving man that he is, but to show Judge Plowman that this travesty of marriage isn't really one at all, and that dissolving it's the only plausible solution for a union that doesn't exist except on paper. Anything you can do, on the witness stand, to emphasize that hollowness would be helpful. I'm going to ask you simple questions, such as whether Walter's ever told you he loves you. Answer them clearly and carefully. All you really have to do is tell the story, simply, with all the detail you can muster."

"Count on me."

"Sincerity goes a long way. Don't exaggerate, don't minimize. Don't assail Walter or snipe at him. Especially not that. But do describe your sadness, your loneliness, your disappointment, the hours you wait for him, your ache for a word of love from him, the lonely meals, the flight of your hopes and dreams, your desire for children, just as you've described them to me. Will you do that?"

She nodded.

"Good. It may not be much of a case in law, but it is a powerful case nonetheless. We'll give it our best, eh?"

"Yes," she whispered.

C H A P T E R   1 4

rom the bench, Judge Plowman slowly explained his verdict. "What this boils down to," he said carefully, "is that Mrs. Kimbrough feels neglected. Mr. Kimbrough's a busy man, and hasn't been as attentive as she may have wished. Now there's no cruelty in that. It's an ordinary fact of life.

"The other bone of contention is conjugal rights. Both the complaint and cross-complaint allege a lack of access to the other spouse. Now, Mrs. Kimbrough's allegation was not supported by witnesses, while Mr. Kimbrough's allegation was supported by witnesses, men to whom he confided his unhappiness over the years.

"Now, I don't discover anything cruel or abnormal in any of this. It is the ordinary condition of marriage that one or another spouse may not seek the embrace of the other for a while. As for the rest, I find nothing to it. Mrs. Kimbrough's lived in luxury, no wish denied. Mr. Kimbrough has been present in the household all along, apart from perfectly normal business trips. It's hardly a ground for divorce that he stays out late, entertaining business associates.

"Now, the State of Colorado has a powerful interest in preserving and sustaining the institution of marriage, so that children may be nurtured, and husbands and wives may nurture each other and preserve respectable society. This court finds no grounds to grant a divorce. Certainly not cruelty or neglect. And no other grounds were brought before the court. Therefore, I rule that the legal grounds for divorce do not exist and these parties remain husband and wife. Let them reconcile and peaceably restore their union. This session is adjourned."

He stood, mopped his bald crown, and vanished into his chambers.

The verdict didn't surprise Cornelia. She felt deflated, a prisoner of events she could not control. She stared at Homer Peabody, who looked to be on the verge of tears, and she wanted to console him. In his way he had made the strongest possible case, she thought. He had tried valiantly, as relentlessly as a man of his courtly nature would permit himself to challenge, rebut, question, and argue. She wasn't sure that the most powerful shark of a lawyer in Colorado could do any better against Walter's amassed power, assorted witnesses, and a law that made divorce very difficult.

"Oh, Cornelia, he didn't buy my arguments," Peabody said.

"You did your best, Homer."

"It wasn't enough."

"I was just thinking, Homer, that no lawyer in town could have done better."

"You really mean that?"

"Walter has ways and means to get what he wants." She eyed her husband, who was shaking hands with his counselors, enjoying some back-slapping. How strange it was that he and the state of Colorado should regard her captivity as somehow a public good, an upholding of the bonds of marriage.

"Send me your bill, Homer, and thank you," she said, feeling a certain tenderness for this portly old gentleman. He looked so white, so stricken, she wondered if he was about to collapse. But then he pulled himself together, smiled, and nodded.

"My dear Cornelia, I would have overturned heaven and earth to find the means . . ."

She feared he would tear off into paeans of sentimentality again, but he didn't.

"I suppose you'll return to domestic life," he said.

"What about a suit for separate maintenance?"

"The grounds are the same for legal separation. The judge would deny."

"I don't even have that option, then."

"No, not at present. You might in the future."

"What's left for me?"

"Three things. A reconciliation, moving to another state and trying again in a year or two, or creating some sort of life within the cage that Judge Plowman's put you into."

"None of them appeal to me."

"Let the dust settle awhile, and you'll have a better idea," he said.

She watched him labor out of the court, a defeated man with his shoulders back and his head erect, and a calm dignity about him that was belying his real feelings. She spent a few moments with her family, who had watched the entire proceeding, and then fled into the sunlight, still a prisoner and a starving woman.

That evening she waited in the parlor for Walter. If she were doomed to marriage, then some accommodation would have to be worked out. The hours ticked by, and he didn't come home. She would wait him out. She sipped a sherry, thinking and planning, rehearsing what she would say to him. She wanted a separate life. It was that simple. She would have it, whether it was court-sanctioned or not. She hated the Capitol Hill brickpile, with all its ostentation, its vulgar display of possessions including a wife. She hated being dependent on him for every cent. This sad day she had been denied the right to begin over, so she would do the best she could with what was left to her.

By eleven, she knew he wasn't coming home that night. He would stay at the Denver Club or someplace, probably celebrating with his cronies. He couldn't do that for long, or she would be back in court with a valid desertion complaint. She had certainly learned a lot of divorce law these past months, much of it from old Homer Peabody. She knew Walter would ignore her more than ever now; he would make not the slightest attempt to reconcile, or reform himself, or alter his domestic life, or consider her happiness. And she knew as surely as the tick of the grandfather clock that there would be no confrontation this evening or any time. Walter would not be available for negotiations.

That shouldn't have dismayed her but it did. After the verdict she had been buoyed home by the thought that she would negotiate some sort of bearable life, an apartment, an income, no demands upon her other than an occasional public appearance on his arm. But now the hope that had buoyed her spirits fled, leaving her weary after a long and bitter day.

Wearily, she turned down the gaslights and retreated to her bedroom. She felt better there in her own chamber, surrounded by her own bric-a-brac, the photographs of her parents, the oaken armoire filled with her gowns, her silky negligees in a drawer, her small but precious domestic freedom there.

She lay abed, just pondering her fate, suddenly grateful to be left alone that dreary evening. Other women might see the pomp around her and envy her, but they wouldn't see the bleakness. She knew that if she were to find happiness in this life, she would have to achieve it on her own. She could not expect help or sympathy from people who saw only the luxury and had no perception of her starved and barren life.

She could flee, couldn't she? Walk out? Head somewhere—Boston, New York? Start over? To ask it was to know that she couldn't do that. She would still be married. She knew herself to be a woman of principles and scruples, and whatever she did, she would not compromise herself.

She surrendered a moment to self-pity, yearning for children, for a loving and attentive husband, for shared intimacies. But then she pushed the hungers out of mind. If she could not have a woman's ordinary lot, she would find something else, a lesser life but a rewarding one. Heartened by her own courage, she finally drifted to sleep.

The next morning Walter summoned her to his offices in the First National Bank Building. She half expected him to be flanked by lawyers, witnesses to whatever he said to his domestic enemy, once a woman who loved and cherished him.

But when she was shown in by a clerk, she found him alone in his enormous lair, horsehair sofas and chairs, decorated with Currier and Ives lithographs, massive oak desks and tables, a gaslight chandelier, and antique maps on the walls. She had been there only a few times, sensing that he didn't want a meddlesome wife in the middle of his business affairs.

"Have a seat, Cornelia," he said.

She settled herself silently, awaiting word from the lord and master. He seemed almost civil. She bit back the sarcasm that welled up in her, and nodded.

"The whole business was embarrassing to me," he said, "especially the testimony about our conjugal life. I was fortunate to find witnesses who heard me lament that facet of our marriage. I wouldn't want that to stand on the public record uncontradicted."

She listened, amazed.

"Nothing is worse than airing dirty linen in public," he continued. "I encouraged my counselors to preserve appearances, no matter what. But you've done a lot of damage even so, and I fear the name of Kimbrough is going to be tarnished."

"I thought you invited me here to talk about renewing our marriage," she said, "as long as you and the state of Colorado seem to think appearances are more important than realities."

"Appearances are very important. We are prominent people, and we must set standards. We must be the very models of conduct."

"I'd like to be separately maintained, even if not by court decree."

"No, you turned down my offer, and I won't maintain you separately. If you had not brought up this whole conjugal business, you could be looking for a suite right now, with my blessing."

"Conjugal business! That's what you call it. I call it love and intimacy, the heart and soul of marriage. What about simple companionship? Friendship? Is a wife not at least a friend?"

"Of course a woman would think that way. No man does. Without children in the house, there's not much reason to be present in your domestic world. What's there to talk about? There are more important things. Even now, I'm taking time away from my preparations to close two major real estate transactions."

"My God, Walter, I'm keeping you from *important* things. I mean, I'm only your wife."

"Don't be sarcastic, Cornelia. I shall be pleased to continue to support you as I always have. I'll be present, either here or at my house, to handle any crisis or need."

"Any need."

"But no, no suite, no separate life, court-sanctioned or not. We'll continue to show the world our affectionate regard for each other. The state of Colorado has ruled that we're married, must remain married, and must perform our marital duties. I'm sure you will. I know I will. Now, thank you for coming. I really must get over to the opera house."

She gaped. Then swiftly gathered her coat and hat, and plunged out of his respectable office.

CHAPTER 15

he first thing Rose Edenderry did was call herself Mrs. Holliday. She didn't think it was proper just to move in with a man and not be his wife. At the Palace, she told all the serving girls she was now Mrs. Holliday, and they congratulated her and Mr. Holliday.

He wasn't even surprised. "She's number forty-seven," he said. "I won her with a nine of clubs."

The next thing she did was domesticate his awful apartment. She put lace antimacassars on the armchair, and tacked a color lithograph to the wall.

"Damn," said Mr. Holliday. Something about him reminded her of a lit fuse, and she wondered when he would blow up.

She found a folding screen of ebony wood and rice paper that would ensure her privacy while disrobing. It had images of Japanese temples on it, which she thought was appropriate because her body was a temple. She and Mr. Holliday didn't make love. He tried to the first night, but he panted and coughed too much, and stopped. That was the only time she ever saw tears in his eyes.

She found machine-lace curtains and put them up at the window to gauze the harsh light of day and keep neighbors from seeing what she and Mr. Holliday were up to at night.

She added some blue-speckled metal kitchenware, because Mr. Holliday had almost none, and then she visited a Chinese herbalist and bought ginseng, jaborandi, valerian, ginger, and other medicinal roots and teas and herbs.

Her work ended whenever the crowd thinned, but he usually stayed at his table until the last player left the saloon. She always waited up for him, wearing her flannel nightshirt and high slippers that hid her varicose veins. The moment Mr. Holliday walked in, she poured some of her medicinal tea.

"There now, John Henry, dearie, this'll halt consumption in its tracks, and improve your digestion too, it will," she would say ritually, as she handed him his cup.

He always laughed, as if she had made a joke. But he always took the herbal concoction and sipped it, and that pleased her.

She usually cooked a breakfast around noon when they both got up. He always ate part of it, but he never seemed to notice what she had prepared. She fed him good things, like porridge and eggs. Before she started feeding him, his usual breakfast had been two tumblers of rye whiskey, which caused him to cough up blood and curse ferociously.

"You shouldn't say things like that," she said, the first time she heard him.

"Like what?"

"Like what you just said. It's a bad start for the day. I'll fix breakfast after this."

He lit a cheroot and coughed spastically until she thought he would choke, and then threw another bloodied handkerchief on her wash pile.

Sometimes, when he was in just the right mood, he became almost sociable, and then she plied him with questions and mothered him.

"Mr. Holliday, why do you deal faro? Couldn't you think of anything else to do?"

"I can think of lots of things to do. Rob trains, a little bunco steering—"

"You're a southern gentleman, like Andre. I think you should practice it more."

"Practice what?"

"Being a gentleman, being courteous to others. You're always mocking people. Someday it'll all come back upon you and you'll get hurt. Now if you want, dearie, I'll sort of signal you when I hear you do that. I could wiggle my fingers or something to warn you."

He laughed himself into another coughing fit.

She confided in him when they lay in bed, telling him all about her family and her executed rebel father and her English mother, both under the Irish sod, and her life in this country. She just liked to have someone listen, even though he wasn't listening very hard. She tried to get him to talk about himself too, but he always brushed her off with a quip or something mean.

She told him she took after her father, who hated authority of all sorts, especially the British, but also the Catholic Church and the local aristocracy, including their wives and children and dogs. Her mother, she explained, had been prim and rule-bound. Rose had gotten manners from her mother, but that was all. She rebelled against authority as much as her father had, and she had a wild streak worse than his.

Mostly she wanted to learn what Holliday's dreams were, and if he still hoped for a better life even if he had consumption. She could never figure out what she wanted from life except to escape from people who made rules and kept her from doing whatever she felt like, and so she often asked other people what they wanted. It felt odd, not having a goal other than freedom. Maybe John Holliday didn't have a goal either, and in that case they were kindred spirits.

"My goal is to croak," he said.

"But that's not a dream, dearie."

"Pain rules my dreams," he said roughly.

"What about money?"

"Enough to feed myself until I croak."

"I'll take care of you."

He laughed, coughed, and lay silently awhile. "I used to be a dentist," he said. "I called it the extraction business. Extract teeth and money. One dollar a tooth. A hole in the jaw and a hole in the sucker's purse."

"Why did you stop?"

"I didn't really. Any sucker who wants a consumptive dentist spitting blood and coughing while he yanks a tooth is welcome to my services."

"Oh. You shouldn't smoke Havanas. If you stopped, then you wouldn't cough, and then you could pull molars again."

He laughed cynically. She didn't much like it when he laughed like that, rejecting everything she said.

"You drink too much, dearie," she said. "If you didn't gulp down all that whiskey, you'd get well."

"Who says I want to get well?"

"You do. I know you do. You're just mired in hopelessness, John Henry. If you'd just take more of my herbs, especially the ginseng, you'd hardly know yourself in a month."

He coughed into his handkerchief.

She lay beside him, troubled by his attitude. Her hand slid over his emaciated body and she wondered how long he could survive now that he was down to bone. She ached to help him.

One night as they lay in the dark, she ventured to talk about the thing that scared her. "Why don't you ever stop me when I drink too much?" she asked. "I get goin' and I can't stop."

"Why should I? You're an adult."

"Andre did. He always told me to stop, and I always did. Just one word and I would quit. It was so nice to have him looking after me."

"Jaysas," Holliday said.

"All I need is a man to tell me I've had enough. You're right there every night. You could tell me. Otherwise I don't, and then I'm always mad at myself for doing it."

"Rosey, you're on your own. Do whatever twangs your banjo strings."

"You just don't care about me, you don't," she said.

During the next weeks she redoubled her efforts to cure John Henry Holliday. She pressed more herbs on him, scolded him for lighting up too many cigars, sneaked whiskey from his bottle so he wouldn't get it, and tried to talk him into heading for a warmer climate that would be easier on his ruined lungs. She cooked and brewed ruthlessly, determined to rebuild his health even if he didn't want to. And when he stared at her culinary achievements and scarcely forked a mouthful, she felt wounded. Here she was doing her best for him, and all he did was grumble at her.

"Mr. Holliday," she said late one night, "you have a dark vision. All you have to do is dream good dreams. We could have a little cottage in San Diego and watch the ocean. You could get well and we could have children. You could run a hardware store or a funeral home or something like that, and I could raise a family, and we could go sailing once in a while and play whist at the card club."

His response was to leap from their bed and pour a stiff rye whiskey for himself and gulp it down.

"Ah!" he said, wheezing. "You give me nightmares. You miserable preaching bitch."

"Oh!"

The end came the next noon, when she tried to make him eat half a peeled and sectioned grapefruit. He growled at her and pushed it aside, but she patiently placed it in front of him again.

"I'll help you, John Henry," she said. "If you'd only let me take care of you, you'd be so healthy—"

"You're nagging me to death. I'll die of the inflated nags before I'll die of the consumption."

"Did you drink your ginseng tea?"

He growled something unintelligible, sprang up from the table, and began stuffing his things into a battered valise.

"What are you doing?"

"I'm crawling into a bottle until you fetch yourself out of Leadville. I don't mean move down the street. I mean get yourself to the railroad station and hop the next train to anywhere. I'm tired of being nagged to death."

"But I was only trying to help you."

"You're killing me faster than the consumption," he snarled. He pulled his drawers on, puffing hard and looking feverish. "And take the damned doilies."

"Where are you going, dearie?"

"Out of earshot."

He slammed out the door.

She stared bleakly at the rooms. They looked nice now that she had fixed them up. He needed her. He could be feeling better now if he'd just done what she asked.

Sadly, she began collecting her things, starting with the lace antimacassars on the horsehair chair.

CHAPTER 16

. . . .

Lorenzo Carthage had a way of making things happen. He opened an office in Silverton, employed mining engineers and contractors to begin the lift, ordered skips—a type of ore car with the bin on a pivot—which were used to carry loads on inclined tramways, started timbering the shaft, built shops and a lift house in the valley below, graded a road out of the valley, and advertised for hard-rock miners. He put the first four to work immediately blasting and mucking the highgrade seam, and used the proceeds to help pay the soaring development costs. He knew the miners were pocketing a little of the highgrade, but he said nothing. That was the price most mines paid for valuable labor. But he would make sure it didn't get out of hand.

Dixie Cotton stayed in her cabin near the mine, guarding it with the ferocity of a terrier. Carthage saw her whenever he hiked to the mountaintop to keep an eye on things. Her shining cabin and uncomplicated cheer became his Mecca, and he spent hours getting to know his senior partner. Dixie, he decided, was a gem. A fountain of good humor helped to moderate even the worst events of her life, which had actually been a hard one.

"Carthage," she said one spring day, "what're you going to do when this mine's up and running? Silverton's a hick town. Throw a party for the locals?"

"I'm going to pay attention to production."

"Yeah, but that's not your way. You need a Leadville to enjoy yourself, not some collection of log cabins and false-front stores. You got style."

"Why, I'll just turn Silverton into another Leadville. Build an opera house, put up a four-star hotel, bring in a blue ribbon chef, buy myself a Pullman palace car and fit it out, start a racetrack, import truffles and caviar, buy a shipload of French wine, hire a string orchestra, build a ballroom, put up my own Versailles out of town and import the lowlifes, make Tabor look like small fry."

"Well that sure beats all," she said. "How are you gonna do that with two thousand a month and the two percent of the net profits? That's what we worked out, isn't it?"

"Two percent is going to be a lot of money. It's a bonanza, Dixie. I'll turn this operation into a real winner."

"Two thousand salary and a small slice of profits won't build opera houses or turn Silverton into Leadville."

"You have to have faith, Dixie. Money attracts money. When I open the Silverton Opera, when I throw the biggest ball in Colorado, the moneymen'll come and the deals will drop in my lap. That's really all Tabor does. It's not luck. He just spends big and collects opportunities."

"You certainly have notions," she said. "Me, I'm gonna bank the stuff, live quiet, and enjoy a few small luxuries, such as a Thoroughbred racing stable and a steamship."

"You're not a bit grandiose. Just practical, right?"

She had an endearing grin that lit up her big square farmgirl's face, and now she grinned at him affectionately. "When I first took up with Army Cotton, I thought just a nice little cabin and a ma-and-pa mine would suit me. We'd just chop out some ore now and then and enjoy each other. But now . . . it sure grows on you, Magnificent. When I was a serving girl at the hotel in Leadville, I thought you were crazy, blowing money like that, showing off like that. But now . . . You know what my dream is? A laundress. I like cooking, but I can't stand half a day over a washboard scrubbing underdrawers and stockings. Give me a laundress, and a nice little house, and good health."

"Well, I'll see that you're properly corrupted, Dixie."

She guffawed and poured him some more tea.

Carthage achieved his goal of opening the mine to full production within four months. Proudly, one dawn in March, he watched a dozen miners collect at the hoist works in the valley, ride the skips to the top, and begin to muck out ore that had been blasted the previous evening. One by one, loaded skips descended the inclined rails and dropped their ore into a chute. For now, the ore had to be wagoned into Silverton, but as soon as he could afford it, he'd build a three-mile spur track right to the works. That first day he shipped enough highgrade ore to collect a five-thousand-dollar check from the smelter. Old Hod Tabor would have a full return on his investment in ninety days, and after that it would be gravy. Dixie would get rich faster than she could spend the loot, and Lorenzo the Magnificent would be back in business, even if on a reduced scale.

The press trumpeted the story of the new bonanza, and within days Carthage was collecting batches of telegrams congratulating him on his new venture. A few unpaid bills from the Leadville days floated in, too, but these he ignored. He had put Leadville on the map; he didn't owe them anything.

Each week buoyed him higher. The mine proved to be as fabulous as any in Colorado, the ore plentiful and easy to reach, the horizontal diggings far less costly than vertical ones, and the assay values actually improving: the ore was getting richer as his men blasted and mucked their way into the mountainside.

Carthage sent for his old Leadville tailor and had five new suits made, plus a dozen shirts. He ordered a gross of cravats and seven pairs of shoes, each styled differently. He bought a whole wine cellar from the estate of an alcoholic banker in Central City and shipped it in. He acquired a British butler who had to take rooms elsewhere until Carthage found a proper place to live. He bought an ebony lacquered phaeton and a pair of high-stepping matched trotters, and hired a stableboy.

He regretted having to go slow—his managerial wage brought him only 10 percent of what the Pandora was yielding before he lost it. Nonetheless, he cultivated the appearance of prosperity, knowing that the image of Lorenzo the Magnificent would swiftly bloom throughout the mining districts of Colorado. Let them think he was a millionaire again.

In July he was able to purchase a white mansion put on the market by a departing mine owner. He bid low, because there were no other buyers, and got it for nine thousand, with only two thousand down. It was set in a park outside of Silverton, with grand views of the San Juans, and resembled an antebellum southern plantation house, with a huge, pillared veranda and a majestic facade that rivaled the White House. He hired two beautiful maids, both of them dancehall girls who wished to escape the hurly-burly life. He hoped that no one would notice that two maids, one butler, a cook, stableboy, and gardener were inadequate for the establishment. But when he got his first bonus from Tabor and Cotton, he could expand.

In August he threw his first bash. It put him two thousand in debt, but that didn't matter. The new mine was minting money. He engaged a private Denver and Rio Grande parlor car and invited half of Denver, including Horace and the new Mrs. Tabor, up for the weekend. He telegraphed dealers on the Atlantic Coast and New Orleans and had them send lobsters and shrimp on ice, via Railway Express. He hired a sixteen-man string orchestra to come over from Leadville. He purchased moose and elk from hunters, added pheasant, duck, beef, pork, and mutton to the menu, and at the last moment received some javelina from Arizona Territory and caribou on ice from Alaska. He planned an impromptu racing meet, and invited a dozen owners of good Thoroughbreds to try their luck on his oval track behind the house.

His partner for the gala weekend would be, of course, Dixie Cotton.

But she had never been to a ball, lacked a ballgown, and was reluctant to come until he arranged for a New York couturier to come out and sew one up on the spot. Privately, he told the seamstress to bring an extra few yards of cloth, because this ballgown was going to be big. Dixie thought it was all pretty comical for a farmgirl to dress up like a Vanderbilt, but she stood still long enough to be fitted in a magnificent slinky gold lamé gown that highlighted her Junoesque figure.

He did not forget to invite reporters from every Denver paper, and told them the gala was black-tie only. Neither did he forget a bit of ceremony: it was time to name the hitherto nameless mine, and have Dixie christen the headframe with a bottle of Piper Heidseck while the reporters scribbled. All the weekend guests would ride up the lift in the skips and witness the event.

"Dixie, what're we going to call this mine? How about the Silver Cloud?"

"Too fuzzy, Magnificent. Call it the Tall Cotton."

"The Tall Cotton Mine? I like it!"

It all went magnificently. The first families of Denver and Colorado arrived en masse: the Tabors, Cheesmans, Evanses, Byers, Hills, Guggenheims, Campions, Woolcotts, Pattersons, Zangs, Tritches, Mullens, and Knights. Walter Kimbrough came alone, as usual. Baby Doe wore a new ermine cape, even if it was August. Everyone was enchanted with the outgoing, hearty Dixie Cotton, and they all cheered when she bounced the bottle of champagne into the headframe. It didn't break. She took another whack, a farmgirl sort of swipe, and sent the shards and fizz everywhere.

"Ladies and gentlemen, the Tall Cotton Mine is now official. May you all be in tall cotton all your days," said Lorenzo. As a parting gift, he handed each guest a chunk of highgrade silver glance.

The reporters scribbled. As an afterthought, he handed them some highgrade too. They leered at him but they took it.

Horace Tabor pulled him aside and congratulated him. "This here little old hole is a doozie," he said. "Magnificent, you've done 'er again. Find me another and I'll give you half."

"I'll find you a dozen, Hod," he replied.

Lorenzo the Magnificent had risen like Phoenix from the ashes, and loved every moment of it.

After that he went back to making money and putting off creditors, as usual. Smarter this time than last, he did the location work on the claims surrounding the Tall Cotton, and primed Tabor's lawyers to land all over anyone filing an apex suit. No one did. He assayed regularly and watched the operation, missing nothing. The highgrade seam, which angled forty-five degrees to the left of the mouth, ran thirty to forty feet wide and a foot thick. He would mine all of that before tackling the enormous reserves of routine ore.

He worried about declining silver prices—between the Colorado mines and the great Comstock Lode in Nevada, silver was flooding the world faster than the world could absorb it. But that was only a small cloud in a sunny sky. The highgrade was so rich that he could make fat profits from it even if silver should drop below a dollar. He commissioned a railroad spur from Silverton, lobbied Congress to increase federal stockpiling of silver under the Sherman Silver Purchase Act, and wooed Dixie. He was getting marriage-minded and thought maybe he could wed two-thirds of the Tall Cotton and polish her rough edges in the process. She was in no hurry to commit to anything, so he helped her move to Silverton and set up housekeeping in a cottage there, and sent her a dozen Denver greenhouse roses every week. She had fifteen or twenty thousand dollars in Baumgartner's bank, and was adding more each week.

He was planning his next gala, a Thanksgiving ball featuring wild turkey, when the thick manila envelope arrived that changed everything.

CHAPTER 17

 lawsuit. The letter from Denver lawyers was actually addressed to Dixie—it addressed her by her maiden name, Dixie Ball—with copies to Carthage and Tabor. It notified her that the legitimate heirs of Armand Cotton, including his mother, a brother, two sisters, and five nieces and nephews, were seeking to recover the Tall Cotton Mine and to be reimbursed for all the ore wrongfully extracted from it by Dixie and her colleagues.

It said no marriage was on record between Dixie and Armand Cotton, and she had no right of inheritance to Cotton's claim. It added that the seven months she had been his consort was not even adequate to establish a commonlaw marriage, not that such a liaison gave her any right of inheritance.

The attorneys had plainly done their research. They said that the value of the ore wrongfully removed from the mine exceeded the value of the improvements connected with the mine. If Ball, Tabor, and Carthage would peaceably surrender the mine and convey the improvements to the rightful heirs, the heirs would not sue them for damages and fraud or tie up other assets of the three in the process. The present operators of the mine were to surrender the mine no later than the first of December, and not ship any more ore to the smelter.

This formidable communication was signed by Gideon Stone, Esq., one of Carthage's guests at the recent party. The man had been collecting information.

Dizzily, Carthage read and reread the allegations, which were supported by affidavits, including one from the county clerk that no marriage license had been issued to Armand and Dixie, and another listing the total tonnages of Tall Cotton ore received by the smelters in Denver, and the amounts paid for the silver and gold from that ore.

Carthage needed a lawyer. Had he no rights, no equity, from developing the mine into a prime producer? He supposed Tabor's attorneys would already be on the matter, and he would hear soon. Meanwhile, he had to talk to Dixie. Sick at heart, he hastened to her plain cottage in Silverton and parked his gig.

She opened even before he reached the steps.

"Dixie! Is it true?"

"I know, I know. Well, you take up with a man and you just think it's marriage. No, we never did go before a preacher, but me and Army, we knew we'd stick together."

"But didn't you understand you'd have no legal rights? No right of inheritance?"

"I never thought of it."

"Did he give you half? Did he write something out conveying some of the mine or all of it?"

"Nope, he plumb forgot."

"Did he ever promise he would? When the right moment came, or something like that?"

"Nope."

"When you were digging in it, did you find that highgrade seam? Was that your discovery?"

"Nope. He had the muscles and the drills and the giant powder and all that, and he dug that tunnel. After he died I just chipped away as much as I could. But he found the ore."

"Dixie, when he was dying, after you brought him into town with pneumonia, did he say anything about the mine? Did he ever talk about a partnership? Did he offer you a share?"

She shook her head. "He just whispered he loved me, and then he closed his eyes and went away."

"Dixie, did he leave a will? In a strongbox, or at the bank, or in his papers?"

"He wasn't hardly thirty, Lorenzo, and he never left a will that I know of. Never told me about one. I have all his papers here—want to look?"

"I certainly do."

They went through Cotton's meager possessions and found no will.

"I guess we're up the creek," Dixie said.

"You're not. You've got some cash banked. Tabor'll be all right, too. He's gotten some of his investment back. But I am. I'm twenty thousand in debt."

"Hod Tabor'll fight," she said, "and then they'll sue, just like they said, and they'll just take my money from me."

Carthage had no answer to that.

"Well, Magnificent, it was a hell of a whirl," she said. "I never expected some gal like me'd ever see the bright lights. Whatever happens, I'll be all right. I got some cash out of it."

Her brightness almost chased his own clouds away.

Horace Tabor's lawyers arrived on the next train, and reviewed everything, subjecting Dixie and Carthage to long, tedious inquiries that confirmed the worst.

"It doesn't look good, Carthage," confided one, Sylvester Lawrence. "If she never married him, and there's no will, and no partnership or incorporation papers, and no witnesses to any promise, and she put no equity into it, and nothing else is in our favor, Cotton's heirs are going to take over. But we'll dicker. We've built the mine, proven up the reserves, protected the property by filing mineral claims on adjacent properties, and so on. Development's worth something in its own right. We supplied expert management. And if the heirs want to protect themselves from apex suits, they'll want to buy your adjacent claims. But we're not holding any high cards. We've got the three of clubs."

"What about my staying on as manager?"

"No. They want their own man, a fellow named Donald Dillon."

The lawyers returned to Denver, and Carthage waited for the results of the dickering. The ax fell a week later, when Lawrence showed up to oversee the transfer of the property.

"We tried to negotiate the sale of the surrounding claims for a good price, but the heirs didn't budge," Lawrence said. "They argued that they've already made us a generous offer, and those unproven, undeveloped claims that lack even the location work required by the government are worthless. In short, without even location work, those claims are nothing but paper. Sorry, Carthage. We're to be out in two days, and they'll have a manager in here tomorrow."

"Is he looking for a nice little mansion?"

"Go ahead and ask him. From what I know of Dillon, I suspect he wouldn't know what to do with a wine cellar and a racing oval."

Lawrence's eye for character proved to be right. The new manager, Dillon, was a deacon in his Congregational church, a teetotaler, and a Civil War historian on the side, specializing in the campaigns of General Rosecrans.

As they walked the estate, Carthage eyed the man beside him, whose bushy eyebrows shadowed the man's brown eyes from the world. "You can move in just by assuming the mortgage," he said.

"Young man, this is one of those glittering altars to hedonism that are poisoning the Republic," Dillon replied.

"Well, you could do your company entertaining here. Or maybe the Cotton heirs would want it. It's handy to the mine."

"The Cottons aren't the sort who entertain notable people. The elder Mrs. Cotton, Armand's mother, smokes a corncob pipe and reads a chapter of the Old Testament daily, and will no doubt give her share of this wealth to the Primitive Baptist Assemblage."

"Well, if you were to assume my mortgage, you probably could liquidate at a profit, Mr. Dillon. That vintage wine in the cellar will appreciate year by year."

"I've never traded in spiritous liquors in my life, sir," Dillon replied. "I manage mines and men, and that's how I earn my keep."

"Well, I'll liquidate all the items that offend you and then you can turn the place into the headquarters of the Tall Cotton. You've got the biggest bonanza mine in the San Juans, better than Tabor's Matchless Mine in Leadville, and you may as well enjoy it. What's money for, if not to enjoy life a little?"

Dillon stopped their stroll. "Mr. Carthage, when we were investigating this operation and you and Tabor and Miss Ball, before bringing suit, we learned that you've acquired the name Lorenzo the Magnificent. Of course I headed for my history books to learn more about this famous de Medici. In some ways, it's apt to apply the name to you. You both lost awesome fortunes and bankrupted yourselves. In other ways, the true Lorenzo was a better man. He wasn't a mere hedonist, but a patron of the arts, and under him Florentine art and literature reached a great peak. Because of him, we have Botticelli and Michelangelo. Lorenzo himself wrote magnificent odes, sonnets, and love lyrics. I truly doubt that you've written one heroic couplet or donated two-bits to the arts. This establishment, sir, is the efflorescence of a mere sensualist. No. Never.''

Lorenzo sighed, knowing he would be adjudged bankrupt soon, and even then his creditors would swoop in on anything he might accumulate in the future.

Over the next two days Carthage hocked what he could of the few items he owned, turned over the offices of the Tall Cotton to Dillon, turned over the trotters and gigs, the racehorses and wine cellar to his creditors, and wept at the mad misfortune that had broken him over the rack twice in a few months. The awful thing about it was that he should have checked: Was Dixie the lawful widow of Armand Cotton? His new blunder ranked right up there beside the apex suits.

Glumly, he packed his bags, salvaged a bottle of '78 Haut Brion before Baumgartner's bank and a dozen other creditors threw him into bankruptcy, locked the doors and headed for the Denver and Rio Grande railroad station with a few double eagles in his pocket and a few banknotes in his purse.

He paused on his way to say good-bye to Dixie. His marital instinct had faded as fast as her fortune, but she charmed him anyway, and they had wrestled the world together.

"Howdy, Magnificent," she said, beaming at him in her cottage doorway. "Come on in and bend an elbow. I was just going to pour me a whiskey and branch."

"I'm on my way out of town," he said. "Just have a few minutes."

"Where you headed?"

"Perdition."

"It must be in eastern Colorado," she said. "When you get to Denver, you look up old Hod and give him a hug for me."

"Well, uh, I'll be looking him up anyway."

"You having some regrets?"

"Of course I am. Wiped out for the second time."

"Aw, life's too much fun to worry about it."

"Worry! I'm liable for around twenty thousand dollars. But enough of that. Dixie, you're a gem. I'll never forget you."

"I won't forget you either, Lorenzo. I sort of knew we'd meet some day, even back in Leadville when you took a drink off my serving tray.

Listen, sweetheart, I'm sorry. I didn't think about legal marriage or anything."

"Oh, don't fret about it. That's the past. What're you going to do? You still have a fat bank account."

"If those Cottons don't attach it. I took a half of it out yesterday and bought city lots and real estate around here and stuff. Instead of me paying the rent, a lot of people here are gonna fork over the rent to me. I'll go to Denver, I guess. Nothing for me here."

"Well, I might see you there. I'm going to talk to Hod about starting up somewhere again. He didn't come out badly on this and I think he'll back me."

"Good luck, Lorenzo. I want to give you a hug."

She swept him into her arms and crushed him until his ribs protested. The woman was no butterfly. He hugged her back, kissed her smooth cheek.

"Off to Denver," he said. "I'll be at the American House for a few days at least."

"Oh, Magnificent," she said, and he discovered a tenderness in her face. "Next time, you'll win, and you're my fella, win or lose."

CHAPTER 18

Nervously, Homer Peabody adjusted his cravat and dusted the dandruff off his old suit. The cuffs and collar looked passable. He wished he might be a snappy dresser, but he just couldn't manage it. He rubbed his black hightop shoes, hoping for a luster, and then set out into the wind.

Cornelia had invited him to lunch at the Windsor Hotel, an act that astonished and terrified him. He had walked through the grand hotel several times before, trying to nerve himself to enter one of its saloons and meet the movers and shakers of Denver. But he knew it would be futile. He wouldn't fit. He rarely partook of spirits, so he would have to order a sarsaparilla and try to make small talk. He had never been very good at that, and he knew his thick old-fashioned suits with their broad lapels and cutaway tailoring would mark him as the outlandish old fogy he was.

Fearfully, yet curious about what she had in mind, he made his way through town and reached the arrogant hotel in a blast of air. The doormen ushered him into the gorgeous lobby, with its frescoes and marble and potted palms. She was waiting for him there, looking perfectly at home and as young and ravishing as ever. She smiled at him from across the lobby, and that was a good sign. He feared she intended to upbraid him for his dismal performance in court.

"Why, Homer," she said, extending a hand, "I'm so pleased to see you again."

He took her white gloved hand nervously, held it limply and dropped it as if it were a scorpion. "Yes, nice, you look lovely, Mrs. Kimbrough."

"We're back to Mrs. Kimbrough are we?" She smiled. "We'll have to change that."

She led him to the electric elevator. He had never been on one and worried that it might crash. A uniformed little man operating brass controls took them upward at a dizzy pace and braked just as Homer concluded they would hit the roof and fall to the basement.

She was taking him to the Roof Garden restaurant. He had heard about this wondrous place, but of course had never ventured there. It cost too much. Nor would he have felt a bit comfortable with its extravagant cuisine.

"A table at the window, Roberto," she said to the cadaverous majordomo, and soon Homer Peabody found himself seated across from the young matron he had failed so miserably two weeks earlier. If she despaired about her fate, he couldn't see it. Her flesh glowed with life and health, her eyes glistened, and she sat erect and bent forward in her soft teal wool suit with a jabot at her throat.

She did something quite beyond his experience. She ordered for him. A lobster bisque, shrimp cocktail, a chicken curry, a spinach salad, Parker House rolls, jams and marmalade, and Earl Grey tea. "You would've ordered oatmeal, Homer," she explained.

He nodded. She knew him all too well. "I'm delighted with your selection, madam."

She smiled wryly at that. "I suppose we should do the business before visiting," she said, pawing open her reticule. "Here. It's your payment. You charge far too little, you know."

He took the envelope. The three hundred something seemed a lot to him. "You didn't need to pay so soon," he mumbled.

"I wanted to. You earned it. Of course Walter wouldn't pay it, so I had to resort to my own devices."

He nodded and tucked the envelope into his breast pocket.

"Aren't you going to ask me how I managed it?"

"Why, no—"

"I sold my wedding and engagement ring." She laughed so gaily that he joined her. Indeed, her ring finger was bare. "I think it's appropriate, don't you?"

"Cornelia, I'm sure that everything you do is well thought out and appropriate."

"The last time I saw you, you were almost in tears. Are things better now?"

"Oh, they're grand. Perfectly grand."

"My dear friend, when an innately truthful man talks nonsense, it's rather painful to hear."

He sighed. "That case. It was a miserable performance. I failed."

She reached across the table with her ungloved hand and touched his arm. "No, Homer, that's not true. You did a good job. Even Walter's lawyers told me so. They said you got as much out of a weak case as any man could. They also said that to their wives, who told me. I heard it several times. You shouldn't be so hard on yourself."

"Really? Did people say that?"

"Yes. I wanted you to know. I sense that the defeat crushed something in you."

"Let's not talk about that."

He was rescued by the waiter, who served a sumptuous meal brought in pewter salvers. He couldn't remember ever having had such a feast for lunch, and scarcely even for dinner. The heady fragrances made him salivate.

After they had devoured the glorious meal, she returned to her topic. "Homer, do you have friends in Denver?"

"Why, I really haven't taken the time—"

"I thought so. We all need friends. You might consider joining the Denver Club."

"Ah, no, that wouldn't be possible just now."

"You want me to think it's the money. But that's not what you're thinking, Homer. You really don't think the membership committee would accept you, and I'm sure you believe that if you became a member, it wouldn't improve your life. You feel awkward. Am I right?"

He stared. "How are things going for you? It must have been hard to return to your empty home, your situation unchanged."

"Homer, we're talking about you now. I think you feel you're socially rather—old-fashioned, and so you don't even try to find friends. You're really quite shy, you know."

"Some people draw others to them, other people—everyone flees when they come into a place," he said slowly. "I've learned my limits. I have certain traits that—"

"Homer, you should count your assets. If you know you've many admirable qualities, then you wouldn't slide into this sort of thinking."

He gazed at her numbly, and chewed on a Parker House roll. "How has Walter treated you since the divorce?" he asked.

"Every time we reach a painful point you try to divert our conversation," she said. "What I see before me is a man of transparent honesty. You're also courtly and gallant and always civil. You're always gracious; I've never heard an unkind thing from your lips. You're an adult, Homer, not a bit childish. You're generous. You praise others, including your adversaries, such as the opposing lawyers. I heard you do it in court and before and after. Women always feel comfortable with you because we know you're a gentleman. And you listen to us, and to everyone. There's not a client who hasn't received your full attention. Now, the first step is to know what's good about yourself and forget what's less good."

He lifted the thick linen napkin to his face, making it look as if he needed to wipe away food, and furtively dabbed at the wetness in his eyes.

"You're a virtuous man, Homer, with a tender side, but you see those things as drawbacks. Your scruples defeat you at law, and they inhibited you when—you were courting young women."

"Please, Cornelia—I must go."

"I'm sorry. I went too far. I came here with a certain mission in mind. Tell me what your dreams are. Maybe I can help. I have all sorts of connections."

"I have none."

"Not even marriage? You gave up on that?"

"I don't expect to live long. It's too late to have dreams."

"But Homer—" She retreated a moment, but then pressed on. "Is it awful? Some terrible disease?"

"No, very ordinary. But I have only a few years. The doctors can't say exactly."

"But what is it?"

"It's not table talk."

"But I'm done. See?" She put down her fork.

He felt trapped. "I can't make water," he said. "Almost stopped up. Prostate."

"Oh," she said, obviously puzzled. "I guess I need to learn about that. I'm sorry. But you must still dream. We all must dream. We all must go on with our life journey, no matter what."

He stared bleakly at her. "God knows, I appreciate your encouragement. And those were the first compliments I've ever—ever—heard in . . ." In his life. No one in Crawfordsville had ever complimented him for anything. And in Denver he didn't know anyone anyway. He dabbed at his watery eyes again.

"Well," she said softly, "let's say you have five years. Let's say there's time to try something new. Let's say you want to focus on your assets, your gifts, the things you give others. What would you do?"

"I'm not aware of giving gifts to anyone."

"Homer, your civility and courtesy are models that others emulate. Your honesty and truthfulness are shining lights. I was very proud to have you represent me in court."

Peabody gathered up his courage and straightened in his chair. "Cornelia, you're overly concerned about me. I've made my bargain with my Maker and wouldn't know how to change myself."

"I think maybe you should try. For one thing, you might look at your practice. Maybe specialize in divorce cases. Maybe you have other talents. Maybe Denver is crying for a man just like you."

He laughed bravely. "Now, you can't teach an old dog—"

"No, I don't expect you to become a hardware store owner. But what if you could put a lifetime's experience in law to good use some other way? What about becoming a salaried lawyer for a company, or the city? Or an administrator? Or running for a judgeship?"

"Abstractions. We must live with our realities. I don't inspire friendship or offer it. My record over a quarter of a century doesn't assure my clients that they're in good hands."

"Have you ever written for legal journals? Or tried poetry? Or written an essay?"

"I have a lucid style," he said. "I've often thought of making a few modest submissions to the law journals."

"Do they pay?"

"No, one does it to make a point in a controversy. Or in some cases, for the cachet."

"I'd like to look around and find some things for you. I just want you to have a happier life. Would you let me look?"

"Why, I suppose, but it won't help."

"I might even find a widow to introduce you to."

"No, not that, Cornelia. It's too late now. I'm on the downslope of life. And it'd be an ordeal for me."

"An ordeal?"

"Yes, baring all my failures to her, wrestling with hope of intimacy, matrimony. My, ah, infirmities. Nothing I've ever done has amounted to much. She'll—No, no, not that."

She looked amused. "Maybe she'll have the same worries. Maybe you're just what she wants. You need a nice hug from a nice widow. Maybe she'll think she's never counted—until you came along, a gallant lawyer and a loving husband.

"Now, I'll just take that check. Walter pays, you know." Her melodic laughter captivated him.

CHAPTER 19

ornelia knew she had to try. As long as the law and the court declared she was to remain married to Walter, she had to find some way of making the marriage functional.

For a week she thought about what she wanted to say to him, and how to approach him. By some unspoken agreement they had divided the twenty-two-room house into separate quarters. They managed most days not even to see each other, carefully choosing different moments to eat or to pass through the rooms that neither of them claimed.

Then, one evening when she knew he was in his study, and the buttery light of the gas jets leaked from under the door, she approached him nervously. She knocked and opened the door, and found him at his rolltop desk reading legal papers. He looked handsome in his waistcoat and sleeves, his thin patrician face somehow radiating power and position.

"We should talk, Walter. As long as we're married, we should try to come to some pleasant ways of being together." She was proud that she had avoided accusation. Her instinct was to say, "as long as you insist on our being married," but she suppressed that.

"What's there to talk about?" he said.

"Well, first, let's make some ground rules. No accusations. I'm here to heal our marriage."

"You dragged me into court on worthless grounds and embarrassed me. Embarrassed the Kimbrough name. Exposed me and my family to the savagery of the press. Opened our bedroom door to public scrutiny. Brought up conjugal relations in court, mortifying me and making me look like—I don't know what. Fortunately, I was able rebut that part of it, and now the record clearly shows the folly of your accusations."

She sighed. He had broken the ground rules with his first words.

"Do you know what that whole unsavory episode meant to me?" he continued. "We're a prominent family here. A thousand malicious tongues gossiped. We've an obligation to set the moral tone of Denver."

She thought better than to reply to that. "Let's talk about making our lives more pleasant, Walter."

"Mine is very pleasant."

"Will you let me tell you what I'd like?"

He stared stiffly at her, not resisting.

She sat down on the horsehair couch, composed herself, and began gently. "I'd like us to be friends and share our lives," she said. "I'd like to begin a family. I'd love to have a son and a daughter, more children if you'd enjoy them. I'd love to bring them up in a way you'd be proud of, and see them mature into their own lives. I'd love to learn about your business, and share it with you—the real estate, the mining, the traction company, and all the rest. I'd love for you to enter into my life, the ways I shape our home, my charity work. I'd love to go on a honeymoon with you, to celebrate our renewed marriage, maybe to Europe, just the two of us, each hug restoring our lives, making our marriage what it should be, our little bit of heaven on earth."

He stared impassively at her. "What you're really saying is that you find me inadequate for all your fancies."

"No, I'm inviting you to join me in a real marriage."

"A real marriage," he said mockingly. "Didn't the courts determine that we have a real marriage?"

She bit back a temptation to retort that the court merely found no grounds in Colorado law for the divorce.

"It's been years since you came to my room. Maybe it's time for you to renew our bonds, joyously and tenderly. I'm yours if you want me."

"There you go again, accusing me. You didn't even abide by your ground rules."

"Where was the accusation in that, Walter?"

"Everything you've said is an accusation, even if it's cloaked in sugar."

"Walter, why did you resist the divorce? If you feel I'm accusing you, why didn't you just let me go?"

"Because it would have been a scandal. Kimbroughs must never be caught in scandal. Your testimony that I had failed in my conjugal duties mortified my entire family. Imagine what the *Rocky Mountain News* would have done with uncontested allegations like that. Fortunately, I was able to rebut them."

"Are you saying you fought the divorce to avoid—public disgrace?"

"Public scandal. Absolutely."

"And not because you want me for a wife?"

"You've long since poisoned the well."

"My life, my future, my needs and hopes are not a consideration?"

"They were before the divorce suit. I offered you an entirely separate life, quiet maintenance apart. To put it bluntly, you would have been perfectly free to enjoy your own liaisons and continue to live in luxury. You chose to disgrace me, and my response now is that your happiness is no longer my concern."

She bottled up a dozen responses to that, and weighed him solemnly. "All right. I'm glad I tried one last time. I've removed any lingering doubts."

"I'm busy. Please don't pester me." He turned to the thick nest of papers before him.

She stood slowly, feeling icewater in her veins.

"And don't try another legal action," he said. "I keep a log of my time in this house. My accountants will witness that you never lack for a thing. Because I'm a gentleman, I take special pains to praise you to my colleagues and associates. In fact, they marvel that I find so much that is pleasant about you. They think I should be much more severe. The record will always be very clear about my conduct. Bear that in mind if you should ever find some rogue lawyer again." He surveyed her coldly. "By the way, you may have these back." He pulled open a cubbyhole drawer and handed her the rings. "You will wear them, of course."

She gaped at him.

"The Windsor Roof Garden is hardly a private chamber," he said, answering her unspoken questions.

"You were spying?"

"I'm a prominent man. People naturally keep me informed about things affecting me. Now, then, I am immersed in business."

"Indeed you are," she retorted, and left him.

She stood in the dark hall, making an important choice. She could put on the rings or not. But it really wasn't a choice.

She retreated to her own suite, actually relieved by the encounter. Walter would always be Walter. She wished she had seen his nature when he was courting her, but all she saw was an unusually serious and adult young man whose reserve formed an invisible wall around him that she supposed she would pierce once they began the intimacies of married life. Oh, what a mistake that was. But she had been so young, and the Kimbroughs so prominent. . . .

In her suite she dropped the rings in her jewelry box and settled into a parlor chair, needing time to reflect on all that had happened.

She had gotten one new fact out of it: he was taking steps to prevent or quash another divorce action, even keeping a log of his time spent in the house. Even telling his associates endless lies about how delightful his wife was to him. Evidence. Dozens of witnesses. A barrier to any more scandal. She marveled at him.

What did it mean? Another divorce effort would fail, no matter what sort of case she put together. If she chose to live honorably, she would never again hold a man in her arms, or know passion. She would never have children to love and nurture. She would never enjoy a shared life, encouraging her husband even as he encouraged her. If she lived honorably, she would throw her life away, the victim of an unconsciously cruel man whose only passion was the esteem of his colleagues.

But she might choose to live dishonorably, and could even justify it. She could desert him. She could leave Denver, leave Colorado, and try for a divorce in some other state. But she knew he would resist as ferociously in California or Nevada as he had in Colorado.

She could toss virtue to the winds. She could take up with some happy and affectionate man and bear his children. Or she could flee Colorado, assume a new name, and marry again, in what would actually be bigamy. She bridled at all that. Oh, why were the choices so cruel?

Not that she lacked the mettle to rebel against this steel cage Walter had built around her. She had the nerve to do anything. But some instinct warned her that she would not enjoy a rosy life if she took up with another man. She would have to live with her own conscience, and it wouldn't be easy. She ached to be freed in the legal and proper and approved manner, and then start over with her head held high, her friendships intact, her honor and virtue unquestioned.

It seemed to come down to whether she was willing to pay the price. She knew it was a question she would entertain for quite a while, while she explored her chances. A decision did not have to be made just yet. Comforted by that, she decided simply to postpone doing anything rash. She intended to get more counsel from a good divorce lawyer, one not even known in Colorado.

She was young! Her life had barely begun. In one sense, she had everything. She had only to sign an invoice or a bill or a restaurant tab and it would all be taken care of. Surely she could turn this caged life into something at least pleasant. She could plunge into charities, as some of her friends had done. She could give her own parties. Walter's absence from them would start tongues wagging, which she would enjoy.

But the awful truth of it was, nothing she did would be very fulfilling. Nothing would release her from her need for a loving husband, and her own dear children. She had gradually come to know her own nature: her happiness lay in giving, nurturing, intimacy, and warmth radiating out to her husband, her family, her friends, and all the world.

She might, to some eyes, live the life of a privileged woman, but in deeper ways she knew she was one of the world's most impoverished and desperate. The bitter truth, brought home to her this evening, was that she had no choices.

CHAPTER 20

fter buying his casket, lot, and monument, Yves Poulenc set about the business of dying with greater earnest. That meant more study of the topic, even though he had to send to Denver for books. He wanted to know what the world's great religions and other societies had to say about death, reincarnation, heaven, hell, and souls and spirits independent of the mortal coil.

But only a poet could speak truly of death, and of these, only John Keats had it right:

> When I have fears that I may cease to be
> Before my pen has glean'd my teeming
> brain,
> Before high-pilèd books, in charact'ry
> Hold like rich garners the full-ripen'd grain;

When I behold upon the night's starr'd
   face,
Huge cloudy symbols of a high romance,
And think that I may never live to trace
Their shadows, with the magic hand of
   chance;
And when I feel, fair creature of an hour,
That I shall never look upon thee more,
Never have relish in the faery power
Of unreflecting love!—then on the shore
Of the wide world I stand alone, and think
Till Love and Fame to nothingness do sink.

Ah, there was truth, and there was a poet who sang his death sublimely. Yves intended to die no less beautifully, and leave behind him the verse that would rival Keats and ensure his immortality.

But his first efforts were interrupted by a change in his routine. A consumptive young woman moved into the cabin next to his, and after that his dying would never be the same. His glimpses of her as she unpacked, bought groceries, and explored the lunger community, were of a woman of unearthly beauty, with great dark feverish eyes, a flawless pallor of doomed flesh, a gaunt angularity of face that gave it a classic quality, as smooth and sublime as a Michelangelo sculpture.

He met her the following day, when they both happened to depart for the hot springs and sulphur steam at the same moment.

"I believe I'm your neighbor," he said. "I'm Yves Poulenc."

She gazed at him brightly, her face cheerful instead of melancholic, which made her different from most consumptives. "Yes, I've noticed you. I'm Maria Theresa Haas. Are you going to the pool?"

"Yes," he said, and they walked down the path together, she in her woolen swimming dress and robe, he in his swimming drawers and robe.

"Have you been here long?" she asked.

"For months. I expect it'll be over soon, now. I can tell. I'm preparing for the end."

"Oh, no, don't say that. You must never surrender."

"Who recovers from this plague? No one."

"Some do. I'm going to."

He wanted to say something cynical and caustic, but he remembered to be polite. He remembered that he had clung to hope at first, having learned of a rare case or two where someone with a hardy constitution had triumphed over the terrible disease. "I hope you succeed," he said kindly.

They reached the side of the rock-bound pool, and she shyly pulled off her robe, revealing a slim, frail figure within the swimming dress. He noticed her ring.

"You are married, Mrs. Haas."

"Yes, my husband couldn't afford to come. He's an apprentice architectural engineer in Philadelphia. He's a genius, and some day he'll design bridges so beautiful your heart will melt at the sight of them. He shows me his drawings. If I need him, he'll come, even if it means leaving his position. But I'm going to try this alone as long as I can."

"You may as well send for him," Yves said hoarsely, stepping into the hot water, his pulse racing as it always did with the slightest exertion.

"So this is what you do," she said. "Breathe the sulphur fumes and soak."

She followed him, exclaiming at the heat. "This is certainly an adventure," she said. "The doctors all recommended it. They said the clean air would help—we live in the sooty city, you know, so much coal smoke. And the hot springs with their minerals would help, too."

"Yes, but I'm afraid they don't help."

He sucked in the steam, and paddled water awhile, weary of the whole repetitious business, his body hurting.

"You're discouraged, that's all. I brought some herbs with me, and I'm going to use them."

"I'm afraid there are no herbs known to cure consumption, Mrs. Haas. If anyone could prove there are, we'd all be devouring them."

"Well, we'll see. Sometimes I take them to lower my fever. Other times as a tonic. I take ginseng. I also eat lots of greens and fruits and vegetables and I take honey, too."

She had an endearing optimism, and he envied her. Of course when the disease had done its work, and ruined her lungs, and debilitated the rest of her fragile body, she wouldn't be so cheerful. "That's all very good," he said, "but Dr. Pierce, one of the foremost authorities, says to eat fat. Lots of animal fat is what slows the disease and keeps us from emaciation. I can quote him exactly. He says oily food's important. Beef should have lots of fat. He recommends plenty of salt. Plenty of eggs and cream and milk. The flesh of fowls is especially good for consumption. I always insist on being fed in that manner."

She eyed him across the water, which rose to her breast. "And did it help?" she asked.

"No. I'm too far gone."

She laughed lightly, a gossamer tone in her voice. "I think maybe you should not take this Dr. Pierce so seriously."

"Oh, he's right; it's just that I'm incurable. I'm doomed. I'm preparing for the end. Writing poetry like John Keats. He died from consumption, you know, and made himself immortal." He coughed, and then wheezed desperately, gasping for air. He was so sick of the endless fever and convulsions and pain.

"Are you all right?" she asked.

"No, I'm sinking. I've made all the preparations."

"What preparations? Forgive me for asking. I'm so new at this, Yves."

He enjoyed being addressed by his own name. "A consumptive has to come to terms with his tragedy," he said. "That means accepting death, buying a cemetery lot, buying a coffin and a funeral service, and putting his affairs in order."

"Oh, I'll leave that to Carl. Besides, I intend to get well. Herbs, greens, and some exercise in mountain air and sunshine. That's what'll do it."

"I have to get out of the pool," he said. "If I stay in too long, I suffocate. It's bad enough not being able to breathe—I'm desperate for air, just some air—but this steam . . ." He clambered painfully up some rock ledges and stood in the chill air, dripping, panting, feeling dizzy.

"I like this heat," she said. "I'll stay. But you come over for dinner. I'm going to start healing you. Mostly, you just need a little mothering." She laughed.

He thought he'd accept. He would have the chance to educate her about doom. "I'll be there. At six, I suppose?" he said.

She nodded. Stiffly, he wrapped his robe about him and stumbled back to his cabin, wheezing desperately. She made him sad. She was so *ignorant*. So frivolous. Putting all her faith in chimeras.

He collapsed on his cot, his heart hammering wildly as it always did now. He was sinking fast, and an elevated pulse was one of the symptoms. Little did that poor woman know what she faced.

He showed up promptly at six, knowing he wouldn't stay but a few minutes. It was past his bedtime. All physicians he had consulted told him to rest constantly; it would delay the inevitable. He carried with him his medical bible, Dr. R. V. Pierce's *The People's Common Sense Medical Adviser,* published in 1876, with all the latest medical information within its pages.

She seemed scarcely affected by the lateness of the hour. "Now,

Yves, I'm going to start curing you. You just help yourself to a glass of that syrup there, and I'll give you more. You should take it three times a day."

He looked at the brown concoction dubiously. "What's in it?" he asked.

"I'll read you the receipt. It's right here. 'Take one part elecampane, one part spignut, one part sage, one part horehound, one part yellow parilla, one part goldenseal, one part Solomon's seal, half part gum myrrh, half part gum guaiacum, half part tamarack gum, all boiled in rainwater, then put one gill of wine to every pint, bottle up, and take one wineglass full three times a day. Also take one quart of St. Croix rum, and one pint honey, alum the size of an egg, boil and skim as long as there is any froth, then bottle for use; dose one tablespoon three times a day with the above syrup.' Now, did you drink the syrup? Good. Take a tablespoon of this bottle here."

He did as he was told, concealing his skepticism because he rather enjoyed her attentions. "There," he said. "Now I have something for you. This is from the best authority, Dr. Pierce. He says that about a seventh of all deaths are due to consumption. Now let me read you this: 'Invalids are seldom willing to believe they have consumption, until it is so far advanced that all medicine can do is to smooth the pathway to the grave. Another characteristic of this disease is *hope,* which remains active until the very last, flattering the patient into expectation of recovery.' Now, the first thing you have to do, Maria Theresa, is to come to grips with the truth."

She laughed. "You're just determined to die, aren't you, Yves?"

He choked back his impatience, and then coughed spastically for two minutes, finally spitting up a large chunk of purulent matter mixed with blood. He wiped away the tears in his eyes, and folded the stained handkerchief and stuffed it back into his suitcoat.

"I'm sorry," she said gently. "I truly am sorry, Yves. You're very sick, and I've been callous."

"You just don't believe you have consumption, that's all," he said.

That astonished her. "Why, I've spent the past year finding out all I could about it," she said. "I've had the disease for longer than that, but I didn't know it. Cough. Trouble breathing. Hemorrhages of the lungs. Emaciation. Fevers. Sore throat. Weariness. All the rest. I know I have consumption. Three doctors told me so. But I think I can help myself."

"Have you children, Maria Theresa?"

She stared into the floor. "The disease made me barren," she whispered. He discovered tears in her eyes. "I must get well. I must!" she cried.

"We all must prepare for the worst," he said gently. "Later, you'll thank me for preparing you. I'm trying to help you. It makes the end easier when you're reconciled to your fate. I never let hopeful talk seduce me from the truth."

"No! I'll never stop hoping," she cried. She whirled away from him, to the little counter that served as her kitchen, and began serving her meal.

"The spinach is for your blood," she said. "This honey and ginseng tea will help you. The tangerine salad, with the herbs in it, will help your body resist. The beef's for your strength. I want you to be sure to eat the skins of the red potatoes. And afterward, I have some rose hip tea."

"Where did you get all this?"

She shrugged. "I brought the herbs. See that trunk? All herbs and decoctions and tinctures. I'm having things shipped from Denver. I knew I couldn't get much here. One look at that little store, and I knew I was right. No wonder you're all dying. You don't get the right foods."

"Dr. Pierce says to eat fats, and I've had plenty, all from that store."

She smiled at him and ate peacefully. He ate slower, having trouble swallowing because of the ruin of his throat and esophagus.

"I really don't know what works and what doesn't," she said softly. "But I like to try. I've had several remissions. That's because I keep trying, I think."

"Well, you'll get past that," he said.

"I have faith," she said. "I'll get well. I'm going to go home. I'm going to have children. My husband is going to welcome me at the train station."

He pitied her. He'd wrestled the demon longer and suffered more defeats. She was putting her trust in herbs and diet, which was foolish, but she'd find that out soon enough.

"Thank you, Maria Theresa. It was delicious. And I'm glad we talked. Thank you for the tonic, too. I'll try it for a few days. Perhaps you've learned a few things. Pierce is the great authority, you know. Half the lungers in camp have his book. I'm very weary now. I must lie down quickly. I'll leave you with one thought: Come to terms with your fate, for the sake of your peace of mind. I'm trying with all my strength to help you."

She nodded and smiled, as he left.

ose Edenderry told herself she was turning over a new leaf. She was done with men. They either bossed her around, or got mad when she did what she pleased. When she got to Denver, she would find rooms for herself and avoid all tinhorns, bunco steerers, sharpers, and sports.

Her figure kept getting her into trouble. She supposed she would be thick some day, but just now she was all curves, and she could tell from the look in men's eyes what was on their mind. At least her assets got her lots of tips as a serving girl or a dancehall girl, and that was fine with her. She didn't have to do what some women did to survive.

The Denver and Rio Grande train wound its way along a looping, tortuous route, but would eventually deposit her at Union Station in the Queen City. Denver was a good choice. She was done with the mining camps and all their rowdy sports. Denver would be more respectable and treat her better. Lots of rich men lived in Denver and maybe she'd find one. But for now, she wasn't going to have a thing to do with any male, except to serve drinks, of course.

She stepped off the conductor's iron stool in a glowing May afternoon and decided to look for rooms at once, and then have her trunk forwarded to her. Blake Street and its alleys was the place to look; Market Street was the one to avoid. The sporting district was close to Union Station, so she didn't get a hack. She hiked eastward on Blake, liking what she saw. Nice cabarets and saloons all cheerfully crowded together; lots of places a girl could work. And just as she expected, she could let a room by the week within a block of the cabarets. She tried several places, ranging from grim and grubby to snappy. Feeling lucky, she took a clean ten-dollar room with chintz curtains, up an alley with some Chinese living on it. She knew they would sell her powders whenever she wanted them.

Getting a job turned out to be the easiest thing she had ever done. She walked into the first likely joint, the Arcade, about five that afternoon. She felt right at home as she sashayed up to the barkeep.

"You need a serving girl, hon?"

The pox-pocked man behind the white apron nodded. "Go talk to himself in the corner there. Jack Diamond's the name, and he owns the place."

Diamond studied her up and down a few times even before she had a chance to introduce herself. "You can start right now and you get tips," he said.

She looked him over. Young, dark, skinny, but she liked the humor in his gray eyes. "Slow down, dearie. I want a buck a day plus tips."

He didn't hesitate. "You'll bring 'em in. You got the looks. All the pretty dollies are in the mining camps, not Denver. All right. Wear something that'll catch the eye. Work from five until we shut down, whenever that is."

"You mean skimpy. A little ankle, a little scoop. All right. I'll come here skimpy on warm days, but I'm not gonna catch catarrh on cold days."

He aimed a tobacco-stained thumb at his chest. "I'm Diamond. I run it. Barkeep's Louis Krivitz and another one comes on in a few minutes, Roman Gans. Fellow at the faro layout's Masterson. You're on."

That settled that. A dollar a day almost paid her rent, and the tips and free drinks and stuff would cover the rest, and she'd have some left over for some powders from the Chinee whenever she wanted. At last! No blasted man was going to tell her what to do, or kick her out of his dump. This Denver, it was a big city, and she'd counted a dozen gin mills right on this stretch of Blake.

The Arcade did a booming business from five to midnight, and she marveled as she swiveled through crowds of males at tables, or around Mr. Masterson's faro layout. Masterson was short, thick, dark, and as good-humored as Diamond, and maybe that was why the Arcade drew a lusty crowd. But she saw a quiet assessing quality in Masterson, not so much menacing as wary. He sometimes favored her with a faint smile, but she ignored him. He was one to beware of, she figured. That was a lady's man if ever she saw one. The tinhorns all thought they were God's gift to women.

She served up lots of fancy stuff in this place, not the usual sour beer or popskull or red-eye, but real bourbon from back East, and two or three good pilseners and ales. This was Denver, not some hick mining camp. And these were city sports, not some hard-rock miners and speculators. The tips weren't as good as she had hoped; Denver wasn't quite as carefree as the mining camps. But they were all right. Soon she'd have some regulars, boys who got mooney and gave her four-bits with each round. Then she'd be in clover.

That night she counted three dollars and three-bits in tips, which was just fine. And she never had to buy a drink, neither. That big masher at the bar kept pushing them on her, trying to take her home.

"I'll take your drinks, dearie, but don't think it'll get you anywhere.

I live with my sainted mother and my twin daughters, I do. My uncle lives upstairs."

The masher had grinned and bought her another round.

She wasn't hungry, and she didn't know where to eat anyway at two in the morning, but walking up the alley she had smelled the sweet smoke, and that was what she wanted. She headed into darkness, knocked softly on the door of a half-basement room, and found herself facing an ancient Oriental whose queue hung to his waist.

"Hop hop," she said.

He smiled, bowed, retreated a moment, and returned with a paper packet that wrapped a small hard ball.

"Two dollà," he said.

Moments later, she examined her purchase. Opium came in solid brick form, or powder. This was a bit of brick, brown colored. It looked like good Turkey opium, made from the milky fluid extracted from opium poppy fruit. Upon exposure to air, the milky fluid turned brown or even black. This gummy piece was spherically shaped to drop into her little clay pipe. She settled herself on her pallet and soon ascended upon a cloud of smoke and didn't come down. The next day she did not feel like working at the Arcade, so she didn't. The following day, she showed up.

"Is this a little habit of yours?" asked Diamond.

"I needed a day off, dearie."

"Don't we all. But someone has to hustle drinks. What's your little weakness? Hop?"

She didn't reply.

He studied her, contemplatively. "All right. You'll work when you want a little hop money or rent money. That's fine. You're a draw here. Just one thing. When you're working, you stay off the sauce—all sauce. You get the orders straight and serve fast. Okay, Rosie?"

She nodded, annoyed. Men always wanted something. No one let her do what she wanted. She liked to smoke hop. It let her escape into pure white joy, like a down-filled bed. It wasn't anyone's business what she did. They all said she'd get hooked. Well, she could take it or leave it.

"One thing more. Since I can't count on you, there'll be another girl or two around. It'll cut into your tips."

She smiled. "Not very much," she said. She could hustle drinks better than any dozen serving girls she knew. She knew how to kid a customer into anything.

She had plenty of business that night. A dozen times Mr. William

Masterson rang his brass bell at the faro table and either ordered drinks for the players or let a player order one for himself. He had a slow, knowing smile, and eyes that saw through her.

"Bring a round for these gents," he said one time. "And you can tip me after we close up."

"I tip you?"

"Out of sheer gratitude," he said.

She laughed. William was a wild card.

Nonetheless she waited with an odd anticipation for the Thursday evening to end, which it finally did when a die-hard player cashed his chips after one.

Masterson was waiting, too. "You can give me my tip now, Rosie," he said.

"You can give me your tip for serving you all night," she retorted.

"Your place or mine?" he asked.

"No place. I'm sick and tired of tinhorns."

He grinned, tugged his derby over his groomed dark hair, and slipped into the darkness.

That night, two of the serving girls, Betsy and Heather, had a party just for the saloon girls, so Rose went, and drank gin, and they all got weepy. They talked about their men, and Rose told them she had sworn off men forever. They thought it was a grand joke. The next afternoon she didn't feel like working, so she stayed in her room and drank tea.

She worked hard Friday because she needed to make her Saturday rent, but she was still over a dollar short on rent day. She dropped eight dollars and ninety cents into Mr. Heilbrenner's calloused hand and said she'd give him the rest in the morning.

He responded sternly. "You get one chance on the cuff. You pay me the rest in the morning, you get one more chance. You stiff me, and out you go. You can make good credit, see? If you're good for it, I don't mind waiting a day or two."

She nodded sweetly and headed off for the Arcade. Saturday nights were always good, anywhere, and she knew she'd make lots of boodle. She'd pay Heilbrenner and have some money left over for hop. The Arcade rocked that night and she had to push through crowds just to serve her drinks, and some boys grabbed her when she squeezed past them. She got a headache and slipped out to get some Dover's powder, which was opium mixed into ipecac and saltpeter. A couple of five-grain tablets helped, but she felt giddy and big-eyed—the chandeliers were so bright—but she got through the night. She didn't even know how much she had, lots and lots for Heilbrenner.

"Your place or mine, Rosie?" asked William, the tinhorn, when they shut down after three.

"I'm off tinhorns," she replied. She felt heavy, and she had pounds and pounds of coins to carry.

"I'm going to walk you to your rooms," he said.

"I don't need your help. You men all think we need your help all the time."

"There's half a dozen footpads in this neighborhood, mostly preying on gambling winners, and this is their hour."

"No, leave me go, William."

He didn't. He walked her up the alley with his hand in the pocket of his coat, and when a yegg crept up in the dark, William whirled, sapped the man so fast he grunted and toppled into the filth of the alley, and they heard the footsteps of another man running away.

She let William in.

"I need some huggin', Masterson, damn you," she said, oozing with maudlin misery.

CHAPTER 22

When Mr. Baumgartner at the bank summoned Dixie Ball, she discovered her troubles weren't over. A little wiry man with a blotched bald noggin, a drooping moustache and wire-rimmed spectacles studied her alertly, fairly bristling with energies.

"This here's Samson Smith," Baumgartner said warily. "He's a lawyer for Horace Tabor."

"You're Dixie Ball?" the man asked, almost nattering.

"Sure am, pal."

"Well, here's some documents for you. The first notifies you that Horace Tabor's brought suit in Denver against you for fraud and misrepresentation. You'll be served soon, I'm sure. The second is a *lis pendens* action tying up your assets. Your bank account, your real estate, your house and personal possessions cannot be disposed of until judgment is rendered."

"What do you mean?" she asked.

"It's a standard measure to prevent a party in litigation from disposing of assets or hiding or spending them until the court decides what to do with them."

That hit her hard. "But why? Why me?"

"Read the complaint, Miss. It says you misrepresented yourself as the proper and lawful owner of the claim upon which the Tall Cotton Mine stands, and by said fraudulent representation induced Mr. Tabor, through Mr. Carthage, to invest considerable capital totaling seventy-eight thousand dollars in a mining claim in which you had not the slightest interest. He seeks to be made whole, of course. Your entire assets would barely do it, given legal fees and court expenses."

She turned to Baumgartner. "What's this? Can he do this?"

The banker nodded. "I've been served. Your assets here are frozen by the Denver courts, Dixie. I can't release them without court permission. Same's true of your real estate."

"I won't sit still for this," she bellowed. "Old Hod Tabor didn't do so bad. He got most of his investment back before the Cottons took over."

Smith began nattering again. "Well, Miss Ball, I've an inducement that might encourage you to cooperate," he said smoothly. "So far, this has all been a civil matter. If you turn over these properties forthwith, we won't file a criminal complaint."

"A criminal complaint?"

"Fraud. You knowingly defrauded and buncoed a wealthy man out of his money. We'll file the complaint right here in San Juan County, within the day, and you'll face a felony indictment. Given the nature of the case, and the prior litigation with the Cottons, I'm quite sure you'll end up doing a two- or three-year stretch."

"But I didn't know I was doing anything wrong."

Smith gazed at her patiently. "Even an adolescent knows that a few months of cohabitation with a man doesn't make you an heir. You weren't married. He left no will. He made no promises. You knew that. Your responsibility as a competent adult woman, at the time of his demise, was to notify his heirs at once, and surrender the property. From the day you dug out some ore after his demise you were stealing, and the entire time you were pretending to be its owner you were engaged in felonious theft and fraud."

She turned to Baumgartner, who was piously steepling his fingers on the desk. "You're my banker. I'm your customer. I want an independent opinion. Is this shyster right? I never was pretending anything. Army was my man, that's all."

"Dixie, Mr. Smith is a counsel of good repute. He's simply defending the interests of Mr. Tabor, and my instinct is that he has a valid case."

Dixie glared at him.

"Now as a further inducement," the rooster continued, "we are prepared to let you keep your household possessions, providing of course that they have incidental value not exceeding a few hundred dollars. We'll give you seven days to sell them and vacate. This depends of course upon your signing the several documents I've prepared here: quitclaims to your various properties, and various releases and agreements. Sign right now, Miss Ball, and we'll tear up the criminal complaint and agree that we've come to a peaceful settlement and Mr. Tabor has been made whole."

"You mean you'll lay off if I turn my stuff over?"

"Exactly."

"For good? No debt?"

"Well, yes, but only if you act today."

"You wrung this hen, gutted her and plucked her feathers, right?"

"Well, ah . . . we're offering a generous way out for you; preferable to facing criminal charges, a trial, debt for representation, and no doubt some time in sequestration. I don't think you'd enjoy prison, and a felony record that would dog you the rest of your life."

"Does old Hod know about this?"

"We keep him informed of overall strategies."

"That's not what I asked, blast it. Talk square. Does old Hod know? I'd like to talk to him. We were partners, him and me and Magnificent."

"He doesn't know the specifics, but it won't matter. He knows we're pursuing every avenue to make him whole. I'm still inclined to offer you the remainder of the day to come to terms."

"Can I send him a wire: Call off the dogs, Hod?"

"You're perfectly free to do so."

"Maybe I'd better find me a lawyer. I've never even talked to a lawyer before. You know one, Mr. Baumgartner?"

"Three of them around the courthouse, Dixie."

"All right, blast it. I'm going to find one."

"Very well. Have him get in touch with me at once," said Smith. "I'll be here or at the Antlers Hotel. Returning to Denver on the five-thirty train."

She hurried to the courthouse square and engaged the first lawyer she could find, a courtly gentleman of about seventy named Loyola Higgins. He heard her out, scanned the documents, and frowned. "Let's go talk to Smith. I'll try to get another forty-eight hours so we can work this out. Maybe we can salvage some of your property, a lot or two, and your house, if we push hard. We can often salvage a domicile. I rarely say a case is hopeless, but I suspect you're as close to that estate as a person can get. I'm wondering if we can't bring a cross-complaint of our own, just to have a little grapeshot in the barrel. I'll do some sharp quizzing.''

He hastened to the bank with her and found Smith dawdling there over a Ned Buntline dime novel. For a while she thought maybe she had a chance: Higgins was twice the size and three times the weight of Smith, and employed a booming basso against Smith's squeaky tenor. But the skinny rooster wouldn't budge, wouldn't even grant a few hours' reprieve, and looked at his pocket watch every ten minutes.

At last Higgins turned to her. ''Your options, it seems, are exactly what Smith says: sign away your property now, or face a criminal complaint and take your chances on an acquittal.''

She had already come to that conclusion just from listening to these gladiators strike swords.

''All right, blast it,'' she said. ''Mr. Higgins, you make sure he's telling me the truth when he says I've got seven days to vacate and I can keep my household stuff, and if I sign all those papers that ends it for good.''

Higgins scanned the documents, nodded, and pushed a pen at her. ''Sorry, Miss Ball'' was all he said. ''It's my painful duty to recommend that you sign.''

She did. Baumgartner witnessed.

Smith leaped up, stuffed papers into his briefcase, and smiled. ''You won't regret it, Miss Ball,'' he said. ''Off to the train now.''

He left a silence behind him, almost a vacuum.

''The Cotton family litigation and settlement didn't help you,'' Higgins muttered at last. ''A pity. If it had just been a little ledge up there, with a few months' supply of ore in it, no one would have given it another thought. But the Tall Cotton's a big mine.''

She turned to Mr. Baumgartner. ''I need a little loan.''

''Ah, have you collateral, Dixie?''

''Some household stuff.''

Baumgartner steepled and unsteepled hands. ''Let me help you arrange an auction instead. We'll do that tomorrow. I think you can sell enough to keep the wolf from your door, Dixie.''

At last the blues seeped through body and bone and soul. She had lost over twenty thousand dollars in hours. She managed to thank Loyola

Higgins and retreated to her cottage, the only house she had ever owned or would ever own. She brewed some tea, and it comforted her.

What a day! She turned the lamp low, so she could gaze into the moonlight. The San Juans glowed silvery and alien in the distances. For an ordinary girl off a farm, she'd already had an adventurous life, and she had no regrets that she had abandoned that dismal plot of earth for all this, even this day's disaster. She was plenty young, and maybe she'd find a good man and hitch up. She figured she wasn't cut out to have a lot of money anyway; too many people wanted it. All she needed was a good time once in a while, a chance to pin on her straw boater and go on a picnic somewhere with someone pretty fine, or see the variety theater, or spend an afternoon in a beer garden.

Still, she knew she was bucking herself up, and not really dealing with her grief. She had lost a treasure that equaled twenty or thirty of her father's farms. And before that she had lost a fortune to the Cottons. She sipped tea, tugged and hauled her spirits around, now philosophical, now anguished, now resigned, now bitter, and once even amused. She didn't know which of these feelings was true—maybe they all were. It didn't matter. She was busted and would have to find some ordinary work somewhere.

But where? She sipped tea and puzzled that one for a while, and decided at last on Denver, not being one to dither over such choices. She'd tried the mining camps; now she would try a real city, with all sorts of people in it, lots of young women like her, maybe a man or two. Life was just too much fun to spend time regretting what she had lost.

The next days went smoothly, thanks to her banker's help. She sold off her furniture, paid Mr. Higgins fifteen dollars for his three hours of valuable assistance—he'd earned it, she thought—and bought a coach ticket for herself and express passage for her humpbacked trunk.

When she left, no one came to the Silverton station to see her off. She took it for an omen. She hadn't really made friends in Silverton, living up on the mountains at first with Cotton and then alone. Friends. She wanted lots of friends. Real friends would be worth more to her than a mine anyway. And the prospect of making a lot of new friends was what led her to choose Denver. She wouldn't miss Silverton.

After a long, slow, rattling trip, she finally stepped onto the brick platform of Denver's Union Station and headed into the great city. She wore a fancy gray silk dress, one of her few mementos of richer days, but it softened her large frame and she thought it might help her find a job.

She had already decided where to start: the Windsor Hotel. She had plenty of experience as a chambermaid and serving girl in Leadville hotels; maybe that would recommend her to the managers of the luxurious Windsor. That was where a girl could get the best tips, so that was where she would begin.

She tiptoed through the gilded lobby, awed by what she saw, found the way to the hotel office, made her case, got herself a job as a chambermaid on the evening shift, met several of the women on shift to learn the ropes, and even arranged to live in a little flat in the Cherry Creek Bottoms area with two other maids. The pay would be seventy-five cents a day, but there were a few extras. Although it wasn't hotel policy to feed the maids, most of them ate leftovers in the kitchen, and that would help. She'd get by, if only barely.

Dixie Ball had descended from a mining queen to a Denver chambermaid in weeks, and she hoped she would be strong enough to cope with it. Dreams died hard.

CHAPTER 23

L orenzo Carthage set about finding Horace Tabor as soon as he reached Denver. The silver magnate had finally shed his wife Augusta and married Baby Doe, and was ensconced in a suite at the Windsor. But he was surrounded these days by politicians, retainers, lawyers, managers of his enterprises, capitalists, and bankers. Reaching him wouldn't be easy.

Hod Tabor had once promised Carthage another grubstake, and Carthage meant to take him up on it. So he haunted the Windsor saloons, sent word up to the guarded suite above, and watched his double eagles slide into saloon and restaurant tills one by one. Finally, a fortnight after he had abandoned Silverton, he caught Tabor, who was sitting in a banquette with Baby Doe and several mining men.

Carthage figured that was good. Whatever Tabor said would be known to the world.

"Well, it's Magnificent," said Tabor when Carthage approached. "Pull up and have a toddy."

"I'll just do that, Hod," Carthage said.

"Fellas, this here's Lorenzo the Magnificent, who makes and loses fortunes every few weeks," Tabor said. "Last time, he lost some of my fortune, too."

"It was worth the risk, Hod."

"Sure, if we had the slightest legal claim to the mine."

Carthage met a water company president, a mining engineer, two lawyers, and a railroad man, who courteously made room for him.

"Well, Hod, are you game to try again? I'll find another one," Carthage said, getting right to the point.

"Oh, you'll do that, no doubt about it. And maybe lose it, too."

"No. That was a fluke. I've got a nose for mines, and I'd like to try it again, Hod."

"Lorenzo, my boy, you've the nose all right, but I'm not going to set you sniffing again. I've got other plans. There's a killing to be made in South American mahogany. These fellows here and me, we're just talking about buying up a few forests or a banana republic and shipping mahogany up to the States. Now if you had a nose for rare wood, why maybe I'd deal."

That astounded Carthage. "You're out of the mining?"

"Not at all, but even dumb old Hod knows there aren't many new properties worth plugging a nickel into. Maybe south of the border, but not here. I'm just plumb out of the grubstaking line."

"How about if I just look over mines and prospects and report to you? Give you the lowdown on each for a flat fee? Then you and your managers can check them out and decide?"

"Well, boy, I've got half a dozen fellers, good shrewd men, doing just that. Don't need another."

Something tightened in Carthage's chest. He saw what the end of this conversation would be. "If you have a place for me somewhere, you'll get the best from me that I'm capable of, sir."

"Well, old Hod Tabor knows that, and I'll keep you in mind, Magnificent. But we're getting into tropical wood. Have another toddy, boy."

The mining engineer, the man called Wilburforce, smiled. "How'd you get to be called Magnificent, Mr. Carthage?"

Tabor answered. "They named him for that Eyetalian, Lorenzo de Medici, the magnifico, when Carthage ran the Pandora in Leadville. Threw parties like you never seen. Style, that's what. Put even an Eyetalian prince to shame."

"Oh, the Pandora. Got eaten up by apex litigation. I remember," said Wilburforce. "Well, if you're looking for a good mine to manage, you should take a close look at the Lucky Strike in Telluride. They need

a manager who knows his stuff. I was in that pit the other day, and saw
more silver and gold tellurium ore than their own management realizes.
Silver ore with tellurides and some gold and half a dozen base metals
in it's tough to reduce. I argued with them for hours about the way
they're doing things. They're losing money on a rich mine. Someone
smart's gotta go in there and straighten them out. It's a good mine,
even if they can't figure out what to do with it. All they see is the red
ink. I'd be buying stock in the Lucky Strike if I weren't so committed
elsewhere. Their bungling is an investor's opportunity. Someone's
gonna turn that money sink around."

Something thrilled through Carthage. "It's on the mining
exchange, sir?"

"A bargain."

"Why's no one buying it?"

"Like I say, they're mining a refractory ore. Durango mill can't handle it well, getting only twenty or thirty percent of the gold and silver,
at more expense than it's worth. Scares off investors. But I know several
chemists who'd crack that problem. What they need is a manager who's
not so bullheaded. And a better mill. They're using the old mercury
amalgamation process and won't even switch to the Freiburg process,
which would help. They say it costs too much."

"Mahogany's my ore, and so's Baby," Tabor said, and Baby Doe
laughed.

She sure was gorgeous, Carthage thought, pure sugar and spice. And
she loved old Hod, doted on him, watched him reverently from those
big blues, her hands always patting and poking and caressing him.

"If you were to send me, I'd go out there and take a look at the
Lucky Strike, Hod," he said. "I know ores. I know milling and smelting.
If I think it can be reduced, and I can prove it in a laboratory, you could
make another killing. Just buy a controlling interest in it and let me try.
I'd do it for a flat fee."

"I think not, Carthage," said the lawyer. "With all due respect, Hod
has his own staff. And he's looking at wood now."

"Lorenzo, I've got the Matchless, and its carbonate ores reduce
right down into thick bars of silver bullion. Thanks anyway, old friend,"
Tabor added.

Carthage finished the whiskey and another just to conceal his itch-
iness, and finally retreated. He hastened through the baronial lobby and
beelined to the stock exchange, wanting information about the Lucky
Strike. He corralled a trader just before the closing bell, found that the
stock was going for seventeen cents a share, and bought a thousand

shares for a hundred seventy and a commission. It happened so fast, and he acted so recklessly, that he felt the fool when it was over.

He had twenty-three dollars left.

He stared numbly at the crowded trading floor. Men in vests and shirtsleeves were tallying accounts, wading through paper, wiping chalk off blackboards, lighting up cigars, writing notes. Carthage had impulsively walked into this snakepit and bought shares in a faltering mine without a serious investigation of its value or condition. Just on one man's speculation. He'd been a fool.

The trader, whose name he didn't know, approached. "Where shall I send your certificate?" he asked.

"I'll pick it up here."

"Suit yourself. Here's a receipt for the trade. Here's my card. I'm Quigg. I've a seat here and my offices are on Seventeenth. Need your name and address."

"Lorenzo Carthage, American House."

"Lorenzo the Magnificent. Didn't know I was dealing with you. Mighty pleased. You're a legend."

"I'd like a margin account"—he studied the trader's card—"Mr. Quigg."

"Sure, we'll fix you right up. Man like you, we'll open it right away—getting into the action, eh?"

"You bet," said Carthage. "See you in the morning, Quigg."

Carthage watched the trading floor empty, and felt the energy of the place ebb as quiet overtook the market. Willy-nilly, he had become a stock speculator, without the slightest preparation or experience. A plunger would be the better word. Maybe that was good—as long as he could turn his slim investment into a living. His remaining cash wouldn't support him for more than three days at the American House.

What if that mining engineer with Tabor didn't know what he was talking about? What if the refractory ores defied reduction and the mine sank? Or what if the mine simply languished month after month while the smelter experimented with its ores? Amazed at his own impulsiveness, Carthage meandered back to the American House through a hot afternoon, so astonished by the swift turn of events that he couldn't make sense of what happened.

At the exchange the next morning, Carthage boldly bought another thousand shares on margin. He had two thousand shares, and thirty days to repay the broker for the second thousand—or lose them all. The price per share hadn't changed, and showed no sign of drifting away from seventeen cents. He peppered the trader with questions, and in between trades Quigg filled him in. The Lucky Strike had been capitalized with two hundred thousand shares, par value one dollar, but had disappointed investors from the start, failing to do much more than meet payroll because the ore wouldn't reduce efficiently. The price had settled around eighteen cents, and stayed there for months.

Carthage headed off to the Windsor for lunch, wanting to think things over. He looked around for Wilburforce, the mining man, and didn't find him. He ordered the dollar blue-plate five-course special, and sat back to contemplate his folly.

Over potatoes au gratin he had his first insight: he didn't have time to go out to Telluride and try to talk the managers into accepting his services as an expert. He was twenty dollars from the streets of Denver.

Over cherry cobbler he had his second insight: he didn't have time to wait for the stocks to rise, which would happen only when management licked its problems and turned around the ailing mine.

Over Columbian coffee and a chocolate mint, he arrived at his third insight: he, the well-known, widely acclaimed, celebrity and genius called Lorenzo the Magnificent, could nudge the stock and make a quick profit. And what better place to start than with Quigg, his trader, and his creditor?

He hastened back to the exchange, and caught Quigg in a slow moment. "Want to talk privately," he said.

"No one eavesdrops around here."

"Well, this is highly confidential. I think I know a way to turn the Lucky Strike around. Next two days, I'll be raising capital among a few worthies who've helped me over the years; plan to buy up a lot of stock, controlling interest if we can, and then go out to Telluride for some talks. I want to manage that mine. When I get the cash together, I'll let you know. Then start buying quietly on my account, little at a time, you know? No rush. Don't drive up the price. Got it?"

"Sure do. Mind if I buy a few thousand for my own account?"

"Not at all, Mr. Quigg, if I can have your proxy when the chips are down. Just keep it slow and easy, and don't give the game away."

"I'm glad I run into ya," said Quigg.

"Mr. Quigg, I'll invite you to my first party," Carthage said. "Put you on the board of directors."

. . . .

T he next morning Quigg had bad news.

"Carthage, I'm calling your loan. That Lucky Strike stock's dropping by the hour. It's selling at ten cents, some of it nine cents right now."

"Ten cents? Why?"

"Stuff's flooding the market. There's seventy thousand shares going begging. No one wants it. Rumor is that the Lucky Strike's bankrupt and didn't meet payroll. No production. Durango mill won't handle the ore anymore—it can't make costs."

Carthage knew he was on the knife-edge of failure again. "Quigg— I'll settle after the bell. You buy every share you can lay your hands on. Buy all seventy thousand."

"You're crazy, Carthage. You'll saddle me with a lot of debt and a mess of bad stock."

"Buy it, Quigg. I'm going to talk to the Guggenheims. Knew 'em in Leadville. Their smelters can handle this ore, plenty of reverberatory furnaces designed for it. But it's a long haul from Telluride. Ben's in town, and I'll see him. Maybe I can track down Meyer, too. Quigg, buy. Don't you fail me now. Don't rob yourself."

"I'll rob myself into a bankruptcy, that's what." He sighed. "I'm crazy. I'm greedy. All right, Lorenzo the Mad, I'll start buying, and by tonight I'll know whether I'm ruint. We got thirty days to pay anyway, that's the rules on this exchange. So wipe me out."

It took a while to track down Benjamin Guggenheim. He wasn't at the smelter, nor at the family's fabulous Leadville mines, nor at his Denver home. But he was at the Windsor Hotel, hosting a reception for his suppliers in a suite on the top floor.

Finding the smelting magnate had taken time, and Carthage was two hours from disaster. He adjusted his cravat, dusted dandruff off his shoulders, rubbed his shoes on the back of his trousers, and plunged into the reception. He spotted Ben at once, the man as serious, formidable, and urbane as ever.

"Why, Carthage, it's grand to see you," Guggenheim said, surprise in his face.

"Need to talk to you fast, Ben."

"Why, after my little soiree, my old friend."

"I'm talking about a fortune, and the chance dies when the exchange closes in two hours."

"Oh, nothing worthwhile dies so swiftly, Carthage. These balloons and bubbles don't interest me. I'm not in the killings business. And it's better to wait for a collapse and pick up the pieces anyway, if that's what's happening."

Carthage ignored that. "I'm buying a valuable, proven mine on margin. The Lucky Strike, in Telluride. It's bankrupt. It didn't make payroll and it's idle. Stock's flooding the exchange today. The trouble is refractory ores—the Durango mill can't reduce them well enough to turn a dollar. You can."

Guggenheim said not a word, his gaze searching Carthage with disconcerting intensity.

Carthage described his purchases and hopes.

"That's a little reckless, isn't it? Buying what you can't pay for? I've been hearing about your troubles with the Tall Cotton."

"Yes or no, Ben. I don't have time to debate it. Make your own deal. I want to manage that mine. I can make it work."

"I know the mine," Guggenheim said. "They sent some sample ores for me to experiment with."

"And what did you conclude?"

"That ore is hard to reduce. And it would have to be shipped here. But it's rich ore, I'll grant that. Silver, gold by-product, other metals too. You wait here, Carthage, and I'll ask some questions. The information I need's right here in this suite."

Carthage ladled rum punch from a cut-glass bowl, and sipped and agonized while Guggenheim drifted from one man to another in that smoky room.

At last the magnate returned. "How many shares did you say?"

"Last I knew, seventy thousand available, at a dime or less, out of two hundred thousand shares outstanding."

"Seven thousand dollars for a third of the Lucky Strike?"

"Seven or more. My broker's still buying."

"Who are the principal stockholders? I know Teller's one."

"I haven't taken time to find out."

"How much debt?"

"I didn't have time—"

"Can the company assess shareholders?"

"I didn't have time . . ."

Guggenheim shook his head disbelieving. "And what do you want?"

"To manage it for a piece, say five percent of net profit and a reasonable salary. For you to cover my margin right now."

"I would own the stock you're buying on margin?"

"All yours, Ben."

"You're a reckless young man, Lorenzo. This doesn't commend you as a manager. Neither does your history."

"Try me for a year."

"I don't know; I'll think about that. No promises. If I cover your purchases, you'll turn over whatever you've bought on margin to me at cost?"

"I'd like a cent a share over my cost. I have a thousand other shares."

"Excuse me, while I talk to a few people," he said, and drifted away.

Carthage watched Guggenheim engage several men in terse, sharp conversations, punctuated by occasional glances in Carthage's direction. Then Guggenheim returned.

"The Lucky Strike's about ten thousand in arrears and losing two hundred a day," he said. "It's defeated the current management, as you say. The stock coming on the market now was in the hands of its operators. They're bailing out ahead of the crowd."

"Well, there's our opportunity," Carthage replied.

"You're a plunger," Guggenheim said. "You think you're going to stanch the flow and turn a profit?"

"I know I can."

Guggenheim smiled, suddenly, like sun piercing some black clouds, and nodded. He headed for an escritoire and penned a note, guaranteeing that he would cover purchases of the Lucky Strike made that day by Carthage.

"There you are, young man."

"You're not so much older than I am, Ben."

"I'm ten times older, I think."

"Thanks. You won't regret it."

"That remains to be seen."

Carthage raced madly through the hotel, and then up Sixteenth Street, back to the exchange and into the bedlam of the trading floor.

"Well, am I ruint?" Quigg demanded.

"How many shares?"

"I've bought the whole lot, starting at seven cents, but the last bunches were going for eleven, twelve. Seventy-eight thousand so far. Am I crazy?"

"Ben Guggenheim's covering." Carthage shoved the marker into Quigg's hand.

"What's the deal? Who gets the shares? You syndicated?"

"He does, except for what I started with."

"What do you get?"

"A penny a share profit, and a manager's position turning that mine around, and maybe a cut of the profits if I succeed."

"But you don't have controlling interest."

"We'll see," Carthage said, at last beginning to enjoy this frantic day.

Just before the closing bell, Guggenheim himself showed up. Carthage handed him a sheaf of receipts, which the smelting man leafed through.

"Price rose," he said. "To be expected, I suppose. What's the total?"

"Seventy-nine thousand one hundred shares, seven thousand five hundred-something dollars, plus my penny a share, plus Quigg's commission."

"Eight thousand," Guggenheim said. "All right. I'll deal with your broker. Tomorrow, I'm going to Telluride and find out what's to be done and where we stand."

"I'll come along."

"No, I'll do this alone."

"But I'm going to manage—"

"Maybe. You're a man of great ability and . . . weakness."

"I won't make a mistake this time."

Guggenheim's disconcerting gaze settled on him again. "Carthage, what do you want from life?"

"I want to turn that mine around, put it in the black, show you I can do it, win your confidence, and make a lot of money myself."

"And what else?"

"That's it."

"I believe you're known as Lorenzo the Magnificent because of your lavish way of living."

"If I earn it, I'll enjoy spending it. It's my cachet."

"Your response doesn't win my confidence. What is your vision? Your larger purpose in life?"

"To count. To make it, Ben."

"And when you make it?"

Carthage didn't enjoy the cross-examination, and merely shrugged for a reply.

"I will tell you a paradox," Guggenheim said. "If your goal is merely to make it, you probably won't. This day you came to the brink of destroying your broker, Quigg, and ruining yourself beyond redemption. You intended for me to bail you out, no matter the risk to me. All for the sake of making it."

"Your family made it in Leadville, much the same way," Carthage replied. "I made a big bet today and won. You'll profit as much from this as you did from the A.Y. and Minnie mines in Leadville. You're still getting a thousand a day out of them."

"We shall see," Guggenheim said. "When I return from Telluride, I'll be in touch with you. Where are you staying?"

"American House."

"Have an operating plan to show me when I return. In my office are assays of that ore, and some cost projections for reducing it here. I'll make sure copies are sent to you."

"I'll be ready."

"All right. Let's go talk to your broker and go over these arrangements. We seem to be harnessed, for better or worse."

CHAPTER 25

omer Peabody prospered. The newspaper publicity, naming him as counsel for a prominent woman, brought him clients even though he had lost the case. For once he didn't have to spread dead files across his work table to look busy; the stacked files held genuine business now. Most of it involved divorces, a facet of law practice that was distasteful to him.

Life had improved a little. There had been moments when he was on the brink of hocking his law books to pay the office rent. Now, though, his income permitted him a few pleasantries, such as a restaurant lunch now and then, although he stuffed most of his spare cash into his bank against the next financial drouth.

But his ascent from financial desperation didn't lift his spirits. His long, lonely life still saddened him. As he aged, doors softly closed behind him one by one, and he had been scarcely aware of those one-way passages. He had come to Denver thinking to remake his life, long after it was possible to transform himself. He had clung to the dream of a wife long after it was probable that he could find one and domesticate himself. He had hoped to become more combative in litigation, long after age had encrusted his solicitous habits of mind.

The only person he ever talked to was Mrs. Kurtz, the widow who cleaned his rooms once a week for fifty cents. Sometimes, when their mood was just right, they exchanged confidences.

"Do you miss your husband, Mrs. Kurtz?" he asked one morning before going to his office.

"Frankly, Mr. Peabody, a man's a nuisance around the house. I miss him, but I'm glad he's gone. I'll tell you frankly, sir. Women don't need men, not in old age. Men need women; you're all dependent on us for your housekeeping and cooking and company. But an old bag like me, all I want is a few old gals to talk to, and it's all the better if we're all widows."

That had shocked him. "I suppose you're right. All I ever dream of is a mate to share my life with."

"Mate, ha! Some poor old woman to cook and make your bed and wash your lavatory, like I'm doing."

"No, I want to share a life with someone. Talk about things, do things together."

"Well, I got over that at age twenty. Women are realists; men are romantic fools. My advice, Mr. Peabody, is to forget women. At your age, they'll all think you're an old goat. Go sit on a park bench and give candy to children if you're a sentimentalist."

She had returned to her featherdusting, and he sat miserably in his chair, knowing she had described a certain truth about old men and old women. Until that moment, he had still believed that somehow or other he would find some affectionate lady who would share his last days with him. But it would never happen. She was right: the most ignored and invisible people on earth were single old men, busy with their dying.

He had nothing to offer a woman, no matter what Cornelia had said to cheer him up. All those dreams, a lifetime of dreams, had been slain by age and infirmity and his own oatmealy nature. No lovely single woman would ever walk into his offices, discover his sterling virtues, and fall in love with her dashing attorney. He would never sit across his office table from a woman he had come to love in the course of his professional service to her. He would never propose marriage; he lacked even the courage to ask. He would never stand at an altar, dressed in a new morning coat and a stiff new shirt, beside a bride in a wedding gown, and recite holy and sacred vows, pledging love and life and support forever unto death. He would never slide a ring onto his beloved's finger. And that tender, lingering hope of fatherhood—why, that had long vanished.

That morning, on his way to work, he realized that if he wanted to enjoy his last years, or discover any meaning in his long, inhibited life, he would have to abandon the youthful dreams once and for all, and try to live for something else. Anything else.

Reality came hard to him. The thought that he still might find a wife had lingered all these years. He could either find something else to do to fill his last years, or else get busy with his own dying, helping it along any way he could, as so many old men, in so many silent rooms, did each and every hour. Mrs. Kurtz had forced him to confront reality, and perhaps he could be grateful for that.

Fortunately, he didn't have to think about that. He was too busy. If Mrs. Kurtz had said the same thing back when he spent his office hours reading *Ben Hur,* he would have brooded and despaired. Work was his salvation. He drafted a business partnership contract, started three divorce actions, drafted a petition to decrease or eliminate alimony, started work on two wills, brought a suit for nonpayment, took on two water-rights cases, and started to negotiate a settlement involving a violation of contract.

He hadn't had that much to do since his earliest years as an attorney. And all because of Cornelia. It came to him that he owed her in many intangible ways, for her cheer, her support, her sensitivity, her invitation to lunch. Perhaps he could return the favor, especially since a lunch at the Windsor would no longer torpedo his budget. He drafted an invitation to lunch, and dispatched it to her via one of the city's many messenger boys, who raced their bikes hither and yon, usually delivering within a half hour. That very afternoon, her response came: she would be delighted to lunch with him on the morrow.

That pleased him. He studied his outlandish old suit, wishing he owned something better. It would have to do. And so would his ancient stock of yellowing shirts and stained cravats, and venerable hightop shoes, with cracks and creases and bulges no amount of blacking could conceal.

The next noon he met her at the Windsor, and they proceeded to the Roof Garden restaurant as before. He marveled at her lavender velvet dress, which transformed her into an imperial, relentless beauty who turned heads as they were seated. But then he noticed more: a graveness and tautness that had escaped him during their first moments.

"Cornelia, you are ravishing today," he said.

She nodded, her mind obviously far away. "How are you, Homer?"

"Why, I've a spate of work, and it's all your doing."

"It was the newspapers' doing."

"Have you and Mr. Kimbrough come to any terms or understandings? Are things any better?"

"An understanding? That's a good way to put it. The understanding is that I'm a prisoner of a man whose life is totally separate from mine. He's very vengeful. He feels the case was a blot on his reputation. If I sound bitter, it's because I am."

"Well, you're fighting."

"I live alone. Do you know what he does? That miserable man keeps a journal, a log, to prove he's been in the house. I suppose it'd also prove he supports me. I suppose he fears it all might come up in court again."

"Nothing's changed, then."

"Yes, it's changed. It's worse."

Peabody noticed again the tautness in her face. A month of isolation had cut deeply into her life. "So I see," he said. "Cornelia, how do you fill your days? What are you going to do?"

She shrugged a faint smile. He grieved to see smiles like that, small, helpless pretensions of happiness.

"You have friends," he suggested.

"Dear friends. But when I'm with them, and they talk about all the happy things they do with their husbands, and how their husbands adore them, or how the children are blooming, or even how they worry about a sick child or a husband who's driving himself too hard—I feel as if I don't belong among them. I thought friends would be my salvation, Homer. Instead, they're my agony. I don't know where to turn."

"Has he taken you anywhere? Do you meet his friends?"

"At this point, I'd turn him down. I won't go through a charade."

"Good. You're a brave woman, Cornelia, and I'm certain you'll find some way, some life."

Her face crumpled for a moment, and then she restored her aplomb, or what was left of it. "Perhaps you have some suggestions," she said wryly.

He knew how utterly incompetent he was to suggest anything to this trapped young woman. "Reading?" he asked.

She shook her head. "Shall I find my solace in romantic novels instead of life itself—shall I accept ersatz life, some author's concoction, instead of my own?"

"You might try education. The women's college."

"Yes," she said absently. "Plutarch or Aristotle. I can't hold them in my arms."

Homer felt very bad for a moment. They ordered and ate silently, scarcely able to communicate. No woman needed a divorce more than she; no woman had a worse husband.

"Cornelia?" he said, sipping coffee. "My heart aches for you. I wish I could wave a wand and make life better for you."

"For us both."

He smiled. "I have some work to keep me busy."

"So you don't have to think about withering on the vine."

"Oh, I'm grateful to be alive, grateful to smell a blossom, grateful to enjoy my freedoms, and walk under the blue skies—"

"Homer."

She had pinioned him with nothing more than his name. "I'm reconciling myself to a lost life, Cornelia. I've a widow woman who straightens up my rooms once a week, Mrs. Kurtz. She has a knack for bringing me down to earth. You know what she said the other day? She said old women don't like to be around old men. Old men need women more than old women need men. When a woman's husband dies, does she yearn for another man, and go looking? No, she gathers her female friends about her, and they go larking the rest of their life, glad they're rid of their old goats."

"Oh, she's talking in generalities."

"She is? Do old men gather together and rejoice to be free of women? No. Old men yearn for women's company right to their deathbed."

"I wouldn't know. But you're finding ways to bury yourself. Please don't do that."

"No, I'm simply coming to grips with human nature. I must abandon the dream. You know what I was thinking about recently? Weddings. Standing up with my bride, saying vows, slipping a ring on her finger. I saw it all so vividly. I ached. I wanted it so much, just once, one holy moment, one moment like walking through the pearly gates—"

"Homer, who was this woman you dreamed of marrying?"

"I don't know. I haven't met her yet."

"She had no face, no name, no character?"

"She was very beautiful and dignified."

"You're smitten by marriage rather than a real woman. She doesn't really exist, except in your heart."

"I suppose you could put it that way . . ."

She reached across to him, touched him with her smooth young hand. "Homer, we both need to make something of what we've left to us. It's no good just to brood or dream impossible dreams."

"No, it's not. I'm weak."

"You're strong. You've kept your cheer all these years, always a kind word, a courteous gesture to everyone around you. Homer, let's help each other. You've become my confidant. I can tell you things I could never tell friends. We each need a better life, even if it isn't the life we dreamed of. I'm so hollow inside . . . let's meet each week. Same day? Same place?"

"We'll wrestle the world together, Cornelia."

She smiled for the first time, but it wasn't the sort of smile he liked to see.

CHAPTER 26

ornelia Kimbrough expected Walter to make trouble, and he did. They had been invited that June Saturday to the Denver Club, for the wedding of Gideon Bancroft and Louise Sneed.

"We'll go together," Walter said. "I'll have the gig brought around."

"I'll walk, thank you. It's just a few blocks."

"No, you come. We must keep up appearances."

"Walter, if you don't like it, divorce me."

"Never," he said, stalking out of her suite. "You'll be sorry."

She felt relieved. But it wasn't over. He would sit beside her at the wedding and stand close to her during the reception, and introduce her to his cronies, all the while heaping flatteries upon her from his dead lips.

Well, she would endure him. The Bancrofts and Sneeds were dear friends and the wedding was the event of the summer, and she would endure whatever she had to endure. She wore her best summer dress, a gauzy white cotton and lace creation, translucent in the summer sun, the light piercing to her petticoats in ways that made her soft, misty, accessible, and racy.

The mirror satisfied her for a change. She hadn't ever liked her looks very much, and these recent months the mirror had shown her a hardness of line and dullness of eye that reflected a captive spirit. But today her eyes gleamed, and she was gladdened.

She found her white fringed parasol and headed north to the club, where Justice Thomas would read the ceremony to the young people.

She had rarely been in that male bastion, the Denver Club, and looked forward to it. She had rather liked the lingering aroma of cigars that clung to the drapes and leather furniture and oriental carpets. That afternoon, women might enter; by evening, immediately after the reception, they would be excluded again. She intended to explore the fusty library, the dark billiards room, the black walnut and frosted glass saloon, and the comfortable parquet-floored lounge where much of Colorado's business was transacted, including this dynastic wedding. Walter spent most of his life there, so she might as well see his male-only lair.

She chose to sit on the groom's side, mostly because she supposed Walter would sit on the other side since he was close to the Sneeds. But he homed in on her and seated himself beside her, smiling pleasantly, silver linings on his black cloud.

Impulsively she rose, moved to the bride's side, and settled there. Walter dutifully followed, smiling at all around him, nodding at the impetuosity of his dear wife.

"You're embarrassing me," he whispered to her.

"Divorce me," she retorted loud enough to be heard.

She listened cynically as old Judge Thomas led the filly and colt through their steeplechase. A ring slid over a delicate finger, and a lot of neighing and whickering followed. But these two were plainly and ecstatically in love. Their tenderness melted her heart, and she envied them as she blotted up the joy radiating from them. But by the end, a hurt had gathered around her heart, and she sat numbly, aching in ways she could not describe in words. Why couldn't she have just the smallest portion of their bliss?

The reception in the stately drawing room, under a pretentious crystal chandelier, gave her a chance to dodge her jailor and see old friends. Such as Jay Graff, an old beau enjoying an inheritance. He looked dashing, his eyes innocent and guileful, his lips caught in perpetual amusement.

"Well, Cornelia, the real entertainment wasn't the wedding, it was you and Walter."

"Jay, let's not talk of that."

"I watched you come in separately, watched you dodge him,

watched him trying to keep up appearances. A much better show than the bride and groom.''

She fought back anger, and turned toward the punch bowl, but he followed.

"My, you're beautiful, Cornelia. Especially when your temper's up. It makes your cheeks bloom.''

"My private life is not anyone's business, least of all yours, Jay.''

He laughed happily. "It's public business. Ever since all the papers in town ran every scrap of contention in your divorce. I especially enjoyed it when he ran in a dozen witnesses who had heard him boast about his conjugal relationship.''

Cornelia retreated fast, but he followed right along. "You're enjoying this, though you'll never admit it. I'm on your side. You don't have the chance to talk about it to anyone," he said.

She stopped at a window, half trapped, half admitting the truth of it.

"Poor Walter," Jay continued. "He was so serious, and the rest of us were frivolous young bucks. He would make the better husband, of course. Seriousness is a virtue. He's serious about business. I know. I'm involved in several of his ventures. But he's a cod, Cornelia. A fish. And you're lonely.''

"Jay, your talk is bordering on indecency.''

"You're weary of decency. That's why you're here and not heading out the door.''

She reddened.

"You should have married me. I like women.''

"That's why I didn't," she said.

"Ouch. At least I'd marry one, rather than marry my business. You know what Walter does these days? He praises you to his business colleagues. He says how happy you and he are. How the divorce case brought you together in wedded bliss. Now he's got twenty more witnesses, if you ever try it again. Some gents even believe him. I think it's a good Barnum sideshow.''

"He says that?" She marveled. "Jay, when he's with men, does he behave—is he a regular man?''

"Oh, sure. Perfectly regular. No fop, if that's what you mean. He's just dead to women and the hearth and children, that's all. He prefers buying railroads or speculating in sugar or spending a week in hunting camp looking for trophy elk. He knows that's strange, that it demeans him among other men, so he goes to all these lengths to pretend.''

She studied Jay, seeing again the perpetual amusement sewn into his face, wondering if life really amused him so much, or whether it really was cynicism and disappointment. With more character he might have made something of himself, achieved things—he was terribly bright and well educated, and she had seen some of his landscape oils. But his life was playing out day by day in froth and foam, and probably would end in dissipation.

Walter had been a disastrous choice; Jay would have been worse. "It's time for me to go now," she said. "Good to see you again. You seem to know more about the Kimbroughs than I do."

"I'll walk you home," he said. "My rooms are on the way."

"I'd rather go alone, thank you."

He shrugged. She thanked the parents of the bride, dodged Walter, found her parasol, and headed into the burning afternoon heat, so scorching that the sidewalk shimmered and she wilted, even in her gauzy dress.

Then Jay was beside her. She wasn't surprised. He had been almost a rogue when he courted her; he was a real one now.

"That dress. You aren't just beautiful, Cornelia, you're ravishing," he said, keeping apace.

She didn't mind compliments. When had she last heard one?

"I've some lemonade on ice. You've never seen my new flat. It's wickedly done," he said.

She let herself be led into a new apartment on Grant, guarded by stone lions, not resisting because she was enjoying the novelty of being courted. Even by Jay Graff. Her pulse lifted slightly. They ascended wide white marble stairs to the second floor. Jay's apartment, with a chased brass lock, filled one entire side.

He unlocked cheerfully, and ushered her into a voluptuously decorated quarters. She smelled witch hazel or some other scent.

He pulled some heavy velvet drapes, flooding the room with white sunlight. She beheld a lavishly furnished drawing room, with wine-colored, flocked wallpaper, matching silk-upholstered settees and a love seat, ornate tables with claw feet, gas lamps in gold sconces, thick, delicately tinted carpets, and gilt-framed paintings thick on every wall. These caught her eye and held it. They were mostly nudes.

He waited, letting her register all that, and led her into the rest. An extravagant kitchen, a baronial dining hall, a lavatory with gold fixtures and an oversized clawfooted tub. Cheerfully, he pushed open the bedroom door, and she beheld a huge fourposter, twice the size of any bed she had ever seen. And more nudes in gilded frames, these blatantly erotic.

"Jay, at least you're not subtle," she said. "I must go now."

"No lemonade?"

"That isn't what you steered me here for."

"That's true. I've never seen a woman so miserable and starved. I was watching you during the ceremony, your lips following the words, your eyes so yearning, your mouth so bitter, your oblique glances at Walter so desolate . . . Cornelia, we need each other. I'm warm, male, and take joy in a magnificent woman. You're desperate."

She should have walked out. But the whole afternoon had stirred her mercilessly. The wedding, Walter's conduct, the summer heat, the thoughts of honeymoons and lovers, the stirring of her own blood in this wicked place, Jay's brash and ruthless pursuit, his scorn of propriety, his nudes on the walls, their aloneness there, a world away from the rest of Denver . . .

She stared at him gravely, afraid, yearning, despising him, feeling the lift of her pulse, remembering back years and years and years to the few blessed moments with Walter at the very beginning of her marriage, remembering her fulfillment, what little there was of it, hating Jay Graff there before her, seducing her, waiting like a knowing fox for her to move.

He plucked her lemonade glass from her hand, and gathered her to him, gently at first, then fiercely. Her pulse soared. Her body remembered, and turned to wax. She clung to him, hot, desperate, needful.

And then the strangest thing happened. A vision of Homer Peabody formed in her mind. Poor old Homer, heavy, jowly, so excessively proper that he could not even admit to his own passions, but innately decent and respectful of her, too much so, as if she were a fragile porcelain doll.

She struggled free.

"No!" she cried.

He wouldn't let go. "Your body tells me otherwise, sweetheart," he said.

"Yes, that's true. But this isn't what I want, I don't want this, I want—what's right."

She pulled free. He stepped toward her again, but she dodged him. "Enjoyed the lemonade and seduction, Jay," she said, "especially the seduction." Then she fled.

She retreated to her rooms, plunged onto her own blessed bed, and spent the rest of that hot day in turmoil, everything within her at war.

CHAPTER 27

. . . .

It didn't take long for Rose Edenderry to know what she wanted: Mr. William B. Masterson. She intended to become Rose Edenderry Masterson. She wanted to run a three-chandelier saloon with him the rest of their lives, and when he was old and dying she wanted to iron his last shirt and bury him with a red granite double marker carrying his name and dates, and her name. She would die later, after she had seen to it that the newspapers paid him proper respect.

William B., as she called him, wasn't like other tinhorns and sports. He was steady and calm. He had been a lawman and had come through bad moments unscathed. He didn't even have a temper. He never lacked for funds, either. You couldn't hardly find a better bucko than that.

She remembered that first night, when he took her home, and fought off the yegg, and then spent the night with her. She had enjoyed that. He gave more than he took.

After that he came home with her often, and she enjoyed it even though she was off men and wanted nothing to do with them. If he got out of line she was prepared to tell him to vamoose, but he never did. He was always calm and soft-spoken and even when she got mad at him he just smiled and kept his peace and put his pants on.

At first she didn't know what to do about her resolution to swear off men. She finally decided that marrying William B. Masterson didn't conflict with swearing off men. He wasn't the kind of man she was swearing off of. She was swearing off of tinhorns and sports who tried to take her money or live on her earnings or enjoy her favors without ever thanking her or doing anything for her. She was swearing off the tinhorns who were always telling her not to dissipate herself, or taking away her bottle, or telling her she was doomed if she took a little bit of coca leaf snuff or smoked a pipe of dark brown opium now and then.

Mr. Masterson wasn't like that. Whatever she was, that was fine with him, and he never tried to change her or lord it over her. But the problem was, he wasn't inclined to marry her. She had tried some broad hints:

"William B., don't you think we're a real pair? Wouldn't you like to open a little saloon with me in Hawaii? I'll be your wahine queen."

"You've got gorgeous coconuts," he replied.

"I know, but no milk," she said.

He didn't move in with her, and she learned right off that he wouldn't spend every night with her. He vanished for several nights in a row, and then returned to her, saying nothing. That made her nervous and she gulped Dover's powder tablets to stay calm. She was used to being courted by sports, but she found herself courting him, anxious about his loyalties, wondering if she was pretty enough for him, or whether she had some habit he didn't like, or if she pleasured him enough. He never said, and she felt jittery. That was one reason she wanted to get ahold of a justice of the peace and tie a big squareknot, hobble that son of a gun for good.

When she discovered that he was spending nights with other women—not one, but two or three, most of them serving girls in the sporting district—she grew frantic. Why couldn't he just settle down with her? A dozen times she had nerved herself to bawl him out when he came over for the night, but she didn't. She couldn't whine at a sweetheart like William B., who was so amiable and steady and good-humored.

William B. just wasn't a one-woman man, but knowing that didn't help her any. She brooded about it. She watched him ferociously every night, especially when one of the other serving girls brought rounds to his faro table. He smiled cheerfully at each serving girl, enjoying them from those dark, deepset eyes, and never showed the slightest partiality. At least until the last customer left and Diamond began turning down the gas lights. And then, with no explanations at all, he'd leave with one dolly or another, or sometimes alone.

She decided he was shy, and so she would do the proposing. The next time he slipped into her room, she was up and waiting for him in her furry robe and ancient slippers.

"William B.," she announced, "we're turning over a new leaf, we are."

"You ironed the sheets?"

"I'd like to iron your sheets the rest of your life."

"This sounds dangerous, Rose."

"It is. Let's get hitched, dearie. I talked to Penrose, the justice, and he'd do it for two dollars, and I'll pay. I'll even say the words for both of us. I love you, William B. All I want is to lie beside you through all eternity."

"Are you contemplating murder-suicide, Rose?"

"Oh, you know what I mean, bound together in holy matrimony, now and forever. You at your faro table, me wiping the bar down and dipping the glasses and lighting your Havanas. I'm yours, I am, Masterson." She felt vulnerable, baring so much so desperately.

He didn't laugh, and he didn't say anything unkind, but he didn't say yes, either. He took her hand and led her to the bed, where they could sit side by side. "Rose, I'm sort of a stud horse, and I'd not do well gelded."

"Gelding you's the last thing I have in mind, William." She reached up to his cheek and scraped a finger across it, knowing how bristly it would feel at the end of his day. "You are what you are, Masterson. If you need to slip your collar once in a while, I guess I could live with it. I'd rather have some of you than none of you. I don't know nothing about love, but I sure'm learning."

He laughed, and squeezed her hand. "This is the first time I've been proposed to," he said. "You're a sweetheart."

"Hold me, William B.," she said huskily.

He did, and for a while things were good and it was like the honeymoon she dreamed of. But she had no answer from him, and more and more she craved one, especially those long bleak nights when he was in Virginia's or Marigold's bed. Those nights she pulled out her long, thin porcelain pipe, and bought a little sticky brown ball to put in the bowl, and floated her way toward marriages made in heaven.

Friday came, and she realized she hadn't worked for two days and was penniless and owed rent in the morning. She felt sick. She fought back cramps and went to work that afternoon, not saying a word to Jack Diamond, who studied her closely. She hustled drinks, smiled at all the men, made jokes, tried for big tips, downed a few drinks at the bar to settle her roiling stomach, served Masterson's table seven times under his calm, penetrating gaze, and when Friday's revelries ended, she was still six dollars shy of her rent.

She waited for him to close his table, needing him badly.

"Come home with me?" she asked. "I need you, William B."

He nodded. They walked through a chill, silent night, Masterson as wary as ever of footpads.

She pulled him into her cold room and lit a lamp, while he watched quietly. Then she pressed him to her and wept, unable to stop a flood of loneliness and fright and agony. "Please, please, William, marry me. I can't make it on my own. When I'm alone I—I can't stop. I just do things I don't mean to."

He pulled her to the side of the bed and held her while she calmed down within the strength of his arms.

"The only person who can help you is yourself, Rose. Some things are poison. They'll kill you sooner or later. Put you in an early grave. But if you're going to drink, and use hop, no one can help."

"If you were with me I wouldn't. I really wouldn't."

"Maybe for a while. But you would, sooner or later."

"I don't know how," she said in a small voice. "Andre would just tell me to stop, and I would. Won't you just tell me to stop?"

"You're not a child, and I'm not your father." He pressed her small hands between his. "Rose, you need to govern yourself. Children surrender to impulse, but adult men and women know how to say no. Until you govern yourself, you'll never have much of a life. If I started to say no, you'd just resent it. And I don't want to be involved with a woman I have to look after every minute. You keep calling yourself a rebel, but that's not it, Rose. You're not yet an adult."

"There you go, preaching at me like all the rest. You all think I shouldn't have a good time."

Masterson smiled and let go of her hands. "I've said what I needed to."

"I'm sick. I'm so broke."

"You didn't make rent? How much do you need?"

"I don't know."

"Here's a fiver, Rose."

"Oh, William," she said, starting to weep all over again. "I can't live without you."

"That's what's wrong," he said.

He stayed that night, although she thought his mind was far away, maybe on some other woman. But he did stay even though she had made a fool of herself and he probably was disgusted with her. They lay side by side, and he held her. He was a kind man, but he wasn't going to marry her, and she wouldn't even be his one and only girl. She knew that now. He didn't want someone like her, who had lots of fun. Her stomach was roiling and she desperately wanted some paregoric to quiet it. But she didn't want him to know, so she endured through the quiet, to the dawn, and finally slipped into a troubled sleep.

She knew she had lost the only man who could ever give her a good life.

During the next weeks she tried hard. She didn't buy any hop from the Chinaman, and she showed up at the Arcade every evening, and she kept up with her rent. She drank a lot, though, because she wasn't taking any powders or smoking hop. There were always some Arcade regulars, like Ikey Foster or Red Bones, eager to buy her a drink and make suggestive remarks. She served drinks to William Masterson's customers whenever he rang his little brass bell. He seemed distant but ever polite. He was so solid, like a rock in a world of slippery, muddy, treacherous people with mean tempers. She wished he would come to her room, but he didn't.

She felt increasingly desperate. She had to find someone to take care of her, some real man who'd tell her not to do stuff. She eyed Jack Diamond thoughtfully, but he had a dolly who worked over to the dancehall, selling tickets. So she kept on at the Arcade, making eyes at Red Bones and letting him touch her every time she approached the bar and laughing at his bawdy jokes.

She always went home sort of drunk after she had done her stint and the night trade left the Arcade. But she was paying her rent after that close call. She sure was miserable, though. Just bad luck with men. She wanted life to be fun, but it wasn't. It just seemed like a dead-end alley, like the one she lived in, always broke, always surviving, but that was about all.

Then one really bad evening she took all the rent money she had saved and bought a lump of black opium with it and locked herself in her room and traveled to another world. She didn't know how long she did that, but finally her landlord came and pounded, and she cussed at him, and finally opened up, sullen right down to her bones.

"You're overdue two days, Rose," he said. "If you need an hour to get it, fine, otherwise I've got to put you out."

"Yeah, and who are you to tell me where to get off?"

"Sorry, Rose. I'm a patient man, but not inclined to charity. You want me to help you pack up?"

"No, I'll do it."

"I'll be back in an hour. And you still owe me for these two days."

Soon afterward, she and her ancient trunk were out in the alley.

CHAPTER 28

ose stood in the alley, in the aching beauty of a summer morning, mad at the world. She didn't like being up so early and her head pounded. She glanced sourly at her trunk, wondering what she could do with it.

Maybe the Chinamen would keep it.

With much pantomime and pointing, she managed to get two of

them to haul her trunk into their dark and smoky cubicle. She had no idea whether she would ever see her clothing again. They smiled, bowed, and closed the door.

A summer zephyr caught the dust in the alley and lifted it. She was glad she hadn't been thrown out in winter. But mostly she raged at the world, doing this to her. She had a right to live, same as everyone else. She hiked to Blake Street and found the Arcade open. A strange bartender stood gloomily behind the bar. Harsh white daylight poured through the front windows, somehow making the rear of the Arcade bleak and dark. At night the gaslights tinseled the place with warm light but now the Arcade seemed like a dump.

She headed for a bowl of hard-boiled eggs on the bar, and took a couple.

"You want a drink, ma'am?" asked the keep.

"I work here."

"Haven't seen youse before."

She didn't reply. She needed something in her stomach and the eggs would have to do. She cracked the shells, salted the eggs, and downed them, all the while wondering what to do. She didn't even know where to go until her shift started. She wished she had befriended the other serving girls, but they had all been rivals, and anyway, she preferred to go home and sample some of the Chinamen's wares. But now she had no home, and no cash. That was all right. She'd make some tips tonight and she could rent a room for the night.

"Could you lend me a couple dollars from the till, dearie? Put it on my tab? I'll pay when I do my shift," she said.

He looked doubtful. "I don't know—"

"I'm broke."

"I'll ask Jack Diamond. He's in back, still sleeping I guess."

"No, forget it. I just wanted some lunch money. I'll take a couple of eggs."

She didn't want to bring Diamond into it. The man had been glowering at her recently, like he was ready to fire her. She retreated into the street. The glare of the sun hurt her eyes. She didn't like daytime. Life didn't even get interesting until sunset. But it was only ten in the morning, and she had seven hours to go until her shift. She needed sleep and darkness so she could close her eyes and stop the pounding in her head.

She started walking, just drifting through the heart of Denver, past

Union Station, north toward the viaducts across the South Platte. She'd hardly seen Denver by daylight. The mountains rose blue and stark, the snow all gone, a wilderness not far from a big city. She didn't care where she went, just anywhere she could find some shade, some grass, a place to eat her other eggs and sleep out of the sun.

When she reached the river she walked along it, following a trail through brush, past dead-end streets, piles of refuse, shanties put up by hoboes, and occasional factories. Denver wasn't pretty. She kept on, not knowing or caring where she was going until she found herself at Riverside Cemetery. There the tawdriness vanished. She walked across emerald lawns, beneath stately trees, past a forest of headstones, monuments, crypts, stone crosses, statues of angels or Jesus Christ, and graves protected by black iron fences.

The city of the dead. Somehow, she felt glad she had come there. Dead. That's what she was. She felt a kinship to all those people around her. She began studying dates, birth and death. So many had died young, often in their thirties, a lot in their twenties, a lot of children. Consumptives, she guessed. She felt uncomfortable around all those expressions of religion, crosses, scriptures graven in granite, and stone visions of heaven. She was nominally Catholic but didn't know what she believed. That was all just stuff. She trusted what she could see and smell and hear. Faith was an utter mystery to her. What good was it?

She found what she was looking for, a velvet carpet of grass beneath a towering cottonwood where she could lie comfortably in the cool breezes and while away a long day. She could see no other living person in the whole cemetery, but she didn't feel alone. She would sit there and watch the mountains and eat eggs and talk to all these people. Maybe they would tell her what her own life was about. She hadn't the faintest idea.

She hated thinking, especially if she had to reach for ideas. But she loved just to sit and feel the energies around her, her soul receptive to everything. That's why she enjoyed drinking. She never had to think, and when she sipped booze she felt everything pouring through her, the sound of talk, the laughter, the gossip, and fun.

She guessed maybe she wouldn't live long. Not if she took a lot of opium. She would turn herself into a scarecrow and die if she did that. She'd die if she became a drunk. She'd die if she went into the business on Market Street. She'd die if she got married to some bore. Living was the problem.

She lay back in the grass and dozed. Then she ate the two hard-boiled eggs. Then she tried to make sense of her life. If she got work as a shop girl she would be bored and restless. If she married some gent, she would ditch him in a month—except for William Masterson. But he didn't want her. All these dead people around her were lucky: they didn't have to figure out what to do with their lives, or who would feed them, or who would cure their boredom, or who would give them money.

She decided to ask the dead. "Should I move to Market Street and sell myself to men?" she said aloud.

They didn't reply at first, but then she decided they were saying no. Especially the man over in that grave with the obelisk. He probably was a preacher.

He was telling her she should do something worthwhile, something that would make her count. Get an education, become a nurse, teach children, care for orphans, be a bookkeeper.

Her father had been too much the rebel to think about doing any-thing with his life. All he wanted was to pull down the rich and powerful, the British oppressors, the fat churchmen, the lords and ladies. That's what she was: she didn't want a long, dull life. She wanted to tear the world down to its cellar.

She watched a distant woman walk to a grave, kneel there, pull a few weeds, and lay a bouquet upon it. Then the woman prayed. The woman loved whoever was there. Rose thought that was the trouble with loving. Pretty soon the beloved went away. The woman lingered awhile and then left, and Rose was alone again, with only the ghosts, the sun, the zephyrs, the shade, the smell of grass, and the rustle of leaves. And tears in her eyes.

At least her headache went away. After a long time, she left, discon-tent. Riverside Cemetery had not revealed the answer to the riddle of her life. She didn't even know where she would sleep that night. But at least the cemetery had been a private haven where she could lie in the grass and no copper would chase her away. Maybe she would buy a plot there if she could save up for one. She had never been able to save for anything. Any time she had a few dollars, she found a dozen things to spend them on.

She got to the Arcade an hour early and began serving the early birds, the boozers who had slid out of their offices to get a head start on the evening. They didn't tip much, but she got a few dimes out of it. Pretty soon the regular crowd drifted in, and Diamond lit the gas-lamps, and the place looked right again. She loved the roar, the clink of glass, the smell of cheroots and beer, the rattle of the roulette wheel, and men's bawdy jokes.

Red Bones had settled at his usual perch at the bar, and told her a new traveling salesman joke.

"You want a little old drink, Rosey?"

"Buy me a double."

"A double? You'll have to come have fun with me later on. I'll feed you six doubles."

"Okay," she said.

"What do ya mean okay, are ya serious?"

"Let's do it up tonight, Red. I got nothing better to do."

His mood changed. He squinted at her. Something hot rose in his lumpy face. "Yeah, we'll have us a soiree," he said.

She laughed and dodged his big paw.

That night she got lots of tips, and she knew why. She'd smiled a lot, joked a lot, and hugged a few men. She avoided Masterson's faro table; he never tipped much anyway.

Then the crowd thinned. Red Bones and Ikey leaned into the bar, along with a couple of bruisers she didn't know.

"Any time you're ready, we're ready, Rosie," Red said. "We got Lilly coming too."

Lilly was a plain, dumpy little serving girl who had hair on her lip and a desperate look about her.

Red held up a bottle of red-eye and winked.

She abandoned the Arcade about midnight, and drifted along Blake with the rest, heading east toward an area with rooms and flats. Lilly seemed almost giddy, tittering too loud.

They all climbed three floors to Bones's small room, and she wondered how six people could party in that cubicle. It was nothing but a square with a kitchen alcove and a wash stand.

"This here's going to be an intimate party," Lilly said.

"Nothing like real close friends," Ikey replied.

They laughed, and settled themselves on the floor, propped up by the walls.

Red didn't have drinking glasses so he just passed the bottle. Rose chugged a swallow, felt it scorch her throat, fought back tears, and passed it to Lilly, who sipped and coughed. The next round was easier. After that she lost track.

She had the sense of things happening, floating, the rustle of clothing, hot ripping pleasures, and then at last, woozy sleep amidst snores. She woke up once desperately thirsty. She was in her chemise and petticoat. She felt cold, but she couldn't find her blouse and skirt, so she crawled back into her corner and clutched herself to stay warm.

When she finally woke up around ten, she and Red and Lilly remained, half dressed and half sick. That had been a pretty wild party, and she'd be sorry all day. But it put a roof over her head, and she wasn't even hungry.

CHAPTER 29

L orenzo Carthage waited restlessly for Guggenheim to return from Telluride with his assessment of the Lucky Strike. Meanwhile he studied the chemists' reports. The Lucky Strike ore contained large quantities of lead, antimony, and zinc, with a trace of copper, making the gold and silver difficult to separate from the base metals. Worse, there were sulfides, greatly complicating the task. Carthage wasn't at all sure what he would recommend, but probably it would be some combination of milling the ore at the mine head and shipping concentrate to the Denver smelter for roasting, and then some refining to separate the metals. Each stage of the refining added to the costs and reduced the value of the ore.

He wondered what it would be like to work for the cautious Guggenheims. Meyer, the patriarch, had perceived that mines were chancy up-and-down investments, but smelters need not be, and had gradually transformed their Leadville bonanza into smelter operations at key points in Colorado, reducing ores from many mines with the best equipment and techniques known to modern mining. They weren't averse to risking capital on a mine like the Lucky Strike, but such an investment would always be a sideline, perhaps only a way to feed the maws of their smelters.

Four days passed before Benjamin finally summoned Carthage to his offices. Carthage went warily, understanding that this would not be a lunch at the Windsor between peers, but something more humbling. And he was right.

Ben was all business. "I probably wouldn't have bought this mine," he began, "but for your get-rich-quick schemes, which deranged my judgment momentarily. But now we have it, or a controlling interest. The rest of the stock is so widely scattered that the Guggenheim interests are the effective majority. We've enough of the shareholders lined up to give us an absolute majority and control. One good thing about the Lucky Strike—its stock is largely held by very intelligent men in Denver. Men we can go to with facts.

"The managers are far more intelligent than they've been given credit for. The mine's isolated and high up; the cost of carrying ore by wagon to the railhead at Telluride, and then to Durango, is unusually heavy. Winter storms often shut down the mine. The cost of shipping ore here is prohibitive. The mine actually collapsed because the Durango mill refused to buy any more of the refractory ore, which it could mill only at a loss.

"We're saddled with a heavy debt that grows even though the mine's not operating. The managers explored the possibility of milling the ore on-site and shipping concentrate here. It doesn't work out. Their assays are accurate, and they've been verified by independent assayers. They know full well what they have—extremely rich ores potentially worth a fortune. They thought to stockpile ore while awaiting developments, or the technical means to reduce it, and have quantities above grass—and there it sits, some of it vanishing in workers' lunchbuckets day after day.

"I talked with the managers of the Smuggler-Union, and looked at some of their assays. Bum ore. Refractory sulfides like ours, but they don't have the base metals to contend with. We do. There's no doubt that the Lucky Strike's the toughest mine in the district—and the most isolated. It's miles from the nearest mine, in its own patch of telluride conglomerate to the north. You sure picked a lulu, Carthage."

He fixed Carthage in his unblinking gaze until Lorenzo grew uncomfortable.

"I find myself owning a theoretical fortune, which is more likely an actual rathole. The obvious reality is that large amounts of capital are going to be required to separate the gold and silver from the sulfides, tellurium, lead, zinc, and the rest. You read the reports. No one knows whether the reserves justify the expenditure of so much money, probably half a million dollars in railroad, milling, and smelting equipment.

"So, Carthage, what's your plan? It had better be good, or I'll put my shares back on the exchange and take a licking. A few-thousand-dollar licking's better than a half-million-dollar one."

Carthage knew the moment of truth had arrived, and he had no real plan. "I'd like to see the mine before I send you a plan. I need more than generalities."

But Guggenheim wouldn't let him off the hook. "Based on what I've told you, how would you attack this?"

Carthage sucked in breath, and plunged in. "The way I see it, you could justify a heavy investment if you have proven reserves. You'll be spending maybe two hundred thousand to start up, and more to achieve some economies. You'll want to know what's in that hole first. All right. I'd like to keep a single face crew on, purely for exploratory purposes. I'd have to look at the setup before I'd know how to deploy them. Put on four good men, and maybe a timber cutter. Spend two, three, six months at it. Then you'll know."

Something amiable filled Ben Guggenheim's dark eyes for the first time. "That's the thing to do. We're not heavily invested in this. But we're familiar with ratholes, and the Lucky Strike is not going to be one." He paused. "There's the matter of your terms. We can't pay you a supervisor's salary with a dormant mine. If you bring it up and it produces, that's another matter."

"Well, I could scale back a little. How about eight hundred a month?"

"Two hundred, yes or no. I was impressed with Baumann and Lipsett in spite of the gossip of all the second-guessers and critics. They knew what they were up against. I'd keep them on, but I'll give you this chance."

"Two hundred?"

"That's it, and I'll review your work once a month. No guarantees. Performance will mean everything. You'll have to clear all large expenses with me."

"Two hundred—"

"That's a comfortable income. The miners live quite decently on a hundred a month."

"All right, I'll show you what I can do, Ben."

That very afternoon, Lorenzo the Magnificent found himself riding a coach on the Denver and Rio Grande, en route to Durango. He bought a *Post* and an apple from the candy butcher, but his mind was on his fortunes. Two hundred appalled him. They were getting the best mine manager in the West for peanuts. Well, he'd show them what he could do with a tough mine.

The train took him to the southwest corner of Colorado and deposited him in Durango in the middle of the night. The next morning he caught the narrow-gauge Rio Grande Southern, which took him on an endless dogleg trip to Rico, Ophir, and Telluride, which nestled deep in the western slope of the San Juans, in tumbled, barren, red and cream rock country.

The little Mogul steam engine, the size of an oversized toy, whipped the miniature train around sharp curves, ran under brooding brown slopes and rust-colored redbeds, passed Dolores Peak, with Mount Wilson ahead, echoed through snow sheds, snorted up mountain-goat grades, topped Lizard Head Pass, entered the Ophir district, a good gold and silver producer, and emerged at last in the valley of the San Miguel, walled by slide-prone rock to the east, and finally into Telluride, brooding at the end of the world under the claws of distant Mount Sneffels.

The mining camp had the rough look of a frontier town, but Carthage spotted the beginnings of comfort. Some spacious, gingerbreaded white houses lined one street. Mercantiles had put up false fronts or were moving into brick and stone buildings. Some fancy hacks with blooded horses in harness dotted the streets. Prosperity had altered Telluride, and would transform it within a year into an amiable if isolated outpost. Surely it was farther from city life and its amenities than any other mining camp in Colorado, barred by Red Mountain to the east from any easy connection with the rest of the state. He knew, after negotiating the tortuous trip, that shipping ore to Denver would be a mine-busting expense. He would have to reduce the ore right there, one way or another.

He rented a gig at a livery barn and headed at once for the mine, located far up the glaciated steep-walled valley. Even at a smart trot it would take him an hour. He carried his satchels and the old trunk, hoping there would be some sort of accommodations there.

Late in the afternoon he spotted the Lucky Strike perched on a high slope, with a mountain-goat switchback road leading up to it. He stared up at it. This was the reality. This was what he had laid out his last cash for, an abstraction called the Lucky Strike, an engraved certificate of ownership of one small fraction of the whole. Was that tiny headframe, and hoist shack, and work shed up there all there was? How humble it seemed compared to the rich arrogance of the Denver exchange and the fevered dreams of wealth that circulated like blood through the floor of the exchange. Had he seen this sight before him— a shack or two, a couple of shanties, some timbers bolted together into a headframe and hoist works, would he have plunged?

And yet . . . he wasn't called Lorenzo the Magnificent for nothing.

This would be his toughest venture, his ultimate challenge. The riches were there if he could get them: that ore would yield a thousand dollars a ton if he could reduce it properly. Which he intended to do.

He let the laboring dray climb the long grade slowly, and rested it periodically when it began heaving. He estimated that he would climb eight hundred feet from the valley floor to the mine.

He arrived at last and found Martin Lipsett on duty there, alone in the works. Everyone else, including Baumann, stayed in Telluride now.

Lipsett, a gray-bearded man with a keen squint, proved to be everything that Ben Guggenheim said he was: tough, knowledgeable, and daring. This mine's problems had simply overwhelmed the old management.

"We're going to do some exploratory work, prove some reserves," Carthage told him. "If the reserves justify the expense, we'll build a reduction works right here, or at the valley floor. The San Miguel offers water power."

"Well, that's what we wanted, but we couldn't put it through the board. When things went sour, they wanted to cut back all expenses, period. Guggenheim knows his stuff."

"I'll want the names of the best men available for the face crew, and a good timber man. I'd also like a tour of the works, and your perceptions of the dip and strike of the ore. And anything else helpful. And also, what your plans are. Will you and Mr. Baumann be staying in Telluride?"

Lipsett shook his head. "No. We'll help you get started, but we both would like management positions of our own elsewhere."

"Well, you've done a fine job. I can see that right off. I wish you all the best. Is there a place up here where I can bunk?"

"Sure, two or three. Take your pick. A foreman's in one."

"Good. That'll save a little."

During the next days, Carthage mastered the Lucky Strike. He visited every drift and crosscut and face, took his own assay samples, studied the books until he knew exactly what the mine owed to suppliers, studied past expenses to see what might be trimmed back—and found nothing. He studied the mound of ore above ground, unprofitable to mill until something better was worked out. He rode up and down the valley floor, studying the rushing creek as a source of power for a reduction works.

He talked to former managers and miners in Telluride, listened to their theories. He talked to some of the thirty-odd stockholders who lived in town, most of whom were eager to sell out. Shrewdly, he bought shares at seven to nine cents, using up the several hundred dollars of cash he had gotten out of brokering the sale to Guggenheim. The additional shares gave him five thousand in all, a significant piece of the pie.

Cautiously, remembering his experience in Silverton and Leadville, he checked incorporation papers, looked for pending lawsuits, easements, and rights of way. He examined the original claims and made sure they were valid. He read the correspondence in the company files, determined this time not to make a mistake that would sink Lorenzo the Magnificent for the last time. He found nothing amiss. The mine simply had fabulous but perverse ore.

Then he let Guggenheim know he was ready.

CHAPTER 30

During the next months, Carthage kept his exploration crew at work in the bowels of the Lucky Strike. The ore body dipped at twenty degrees, and had been mined from huge galleries, well timbered, that descended stair-step fashion deeper and deeper. The previous management had followed the ore seam at its thickest, usually around eight feet, and ignored thinner ore at either side, because it was less profitable and could be extracted later.

Carthage had his crew drive drifts to either side of the galleries, often fifteen or twenty yards, to determine whether the seam pinched out. Usually it did. The previous managers had mined intelligently. The ore body wasn't wide enough to extend into neighboring claims, although the company owned those as well as the discovery claim.

He had a good crew, cheerful and experienced men who knew mining, blasting, mucking, and how to read the rock in the dull light of their carbide lamps. The dip was shallow enough so they didn't need to use the power hoist at the mine head, and simply stockpiled the ore in the huge galleries. Carthage spent a large part of each day with them, and always showed up after each blast to see what the newly exposed face looked like.

The pinching at the sides probably limited the reserves to whatever lay ahead, deeper into the mountainside. There would be little prospect of a parallel seam of ore above or below the present one, but as a last resort Carthage intended to sink a vertical shaft a hundred feet to see what lay below. He reported to Ben Guggenheim once a week, confining himself to fact and avoiding all speculation as to whether there was enough ore to justify any major capital expenditures.

By the end of three months, he had completed the lateral work and was driving a drift straight down the seam at its thickest, in essence peering into the future. The thickness held for another thirty yards, and then diminished slightly, while the ore values remained uniform. That was not a good sign.

In Denver, Ben Guggenheim had put his best smelting men on the problem of reducing the complex sulfide ore more efficiently, and Carthage eagerly awaited their conclusions. Even if the mine's ore body wasn't as large as he hoped, it still might be a profitable venture if a cheap way to reduce the ore could be employed.

During all this period, Carthage lived quietly in a small manager's house at the mine site and patiently bought more shares at seven or eight cents, bringing his holdings to ten thousand. But on occasion, when sheer loneliness got to him, he took the company gig to town for a steak and some camaraderie in the saloons. He didn't know the locals, but they certainly knew him, and always crowded around him, inquiring about the fate of the Lucky Strike. "It's all confidential," he replied one September night. "We're making progress. In Denver, they're working on a way to reduce that ore, and we're looking at the reserves."

"Well, is the stock going up or down? I bought it at a dollar and look at it now. Eight cents, last I heard," said a local banker.

"I'll buy it," Carthage said. "How much do you have? How about seven cents?"

The man eyed him shrewdly. "Don't think I want to sell," he said. "Not if you're buying."

"Well, I'm not saying it'll go up," Carthage said. "In fact, it might drop further. Company's deeper in debt each day we explore."

"That's the sort of thing I hear from other managers when they're itching to buy every share they can lay their mitts on," the banker retorted.

The next time Carthage got to Telluride, he learned that someone was buying every share of Lucky Strike that came onto the Denver exchange, paying fifteen and even seventeen cents. Carthage marveled: his ten thousand shares had almost doubled in value.

His crew punched deeper along the dipping seam of ore, with inconclusive results, which he duly reported to Guggenheim.

"Why is the share price of Lucky Strike rising?" Guggenheim wired back.

"Speculation," Carthage replied by wire. "No matter how much I discourage it, local speculators are buying it up. Come out here for talks. We need to come to some decisions."

The next day Lucky Strike stock topped a dollar a share, and Carthage learned that a flimsy of his telegram to Guggenheim had been smuggled out of the telegraph office, circulated around town, and had triggered a minor frenzy that had reached the Denver exchange. The sentence about making decisions had done it.

He marveled. His shares were worth over ten thousand dollars. And all he had done from the beginning was to deny that the Lucky Strike had been turned around. Had his four miners been talking? If they had, the gossip would be negative, not positive; they knew that the ore body wasn't wide, and they were running into water problems that required constant pumping at great cost to the mine.

A reporter from the *Denver Republican,* the daily owned by smelter magnate Nathaniel Hill, showed up at the mine office and inquired about the Lucky Strike's future and the meteoric rise in its stock. Carthage set a cup of ancient java before the skinny fellow and flatly denied that the Lucky Strike's known reserves justified any such movement of the stock.

"Our findings are confidential, but I can say categorically that we do not at present have plans to resume full-scale mining."

The fellow laughed cynically. "Just drive up the stock and get out, eh?"

"No, I'd just as soon not drive up the stock and disappoint a lot of people."

"But you bought some soon after you arrived here."

"Yes, it was a bargain, and people were willing to unload it. Now they're hanging on to every share. I'd advise them to sell before they take a bath."

"So you can buy more, eh?"

The man was going to believe what he wanted to believe. "Let's go into the pit and I'll show you some things," Carthage said.

"Naw, I don't know enough to see through your Potemkin village. All I know is that you're telling the world there's nothing going on down there that changes anything, but you bought some shares."

"I bought them as a speculation when I got here. That was months ago. Have you talked to Benjamin Guggenheim?"

"He won't say nothing."

Carthage glared at the man. "I can't stop you from writing what you want. But I want it on record that nothing we've done merits the speculation in this stock. Now, let's find my timber man, Judd Grover, so I can repeat it in front of a witness: *we have no plans at present and I have no information about reserves that would drive up share prices.*"

"That's not necessary: I got it in my pad here, and I'll quote ya. Give me a tip: when do you start building the reduction works?"

"We have no plans to build—"

"Yeah, yeah. I talked to that broker, Quigg, at the exchange, and he says maybe you're going to reopen this outfit soon."

"I've never told Quigg anything of the sort."

"Are you gonna issue more shares?"

"That's up to Mr. Guggenheim. I'd say not, based on what we know about reserves here now—and other difficulties."

"Yeah, well, he's got every chemist in Denver working on that sulfide ore, including half the professors in the state. That means he's on to something. I know that much."

"It could mean just the opposite."

"Word is, you're going to build a spur track up the valley."

"This valley's probably too steep for that. The San Miguel River drops five hundred feet a mile."

"Well, I'd expect you to say stuff like that, but we hear different. The Lucky Strike's the biggest news in five years. This'll make Guggenheim's Leadville mines look like penny-ante deals."

"I see that you aren't interested in facts, so there's nothing more for me to say. I have better things to do. Just remember this: stock bubbles collapse. If you publish all this rumor as fact, you'll hurt a lot of people more than you'll hurt this mine. And you just might hurt yourself."

The reporter laughed, baring tobacco-stained teeth. "I'll believe it when Guggenheim sells out," he said.

"What about if I sell out?"

"You won't. You'll ride it up to a hundred smackers a share, and never blink."

The newsman left, and Carthage had the uneasy feeling he should have done something differently, and that he would regret even talking to him. But he had no time to fret. Each day, his face crew was boring another three feet straight down the seam of ore, and was now three hundred feet ahead of the lowest gallery. And each day the seam was shrinking a tiny bit. If it petered out soon, he would recommend that the existing works be shut down but not sold, and nothing be done until technology and transportation made it feasible to work the mine again.

The *Denver Republican* published a sensationalized front-page story two days later, alleging that Guggenheim and Carthage were doing everything possible to conceal a new bonanza and drive down stock prices while they bought up every Lucky Strike share that reached the market. The story said that Carthage had been buying shares in Telluride, but didn't say when or in what quantities. It traced the rise of the stock from the seven cents a share where it had languished to its present dollar forty cents a share. It alleged that the new managers now held an absolute majority of shares and that the mine promised to be the Golconda of the 1880s.

Carthage looked it over, not finding any outright lies, but endless distortions of everything he had said, all of it recorded with a knowing wink of the eye. He wished he hadn't even talked to the man, or at least had done so in front of some impartial witnesses. He didn't mind seeing his stock balloon upward, but the bubble endangered the mine and invited lawsuits from stockholders who would claim they hadn't been informed of the bonanza. The Lucky Strike was a publicly held corporation, and required to keep shareholders properly informed. He saw nothing but trouble, but there wasn't much he could do about it. His first-phase exploration would be done in a few days, and he and Guggenheim would have to decide whether to enter a costlier second phase, which would mean sinking a shaft downward to see whether there were parallel bodies of ore at lower levels.

But on the heels of the story he received a wire from Guggenheim asking him to come to Denver as soon as possible.

He knew he would have to defend himself. He didn't doubt that the mine's principal owner would believe much of what he read in the papers. He turned the mine over to his crew foreman, Otis Frederick, and caught the little Rio Grande Southern train south for Durango, certain that nothing good awaited him. He had tried hard, made no mistakes, and had acted entirely properly in all circumstances, but that wasn't going to alter the verdict in Ben's court.

CHAPTER 31

. . . .

Yves Poulenc was eager to get on with his dying, but Maria Theresa Haas had other ideas. She appeared in his doorway about five times a day, always laden with some new concoction she insisted he consume.

One moment it would be a glass of liquid she called white vitriol, which he was to gargle. The next moment it would be an herbal tonic, full of such things as chamomile, gentian root, dogwood extract, goldenseal, columbo root, gold thread, and heaven only knows what else.

The next hour she would appear with tincture of muriate of iron, or extract of mandrake, tincture of black cohosh, or a decoction of tag alder.

Then, en route to the hot springs for their daily therapy, she would exhort him to abandon his fatty diet and eat citrus, or tomatoes, or lettuce. She sounded more and more like a tent evangelist preaching to the skeptical multitudes. He wondered when she was going to pass the hat to pay for all these herbs that kept arriving on her doorstep each week.

Let him complain of pain, and she would reappear with an extract of *Hyoscyamus,* which she said was better than opiates and would not constipate him. The stuff worked, whatever it was. It was the best anodyne he had encountered. He rather enjoyed the prospect of dying without quite so much pain.

But she annoyed him more and more with all her optimism and mothering. "Where do you get all this stuff?" he asked.

"My husband ships some of it. Some comes from Denver. I get the herbs and do my own decocting. I make my own extracts and tinctures. My cabin looks like a laboratory now. Are you feeling better?"

"If I was, I wouldn't tell you. It'd only add to your dangerous delusions. I'm croaking; you're croaking. You should be buying a cemetery lot instead of wasting your funds on all this nonsense."

She laughed. That annoyed him. She should be preparing for death. Well, she'd get her comeuppance soon enough, when the disease began boring holes in her esophagus. He had to admit, though, that since he had started the white vitriol gargle, his throat seemed a tiny bit better. But he knew it didn't mean a thing.

They slipped into the hot water again. He always liked to see her in her woolen swimming dress. He decided she was beautiful, marked by the special, unearthly beauty of the consumptive: hollow-cheeked, pale, hot-eyed. Sometimes she coughed as they sat in the purling water, her slender body convulsing while she struggled for breath. Afterward, she always smiled at him apologetically, as if she had done something wrong. He thought she had a divine beauty, and he almost wished she would just stay that way, feverish and consumptive, dark under the eyes, tragedy-bound, just so he could relish her exquisite grace. Of course, he couldn't really hope for such a thing; he could only hope she'd have a swift and painless death.

He wondered if he was as attractive to her in his gaunt, feverish condition. Some might find him handsome, even dashing, surely haunting—and unquestionably more galvanizing to the eye than a merely healthy male of nondescript physique. Yes, he decided, the reason she was mothering him was because the fever made him dashing, a lover crêped with death, a doomed Romeo. Sometimes her gaze glided over his emaciated body, and he hoped she found unearthly beauty, a spiritual power radiating from him, the thing not evident in ordinary mortals in detestable good health.

Maybe, just maybe, as he lay dying, gasping for air, she would lean over and kiss his cold lips, and that small, sweet token of love would be what he would take with him on his journey across the River Styx. Of course, since he was all but dead, she wouldn't violate her marital vows, kissing a departing soul tenderly in his last few seconds. Yes, he would encourage her toward that final intimacy.

"When I die, I hope you're beside me," he said.

"Who says you're going to die?"

"There you are, denying our fate, Maria Theresa."

"You're looking better. You're not coughing so much. I'm keeping track. You used to cough constantly. Now it's every ten or fifteen minutes."

That annoyed him. "That doesn't mean I'm not dying. It means that your anodynes have calmed my throat a little. I still cough up acres of lung every day." As if to prove his point, he convulsed in particularly violent spasms, and coughed up blood. "There, you see?" he whispered.

"Yes, I see you're better. Not much blood that time, and not much of that yellow stuff."

That so antagonized him that he bolted out of the hot pool, breathing hard, threw his robe over his shoulders, stuffed his feet into sandals, and headed for his cabin. If there was anything he hated, it was hope. He had wrestled hope the way St. George wrestled the dragon, and had finally slain it so he could die in peace. Behind him he heard her light laughter.

She left him alone that afternoon, and he spent time in repentance for his hope. He wasn't at all sure about God, but if some God existed, he would want honesty from Yves. "I've let this woman delude me," he said into the quietness of the afternoon. "I know I'm going to die soon, maybe in a week. That is your iron law and the only truth. I've prepared myself for months, and now this woman is my temptress. I suppose she means well, showering all this attention on me, but God, you and I know my fate, and I promise you I'll exorcise this wicked hope immediately."

She burst in, unannounced, as she had been doing lately, and caught him at his prayers. "Oh, you're asking for help. That's good, Yves. God heals. I pray all the time."

Wearily he turned to her. "I was asking for forgiveness for deluding myself," he said, pain in his throat.

"You're being healed, that's what. I can see it. You have better color. You don't look so feverish."

"It's not true, but even if it were, we all have brief remissions, especially just before we die. I've studied this at length. The disease seems to remit, give us a moment of peace, and then the end comes in a rush."

She smiled and sat down on the bed beside him. "Yves, let me ask a question. If you were to live, what would you do with your life?"

"I won't live, so it's not worth thinking about."

"What would you want to be, healthy?"

"I refuse to consider the matter."

"But you dream. We all dream. One thing most of us want is a mate. Don't you ever dream of a woman, a sweetheart, a wife, a friend to share your life with?"

"I refuse to consider—please leave. You're upsetting me."

She pulled back a little, obviously reluctant. "All right, but drink this first."

"What's that stuff?"

"It's a vegetable juice tonic. I ran carrots, tomatoes, spinach, corn, lettuce, radishes, apples, turnips, peas, beans, and parsley through my grinder and you're getting the juices. I had a glass, and it was almost as if my body leaped."

Angrily he swallowed the tumbler of the vile stuff and thrust the glass back to her.

"I don't know why I drink this."

"It gives you hope. You care about me in your own way, and that gives me hope. I'm glad you care. The more love I receive, the more I can struggle with this disease. My husband loves me, and writes me almost every day. It's beautiful. Each letter heals me. Every crate full of herbs that he sends comes with his love. What you need is someone to love you, Yves. You're so lonely. You've given up, just because there's no one to be with you when you're suffering. I can help; I can love you in my own way, because we are fellow travelers on a dark path that leads—who knows where?"

"That's sentiment. Love has nothing to do with it. We must ruthlessly drive sentiment out of our minds. Fact prevails. Science explains everything."

She coughed a moment, and then smiled. "When you're better, Yves, I'll introduce you to some lovely women I know, who'd love to meet a fine, sensitive man, a poet like you. You'd give them something beautiful, maybe a sonnet written just for them, like Shakespeare's sonnets to his mysterious lady. How she must have loved to receive sonnets written about her. I know if you'd write a sonnet about me, I'd have new reasons to live. Living requires reasons. Even a poor excuse of a reason sustains life. All you need, Yves, is dreams. Dreams give us our life. Maybe your dreams'll come true after all."

She turned to leave just in time, because he didn't want her to see his crumpled face. When she shut the door he leapt off his pallet, his heart racing, in a delirium of pain and need and loathing and hope. He would need to move, at once, to some other lunger camp. Madly, he stuffed his clothing into valises, but then a paroxysm of coughing stayed him. He convulsed, flung himself back on his bed, and lay quietly, starved for air, his lungs on fire, wishing himself dead.

He could not bear this suspended life one more hour. Did no one understand his condition, dangling month after month between life and death, doomed neither to die nor to hope?

He lay quietly, listening to the struggle of his heart and the desperation of his lungs. He felt destroyed. He didn't know who he was or what he believed. She had wanted only to be kind, but she had demolished him, and now he lay as helpless as an infant, small, lost, alone, frightened, disappointed in himself, unable to see good in anything.

Up until this day, he had a few small things he could be proud of. He knew he would die well, not afraid, not whining, not terrorized, not desperate, not bitter. He had taken pleasure in it: he would die better than most men. Now even that had been demolished. She had flooded him with hope and love, and now he would die regretfully. He could no longer be brave. She had turned him into a rag doll with no spine and no courage, seduced his virtue from him with talk of hope and love.

He knew he was enjoying a modest remission. Yesterday, for the first time in months, he had not coughed up blood and foul matter from his lungs. He felt less fevered. And her gargles had helped his throat. This gentle improvement did not please him. On the contrary, it would only delay and prolong his agony.

She entered after a brief knock, as was her wont, and found him lying almost inert.

"Yves, I've hurt you," she said. "Forgive me."

He scarcely had the strength to nod.

"Here's your ginseng tea," she said.

He shook his head.

She set down the cup. "I'll help you sit up."

He shook his head, but she tugged him up, and handed him his steaming mug. He drank. What difference did it make?

"Yves, this is an important day for you. And for me, too. My temperature is almost normal today. I'm feeling a little better. See? I have some color in my face."

He stared, discovering a beauty he had never seen. Before, he had always examined her for the signs of consumption—the feverish eyes, the darkness under them, the difficult breathing, the waxy pale flesh. But now he was seeing a woman for the first time, young, her brown eyes shining with life, her lips gently smiling. Now she was an alien.

"You've helped me, you know," she continued. "You've given me reality, Yves."

He nodded, his soul far away, unattached, and all his certitudes gone. Maybe he had not given her any reality at all. Maybe her reality, that this disease could be conquered, was the only reality.

"Yves, you've scarcely said a word. Would you mind if I sit beside you for an hour and hold your hand? You would comfort me, holding my hand. And I would like to comfort you with my hands."

He lay back on his miserable pallet, uncaring. She found his cold right hand with her own hands and grasped it tightly. No woman had ever held his hand like that before, at least not since he was a little boy. Her fingers clamped around his hand and conveyed warmth to him, somehow transferring life from her soul to his. Filled with wonder, he looked at her hands holding his, and found something sacred in this moment of touching and connection.

She sat quietly, minute upon minute, while his empty soul nursed upon her sweetness. Was this what it meant to live?

CHAPTER 32

On her first day at work, Dixie Ball discovered that Horace Tabor owned the Windsor along with an English syndicate, and that he lived in a suite in the hotel.

As she made beds, she pondered that. There she was, working in a menial job for the man who had extracted the last of her bonanza from her. Or at least his lawyers had. She wasn't sure he had anything to do with it.

She had fled the farm to find something better in the world than cooking and making beds and sweeping floors, and now she was doing just that.

She had found out about Tabor on the second floor, cleaning rooms with another chambermaid named Clarice, who loved to gossip as they worked together, and who had a lively curiosity about each of the people who had inhabited the rooms. She was forever looking for clues about them, the color and length of the combings of hair, the type of cigars in ashtrays, the papers or books they had abandoned, the notes they had crumpled and thrown into wastebaskets. A gossip like that knew everything, and that is how Dixie learned about Tabor's interest in the Windsor, and Tabor's suite there.

Clarice might fashion a life out of such drudgery, but Dixie knew a chambermaid's life was not for her. Not only had she fled it before, but she had glimpsed better things in her brief noonday of wealth. She would not stay long at the Windsor, not if she could better her condition. But that would not be easy: few avenues opened up for a woman, especially a woman without much schooling or polish.

And now there was a stronger reason to leave: Tabor. She wondered if he would recognize her. They had met only once, at Magnificent's big bash in Silverton, when she wore her one and only ballgown and had painted her lips and rouged her cheeks for the first and only time.

She doubted he would recognize her in her black maid's dress, with her face unpainted. And she would be busy in the obscure corners of the great hotel, not in the saloons or in the Tabor suite.

But it rankled that she was working for him instead of enjoying the fruits left to her after the Cottons took away the mine.

"Do you serve Horace Tabor?" she asked Clarice. "I mean, who cleans their suite?"

"I don't know. I never did," Clarice said. "I wish I could. I'd like to see what's in Baby Doe's wardrobe and what's in the wastebaskets."

"Oh, Clarice, what a little old curiosity shop you are."

"Well? Wouldn't you like to see Baby Doe's stuff? She's got thousands of shoes, and more petticoats and stuff than we'll have in ten lifetimes. I want to see Horace Tabor's nightshirts. They're supposed to be made of lace."

"Lace? On a man?"

Clarice laughed and tucked the counterpane under a pillow.

"They call him Senator Nightshirt."

"I guess I want to see that. But I really want to see Baby Doe. Is she as bold as they say?"

Clarice shrugged.

Day after day she toiled. After six days, she received four dollars in a brown envelope. Her share of the rent cost two; the rest went for food. She marveled that women survived at all on so little. But maybe they didn't survive; she wondered whether chambermaids just faded away, unknown, unloved, wasting away in hopelessness. Were it not for the scraps she and the others sneaked out of the kitchens, they would all starve, too, especially a big, bulky woman like her.

Clarice told her of the two Windsor saloons, where the serving girls collected more than a chambermaid's daily wage serving a single round of drinks to those rich men. And the restaurants, where the waiters collected five or six dollars a day serving fancy food to rich people. And the bellboys and flunkies, who got rich hefting bags and running errands for the guests. And Dixie swiftly discovered the hellish laundry, where dozens of foreign-born women who couldn't speak English wrestled sheets into steaming vats, stirred them, extracted them with lobster-red hands, wrung them, dried and pressed them, all in a gray forest of steam pipes, wet concrete floors, and roaring noise. Maybe she was lucky to be cleaning rooms instead of stirring sheets for sixty cents a day.

The head matron gave her half of the third floor to work on her own after a week of orientation. At first Dixie reveled in it, being her own boss and working at her own pace. She yanked up dirty sheets, made beds, ran her carpetsweeper over the rugs, polished the white porcelain of the lavatories, and dodged guests' bags, stray clothing, underdrawers, cuff links, and jewelry. The valuables frightened her. She dreaded the moment some guest lost a brooch or necklace and pointed a finger at her.

She survived, made friends among the maids, smiled at the miserable sweat-streaked laundresses, hauled sheets, lifted blankets, toted cleaning things about, until all she wanted at the end of her ten-hour shift was to collapse into her cot in the grubby flat in the Cherry Creek gulch. She wondered how long she could endure a life like this, every dream crushed by the sheer need to keep herself sheltered and fed and clothed. She dared not dream.

Once in a while she encountered a man who appealed to her. Sometimes she knocked and opened a door upon half-dressed people. One man in his drawers grinned shamelessly and beckoned her in. She slammed the door, angry at him. He should have warned her. She wished he hadn't been so virile and cheerful and strong-looking.

The second and third weeks of her new life passed with no improvements in her condition. She lacked the time and strength even to seek other employment. But she knew she wouldn't find any: Denver teemed with unemployed people, many of them consumptives who had heard that Colorado miraculously healed people, desperately hanging on, living upon the charity of some churches that had set up soup kitchens.

Was this life? Her fate? Toil without hope, and drop dead of weariness? Even her innate cheer and buoyancy deserted her at last. Her world seemed divided between the desperate and the rich, and she had the misfortune to live and work and suffer in the midst of extravagance.

By all accounts, Horace Tabor was a generous man who would grubstake anyone who asked for help. But why did he employ women who were no better off than slaves? She raged at him sometimes, embittered that his lawyers had plunged her into this life, and she raged at pampered Baby Doe, in her ermine cape or opera gowns, her every whim instantly satisfied.

Dixie endured another month, suffering the occasional examinations of the stern housekeeping matron who vigilantly checked rooms, discovered a strand of hair or a bed imperfectly made. But Dixie endured that; she had to. And when she thought about it, she still preferred being a maid to working in some filthy workshop, or a laundry, or taking in mending, or clerking in a store. She could enjoy her friends during the brief lunch break, and sometimes even squander a dime for a phosphate or a sundae after work, at the ice cream parlor. But was this all that life would give her?

Then one day the matron directed her to the top floor, and the Tabor suite.

"You've done well, Miss Ball. You learned your trade well at the Clarendon in Leadville. Now you'll be put to the test. You'll be straightening up the Tabor suite. You must never say a word about what you see there. Any indiscretion will terminate your employment. You must remain silent and invisible, keeping the suite immaculate. You'll check the suite four or five times a day, never letting more than an hour or two lapse between your visits. You'll have two other of our best suites to look after also, but Mr. Tabor owns this hotel and you must serve him perfectly."

She gulped back an instinctive response to quit on the spot. The last thing she wanted was to serve the man whose bloodhounds had stripped away every penny. He might recognize her because she was uniquely big-boned. But she doubted he would, not after so many months, and not while she wore her plain black chambermaid's dress. She would be cleaning the great man's toilet, carpetsweeping his rug, no doubt collecting and delivering his laundry, washing his dirty dishes, and picking up after Baby Doe.

The new direction of her life flabbergasted her. She had no idea why she had been selected to be the Tabors' maid, but it had happened. She agreed to remain discreet and headed up the stairs—maids weren't permitted in the famous Otis elevator—wondering how she would manage the next hours.

She had never been on the top floor, and marveled at the view of Denver from that dizzy height, which made her feel like one of the very rich who could look down on everything. She found the door and knocked. No one responded. Tension crept through her. What would Horace Tabor do if he recognized her?

She tried again, marveling all the while at the rococo decor of the hallway. Finally she opened the door with her passkey and announced herself.

No response. Timidly she let herself and her cleaning cart into the suite and announced herself again, into a soft silence. She peered about her upon the love nest of the wealthiest couple in Colorado, trying to make sense of this opulent place, crowded with knickknacks, lavish furniture, bric-a-brac in every corner, so much of it that it oppressed her spirit. The rooms burst with things of all descriptions, whatever the new Mrs. Tabor's whimsy required at any moment.

She wandered the rooms, finding nothing amiss, scarcely even a speck of dust. And yet she couldn't just close the door and leave a place so compelling in its mysteries, so exotic, so filled with a wanton sensuality. She employed her featherduster vigorously, somehow fearful that her raging curiosity would get her into trouble if she merely looked instead of dusted. She could barely fathom such extravagance, the gilded frames, silver side service, oriental carpets, cut glass chandeliers.

A gorgeous oil portrait of Baby Doe hung on the parlor wall, revealing peachy flesh in awesome amounts, identical brooches at her neck and pinning diaphanous cloth at her bosom, earrings the size of saucers, a dimpled wistfulness in her face. For some unknowable reason, Dixie lifted her featherduster and drew it over the oils, gently and carefully, dusting Baby Doe's image.

They had separate, connected bedrooms, and Baby Doe's fascinated Dixie. Here her featherduster wasn't needed, so she brought in her carpetsweeper as the fig leaf over her wild curiosity. For here, in armoires and closets, was Baby Doe's wardrobe, the likes of which Dixie would never see again. She gently plucked her way past ermine stoles, ballgowns of silk or taffeta, diaphanous afternoon dresses, ostrich-plumed hats, scores of pairs of shoes, filmy negligees, lacy peignoirs, monogrammed petticoats and chemises, blouses with great jabots, skirts and suits, all in such abundance that Dixie knew she could spend hours marveling.

But she had barely begun her exploration. At Baby's dressing table stood scores of bottles of perfume and cologne, and in her wardrobes hung sachets, all of which burdened the quiet air of the room with oppressive scents. The three hairbrushes contained strands of her brassy blond hair. Dixie lifted two or three strands and tucked them into a pocket, not knowing or caring why. Next to the amassed perfumes stood a small jewelry box of quilted yellow silk. Dixie ached to open its six drawers, but didn't dare, in terror of being discovered and accused of something. So she touched it with her featherduster and tore herself away, yearning to see some of Baby's legendary diamonds and emeralds and rubies and pearls, her tiaras, rings, bracelets, necklaces, earrings, and brooches.

Baby slept in a small bed, but one heaped with spare pillows and draped with a rich, heavy spread. Was this the altar where the richest man in Colorado came to worship? Or did she venture to his room?

Suddenly Dixie laughed, embarrassed at herself for wondering such things, but curious, too. Baby's favors had won Horace to her, had caused a scandalous divorce. What did she offer Horace? What did he offer her?

A whole bureau top had been devoted to tintypes and photographs, Baby Doe and Horace, the man who called himself Hod, or Haw, after his initials, H. A. W. Tabor. Baby and Hod, formal before the portraitist's lens. H. A. W. standing before the headframe of the Matchless Mine in Leadville with business associates. Tabor being sworn into the United States Senate for his one-month term, surrounded by politicians. Baby in an ostrich-plumed hat, a tinted photograph mounted in a pure gold frame. Baby, her lips slightly parted, leaning into the lens, frankly seductive and inviting. Baby, lying on a chaise, a diaphanous gown keeping her barely covered, a faint, piquant, erotic smile on her face. Baby's own family, all in a row, before the veranda of a large house. That one had been photographed in a place called Oshkosh. Yes, Dixie remembered, Baby, Elizabeth McCourt, had been born to an Irish Catholic family, clothing merchants, of Oshkosh, Wisconsin. After marrying a young man named Harvey Doe, who was a Congregational Church Protestant, she and her hapless husband had come to Central City, where she ultimately had confronted Harvey Doe's ineptitude and failure, and had divorced him.

She drifted into Horace Tabor's bedroom, and discovered a high fourposter with a distinctively feminine frill about it—Baby's hand no doubt—and an armoire with a dozen dark suits in it, and a dresser laden with images of Baby, some of them exquisitely rendered miniatures in oil, each of them transforming a naturally handsome woman into something resembling an angel. Dixie poked around, looking around for the famous lacy nightshirt that Eugene Field had made such fun of in the *Herald,* forever branding Horace Tabor as Senator Nightshirt. But she found no sign of it; no doubt he had cast the effete thing—probably a gift from Baby—away.

She examined the rooms again, finding everything immaculate, and left bearing three strands of Baby's glorious hair in her pocket. Once she had closed the door and stood in the hallway, proportion returned to her. Her entire week's wage wouldn't have purchased one of Baby's monogrammed pillow slips. Who was Dixie Ball, anyway? A big, rawboned woman off a farm, that's who.

But it had been fun, for a few precious minutes, to be transported into a magical world where merely mortal people became gods. She didn't know whether she would enjoy serving these two, but she would find out soon enough. She was due back at the suite in a couple of hours for another straightening. Then she might learn what fate had in store for her, whether Baby was a tyrant, or whether Horace required the impossible. And whether her fate had somehow become entwined with that bumbling love-struck multimillionaire who owned this place, and her domestic service.

CHAPTER 33

omer Peabody suffered through a series of bad nights. He could scarcely make water. He stood impatiently in his necessary room, awaiting the dribble that would relieve his bladder. His enlarged prostate was getting him up three or four times a night now, though daytimes were better and he could sometimes manage several hours between trips to the lavatory. Usually, during the night, he couldn't get rid of the contents of his bladder no matter how patiently he waited, or how subtly he relaxed the muscles of his abdomen, seeking the exact posture that would give him relief.

It frightened him. Pain radiated from the base of his belly. The oversized gland was inflamed and so was everything around it. He wondered what quirk of nature caused males to suffer such a terrible disorder. According to his doctor, Jack Meek, the current theory was that an excess of sexual indulgence caused the onset of the usually fatal disease, the punishing use and abuse of the gland causing it to expand irreversibly. Homer Peabody found macabre humor in that. If he was to suffer and die from an enlarged prostate, then he should at least have gotten some pleasure out of it.

In tears, in the middle of one night, he sat on the edge of his bed and despaired. He was suffering such an ignominious disease, a disorder of his private parts, a hurt that sent him to a water closet a dozen times a day. And it would only get worse. Meek had bluntly warned him about what would come. When his flow was cut off entirely by the angry gland, he would have to resort to catheters. He would need to learn how to insert these each time he needed to make water. They would provide him with blessed relief but at a terrible cost, because they would abrade and inflame the urethra, infect him, and swiftly debilitate him even further. He would soon be discharging milky, offensive material. Very likely he would begin to suffer renal failure, uremic poisoning, and other complications leading to swift disintegration and death, with terrible pain accompanying the decline.

The doctor had given him various anodynes for pain, and they tempted Peabody now. He had morphia tablets, and if worse came to worst, he had suppositories containing opium and belladonna, which Meek assured him would provide swift relief from pain, but not from the general disintegration occurring in the late stages of the disease. The antispasmodic belladonna might even help him pass a little water, the doctor thought.

But he took nothing that night. He would resist doping himself for as long as possible, just as a matter of principle. He felt frightfully alone, an old bachelor in his cold-water flat, barely able to help himself, and deprived of the comfort of those who might share his ordeal. Meek had urged him to get into a hot-water apartment with a tub, because sitting in a hot tub was one way to relax his abdomen and that would help him to pass urine. But flats with hot water cost more than a struggling old man like Peabody could afford. Still, the idea lifted his spirits. He was earning a little more, thanks to all that publicity in the papers about the Kimbroughs. If he could get some relief just by sitting in a hot tub, maybe he should try it regardless of the cost.

He tried dribbling again, standing desperately for minutes, achieving a few miserable squirts. Then he gave up, in tears, and clambered back into his narrow bed, exhausted. No one could help him. He would have to face his torment all alone over the next year or two. He was reminded that everyone dies alone.

He wished he could die a good death instead of this miserable one. A good death was a blessing not much appreciated by those who hadn't thought much about dying. And yet it was the ultimate gift. A good death would be a gift from God, a thing to pray for devoutly. A good death would be swift, serene, painless, and devoid of terror or regret. He would not have a good death but a terrible one, full of pain, lingering nausea, fever, helplessness, desperation, and regret. Especially regret.

Still, he was not some whining coward. He was Homer Peabody, of the Crawfordsville Peabodys, good substantial law-abiding folk, assets to their community, respected and admired. He may have failed at life, but he could be brave at the last. He resolved then and there, in that painful darkness, to die courageously, uncomplaining, with a smile for the world—whether or not anyone would notice.

And he could count his blessings. He had thirteen clients at the moment, seven of them women who were filing for divorce. They had decided that an attorney good enough for Cornelia Kimbrough was good enough for them. The rest of the cases were wills, contract disputes, inheritance litigation, and partnership litigation. He hadn't yet seen much cash from all that, but it would come in, and he could think a little about getting a flat with hot water and a tub, so he could sit in hot water and enjoy better times.

It embarrassed him even to think about such things. His inability to drain himself was a metaphor for his whole failed life. His illness afflicted his private parts, almost like some venereal disease, and thus was something to conceal from the world. Did stronger men suffer prostate trouble? He couldn't imagine it, but Jack Meek had told him they did: old cowboys and ranchers famously suffered prostate disease after a lifetime on horseback had pounded their lower anatomy. Maybe prostate disease wasn't just the bane of soft old men.

Days and weeks dragged by as Peabody tackled his cases one by one, sometimes after bad nights, sometimes when things seemed a little better. Constantly he left his desk to trudge down to the end of the hall and stand almost helplessly for minutes. Sometimes these needs arose in the middle of an interview, often with a woman seeking a divorce, and then he had to excuse himself, which he did lamely, while she sat in his office and waited for an old man to return. These episodes so mortified him that he wished desperately to conduct the interviews with one of the new telephones, which he couldn't afford even though the office building had been wired. Denver had employed telephones since 1879, and one could even call Colorado Springs in 1884. The *News* called them "galvanic muttering machines," but they were proving useful, and gradually putting costly messenger boys out of business.

The improved workload didn't really brighten his life, though. He wanted only to fade away as painlessly as possible. The few years remaining to him had none of the excitement of youth in them, nor did he look into the future with pleasure. The landscape ahead was a bleak desert of pain and hopelessness and regret, with the night just beyond the horizon.

Then one day a young man wandered into his office and introduced himself as Richard Peabody.

"Well, sir, it appears we have the same surname. I don't suppose we're related," Homer said as the lean young fellow sat down across the big table.

"Maybe we have a common ancestor in our family trees," Richard Peabody said. "I'm from upstate New York."

"Why, we're from Crawfordsville, Indiana, and before that, New Hampshire."

"I guess we're not related," the younger Peabody said.

"What brings you here?" Homer asked. "I practice the usual branches of law, family matters, business affairs, contracts, wills; perhaps I can help you."

"Well, in fact, I'm not here with a case. I'm an attorney myself. I got out of law school at Columbia University four years ago, and spent these last years clerking for a federal district court judge, and a New York appellate court judge, and most recently clerking for Vice President Wheeler after he left office in 1881. Now I want to go into private practice. My wife—Alice—and I decided to come west, where there's opportunity, new life, a chance to put down roots. I'm looking for a law partner."

Homer marveled. "A partner? Me?"

Richard smiled. "I followed the Kimbrough case in the papers, and it was obvious you did a creditable job under tough conditions. I've been looking around, but you've been in my mind since then."

"But Mr. Peabody, I couldn't possibly support—I have never had a large practice—"

"I'm aggressive; I can support myself. I do need to learn things from a veteran, and that's one reason I'd prefer a partnership to joining one of the large law firms, where I'd be a flunky in the library for ten years. I suppose this is a two-way street, so I ought to ask you about yourself, your practice . . . That was quite a coup, representing Mrs. Kimbrough."

Homer Peabody knew he could never go into partnership, not with his own demise looming over him. "Why, she came to me simply because her husband was too close to the other lawyers in Denver. It wasn't my skill, but my obscurity, I assure you. Mr. Peabody—Richard—I don't see much opportunity for you here, though of course I'm flattered to be considered."

"Why not?"

"Why—why—I might drag you down, fine, eager young fellow like you." Homer waved a hand at his surroundings. "Does this office strike you as the workplace of a successful attorney?"

"May I ask why you're . . . disinclined? If you'd rather not talk further, just say the word. I rather fancied getting together a Peabody law firm—Peabody and Peabody. It'd give us a head start."

"Sir, I couldn't afford larger quarters."

"I'm not without resources."

Homer Peabody blinked at this young Ivy League lawyer, and knew sadly that he could not saddle the young man with his tribulations. "Mr. Peabody, sir, I suffer from a disease that my doctor expects will take me off in three or four years, maybe sooner. It's an embarrassment even to discuss it, but for the sake of candor I will. It's an enlarged prostate, and it becomes more and more agonizing. I can barely, ah, make water. So, surely, you should find a law partner who's in blooming health, young like yourself—"

"My father died of uremic poisoning and complications," Richard Peabody said. "I'm afraid I know all about your problem, and if it's inheritable I face the same thing some day."

"I'm sorry. But you see why I can't even think—"

"I don't see why not. If you really don't want me around, I'll go. But you've things to teach me, and when the time comes for you to retire, a partnership would help sustain you during your time of need."

"Surely you're not suggesting that you'd take care of me?"

"Partnerships usually involve pooling some earnings in the firm for retirement purposes. Isn't that standard among attorneys?"

"Nothing's standard, but it's common. Now, if you'll permit me, I must excuse myself for a few minutes. If you end up my partner, you'll discover that I must absent myself frequently."

Homer retreated, less because his bladder hurt than because he felt off-balance and needed some privacy. In the quiet of the lavatory down the hall he pondered this astonishing turn of events, found himself oddly liking it, and decided that the whole question would bear serious exploration. Of course, as an honorable man, Homer would delve into his failures, his long penurious past in Crawfordsville, the veiled mockery of the Denver attorneys who knew him, and all the rest. He'd bare his soul, and let the young man draw his own conclusions. No secrets between partners. And of course, he'd question the fellow about his own background, and write those judges, and Vice President William A. Wheeler, too.

Homer returned to his shabby little office and found Richard Peabody waiting patiently. "All right, sir, let's explore this. Tell me about yourself, your upbringing, your schooling, your law clerking. And what you want and expect from a partnership with an old lawyer like me. And I'll make my own confessions, so that we have everything on the table. Maybe there's something to it."

Richard Peabody smiled, opened a briefcase, extracted a sheaf of recommendations, and began.

CHAPTER 34

. . . .

In the space of an hour, Homer Peabody learned a great deal about the young man with his surname, and perhaps Richard Peabody learned even more about Homer. The younger Peabody had married after acquiring his bachelor's degree, and now he and his Alice had a child, a six-year-old girl named Cecilia, and were expecting another.

Homer also learned how it came to pass that Richard Peabody landed on his doorstep.

"I arrived cold," he said. "We knew no one. So I began soliciting the various firms, including your adversaries in the Kimbrough case, Roderick and Hamilton. Well, I soon learned you were the brave fellow taking on the most powerful family in the West, or at least Colorado. And that your litigation was surprising them."

"I didn't do anything much."

"You boldly presented some novel theories of desertion in divorce law, and raised some equity considerations—most unusual. It caught them off-guard. You managed to put on the record much more about Walter Kimbrough's marital failures than they had bargained for. That suit wounded Kimbrough and he still chews on his attorneys. None of them had anticipated the tack you took and weren't prepared to rebut it. You might have won that case with a judge who was a little less traditional."

"Richard, I lost that case. I must tell you, before you get too enthralled by all this, that I'm not a litigator. I lack a certain instinct, a certain manner when I'm in court."

"I know what you mean. You have intellect. But I have that litigator's nature. So they tell me. If we form a partnership, you'll be the brains and I'll be the teeth."

"But Richard. Let me tell you candidly, bluntly, I'm something of a—I have no reputation among the attorneys in this town. I'm not blind to it. It's in their tone, in their casual dismissals, in their—"

"I heard only respect for you when I interviewed some of those attorneys. We can't all be litigators, and if you feel that's a weakness, then our partnership makes all the more good sense, because I'm not much of a strategist."

"You know, that makes sense. I've always prided myself on my preparation. Maybe I could help you prepare. I also have the gift of anticipation. I simply know what the other side's going to do, and how to deal with it. Well, you'd teach me some things, and maybe an old mutt like me could pass along a few tricks. But Richard, I don't have a future. Why would you want to tie up with a doomed man?''

"Well, let's look at it this way. You say you have a few years. Time to train me, season me. Time to establish Peabody and Peabody as a going concern. Wouldn't you like to bequeath a living, prospering law firm to the . . . future?

"You're independent. My family's firm in Albany was like that. My father, my uncle, and a brother. My father's gone now, and my uncle's going to retire. They wanted me to come in, next generation and all that, but—here I am, beneath these snowcapped blue mountains, in this golden mile-high plain, in a new city bustling with life. This is where Alice and I have come to nest forever, and we'd really like to join with you. My other option is to start an independent law firm, but why should there be two Peabody firms?''

"Are you sure you want to do this?''

Something gentle filled the younger man's face. "Maybe you're right. But I see things in this I like. Would you consider trying it for at least a while? If it doesn't work, we'll go our separate ways. I'll look for some office space and take care of the move. Chances are, your share of the rent will be less than what you're paying here.''

Homer nodded. "All right. I'm open to change. You're a fine man. I just wanted you to understand about me.''

The younger man beamed. "I'd like you to meet my wife and girl. We're camped in a small residence hotel for now, but we'd like to take you to dinner. Alice would love to meet you. She's never had a father. He died when she was an infant. She'll be a bit shy. But Cecilia's a bold child, and she'll make up for any shyness in my family. She's five, and a brunette beauty.''

Homer nodded, joy and dread stealing through him. Things were happening much too fast. "But don't you want to examine my books? See my records?''

Richard Peabody smiled. "All that exists is the present and the future," he said.

Homer agreed to meet them in the Roof Garden of the Windsor at six. He couldn't concentrate that afternoon and continually popped his pocket watch out of its nest in his vest and examined it. Once the younger Peabody had left, Homer swiftly concluded that this would all unravel. A bright young couple shouldn't become ensnared by the dead and dying.

He closed his office a bit early and hurried to his flat, intending to dress carefully for dinner. All afternoon this event had loomed larger and larger in his mind, becoming frightfully important, crucial to his waning life, though he couldn't quite say why. This proposed partnership didn't make sense. Let the young associate with the young and the living. But the impending dinner took on a mysterious meaning of its own. He dreaded and yearned for it at the same time. He dismissed it as an ordinary business dinner, while knowing it was infinitely more. He intended to assess the young fellow and his wife, but he knew he would be scrutinized himself, and it made him so nervous he wondered how he would get through the meal, or even taste it.

He set a teapot of water to boiling over his gas stove, and stripped to give himself a sponge bath. He knew old men exuded odors, some of them offensive, and his inability to bathe properly only made them worse. He would check his clothing, too. His wearisome dribbles usually stained his underdrawers, and he would put on fresh.

He scrubbed himself with a hot, soapy towel, scraped his face, rinsed his grimy white hair, examined his white, flabby old carcass, seeing in it the doom of a lifetime of dreams and hopes, and finally dressed, paying close attention to his clothing, lamenting stains on his ancient suit, his frayed cravat, the worn and yellow cuffs and collar of his shirt, and the missing button on his waistcoat. At the last he realized his black hightop shoes were as dull as asphalt but he lacked the means to shine them. He rubbed them down with an old rag, hoping at least to remove the grime, but it did no good. His ancient, cracked, prim black shoes would shame him unless he could find a bootblack at the Windsor beforehand.

That thought solaced him, and he hastened through the rest of his toilet to give himself a spare fifteen minutes there. Then he hurried through a windy twilight to the elegant hotel, found the bootblack stand closed for the day, and waited in the gilded lobby for the young people, feeling like a bridegroom about to marry someone from a social station far above him.

They arrived on time, Richard genial and trim in a handsome dark suit, the blond Alice lovely, almost beautiful, her pleated skirts artfully concealing her condition. And holding her mother's hand was little brown-haired Cecilia, a child with great eyes and curiosity written in her face.

"Well, this'll be a treat," Richard said after introductions. "We rarely step out, and there's no place we'd rather come than here."

They took the Otis elevator, enjoying the novelty, Cecilia almost ecstatic from the kinesthetic sensations she experienced, and then the wiry elevator man swung open the doors onto the restaurant perched above the lights of Denver.

As soon as they were seated at a window table, the younger Peabody took matters in hand.

"How about a libation, Mr. Peabody? We always enjoy a glass of wine."

"Why, ah, yes, indeed," Homer said. He had sampled wine only a dozen times in his long, virtuous life, but this was a time to relax a little.

Mrs. Peabody chose a sherry, while the men ordered a good claret, and sarsaparilla was provided for Miss Cecilia. Now, at last, Homer could survey these two. Here was a green young lawyer, but well seasoned as a law clerk, thirty years his junior, the age of a younger son if ever he had had a family. And beside him sat his gracious woman, thirty-two years Homer's junior. They made the world seem so young, and made Homer feel so old and decayed.

He turned to her. "How do you like Denver, Mrs. Peabody?"

She responded without hesitation. "Denver is whatever we'll make it, Mr. Peabody. It's new, it's flexible, not hardened into an old, stratified city the way Albany was. I think we'll find a country place with a view of the mountains, and people from all walks of life we'll come to call friends. Richard thinks this is the perfect place to be an independent lawyer, not some small cog in some large law firm. I think it'll be a place to raise an adventuresome family. We won't be sitting at home much when there's so much beauty to absorb."

"Richard, how did your family law firm take your decision?"

"They breathed a sigh of relief and made jokes about being rescued. Most jokes conceal a grain of truth, and I think they worried about my entering the firm. I don't have the right attitudes, you know. They knew I would tread on the toes of the mighty."

How young, how very young, that seemed to Homer. He turned to the child, who was all dolled up in a blue dress with ruffles down it. "And how do you like Denver, Miss Cecilia?"

She smiled coyly, suddenly silent. It would take a while before an old man would put her at ease.

"I think Denver's prettier because you're in it," he said to her.

She grinned, checking with her mother about all this. "I'm very pretty," she said.

They feasted on a standing rib roast, asparagus in hollandaise, twice-baked potatoes, pearl onions in cream sauce, and various pastries. Homer Peabody could scarcely remember such a meal. And all the while he absorbed this young couple and their child, who peered solemnly at him as she swallowed potatoes.

He learned, to his astonishment, that Alice had urged the move west at a time when Richard was debating whether to join the family firm.

"He needed to strike out on his own, Homer," she said, at last resorting to first names. "He's different from his family, more experimental, more willing to take social and legal risks. He'd take an unpopular suit that other attorneys would turn down. And I'm like that. I guess I'm the typical American, ever looking westward for a better life. I was dreaming of Denver before we ever saw it. When we got here we looked around, and then at each other, and laughed. We'd come home."

"What's your background . . . Alice?"

"My family's operated Hudson River and Erie Canal barges and ships for years, but the railroads are cutting into that. Grain, coal, gravel, things like that, from New York City clear out to Michigan country. We're getting into real estate now. I'm not much of a person for barges, except I'm famous for barging in where I don't belong."

"She's a Farnsworth. They're Albany people too," Richard said. "We met at a Christmas dance at the Schuyler Mansion, and I snatched her from the arms of ten jealous rivals who were camping on her doorstep."

Something in her glowed at her husband's remark. Homer gazed at them each, remembering his own longings, his own shy failure to snatch any woman from anyone's arms, and his long, lonely life after that. He could not heal that desolation, but he could rejoice in the bright fortune in these strong, healthy young people. He discovered some envy, but knew he was too old, and it was too late, and he could put that aside and find simple pleasure in these vivacious people.

"Richard, you speak of being independent," Homer said tentatively. "You know, Denver's just as bound by faction as Albany, and it's a state capital, like Albany. You can't expect things to be very different. Certain interests will employ certain law firms, leaving the dregs to the rest. You might find yourself making less than you'd imagine. I take cases I don't believe in, just to pay my rent."

"Homer, I wouldn't want you to think that I'd be governed by my own preferences. One thing I inherited from a family of lawyers—the knowledge that it's a business like any other. It's just that, once in a while, I'd love to take a case just for the good in litigating it."

"There's plenty of those," Homer said. "You're an idealist, and idealists face costs and tribulations that more pragmatic attorneys don't worry about. Are you up to it?"

"You were up to it."

Homer shook his head. "Cornelia Kimbrough's case was simply one I believed in."

Richard continued. "We've our eye on a house east of here, a big brick three-bedroom, with a sunny room for a nursery. But I'm hesitant to pay down until I've settled my future. I think we'll just have you as our first dinner guest, Homer . . ."

Richard gazed mischievously at Homer, displaying a humor the older man had not seen before. There had been a question mark in his invitation.

"Well," Homer heard himself saying, "your future's settled, here and now. I guess you'd better put some money down, and invite me to dinner and let me bring you a little housewarming gift."

CHAPTER 35

Cornelia Kimbrough endured dragging dark days, and then in January of 1885 came her birthday. She knew she would celebrate it alone.

At Christmas she had put up a tree and decorated it with strings of popcorn. She had bought Walter a silk paisley scarf and wrapped it and put it under the tree. And there it sat through Christmas. He had given her nothing. She rarely saw him, and gathered he was in Leadville over the holidays.

She thought her birthday would be the same, but it turned out not to be. Her parents invited her over to their spacious home on Downing Street to celebrate her twenty-sixth year. That sounded just fine to her. She hadn't seen enough of them anyway. Davis and Claire Montfort still enjoyed good health and every comfort, and they especially enjoyed each other and an extensive family. Cornelia expected all the family to be at hand, but was surprised when Claire led her into the parlor and only her father greeted her. He looked the same as ever, a little shaggy-haired and boyish, even at fifty-eight, and still affecting the look of a country squire.

"Cornelia! Come in and have a toddy. We'll have a grand evening," he said. "Happy twenty-fifth."

"I'm twenty-six, father."

"Ah! You're not used to flattery. A man should make a woman feel young."

She knew something was up; small birthday gatherings weren't ordinary at the Montfort residence. Her father busied himself at a dry sink, pouring liquors as if he were operating a chemical laboratory, while her mother settled herself.

"We'll have dinner in a while. I told Placida about seven," she said.

Her father handed Cornelia an amber concoction in a tall-stemmed glass, and another to her mother. "Here's to your birthday, and may your next year be better than this one," he said, toasting her.

She nodded and sipped the liqueur, not knowing what it was.

"How are things, dear?" her mother asked.

Cornelia expected that. Every little while her parents inquired about the marriage, but Cornelia had been reticent about telling them things. It was not easy to talk about her private life, even though it had been plastered all over the papers a few months before.

"Not very good," she said.

They wanted to talk about her life on her birthday and she would oblige as best she could.

"That's what we thought," her father said. "We're going to have just a little private birthday party so we can talk about it. We have something special in mind."

That piqued her. "Thank you. We'll have a cozy evening," she said, wondering if it would be cozy at all.

"Cornelia," he said, "we've hardly dared to ask, but are the allegations you brought up in court accurate?"

"Of course they are."

"Ah, don't misunderstand. But lawyers tend to, well, maximize a case. You have no marriage at all, I take it."

That was his polite way of rounding a delicate topic, and she was grateful he didn't press further. "I'm simply property," she said.

"Does he treat you civilly now?"

"He doesn't treat me at all. It's a large house. He keeps to his own rooms. I rarely see him, although he makes a show of being there now and then. That's so that he can demonstrate that he hasn't deserted me."

"Walter does that? Act for the record?"

"Reputation's everything to him. He makes a show of it. He keeps a journal. He even told me about it right after the trial. It records each day he's at home."

Her father laughed, astonished. "I always knew Walter's odd, but not that odd."

"He fears I'll go back to court with a stronger case some day, so he's building an elaborate rebuttal."

"But why on earth—"

"It's important to him."

Her father paused, sipped, weighed his words, and finally plunged in again. "Ah, we don't know your case exactly, and we won't probe. But Cornelia, we know you're living in isolation there, and that it's ruining your life. We've talked about this, and what we'd like is for you simply to come back here and live with us. We'd be a fine threesome! We'd enjoy having you. We'd enjoy entertaining your friends. We'd give you whatever you need, a little cash too, so you'd not be dependent on that bounder, not for anything."

"Oh, father—"

"Do you ever entertain, Cornelia?" her mother asked.

"No. I don't feel like it. I don't even feel like it's my house."

"That's what I thought. You come here, and we'll entertain. I'd just love to have your old friends here for tea, or dinner. I'd just love to see you in touch with them again. You're so isolated over there."

"It's hard. I don't see anyone."

"Then we'll do it. You'll be happier. And we have our reasons, you know. Walter's said such terrible things, we just think it's time for you to be with people."

"Yes," her father added, "and family, too. Your brothers are always wandering through here. You've nephews and nieces you've hardly seen. You come back here, and your life'll brighten up."

Cornelia's heart ached. It had all come out in a rush, and now her nervous father and mother waited for her decision.

"It's a wonderful plan, but it's not quite that easy," she said. "I've things to think about."

"Surely not Walter's feelings, I hope."

"No, his feelings don't matter."

"We'd love to have you."

"I'd love to be here. But I want a real husband and a family. That's my dream. Unless I can divorce Walter, I'll never have it. I need new grounds—and maybe a different judge. My attorney, Mr. Peabody, explained it to me. If I were to move in here with you—desert him—I might lose my chance."

Her father shook his head. "I just can't believe that's the whole law. Have you tried another lawyer?"

"No," she said.

"Well, let me talk to a few."

"All right. But it'll get back to Walter, you know."

"I've a friend or two who'll keep confidences." He eyed her. "We thought we might give you something real for your birthday—a little love and a little hope."

"Oh, Father . . ." She was touched. "Let me think about this."

They ate quietly, and she enjoyed a small chocolate birthday cake with her name frosted on it. When it came time for her to return to her Capitol Hill home, she had the feeling she was walking out of a warm house into an ice chest.

Later, in her own bedroom she lit a fire in the stove, trying to get warm, but something colder than temperature pervaded this place, chilling it and her body down to the marrow. She had promised her parents she would think about their offer, and now she tried to.

Vaguely, ever since her attempt to divorce Walter, she had thought she would try again, find new grounds, go back to court in a year or two with a stronger case. That meant she must live blamelessly, giving his lawyers no ground for a cross-complaint. But now she wondered about that. His aggressive lawyers would file one no matter what she did or didn't do. They would make a war out of it.

She shivered, and wrapped an afghan about her. The January cold seemed to penetrate even to this well-heated room.

She had never felt so helpless, so trapped. She examined her goals carefully: she wanted to remarry and have a family. But if she could not have her first choice in life, should she therefore give up and suffer? No, she was too young, she had too much robust living before her, ever to do that. If she could not win a divorce, was there any reason to remain the perfect wife? No. Did it matter whether she deserted him? No!

She resolved then and there, that evening of her twenty-sixth birthday, to accept her parents' offer. She would move back in with them and start living again. Maybe it wasn't her dream; maybe it even looked like a step backward, this return to the parental nest. But it was her only option, and maybe life consisted mostly of second choices at that.

She discovered another reason for moving to her parents' home: that simple act would put the lie to Walter's elaborate tissues of deception, put the lie to every entry in his journal, put the lie to all his public flattery of her among his business colleagues.

In the morning she would tell her parents. In the afternoon she would have draymen load her private possessions into a cart and haul her goods, her life, her dreams, her hopes, her soul and body, out of the monstrous lie.

That night, far from feeling desolated, she felt the first glow of joy. In surrender she had found hope. In giving up her dream, she had found a path out of Walter's cold house.

CHAPTER 36

ornelia moved into her parents' home, not entirely comfortable with the arrangement. It seemed a step backward. She could not become a dutiful maiden daughter again. She knew she would need to establish her independence, come and go as she chose, and resist the kind but encroaching governance of the parents she had left years before. Still, this warm home on Downing was a sudden, precious blessing of warmth and tenderness, of brothers and sisters and nieces and nephews, of life lived well.

It would do for the nonce. It could not ever be a permanent way of life, and if she stayed too long she would be diminished by it, losing her sense of self-determination little by little. Her spirits lifted at once, though, and she barely thought about Walter. All that was over.

But not entirely. One day she received a letter from Walter's attorney, Fisher Roderick. The tone was less than friendly, and no doubt the letter had been dictated by Walter himself.

"Mr. Kimbrough had requested that I inform you that you must return to your lawful domicile at once, or else you might find the consequences painful. Mr. Kimbrough takes your desertion as an affront to his excellent reputation within the community, and wishes at all costs to preserve it.

"Of course, if you should not return, your reputation would be at risk. But that could be prevented by a prompt return to his domicile. He wishes at all costs to avoid a public scene that would only fuel gossip and offend the Kimbrough family."

Long ago, a letter like that would have evoked rage. But now her anger had been melted away in the crucible of life, and she felt only scorn. He didn't deserve anger. This was nothing but a threat wrapped in lawyerly rhetoric. Reputation above all else. Her desertion had already become public knowledge, and the gossipers were making the most of it. On reflection, she knew she didn't really care.

She showed it to her father. "A veiled threat. No lawyer in his right mind would compose and send a letter like that, so Walter must have dictated it to Roderick, and Roderick must have swallowed a few bitters before putting his name to it. Painful consequences, eh? Let him do what he will. Maybe you need a day or two in court. I reckon you'd have some fun on the stand, sweetheart."

She loved her father's bravado.

A week later she received another letter from Roderick, this time demanding that she return "all property she unlawfully removed from the residence of Mr. Walter Kimbrough," or face legal consequences.

"All property! What does he mean by that?" she cried after showing it to her father.

Davis Montfort grinned. "Everything, including his gifts of jewelry. Your wedding ring. The pearls. Every item of clothing you bought while living under his roof. I tell you what, Cornelia. Ship it all back, right to the last slipper. You and your mother go out and buy some ready-mades for now, and we'll get a seamstress in to make you some good things."

"I'll do that," she said, rejoicing in the chance to remove every last item in her wardrobe that Kimbrough money had paid for, especially the wedding ring. The next day she packed every dress, suit, sweater, shawl, bonnet, purse, earring, bracelet, ring, brooch, and glove she possessed. She enclosed six pairs of shoes, some of which she loved. She even removed some tintypes from their gilded frames and sent the frames on their way, too, because Kimbrough money had paid for them.

But after she gave her father's trusted secretary the jewelry to deliver to Walter's attorneys, and watched the draymen haul the rest of the stuff away, she wondered what would come next, and whether that powerful, obsessed man who loved his reputation more than anything else would strike at her again, or begin some terrible whispering campaign to blacken her reputation.

But did it matter what others thought? She was free, after a fashion. Life in her parents' home presented its own limitations. Her friends scarcely knew how to take it. They were used to inviting couples to dinners or parties, and didn't know how to handle the Kimbroughs, or whether to invite one and not the other. Mostly they didn't invite Cornelia at all, and she found it awkward to entertain them in a house not her own. The result was a deepening isolation, only partly recompensed by the love and warmth and loyalty of her family.

She arranged one day to lunch with Homer Peabody at the Windsor Hotel, just as they had before. It had become almost a ritual, meeting the portly old gent in the lobby, lunching in the Roof Garden, refighting their wars and sharing their losses amid the luxuries, the potted palms, the linen napkins and cloths and pewter service and yellow hothouse roses on each table.

This winter day of 1885 he surprised her, simply by looking a little younger and more buoyant.

"You're looking marvelous," she told him over a seafood platter.

"Oh, I've a new partner, and I've moved to new offices. Here's my card."

"A partner?" She marveled at his news.

He described the change in his life with relish, not leaving out his efforts to forewarn the younger Peabody of his health problems. So far, it was working out admirably. The young man had taken hold, made himself known, and was garnering business. And twice now, Homer Peabody had been a guest at their new home, and was coming to enjoy the young people. Maybe, if all went well, he would almost be family to Richard and Alice . . . he paused, leaving things unsaid.

"And that's not all. I've moved to a tidy little flat with hot water. Doc Meek recommended it. The hot soaks help, you know. I'm getting a tad of relief."

"Oh, Homer, so many good things. Your life's really taken a turn for the better."

"Thanks to you, Cornelia. Your case did it. The publicity." He peered intensely into her eyes, his caring obvious to her and very welcome. "How are you doing? You've escaped the demon in his castle, and you're living with your parents. Is that better?"

She shook her head, exasperated. "It should be. They love me and look after me. But I'm half mad with the need for my own home and some sort of social life. They've been a godsend, Homer, but I'm more restless—I should say desperate—every day. I haven't a life of my own. I'm trapped."

"What does Walter think of that?"

"He can't stand it," she said. She told him about Walter's threats, how she returned every item she had acquired during the marriage.

"And not even that was enough. His attorneys still send me letters—harass me—every few days. They're trying to frighten me, I guess. I don't understand Walter. Why is he so obsessed? I have no answer."

"A man who lives for images would do that. You've been in the Polly Pry gossip column a dozen times recently. He obviously hates it. She's rather mean, actually, writing all that twaddle. Marriage may mean nothing to him, but the pretense means everything."

The gossip columnist who wrote as Polly Pry was really Mrs. Leonel Ross O'Bryan, of the *Denver Post,* and she had been having a merry time with the travails of the younger Kimbroughs, Denver's leading social lights.

"Well, Homer, what should I do? Buy a ticket to Tahiti?"

"There comes a point when a lovely young woman must decide what she wants, and whether that will excite social censure and family disapproval, and whether to risk that. Cornelia"—his eyes moistened—"I made a mistake long ago of heeding all those arbiters of good conduct: my parents and grandparents, my teachers, the ministers, the grand dames, the gentlemen in power, the idealists, the Bible tract writers who passed out pamphlets, the magazine moralists. They stole my sovereignty, my right to make my decisions, with all their rules, which I dutifully and foolishly heeded. I couldn't permit myself . . . I'll never forget what that lovely young woman said to me, so long ago. I lacked passion. It seemed to her I never cared because I didn't reach out and kiss her, take her to me. But all I was doing was being proper. Proper!"

His face clouded. This man was talking about the most important thing in his life, his greatest tragedy, and she listened intently.

"Cornelia, do you know what the worst sin against yourself is? Putting words in the mouth of God. Especially *no.* Don't put *no* in God's mouth. You hear *no* from everyone—parents, Chautauqua speakers, idealists, revolutionaries, visionaries, evangelists, professional societies, arbiters of morals. I listened to them. Their message became God's message written in my soul. Don't . . . don't . . ."

He couldn't finish.

"Homer . . ." She slipped a hand across the table and caught his and held it.

"Don't wait for the world to approve your every act. That's what I must say. Don't wait for Walter to make you miserable. Don't seek your parents' approval. Don't even consider your reputation. Do what you must."

She absorbed that solemnly, knowing she had been driven by events closer and closer to that recklessness. It seemed odd that the man urging her in that direction was the most scrupulously proper man in Denver, the most careful of his conduct. But what a price he had paid for all that virtue.

"Homer, you've given me courage. I'll find a way out of this maze, and I'll make my own decisions. I'll find a way. I need an independent life apart from both Walter and my parents. Money's the problem. Help me think of what to do before I die on the vine."

"I can't help you. Those decisions are yours to make. You can only decide what you want the most, and what the social risks are, and whether you're willing to face the consequences."

CHAPTER 37

Lorenzo Carthage arrived at Ben Guggenheim's office at the smelter north of Denver and was ushered in at once. There was a quality about the Guggenheims that Lorenzo admired: they were utterly straightforward. In moments, Lorenzo would know his fate, and the fate of the Lucky Strike.

"Have a seat, Lorenzo. We've quite a bit of business to go over. Did you have a good trip? How are you doing?"

Carthage sighed. "Easy trip. All rail now, thank heaven. Here's some samples off yesterday's face. You can assay them," Lorenzo said, handing his employer a canvas satchel.

"Good," Guggenheim said. He pressed a button that rang a bell. Within moments, the satchel was dispatched to the chemists. If the meeting lasted the afternoon, they would have the result before it concluded.

"I'll get right to the point," Guggenheim said. "Because of this bubble in Lucky Strike stock, we could sell out at a handsome profit, and I'd have you to thank for it. You'd profit too. You're on record now as the owner of ten thousand shares—now worth between fourteen and fifteen thousand and going up. Not bad for a few-hundred-dollar investment. With us, it's even better. I've already sold enough to hedge my investment and exploration expense. The rest is frosting."

His warm eyes bored into Carthage. "Do we invest in the mine, or do we get out?"

The question frightened Lorenzo. His career hung in the balance. A mistake now and he would never see the inside of a mine again, unless to muck ore at three dollars an hour. "I don't have an answer," he said bluntly.

"I was afraid of that. What's your reading?"

"Inconclusive. Within the existing works, there's not much ore laterally either direction. There's a year or so of mining highgrade straight down the ore seam—so far. Another year's worth of lower-grade ore. The tenors are good but the seam is gradually narrowing. We're encountering water, and that means we're running the pumps now, and that means we're using coal that's dragged up there by mule power. There's hydropower there for a mill. A flume would power a mill, the pumps, electric lights, compressed air drills, and a bucket tram down the slope."

Guggenheim nodded. "It's this bubble. It won't last. I can get out with a good profit, or I can mine silver. And the decision won't wait. It's that simple. I understand your reluctance, but tell me what to do."

"I have a pile of data in my portfolio," Carthage said. "But they won't help us much. I can sum them up in a few sentences."

"All right, we'll go over them. But let's talk about this bubble. Did you start it?"

"I did everything possible to discourage it."

"But you bought some shares in Telluride?"

"Nine thousand, for peanuts, around eight cents, before the bubble. From a local doctor and others. It seemed a good risk. That's all there was to it. Since then, I've done nothing but tell people no decisions have been made, period. The rally is the result of your wire calling me here, and the distorted reporting of that ferret that Nathaniel Hill sent out there. I must've denied ten times that we were manipulating the stock, but he turned it into a conspiracy. A flimsy of your wire found its way through Telluride, and that was all it took. I don't doubt that some locals out there pay the Western Union man some fancy cash for good tips."

Guggenheim grinned at last, and Carthage felt himself relax slightly.

"The reporter applied the tarbrush pretty thick," Guggenheim said. "My family avoids all publicity. In the future, just refuse to talk to reporters, even to set the record straight. In the end, unsubstantiated rumors are better than damaging misquotations that can get us into trouble."

"Yes, sir."

"All right, let's go over everything you've brought. Before I see you out the door, I'll decide whether to mine, sell out, or something in between, such as limited mining and stockpiling ore. I figure this balloon'll last maybe forty-eight hours at the most."

"I agree, sir. Unless we stoke it and stroke it. We could keep it going for weeks. Double the value of our stocks."

Ben Guggenheim's face became a mask, his silence a ticking bomb that made Carthage shrink. Carthage knew he had said the wrong thing. The Guggenheims had built their empire through fair dealing, hand-shake commitments, faithful execution of agreements, and sheer recti-tude.

"We'll make our decision today," Guggenheim said.

"It shouldn't be either-or," Carthage said. "It should be based on more exploration. Another hundred yards on the seam, and a hundred-foot exploratory shaft straight down. Another three or four months. Another twenty thousand in exploration before we commit to a mill and other capital investments. And that'll give your chemists time to figure out the best approach for that sulfide ore."

"We already know what we need to do here; the question is what to do in Telluride."

"I can't say now. How about another thirty days?"

Guggenheim stared through a high window opening over the smelter. From it one could see the tall stack belching smoke, and several smaller stacks. "My family doesn't trust mines. They come and go. But smelters reduce the ore of hundreds of mines, new and old, and live on, a stable enterprise that'll serve my children and grandchildren. Our instinct is to unload the Lucky Strike. But sheer greed deters us. The Lucky Strike has spectacular ore. I've rarely seen anything like it. You've a nose for ore, you say: how much ore's in there? If we sold out, would we be throwing away a bonanza like the Minnie in Leadville?"

Carthage squirmed. "Let's look at these figures, and you can decide, Ben."

Guggenheim grinned, knowingly. "You don't like to catch the hot potato," he said.

They examined Carthage's daily reports and assays, but the whole exercise seemed sterile, and was. It was boiling down to Carthage's nose for ore, and the amount of investment the mine would require.

"Well?" asked Guggenheim.

"Have you been in touch with the other directors? What do they want to do?"

"They've been heating up the Western Union wires and the tele-phone for two days. The mine's got a pretty fancy directorate, Lorenzo. Kimbrough, Teller, Cheesman, Byers, Evans, Moffat, Henry Brown . . . Denver Club people. The ones who won't let Meyer and Ben and Simon Guggenheim in the door. Suddenly I'm their friend. And they all want to know if it's a bubble or if it's real. And they're talking to each other. Between them, they could put together a majority and pitch us out. As long as the Lucky Strike was failing, no one much cared. Suddenly they all care, and they're looking at you, and wondering whether to keep you around. What're we going to tell 'em?"

"I didn't know they were on the board."

"You researched the Lucky Strike exhaustively before you plunged," Ben mocked. "And you knew your major stockholders before you decided to manage it."

Chastened, Lorenzo stayed silent, but his mind was awhirl. If he turned the Lucky Strike into a success, he'd be on the top of the heap, perhaps for the rest of his life. And if the mine failed . . . he would be no worse off than now.

"Let's make it work. I want an amalgamation mill on-site, a hydro plant, a bucket tram up that grade, and a spur track to Telluride. You'll handle the smelting and the refining here."

An unsubtle mockery spread through Ben's face. "Name a few prominent people you can invite to parties, and suddenly you got courage."

"I've been on the brink of saying we should try it."

"Then we'll do it. I'll tell them we think we can make the Lucky Strike work, and we're going to invest heavily. I'll call an emergency board meeting and propose floating three or four hundred thousand more shares to capitalize the development. I'll also put this material before them. I'll also tell them it's your decision, not mine."

Carthage had the dizzy feeling he had just put his neck into a noose. But no trap would spring for a while. They gossiped for another fifteen minutes, and then the assay report arrived. The tenors were better: sulfide ore containing two thousand five hundred dollars of gold and silver to the ton, plus lead and other base metals. And just as refractory as ever.

Carthage left that meeting knowing that the Lucky Strike had suddenly catapulted into a major mine, and its success or failure would affect Colorado's elite. And that if he failed, he would look forward to a career as a shoeshine boy.

He stopped at the exchange and talked to Quigg, hinting but never saying the Lucky Strike would be a bonanza mine. He talked of development, investment, continuing good tenors, and left instructions to Quigg to buy a little more stock on margin. At its blossoming price, he couldn't afford much of it.

Lorenzo wasn't a man to waste a moment. While still in Denver, he commissioned a firm of mining engineers to begin the project, and persuaded one of them to return to Telluride with him. True, he was acting ahead of the board's decision, but that had always been his method. When you move, you move fast.

Back at the Lucky Strike, he set the engineer to work, hired an additional face crew, and talked to the Rio Grande Southern about starting a spur up the steep valley to the mine. The spur was going to cost plenty because of rough terrain, bridges, and grades. The Lucky Strike would have to pay for most of it.

Each day during that hectic time he watched the progress of the exploration work. The main drift along the seam was extended another hundred yards, and then water became an acute problem roughly four hundred yards from the lowest gallery that had been worked by the previous management. Water now had to be pumped over half a mile upslope to the mine head and the volume of it was straining his pumps and boilers. He put the face crew to work on lateral drifts again, wanting to know the exact width of the ore seam.

Another crew, sinking a shaft straight down, had encountered nothing but country rock or slightly mineralized rock too poor to mine. He suspected that this mine would not have layered ore bodies. The bonanza seam had been deposited by percolation along a major fault that would not be duplicated lower down. But he doggedly kept the crew at work and sent the bills to Guggenheim, who was paying for it out of his family funds. The cautious directors had not approved a new flotation of stock, but had accepted an increase in exploration work, and the engineering costs for the capital improvements, to be paid through loans.

Lucky Strike stock drifted upward, past two dollars, three, four, and settled at five a share. Lorenzo was rich. He sold some shares and started work on a five-thousand-dollar replica of an antebellum plantation house, with a grand veranda, over on carriage row. Townsmen drove by, gawked, and hunted around for more Lucky Strike stock to buy, but it was scarce now.

Guggenheim showed up a month later, a quizzical smile in his face. Carthage was ready for him this time, armed not only with a better knowledge of reserves, but with the engineering estimates as well. And a new plan.

"How do you interpret it?" Ben asked.

"If the ore weren't refractory, we'd have a sure thing with the reserves we have. Right now, I don't know. The engineers are estimating expenses much higher than I anticipated. The flooding in the lower levels will require heavy pumps. It'd cost four hundred thousand to do what we want to do."

Carthage knew the moment had come. He had engineered a way to turn the mine into an El Dorado. All he had to do was persuade Ben Guggenheim to invest even more venture capital. "This water problem's started me thinking. The way to deal with this is to drive an adit, a horizontal tunnel at the base of the mountain, straight in until it strikes the seam. I calculate that the seam would be about twenty-two hundred feet in. Then we'd need to drive a winze down from the existing works, and use the adit under the works to drain the water, and use gravity to bring the ore out. Most of the reserves would be above the adit. And the mill would be down near the valley floor, using water from the adit. We wouldn't need a bucket hoist up to the mine head. We'd be employing gravity, not fighting it.

"One of the problems with the Lucky Strike is that snows shut it down for weeks every winter because the mule trains can't get through. The adit would solve a number of problems, including winter shutdowns, and radically lower the cost of mining and milling and transportation. We'll mine year around. We can board the miners down below and abandon the mine head up here. We'll cut transportation costs by two-thirds, get rid of about a hundred mules, a fleet of wagons, and thousands of dollars' worth of hay and feed.

"The adit more or less doubles our reserves, by making low-grade ore profitable. It'd cost more than the first plan—two thousand feet of tunnel, a mill and an electrical power plant—but it would guarantee a highly profitable mine—if we can break down the sulfide ore. That's up to you and your chemists. We can concentrate here, extract about thirty percent of the gold and silver, the engineers tell me. And we can ship the rest to you—a ton of concentrate out of five tons of ore, they say. You'll have gold, silver, lead, zinc, and some iron pyrite just to keep you on your toes. You'll need a Bessemer oven for that.

"With three crews going around the clock, we can drive the adit at about eighty feet a week—if we're lucky, and if we have first-rate powdermen and compressed-air drills. It'll take seven months or so to bore, timber, install tram rails and drive a winze up to the works, but we can mine the highgrade all the while for cash to support the venture—providing you can deal with the ore."

Guggenheim studied Carthage's plans for two hours, paying close attention to the projected savings, and gazed off into space for a while. "All right, Magnificent, start the adit," he said. "I'll push it past the board. It's brilliant."

CHAPTER 38

. . . .

Work on the adit proceeded swiftly. Carthage had selected a site about a hundred feet above the San Miguel River. That left room for the gravity-operated mill and power plant below the mouth. His engineers completed the plans for the mill, and Carthage started construction. Meanwhile, the Rio Grande Western began building narrow-gauge tracks up the steep valley. The cost would be formidable because of the numerous bridges and trestles, and the need to gouge roadbed out of cliffsides.

Ben Guggenheim showed up fortnightly, and one weekend all the Guggenheims, old Meyer, Ben, and Simon, came to inspect the progress with unsmiling faces. Likewise, the whole board of directors showed up at one time or another, Kimbrough, Cheesman, Evans, Byers, and all the rest, frowns on their faces. None of them was comfortable making capital investments of such magnitude on a risky project like this. But if all went well, the adit would strike the ore seam twenty-two hundred feet into the mountain, and then there would be rejoicing among the owners.

Meanwhile the stock gyrated up and down, and Carthage sometimes gained or lost a thousand in a day. His paper profits ranged from twenty to thirty thousand and he was tempted to sell some of his shares. He was feeling grand again, a man on top of the world, a potentate of the mining industry. Whenever he made an appearance in Telluride, men of affairs gathered around him wanting news of the mine's progress, eager to discuss assays and shares and above all, the adit.

"We're on schedule," he told them one evening. "Hit some water, which we diverted to the ditch—valuable stuff, actually, a hundred gallons a minute just from that source. It's enough to power a small turbine, and we won't need to divert the river."

That sent the stock higher, though it should have sent it lower, because any mining man knew that so much water could be unmanageable. It threatened the whole project.

Everything about the Lucky Strike was exhilarating him. He was still making two hundred a month, but that would change when the mining began and the stamps started crushing the ore at the mill and the narrow-gauge hopper cars began hauling the concentrate to Denver. He had free time now, and spent it creating his new estate just outside of town. His new white house radiated glory, and he loved to wander through its unfinished confines, enjoying the high ceilings, the tall windows with their views of the mountains, the ballroom and dining hall. Now that he was once again Lorenzo the Magnificent, tradesmen scarcely bothered him about payment; he ordered chandeliers, gold-plated faucets, white clawfooted tubs, black walnut wainscoting, Brussels carpets, parqueted floors, ebony chaises, matched white trotters, a Thoroughbred saddler, a graveled drive, brocaded draperies, and anything else that he fancied. True, the bank required eight thousand shares of his stock for collateral, but everyone else cheerfully put his expenses on credit, knowing that once the construction of the Lucky Strike was complete, they'd be paid. His debts passed ten thousand, but it didn't matter.

One day he took Ben Guggenheim out to his estate and led him through the whole project. He showed Guggenheim the new carriage house, the stables, the peacocks that had just arrived, the lawn statuary, his new silky black Thoroughbred, the mahogany bar and back bar in his ballroom, the shining parqueted floors, the household electrical wiring which he installed even though Telluride had not yet received electricity.

Through all this, his employer said not a word, and when at last the grand tour was over, Guggenheim looked particularly solemn, which amused Carthage.

"Good luck, Lorenzo," said Guggenheim at last, as he stepped into his hack.

A little chagrined, Carthage watched him drive smartly back to Telluride. The Lucky Strike would be a bonanza mine, and his thousand-a-month salary would easily pay for his amusements. His stock would no doubt be split and split again and continue upward once the rich ores were mined with the help of gravity, and shipped off to Denver on the new spur track. Prudence was fine, and he approved of it, but it shouldn't get in the way of an exuberant optimism. Reticence wouldn't conquer anything.

The day came when his estate was about done, at least for the moment, and he was ready for his first grand soiree. As it happened, the tunnel would be driven past the two-thousand-foot mark, and was nearing completion. That was cause enough for a real champagne-popping celebration. His mind hummed with the glory of it. He sent invitations to the whole of Denver's elite, including every director and major stockholder, as well as those in Telluride and Leadville. He made sure his contractors and engineers were invited. He employed Denver wine merchants, Pate and Jameson, to ship him the finest champagne available.

He hired a string orchestra for the dances and paid its fare to Telluride. He found a Leadville caterer, paid for the rail tickets to Telluride, and gave them a free hand to put on a royal feast. He hired temporary maids and groomsmen, rented some fine carriages so his guests could take the country air, arranged for tours of the other great mines in the district, planned a ceremony in which the first Lucky Strike ore would come under the hammers of the new stamp mill, hired a Shakespearean company playing at the Tabor Opera House in Leadville to perform each evening, and hired a pianist and harpist to perform the whole weekend. He swiftly commissioned the construction of a shooting range and bought six Purdys and a mountain of clay birds and ammunition for his guests. And oh, yes, he had a tailor complete three splendid outfits: formal evening attire, afternoon sporting dress, and a rather rakish field outfit suitable for mine tours and picnics.

Lorenzo the Magnificent was back in business.

The adit proceeded quite nicely. The crews hit an area of rotted rock, which required extra timbering and lagging, and of course water remained a threat, a turbulent stream flowing angrily in the ditch on the left side of the tunnel, and tumbling into the river from the mouth. But the crew had cut through an unexpected narrow seam of ore, several inches thick, not enough to mine but a promise of good things to come. He sent word of that back to Denver at once, along with samples. Guggenheim was pleased by the auguries. The ore, while not rich, was additional evidence of mineralization.

At the end of six months, the tunnel was nearing two thousand feet, the mill was up and the last of the jigs, stamps, and tables had been installed; the turbine and generator were ready to power pumps and make electricity to light the mine, the railroad spur was only two miles distant, and the Lucky Strike was poised for its great blooming.

The first of Carthage's parties, during the first week of October, 1885, was an event that set all of Colorado to talking. He put up all the directors and their families in his own spacious manse, while the rest of his two hundred guests were housed in a string of luxurious sleeping cars rented from the Denver and Rio Grande Railroad and parked on a Telluride siding. These and some parlor cars had brought the Denver crowd to Telluride. Colorado's elite had never enjoyed itself in such posh surroundings. Gorgeous peacocks strolled the new lawn, their feathers an iridescent green. The bird hunting crowd banged away at clay pigeons each afternoon. And when it came to viands, Lorenzo had outdone himself. Guests could partake of lobsters shipped frozen from New England, clams, Alaska crab, Virginia smoked ham, fresh elk and mountain sheep and bear and venison, wines of every imaginable sort, pastries and rolls and tarts, chocolates and pies, one course after another, all day each day.

There were excursions to mines and picnics in hanging valleys, the dedication of the adit and mill, and dances each evening, in which Lorenzo did not fail to waltz each of the lovely daughters of Denver, intending to find himself a mate at last. Gentlemen talked of stocks, and tunnels, and assays and sulfide ores and driving railroads up mountain valleys, while the ladies talked of men, and suitors, and children, and whist, and new dance steps, and rattlesnakes, and picnics, and whether life in palace cars was bearable, and schools.

Carthage had discreetly invited the press, and here and there a rumpled reporter wandered about, looking like some poor tradesman or teamster. They jotted notes and wolfed the food. That was all fine with Lorenzo; it was high time the world knew he was back at the summit where he belonged.

"Yes," he told one rather grimy fellow, "this is but the first of my little at-homes. Why, the next one, in a month or so, we'll be celebrating the completion of the adit—we're only two hundred feet or so from the seam now, although, of course, the dip and strike might have varied down there, seven or eight hundred feet below the headframe. But we'll have a little ceremony, and then an intimate little soiree, maybe just the directors and myself, and open a few bottles of the bubbly. Why, when you uncork a bonanza, you may as well uncork the Dom Perignon."

All of which, he knew, was quotable.

He saw to it that his guests enjoyed every minute, and made sure that the ones who counted—the directors and stockholders—got into the adit, right to the working face, and saw with their own eyes the entire magnificent project on the brink of its glory. There, deep in the bowels of the earth, in the eerie light of carbide lamps, Denver's elite abandoned their jovial demeanor and asked hard questions: How long would it take to amortize the cost of the investment, given ore tenors the same as above? What about the water trouble? How profitable would these sulfide ores be? What was the projected life of the mine? Why was the Rio Grande Western so far behind in building the spur?

Carthage had prepared himself for all these and worse, and smoothly rattled off data, offered projections, and exuded a certain subdued and cautious optimism he knew would find favor in the bosoms of his auditors. It was all performance. Life was a performance. His parties were a performance for those with eyes and ears. All his soirees, those in Leadville, the one in Silverton, and this one, had been more than entertainments for the rich; they had all had an underlying business purpose, not only to promote a mining property, but to promote Lorenzo the Magnificent.

He saw his guests off that Sunday, as one by one the carriages took them back to the sleeping cars on the siding. They seemed a happy, euphoric lot, having danced and wined and dined away an extended weekend. But some of the grandees of Colorado eyed him coolly, as he knew they would. There would always be those who objected to having a good time, and those who simply couldn't enjoy a good time or the fruits of their own wealth.

Senator Teller, among the last to leave, was one of the skeptics. He had made his pile in Central City and had served Colorado well, especially the mining interests. And he was a major stockholder in the Lucky Strike.

"Been just dandy, very pleasant, Carthage," he said. "Very impressive show. I hope there isn't a hard lesson in it."

CHAPTER 39

Rose Edenderry resented losing the money. Every night she earned some good tips at the Arcade, but the money always vanished during the binges that followed in Bones's room. All it took was a couple of drinks and then someone stole her coins, which made her mad.

She wasn't even having a good time. She got sick on that rotgut they swilled right out of the bottle, and she usually didn't remember anything after an hour or so. Each party lasted until they all were too drunk to stay awake. First it was Bones and Ike sharing a bottle of red-eye and stuff, then others, so many she didn't know their names. But at least she was out of the weather, which was growing colder and meaner. She could hardly remember having a regular meal, or sleeping in a regular bed. She hated this life, but couldn't even slow down.

She had trouble keeping clean, but she kept trying even though it was a losing battle. Bone and Ike didn't have a washboard or soap. Her clothing was falling apart and her shoes had holes in the soles. She was constantly sick, and sometimes feverish or nauseous. Food barely interested her, and she couldn't even remember sitting down to a good meal. Strange red and purple bruises appeared on her arms and neck and face. She couldn't remember how she got them. In a few months of riotous living she had aged and sickened, and it showed in her yellowish, puffy flesh and the black pits of her eyes. She couldn't bear to look in a mirror now, loathing what she saw there. Not long ago, she had been pretty.

She was earning less, too. Customers at the Arcade summoned other girls. The gamblers, like William Masterson, refused to let her serve their tables. She wasn't attracting men into the Arcade anymore, and one of these days Jack Diamond would throw her out. She had moments of utter desperation, but saw no way out of the life she was living.

One November night, when she arrived at the Arcade, Jack Diamond motioned her toward his back room. She knew she was about to be ousted, and she didn't give a damn. She intended to give him a tongue-lashing just because she was sick of men telling her what to do and how to live.

Diamond rounded his old desk and waited for her to settle herself. He was a rough, hard, black-haired man with a ruthless quality about him, and now he radiated something stern.

"You're gonna get rid of me," she said, defiantly.

"I hate to see you destroy yourself."

"Don't gimme no lectures, dearie."

He stared silently at a wall calendar, and she wondered what he was thinking. He wore the mask of a poker player.

"All right, no lectures, Rosie," he said. "You were quite a draw here. Lot of men came in just because you were so pretty and full of smiles, and eager to trade a few words with 'em. Well, hell. Look at you now."

"Don't you say a damn word, Diamond. The dudes keep stealing my tips so I can't buy a dress."

"I like you," he said. "Liked you more half a year ago."

"You're preaching. Like Masterson, like Holliday, like all the rest."

"Do you want to work here, Rosie? Yes or no." Diamond's voice broke through her defenses roughly.

"I don't give a damn about this hellhole."

He grinned suddenly. "That wasn't what I asked."

She hadn't expected the grin, and grinned back reflexively.

"You can work here—if you shape up."

"I knew you'd say that. What I do is nobody's business but my own."

He was not deterred. "Here's my proposition. You're not gonna

work here looking the way you do. You should burn that dress. Get off
the sauce and quit the wild life. Look at the bags under your eyes. You're
hell warmed over. You can stay if you'll get ahold of yourself and start
drawing customers again."

"No one tells me what to do."

He shrugged. "Here's the rest of the deal. I've got quarters in the
rear. You come live with me. I'll buy some clothes, feed you, help you
get your health back. You'll serve, make tips—that's your cash—and
stick to the straight of it. No booze, no parties, no hop or any of the
rest."

"Go to hell, Diamond."

Jack Diamond smiled faintly. "That it?" he asked gently.

"That's it, damn you."

"What are you going to do? Maybe I shouldn't care, eh?"

She started to cry. "Leave me alone, Diamond," she said through
her tears.

"I thought I'd give it one last try," he said. "You're a sweet girl,
Rosie, when you're sober. All right, you're not going to work here.
You're out."

"I'm not going to work anywhere. I quit."

"No, you're fired."

"I want a drink before I go."

He shook his head.

"You damn cheapskate," she snapped.

"Saving a nickel of booze isn't the reason," he said.

Moments later she found herself standing on the street, watching
the sports head for the saloons after a long day's work. She knew it was
futile to try for a serving job, looking the way she did. And anyway, every
saloon operator on Blake Street knew her by now. She seethed at Diamond, kicking her while she was down, treating her like that.

She itched for a hot bath, with fragrant soap, and some clean crisp
clothing, and shining new shoes, and a dab of perfume, and a beautiful
flat full of shining furniture, with glowing wooden floors and steam heat.
She wanted a whole market basket full of food; fresh yeasty loaves from
the baker, a rib roast from the butcher, and some new red potatoes
from the greengrocer. She wanted a heap of money in the Denver
banks, and a maid to come clean, and a laundress to do all her things.

A man jarred her and laughed when she tumbled into the slime.
She cried out at him, but he never apologized, and vanished through a
pair of double doors into the Occident, a high rollers' gambling house.

She picked herself up and didn't bother to brush off the slime. If she was going to freeze like pond ice, it didn't matter whether she froze clean or filthy.

She shivered. The night would be frosty and she lacked a coat. She possessed nothing but the clothes on her emaciated body. The high plains air eddied through her thin, smeared skirts, numbing her legs, chilling her feet. Weariness stole through her; she had so little strength anymore. The night wind whipped a ragged newspaper and rolled it along Blake, past the yellow light spilling from the saloons and variety theaters and gambling parlors. She felt like that yellowed old paper, a worthless rattling thing bullied by the breeze. She craved a drink; craved any powder that would let peace steal through her. But she could not satisfy her cravings now, and never would again.

She laughed suddenly. This woman, this Rose Edenderry, was nothing but a bag of bones. She saw herself from a distance, her whole life before her, the starving childhood in Ireland's County Offaly, where she grew up in a wee house beside the Bog of Allen. How innocent she was. Little did that girl-child know what fate awaited her on a foreign shore.

Her father had been an ally of the O'Connors, those legendary rebels, and she had rebellion purling in her blood. No law of man or crown or God or Protestants could contain her. She would do what she would do, and the devil take those who tried to stop her. Devil take William Masterson. Devil take Jack Diamond, him who wanted to clean and dress her and turn her into a puppet again. Devil take them all! Better to freeze this miserable cold night than to surrender to all their rules.

She wandered out of that district, past the quieter and darker bordellos and parlor houses of Market Street. They didn't tempt her. She'd rather die than become an inmate in one of those. Not a good girl, she was, but not one of those.

She drifted south and west, through the center of Denver, past the haughty buildings. She tried to enter the Tabor Opera House to warm up, but a doorman chased her away. Maybe she could beg. She stood in the wind, with not even a shawl to warm her, waiting for the theater patrons. But whenever she approached, they recoiled.

"Help a starving lady," she cried to their backs.

She spotted another likely mark. "Keep a woman from freezing to death," she said.

"Get a lawyer," said the gent.

She spotted a church and thought to warm herself within. It was some Protestant denomination and the big door was firmly locked, keeping the faithless out. Maybe if she could find a Catholic one, it would be open and she could curl up on a pew until some fat priest booted her out. If she was going to croak, it might as well be in her own Catholic Church, so that God could get right down to the business of sending her to hell. God was on the side of the lords and ladies and the crown and the gentry and tinhorn gamblers, and if she was going to spend eternity in hell, she'd shake her fist all the way down there, and every time they peered down on her, she'd be shaking her fist. In a thousand years of hell she'd still be shaking her fist.

She didn't find any more churches, but she kept walking to stay warm, drifting toward Capitol Hill and the great homes nearby. A notion was forming within her. If she could find a livery barn, or someone's carriage house, she might find warmth. There would be horses, radiating their body heat, and a hay pile she could burrow into. Her hands had numbed, and her whole torso seemed naked to the weather beneath her thin cottons. She knew from the darkness of the neighborhoods that the hour had grown late. Fewer lights filled windows.

She turned into one gravel drive, heading toward the carriage barn at the rear; anything, any shelter now, any resort would do. She studied the gloom for clotheslines, for any garment she might borrow for the night, but the gloom defeated her. She found her way to the carriage house only to awaken a dog, which barked viciously. She fled back to the street and drifted toward another house, shaking now, the shivers quaking her body uncontrollably. This time she reached the carriage house without arousing a canine chorus, but it was frightfully dark. She felt her way into pitch blackness, and heard horses shift around nervously. It felt a little warmer there, but not much. She didn't stop shaking.

"It's just me," she said to the horses, from clenched lips. "And I need you."

A horse snorted softly. She ached for light; ached to find a ladder to a hayloft, or a horse blanket. She felt cautiously along the walls, desperate to find anything that would warm her, and finally found several burlap bags. They seemed a miracle, even if they were coarse and porous. She wrapped one about her chest, and pulled the other around her shoulders, and carried several more.

She worked her way around the carriage house until she found the stalls, and suddenly felt the wet muzzle of a horse sniffing and snorting softly. Warmth. At least a little. Enough to keep her from freezing.

She found the stall latch and opened the gate slowly, worried that the animal would attack her, or bolt, or rear up over her. But it didn't.

She eased past the animal, talking softly while it sniffed her nervously. She found a manger at the head of the stall with some hay in it. She spread the hay the length of the manger and crawled in. There she settled for the night, under the nose of a large warm animal, the thin burlap bags her only blankets.

Was not a manger the place where the Virgin had laid the Christ Child when there was no room at the inn? She was neither a virgin nor a holy infant, but the image brought tears to her. Her shivering slowed, but did not cease. She waited for warmth that didn't come, and knew that she had to change or die.

CHAPTER 40

Maria Theresa Haas was packing. Yves Poulenc watched her dolefully as she filled leather trunks with her wardrobe, chattering all the while.

She looked radiant. Color had returned to her flesh, and a shine to her eyes. She had stopped coughing. Even her brown hair glowed. She moved about her cabin without breathing hard, excited at the prospect of returning to her family. She had been free of fever for two months, and while her lungs were permanently weakened and scarred, she could hope for years and decades of joyous life. She had been at Glenwood Springs less than a year; only a third of the time that Yves had been there.

Yves grieved, but there was more to it. He was envious, and knew he would miss her terribly. He was secretly in love with this enchanting woman, but it could never be voiced. No longer would they march down to the hot springs and soak, and gulp the salubrious fumes, and talk, and forge a bond that Yves had thought was sacred and profound.

She stopped her busy packing at last, and turned to Yves. "The herbs are next," she said softly. "Would you like them?"

"Why—I . . . I suppose so."

She eyed him wryly. "You only suppose so. You're almost cured yourself, but you only suppose so."

"No, I'm not cured. This is just a temporary remission."

"Would you take them—all the things I've been giving you—after I'm gone?"

"I don't know. If you want me to."

"Yves Poulenc, if you don't want them, I'm not going to waste them on you. I'll give them to others. Old Heinrich Blatz would love to have them. Mrs. Pickerell wants them, and she's always over here learning about them. I'll give them to her if you don't want them. She wants to get well, which is more than I can say about you."

"Of course I want them. Who said I didn't?" he replied crossly.

She gazed solemnly at him, and then sat down beside him. "Yves," she said softly, "you don't really believe these help. Maybe some don't. I can't tell. But some do. I don't think I'm going to give them to you—at least not unless you promise—a real promise that binds you—to continue with them just as I've given them to you." She reached over and touched his brow. "Your fever's down. You've color in your flesh. The dark circles under your eyes are gone. You're not coughing very much. Your pulse is slower. You walk easily to the hot springs. Before, you could barely do it. And yet you're not happy. Why is that?"

"Of course I'm happy," he said shortly. "I want to get well even worse than you."

"Do you?"

He glared at her.

"When you're healed, what are you going to do with your life?"

"How should I know. Write happy poetry, I guess. I won't be able to write tragic poems." Why was she annoying him so?

"Yves, if you give me your word of honor that you'll continue what I've started—I've got it all written down for you—I'll give these to you right now. But I want more than a promise from you. I also want you to believe in the future. Soon you'll need to get on with living, and that frightens you more than the thought of dying."

"Well, I won't need to worry about that when this remission is over."

She didn't reply, but her gaze was searching. She peered out the tiny glassed window into spring sunlight. "I'm going to divide my herbs three ways," she said. "You'll have enough for maybe a month. Then it'll be up to you. I'll share the rest with the others."

He felt stricken, as if she had plunged a knife in his back.

"I promise, I swear, I'll take all the herbs, and eat what you suggest. I promise it, Maria Theresa."

She smiled. "I think Mrs. Pickerell needs some things," she said. "She aches to return to her children. She cries each night because she's alone and sick. She's very poor, and every cent counts."

"Who hasn't cried in the night?"

"You."

He reddened, but he had no answer. He had reconciled himself to doom long ago, and since then had considered weeping a weakness.

That afternoon she brought half of her tins and decanters to him, and the little burner that she used to boil up decoctions, and the raw alcohol she used to make tinctures, and other of her elixirs and tonics. He placed all these on a shelf after removing his cherished library of poets, including Keats and Byron, who had also died young, Browning, and the French Romantics. She watched silently, a smile on her face but questions in her eyes.

"Yes, I'll use them all," he said, as if to answer her silent question.

She nodded. "Here's all the instructions," she said. "I made copies for the others. They may be coming to you for things. I've included the addresses of firms that supply these herbs. Please share."

"Of course I will. We're all in this together."

"Will you eat well, too?"

"What you call proper diet goes against the doctors. It's not scientific."

Again she paused, and then addressed him quietly. "You'll get well if you want to. If you don't, you won't."

He choked back a reply. It came to him that he ought to be grateful. He had failed to let her know. "I want to thank you," he said. "You've done a lot for me. These herbs—they help."

She nodded, tenderness in her eyes.

Maria Theresa left the next morning in a hack, surrounded by her trunks, leaving a lot unsaid. Yves watched her go, desolated and lonely. He loved her, but it was his lot in his brief life never to know the joys of requited love. Somehow the parting had gone badly, and neither of them said the things he had expected would be said as she stood beside the hack. Instead of rejoicing in her bloom and beauty, and her excitement at returning whole to her family, he felt envy and desolation and bitterness. Good things always happened to others; never to him. She had been a good thing in his life, the first good thing that ever happened to him.

He watched the hack head down to the Colorado River and strike east, leaving eddies of dust. She grew smaller and smaller, and then he couldn't see her anymore, and knew he would never see her again.

He returned to his cabin and stared at the array of herbs. It was time for his gargle of white vitriol, and later he should brew some ginseng tea, but he didn't feel like it. He sat angrily on his bed, trying to make sense of a ruined life. She shouldn't have asked him what he intended to do with his life when he was cured. That was like driving a sword through him. Dolefully, he clambered into his swimming drawers and headed toward the hot springs, ignoring the glorious Rocky Mountain spring morning, and the lusty trills of the birds, and the blooming grasses. He dipped into the hot water, enjoying it now that it didn't wear him out to walk there, and he didn't have to struggle to breathe or feel his clamoring heart while he took the heat and steam.

A certain peace crept into him at last. He had to get on with his life and his dying. She was gone. He missed her terribly, but what could he do about it? Maybe it was a good thing she had left. Now he could get back to reality.

He returned, dressed, and gargled with the white vitriol, determined to follow her regimen even if it was ultimately futile. Then he went for a walk. He could manage half a mile now, and the little excursions always filled him with a sort of melancholy joy. Glenwood Springs, compressed between arid slopes, was no place of beauty, but even there the lusty Rocky Mountain springtime brought riotous blooms and growth.

As spring dissolved into summer he stuck doggedly to Maria Theresa's formulas, sometimes ordering herbs and elixirs and sharing them with Mrs. Pickerell as she had asked. He could no longer deny the bloom of health in him. His pulse slowed more and his heart beat less desperately. His face took on color and lost its waxen look. His fever vanished, even in the evenings. The assorted physicians who came and went pronounced him well enough to leave, and yet he clung to Glenwood Springs, afraid to go anywhere lest this whole bloom of life be nothing more than a mirage, a remission.

He eyed his casket sourly. He would not be lying in it soon. He scarcely knew whether to keep it or sell it to any of the unfortunates who continued to pour into the springs. The gossip was that soon the British syndicate would be building a resort at the springs, and evicting all the squatters who rented or owned cabins on its land, including himself. He abandoned his studies of death, at least for the moment. The sheer vitality bubbling through him discouraged morbid thoughts. It made him heady to realize he could climb a hill, or hike along the river, or plant an herb garden behind his cabin.

He heard nothing from Maria Theresa Haas, and didn't write her. She would be in the midst of her loved ones now. Her relationship with him had been purely platonic and tender, nothing more, and he secretly understood she disapproved of his attitudes anyway. She had no use for science, of course, and he prided himself on being a strict rationalist who never succumbed to fancy or myth. But he missed her terribly, especially during his dips in the springs, when they had shared some sort of intimacy of the soul, talking quietly in their swimming attire.

"Why don't you pack up?" asked Dr. Bellingham one day. "I doubt that you'll relapse. Whatever Mrs. Haas prescribed, it must have had some merit in it. Leave that list with me, will you? Whenever something works, I want to know about it."

That decided Yves. He would leave. He knew he wasn't cured; he was much too fragile. But he had been given some tentative lease on life, and now he faced the ordeal of doing something with himself. It annoyed him more than it pleasured him. Whatever would he do with the year or two he had won? He didn't doubt that eventually the whole shaky edifice of health would tumble on his head and make things worse, having given him a sampling of a vital life.

He took passage one day on the Denver and Rio Grande Railroad, now that the narrow-gauge tracks had been laid up the Colorado River. For weeks, consumptives had flooded into Glenwood Springs because the railroad was promoting the place. He didn't like the changes, or the crowds of sick, coughing, feverish newcomers he saw everywhere. They would pollute the springs and spread fever. Reluctantly, he sold his casket to one of them.

He arrived in a Denver he didn't recognize. The city had a way of building and rebuilding itself. He eyed the stacks of the smelters north of town and decided to live as far from them as he could to protect his delicate constitution and his weakened lungs. He found a pleasant hot-water flat in the Cherry Creek district, in a sunny apartment building, and settled down. He continued to follow Maria Theresa's herbal regimen, and to eat the vegetables and fruits she had insisted he eat.

As soon as he was settled he hired a hack to take him to Riverside Cemetery, where he located his burial plot. He stared long and hard at the little bit of land that the caretaker had shown him on a plat map, and felt cheated that he could not immediately lie there, a famous poet who was celebrated for the genius he had shown in his brief, tragic span, an American Keats. But he was satisfied with the plot. It lay on a gentle west-facing slope, and the views of the towering blue mountains were just as the promoters had described. But all that would have to wait.

Now he had to live. And he didn't have the faintest idea of what to do with his life. What would he do now? He still could not answer Maria Theresa's question, and the question still aggravated his soul.

. . . .

ate in the afternoon, Dixie Ball returned to the Tabor Suite to straighten it. She let herself in with the passkey.

"Chambermaid," she said.

This time she encountered Horace Tabor himself, standing in the middle of the parlor. He had pulled off his cravat, and looked slightly disheveled, but otherwise was just as she remembered him from the party in Silverton, a soft, middle-aged tycoon with a drooping mustache and a receding hairline. His eyes reminded her of a deer's eyes, and now they were taking her in. He was plainly puzzled.

"You're new," he said.

"Yup, been here awhile, but not on this floor. Anything need cleaning?"

"Mrs. Tabor made some tea. She's in her room. Please don't disturb her."

"I'll straighten things up," she said.

"Where've I seen you?"

She shrugged and featherdusted furiously. She feared her job hung in the balance. Bad luck, being assigned to this suite, of all the crannies in the hotel. She'd be on the street looking for work.

"I know you from somewhere. What's your name, eh?"

She stopped and confronted him. "Dixie Ball."

"Dixie Ball." Recognition filled his face. "Yes. Silverton. What are you doing here?" He had become agitated.

"The Cottons took my mine from me. Then your blasted lawyers cleaned me out. I used to be a chambermaid in Leadville, so I got a job here."

"What do you mean, my lawyers cleaned you out?"

"Why, doggone it, Hod Tabor, you sent the vultures. You should know."

"Yes, certainly," he said, puzzlement in his face. She realized he wouldn't admit he didn't understand. Male vanity.

"They said I'd taken you for a ride, and if I didn't turn over all I had left, they'd press charges." She shrugged. "You won. You cleaned out this old farm gal, Hod."

He squinted. "And now you're trying to steal it back. That's why you're here."

She got mad. "Hod Tabor, if I'd wanted to steal it back, I'd have cleaned you out earlier this afternoon. Who's stealing from whom, that's what I want to know. I was just a gal with a mine, and next thing I knew the whole blasted world landed on me, you worst of all. You think I'm a thief? You look around and see if anything's missing. Then fire me!" She stood before him, hands on hips, her featherduster wagging with every word she spoke.

"Ah, what did my attorneys say?"

"It was that skinny one, looked like a broomstick. He said any adult woman—that's meaning me—she'd know that if she was cohabiting, that wasn't the same as being hitched, and so I'd cheated you and Lorenzo the Magnificent because I didn't own the mine, and he said he'd throw me into the jug if I didn't cough up all I had—which I did, twenty thousand or something. So you got it. How was I to know? My fella, he died, and I just kept on a-going with the mine. Now I'm gonna quit here. I'll be damned if I'll be called a thief by you or your snot-nosed lawyers."

Some faint amusement lit Tabor's eyes. "Whoa up, Dixie. I got six, seven lawyers fighting off vultures all the time. A man like me earns his pile, and everyone wants a piece, and they're protecting me. Ain't this something. Here's old Hod and one of his partners in a mine, getting together, only now you're pushing feathers!"

"What else can I do?" she snapped. "I'm pushing feathers and running carpetsweepers, and whipping the dish towels because of you."

"And the Cottons."

She fumed. "No, because of you. I had enough left over to fix me up, and I was living real peaceable in Silverton until your rattlesnakes showed up. You want this place cleaned or not? You can just have me assigned to some other floor. But I suppose you'll throw me out of the Windsor."

Tabor peered off into space for such a long time she wondered what he was doing. "We'll be out of here in a fortnight," he said. "We're moving over to Capitol Hill. Got a little place there, just about done."

"Little place, my eye. I bet you could fit a twenty-mule team in the dining room."

Tabor laughed, at last. "Two twenty-mule teams, actually. I just ordered a hundred peacocks today. For the lawn, you know. Baby—Mrs. Tabor—likes to watch them. She's, ah, well along now, you know. We'll have us a little Hod pretty soon."

"Well, he'll sure grow up with a silver spoon in his mouth," she said.

"Silver spoon, eh? Say, Dixie, you just keep on here. We'll be out soon. Me and Mrs. Tabor, we'll need a lot of help, seeing as she's mostly indisposed and complaining she's carrying around triplets at least. I tell her she's just got a big old Hod in her."

"Maybe I can help," Dixie ventured. "I birthed a lot of calves and foals in my day, and a mess of piglets. Sows are just like people, you know. I've pulled out little porkers by the gross. If Baby—if Mrs. Tabor's going to have trouble, you just give me a holler. I never midwived a woman before, but I've sure fixed up some unhappy sows, and unplugged a few breech births and all that."

Horace Tabor stood there, rooted to the floor. Dixie whisked her featherduster over some portraits, and headed for the spacious kitchen to wash the teacup.

He followed her there, a certain delight in his sagging face. "Ah, would you tell that to Mrs. Tabor, just as you told me?"

"Why? Do you want me to midwife her?"

"No, I just want her to know about your skills."

Dixie shrugged and followed Tabor to the closed door.

"Baby, darling, sweetheart, I've someone here."

A muffled sound came from within.

"It's our new maid, Baby."

Another sound Dixie couldn't interpret, and Horace Tabor slowly opened the door. Baby had arrayed herself across her bed, in a peach peignoir. She was supported by about twenty pillows and bolsters. She wore huge pearl earrings, a gold crucifix at her throat, some gaudy rings, and a series of gold bracelets. Other than that, she was gorgeous, Dixie thought.

Tabor led Dixie in. "This here's Dixie Ball, Baby," he said. "She'll take care of us. Dixie, this here's Mrs. Tabor, but she answers to Baby."

Dixie nodded, fascinated by the apparition lying upon the mound of pillows. Baby Doe had a gorgeous, pouty face, electric blue eyes, and an aura of sugar and spice. That brassy hair held the light and caught the eye.

"Dixie Ball, here, she's an old acquaintance, Baby. Dixie's had a lot of experience birthing."

"Oh, a midwife. I don't need a midwife when I can have a dozen Viennese doctors."

"Ma'am, you're right as rain," Dixie said.

Tabor eyed her. "You should know, Baby, my sweetie pie, that Dixie has a lot of experience with domestic animals, and has helped many a sow give the world many a piglet. She says sows are just like people, and she's helped sows in their time of need. She's delivered more porkers than she can remember.''

"She has?"

"I just get in there and tuck a head around, or push a little piggy hoof back, and then they all pop out, ma'am.''

"Oh," said Baby Doe, "that's nice."

"Baby, I was just thinking, honey pie, that we ought to take Miss Ball with us over to the new house. She thought that our dining room would probably hold a twenty-mule team.''

"At least that," said Baby. "And I'd invite mules before I'd invite all these Denver jackasses.''

"You mean you want me to work for you?" Dixie asked, astonished.

"Well, Baby and me, we'll talk it over, of course," Hod said, retreating. "Are you good with babies?''

"Me? I'm not even good at makin' 'em.''

Baby giggled, and then touched her crucifix.

"Well, Baby, I just wanted you to meet Miss Ball. Me and her, we go back a long way.''

"You do?"

"She worked in Leadville at the Clarendon.''

Baby's gaze turned glittery and cold, and Dixie figured her employment with the Tabors had come to an abrupt halt.

"But we never met there," Tabor continued. "At least not so's I heard of it. Anyhow, honeybun, I just thought you'd enjoy having someone around who's better than a dozen Viennese doctors.''

Baby Doe studied Dixie. "You should charge five hundred dollars a day for midwifing," she said. "Then I'd pay attention."

Tabor led Dixie back to the parlor. "She likes you," he said. "Baby doesn't like everyone. Especially if they're snubbing her. But when I'm president they won't dare snub her. It's all because she's so beautiful. The biddies can't stand it.''

"President?"

Horace Tabor rared back and smiled. Then he lifted a finger to his lips. "You work for old Hod, you gotta keep a few secrets," he said.

She glared at him. "You're taking a lot for granted, Horace Tabor. Maybe I don't want to work for you. I got a few nits to pick with you.''

Tabor chewed on his droopy mustache.

"And besides, you took everything I had from me. Maybe you should repay me instead of tossing me some old soup bone. Maybe I wasn't married and didn't have a right to that ore, but I wasn't trying to cheat you or Lorenzo Carthage. I just hadn't thunk it out. But you took it, or your shysters did. I can make my way without any old Horace Tabor, I'll have you know."

"You're feisty," he replied. "We're moving end of the month. You give notice here, and show up first of July. I don't know what you get here, but I'll raise you a dollar a day and you'll get meals and board."

"All right, I'll try it," she said. "I don't know why, though."

"Baby needs you," he replied.

CHAPTER 42

Partnership wasn't easy for Homer Peabody. In some respects it compounded the amount of pain in his life. As the months rolled by, he found himself facing troubles he had never encountered in his decades as an attorney in single practice. Young Richard was the rising star, and he was the fading one, and he tried to keep that in mind. But in the end he knew he would always be uncomfortable in a partnership.

When the telephone jangled, the operators always asked for "the younger Mr. Peabody," which shot envy through Homer. Richard had swiftly made himself known in Denver, joined clubs, lunched with other attorneys, become active in his Presbyterian church, while Homer, portly and formal and aware of his social shortcomings, remained isolated.

They wrangled about the office, too. Richard wanted a secretary, but Homer didn't need one and didn't want to shoulder all that expense. Richard wanted to employ a Miss Violet Stutz, a woman trained in stenography and adept on the typing machines for the job, but Homer insisted that a law firm should employ only males; some things, such as the substance of certain criminal cases, or divorce matters, weren't for women's ears.

But Richard prevailed. "Homer, women are realists, and know all about these things."

Homer retreated, ill at ease to have a young woman present while he worked; a woman who was all too aware of Homer's frequent journeys to the water closet at the end of the corridor. He never quite got used to Miss Stutz, although she proved to be an efficient worker and a fine receptionist.

All these changes seemed to come at a dizzy pace, and Homer had trouble concentrating on his work. How could he when Richard popped into his office twenty times a day, asking questions, offering advice, stopping to comment, or drawing Homer out on the wisdom of one tack or another in litigation.

Richard proved to be no fireball at litigation, either, and lost most of his cases.

"Why did we lose, Homer?" he asked one day. "We had the facts and the law on our side."

Homer suspected he knew why, and when Richard litigated his next case, a bitter divorce suit, Homer sat beside him and watched closely. It was easy to see what the trouble was, but it would be hard to tell Richard about it. After the court session was over, Homer spent a day phrasing and rephrasing his message to the young man, and finally gathered up his courage and entered his partner's office during a break.

"Richard, I can offer some counsel," he said. "Not that I'm any great shakes as a litigator, but I have the vantage point of an older man . . ."

The young man grinned. "I can take it, Homer."

"Well, you're—too harsh. Your combativeness makes you seem . . . unpleasant."

Richard stopped smiling.

"I would suggest, young man, that you stop finding fault with opposing counsel and the judge. No matter how you feel, next time I hope you'll praise opposing counsel for a lucid presentation or a good argument, and thank the judge, and—this gets to the heart of it, Richard— stop hectoring the witnesses."

"But that's weak. I want to punch holes in their case. I'm out to win. I represent my client, not the other side. This isn't a love fest, Homer. Maybe your view is why you've been frustrated yourself all these years."

Homer shook his head. "You're not winning. You're not helping our clients. Think about it."

With that he fled, unable to help his young partner further. The young man would have to learn, and was going to learn only when he bloodied his nose enough.

Homer studiously refrained from going to court, and for a while didn't know whether Richard had heeded his advice. But the younger man started winning more often, and Homer concluded that the young lion had listened and changed his conduct, at least to some modest degree.

The new partnership did not run smoothly, and Homer felt new weight on his weary shoulders. He felt like an antique, a superannuated old man whose courtly demeanor suggested an earlier time and different beliefs. His income had improved a little, but even that was really a spillover from Richard's aggressive practice. The younger man often turned over the paperwork tasks, such as drafting wills and contracts, while keeping the litigation for himself. Homer wrestled with new feelings of dependency, and ultimately, failure.

He purchased a new ready-made suit, but somehow his bulging old body and old habits turned the new black gabardine into an outfit as disreputable as his earlier ones. But at least his hightop shoes were regularly blacked.

Alice's time came, and she was delivered of a blue baby, a girl, who died moments after birth. The child they had named Denver was buried in a tiny coffin. Richard was grief-stricken and took time off. Homer suddenly found himself running an office he barely understood, trying to cope with his own sorrow over the younger Peabodys' tragedy, and thinking long thoughts about what he had missed in his single life. Marriage, as he had visualized it all those years and decades, was as heady and fragrant as lilacs in spring, but now Homer was discovering that the reality was far from his fantasies. Marriage involved pain, frustration, shattered hopes, constant awareness of the will of one's mate, and moments of drudgery and sadness. Maybe he hadn't missed so much. But to think it was to deny it. His long, single life, beyond redemption now, was a disaster and a cross too heavy to be borne.

Richard returned to work, but pale, shaken, and somehow more mature. Each day, he came to Homer's office to consult, and now Homer found the young man quieter and different somehow, more absorbent, more subdued.

One day, a month later, Richard invited Homer to dinner. "Homer, Alice and I want to have you soon. She's about ready for company now, and you're like family to us. Would you come over Saturday night?"

"I'd be happy to."

It pleased Homer. The younger Peabodys had found a circle of young friends and Homer had found himself alone again. But now perhaps he would enjoy some company.

He found Richard and Alice more grave. The death of a child had changed them. Their youthful gaiety had fled, but not their courage. It was as if, in their upper twenties, the Peabodys had reached adulthood. If Alice felt strain at this first social outing since the baby's death, she didn't show it. She quietly served a fine pork chop dinner, and gently admonished Cecilia to clean up her plate. The conversation seemed impersonal, though. It was about Denver's precarious water supply, and politics.

But over a delicious caramel-flavored pudding and coffee Richard turned the conversation to law.

"You know, Homer, you helped me more than I can say when you advised me to pull in my fangs. That wasn't easy for me to absorb at first." He smiled, apologetically. "A little too much swagger for my own good. But I tried it. I thanked a witness. I publicly told Darryl Riley his cross-examination was excellent. When I objected to a line of inquiry, old Justice Hughes overruled me, so I expressed my appreciation for his reasoned ruling. It worked. He sure was surprised. I won. The jury didn't think I was a leper. And you did that for me. It's a lesson I'll never forget, Homer. You pulled that out of your bag of experience, your lifetime at this profession, and got it across to me even when I wasn't ready to hear it."

Something melted ice floes in Homer's soul. "Oh, it was nothing," he said. "It just comes with age."

But it was something. In his long, feckless life he had rarely done anything that counted. But this time he had made his mark.

Then it was Alice's turn. "We're going to have more children," she said. "I didn't think I ever would want another. And I hope one doesn't come along for a while. But we want a little brother for Cecilia, and we've decided that if we're blessed again, the child's middle name will be Homer."

"Oh, my," said Homer.

"All in the family," said Richard.

At the end of that pleasant evening, Alice hugged him at the door. Just a quick, affectionate hug, a woman's way of expressing tenderness and love. But for Homer, it was ambrosia. He had stood there, too hidebound to hug back, but enjoying the squeeze of her arms and the softness of her body. And then the moment passed. No woman had hugged him like that since his childhood, and it was as if a meteor shower had lit the heavens.

Homer lumbered home on foot rather than calling a hack, even though the two-mile walk would be hard on him. He felt inspired and animated, and he felt some sort of release from his underlying despair.

At home in his flat at last, his old heart pounding from the hike, he sank into his armchair and undid the laces of his hightops. Then he sat in the darkness, letting the evening's events drift through his mind. He reprised Richard's appreciation, over and over, cherishing the praise as if it were the most beautiful gift in the world. And that is just what it seemed to him; precious evidence that his long sojourn on earth had been something more than failure.

Was he happy? No, it was too late for that. He had spun out a long life in a sort of impotence, a cage wrought by parents, social arbiters, and hosts of naysayers. He had precious little to show for all those wasted years. Could he be happy in the future? Not with his doom looming ever closer. He had reached his late fifties now; his prostate was slowly tightening its grip and he was growing more and more breathless, too. He was too much the realist to imagine he would ever marry or have the things he had pined for, year after year, night after night, all that terrible life.

But he still had a little time, and he had a young couple to dote upon and give to. Birthdays and Christmases and Thanksgivings. He had no dream of his own, but a good father could nurture the dreams of his children, and find some joy in it, and pass along something of himself to the world. He knew that this last chapter of his life was good, a blessing, and a benediction.

CHAPTER 43

ornelia Kimbrough thought she saw a way out, and arranged to have tea at the American House with two women her mother's age, Elizabeth Byers and Margaret Evans. Both of them were not only at the core of Denver's elite, but had founded the Ladies Relief Society in 1874 to cope with some of the growing city's acute needs.

They greeted Cornelia while a serving woman brought them tea and tarts. Cornelia eyed them anxiously, knowing what doyennes these women were, how much they reflected their husbands' political and social instincts, and how motivated they both were by noblesse oblige.

The wife of former governor Evans would, she knew, be both blunt and imperious, but also the woman who would say yea or nay to what Cornelia had in mind.

"And how is Walter these days?" Mrs. Evans asked.

"I have no contact with him."

"A pity. We can only hope that your divisions heal, and you can return to the bosom of his family and his hearth."

"That will never happen, Margaret."

The older woman frowned. "Walter's an exemplary man, diligent in business, a visionary with the future of Denver in his heart. A sterling man. He's helped our aid society each year—substantially, I might add. You are a lucky woman to be attached to such a man as Walter Kimbrough."

"I'm sure that Walter thinks so," Cornelia replied.

"You must pray," Elizabeth Byers said. "That will solve anything if you put your heart into it."

Impatiently, Cornelia turned the chitchat toward her purposes, particularly the matron's position at the children's home on Logan Street that the women had constructed and now operated. "I understand the matron at your orphanage is leaving, and you're looking for a new one. I'd like to be considered."

"But . . . Cornelia!"

"I would enjoy caring for those children. I've never had any and never will."

"You won't as long as you're away from Walter," Elizabeth Byers put in.

"It's those miscarriages," Margaret said. "I'm sure, when you're ready, and your heart is no longer broken, Walter will joyously start a family. That's the thing for you to get over, you know. We're all rooting for you and Walter."

Cornelia ached to tell her that she would have no children even if she managed to repair her marriage, but she kept silent about that. Surely these women had read some of the gossipy material published during the divorce trial. "I'd like the position, and I'd like to move into the home," she said.

"Why, Cornelia, it isn't really suitable for a person with your background."

"I believe that nurturing children, especially unfortunate ones, is suitable to a woman of any background, Margaret." Cornelia sipped the strong hot tea and waited.

"What does Walter say about this?"

"I haven't consulted him."

"But we would have to have his approval, you know. You're his wife. We wouldn't want to cause a domestic tiff. And he's our most important contributor."

"I don't think he would be interested one way or another. I would like an independent income, and a worthy mission in life, and I know I could do a good job."

"You mean you would want the salary? Not just make it a contribution?"

"It would be the only income I have. Walter does not support me, and I wish to be independent of my parents."

"Oh, that would be quite improper," said Margaret Evans. "A woman who's reached a certain station gives rather than receives. And how would Walter feel, knowing you were reduced to wage labor? You, who need only to return to his yearning arms to become one of the richest women in Colorado."

"His arms don't yearn for me, Mrs. Evans, and never have. His feelings are not the issue here. And I believe I would be giving more than receiving. That's a large building, with many hungry little hearts within it, and I think I could give many a child a good start in life."

"But of course Walter's feelings are an issue, Cornelia. He's your husband."

"No, he stopped being a husband long before my divorce action—about the time our honeymoon was over. It's no marriage, except that the courts say it is."

Margaret Evans stared glacially at Cornelia. "What the courts say just happens to count among people."

Elizabeth Byers was growing more and more nervous, sipping tea and shifting uncomfortably in the ladies' parlor of the old hotel. "I really think we can't go ahead—I mean the Ladies Relief Society—until we consult with each other, Cornelia. We have certain things to consider. I'm sure you understand."

Cornelia did understand. The women weren't going to budge. And Walter's financial power and ruthless will were reaching into every nook and cranny of Denver life. "Very well, let me know. I want the position. And I want an independent means."

"We do have several candidates you know," Margaret Evans said. "Very suitable, and experienced."

That was that. The three gossiped for a while more and then abandoned the old hotel. Cornelia knew that she would never have that position because the women thought it was unsuitable and because of

Walter's influence. She had asked the unthinkable of these powerful women: actual employment as a wage-earning person. That would be demeaning to a woman of their—and her—social caste. If her request were considered at all by the Ladies Relief Society, it would also be considered by every husband, and every lawyer, and every merchant prince even remotely vulnerable to Walter Kimbrough's power and wrath.

The response came the very next day, via messenger boy. The note, written on Margaret Gray Evans's monogrammed stationery, simply said that the Ladies Relief Society had hired an experienced matron for the orphanage that morning.

Cornelia wasn't surprised. She knew what the result would be. In the next day's *Rocky Mountain News,* editor William Byers announced that Walter Kimbrough had given a thousand-dollar charitable gift to the Ladies Relief Society to continue its good works. She wasn't surprised by that, either. Byers had been currying the favor of Denver's elite ever since he had been caught in a dalliance with a milliner. It was a wonder that Elizabeth took him back.

Walter Kimbrough would frustrate her dreams and thwart her hopes no matter what she did in Denver—unless she returned to the cold comfort of his iceberg home, and thus repaired his wounded reputation. She stared from the window of her parents' home onto the bleakest of futures. But one truth did form in her mind at that moment: if she were ever to acquire a life of her own, or independence, she would have to leave not only Denver, but Colorado—wherever Walter's writ would run. That seemed so impossible, without so much as a dime to her name and no particular training that would sustain her. And yet the very thought filled her with hope. If Colorado lay in the thrall of Walter Kimbrough, she would leave the state.

But where would she go?

First to the top of the Windsor Hotel for lunch with Homer. She had grown fond of the shy old man, and discovered a sagacity in him coupled with a transparent honesty and realism. And in recent months he had changed, too. The starchy lawyer she had first encountered had given way to a more accommodating mortal, willing to try new things.

She met him at the Roof Garden, and they took a table beside a window opening on the purple mountains in the west. Homer looked almost natty these days, though his flesh looked soft and gray, and she wondered whether his health was declining.

"Cornelia, you grow younger each day. It must be living at home that does it," he said.

"I had to talk to you," she said over sherry. "I'm feeling so trapped. It's as if Walter's everywhere. As if he has spies and informants. As if that waiter there's going to tell him about this lunch, and get a dollar for the information."

She described her attempt to obtain a position, and the wall she ran into, and she didn't leave out the fact that Walter Kimbrough had donated a thousand dollars to the women's group.

"I can't even work! It isn't just that all those women think I shouldn't; it's that Walter's going to stop it if he can. He wants me in the house or dying on the vine."

"I wish I'd known earlier you wanted a position," Homer said. "We hired a secretary and receptionist a year ago. Miss Stutz. She's Mrs. George now, and leaving us to start a family."

Cornelia's heart skipped. "Homer! Do you think—"

"It'd be demeaning to you, Cornelia. A woman in your position. And the pay—"

"Don't you put me in the box that Margaret Evans put me into," she fumed. "I could do that work very well. I was even a Latin scholar. There isn't a legal term that'd throw me. And I'll master the typing machine. Just let me at it."

He laughed softly. "You couldn't manage on six dollars a week."

"Other women do!"

"Cold-water rooms, nothing left over . . . I wish we could offer you more—I'll need to talk to Richard, of course, but at this moment the position's unfilled, and we were going to advertise." He studied her quietly. "And you must think about the implications. What will Walter do or try to do?"

"Maybe you should be thinking the same thing," she shot back. "If you employ me he just might find some excuse to cause trouble."

"That's fine. We'll just turn it into the divorce retrial you've been wishing for. And with some garnish for the potatoes."

The idea startled her. This wasn't the timid old Homer she knew. As if reading her mind, he smiled.

"Richard Peabody influences me these days, Cornelia," he said softly.

"Homer, if you'd hire me, I'll find some little place. I'll work hard. I'll bring in business. I'll take a shorthand course and learn to type. I've always been curious about law. Teach me how to clerk, how to look up precedents, and I'll master that. I was a good scholar in school, and I'll be a better scholar working for you. Try me!"

"I will," he said, "with or without Richard's approval."

"I want to scandalize Margaret Evans!"

"I don't doubt that you'll scandalize much of Denver, including your parents. And especially Walter Kimbrough."

They laughed. She felt life flow into her like a sparkling mountain stream. But she felt the poignancy of it, too. She was pinning her whole life on such a small and humble thing: a dollar-a-day job.

CHAPTER 44

During the following days, Cornelia was assailed by more doubts than she had ever faced in her life. She hunted for a place where a woman making around thirty dollars a month might survive, and found the options dismal. She located a few tiny cubicles, none with a kitchen or lavatory or hot water. Most were in unsavory buildings where she would be rooming next to dubious neighbors, some of them drunks. The hallways somehow smelled of vomit, or violence, or sweat, or cabbage. The landlords looked unkempt, and some eyed her with frank, demanding gazes. One rooming house operated by a landlady harbored mostly female tenants, some with no apparent means of supporting themselves.

Could she bear to move from a comfortable life to that? Her social life had long since disintegrated; the young people she had grown up with scarcely knew how to treat her ever since she deserted Walter, and living at home with her parents hadn't helped matters any. But moving to any of these places would seal her social isolation, signal her drop from Denver's haut monde to utter obscurity. She would have to make new friends, somehow, and meet people for a three-cent vanilla at an ice cream parlor instead of lunch at the Roof Garden.

Young Richard Peabody gallantly attempted to rescue her from that, offering her room and board in the Peabody home for four dollars a week plus a little baby-sitting whenever the young couple wanted an evening out or a Sunday free. Cornelia considered that carefully, and rejected it. She was weary of being an appendage of someone else's family, even her own. And she had fled Walter Kimbrough's cold house for much the same reason: she functioned there merely as decor. No, she decided, if she could find the courage to make this leap, she would want its meager fruit, which would be independence.

Still, doubts piled up like snowdrifts in her mind. She asked herself the most aching questions: Why didn't she just go back to Walter? After all, he largely ignored her and she could fashion a comfortable life with her old friends, and enjoy the Denver Country Club, the outings, the balls and dinners, and all the rest. And why didn't she just stay with her parents on Downing and make a comfortable life, even if a spinsterish one? And what did she really want from life, and was it so important that it was worth abandoning everything she had known? Was being a factotum in a small, struggling law office worth the sacrifice, the poverty, the pinching of pennies to buy a new dress? She had no answers to things like that. In truth, she loved her comfort, and knew now what it had meant to live in affluence. Not that the Montforts were rich, but they were certainly comfortable.

Something drove her to go ahead. It would take all her courage, but the challenge of independence, and the joy of being free at last from Walter's webs, filled her with affirmation. She rented a little room in a boardinghouse operated by a Mrs. Slade, trusting a woman more than the landlords with their calculating gazes.

The moment came when she had to tell her parents. She dreaded it. They would disapprove of her becoming a salaried woman, especially one who toiled in a law office. She chose a moment after dinner one evening, while she and her mother and father were still at table.

"I've some news for you," she said tautly. "I'm going to be working for Mr. Peabody, and I've rented my own room."

Davis Montfort stared at her, astonished.

Her mother objected at once: "But you mustn't do that. It's just not proper for a woman in your circumstances."

"I want to be independent. Oh, Mother, you know how grateful I am to you both. You and Daddy rescued me when I needed to escape from Walter. But I really need to be on my own."

"Have you really thought this through?" her father asked. "I mean, all the implications? You'll be something of an outcast among your friends, all the people you grew up with. Working, you know."

"I already am an outcast. They don't know how to treat me—still Walter's wife but alone and separated. They think I'm a deserter, and I am. Do you see me getting invitations?" she asked, and silently added, Do you see me inviting others anywhere, or here to your house?

"You can't possibly earn a decent living in a law office."

"It'll be a struggle, Mother."

"But where'll you live?"

"I have a room near the railroad tracks."

"In that area?" Her mother was shocked.

"I have a landlady. It's three-fifty a week."

"I suppose it's some little hole in the wall."

Cornelia nodded. It was that, all right.

Her father jumped in again. "I don't think this is wise, Cornelia. Now, if you need a place of your own, we can afford that. We'd gladly put you into a nice flat in a good safe part of town, and give you a competence, too. You think about it. I know you're a married adult, but I'm feeling a little paternal about this. I just don't want you crossing certain lines, burning bridges behind you."

"I'm looking forward to the position, Daddy," she said quietly.

"A wage-earning woman wouldn't be welcome at the Denver Country Club, Cornelia," her mother said. "You'd be considered common. You have advantages now; you can throw them all away, and when you do, you'll be just like thousands of other women, yearning for a better life, but barred from it."

"The good life stopped when I married Walter."

"I understand. Walter's not a warm man. But you've had everything, from jewels and opera seats to the best clothing—and acceptance. No one in Denver ever shut the door to you."

"Walter shut the door to me."

They wrangled it for another few minutes, and then set it aside. Cornelia didn't budge, and her parents grew more and more distraught.

She thought it was over, but the next night she learned otherwise. After their dinner, her father gruffly summoned her to the parlor for a private talk. She followed, hoping she wouldn't have to reassert herself.

He looked uncomfortable but determined as he settled in the wing chair across from her. "I wonder if you've thought about your goals," he began. "Is independence your actual goal?"

"It is now."

"Your mother and I've been under the impression that what you yearn for the most is a divorce from a man you can't abide. And after the divorce, a time of considering new beaux, and remarriage, and the beginnings of a better life as a wife and mother. Ah . . . have we got that wrong?"

"I've wanted that all along, Daddy, but I've come to the conclusion that it won't ever happen. It's not just Walter; it's the state law and Judge Plowman."

"Yes, the courts don't like to grant divorces," her father agreed, "especially when both parties are to blame. Now what I'm saying is, once you become a shop girl—"

"A law secretary, daddy."

"Well, same thing. Once you do that, you've really deserted. It's not the same as staying with your family for a while. If you take that job, you've weakened your case for a divorce."

"I understand that. It doesn't matter. Nothing I do's going to alter anything."

"How do you know that?"

"I just do. You don't know what's passed between Walter and me."

"I have a pretty good idea," he said. "I have a pretty good idea that he hasn't, ah, come to you, ah, as a husband for many years. And dislikes the whole business. And hides his disinterest from the world."

She glanced away, unable to reply to her father.

He banged a pipe on a glass ashtray noisily. "A man knows these things, and sometimes aches for his dear child. You're denied the pleasure of marriage and family unless you can get a divorce."

She nodded.

"Now, if your goal is that—divorce, remarriage to some fine fellow, family—then I beg of you to let me go talk to Walter. I'm going to ask for his consent to a divorce. Maybe if he cooperates the court will come around. This situation doesn't do him any good, this constant charade of his, pretending to be a husband. I'm going to lunch with him and put it to him. I'll say it delicately, so he can keep his tender pride intact, but before you move away, and cut all the cords to a good life, I'd like a crack at Walter. With your permission. Do you grant it?"

She nodded. "I'm glad you're trying."

"I'll do it, then," he said. "Now, if this fails, and you are determined to embark on this new course, we'd like to help you. You can do better than that miserable room. Take your job, but let us put you into a safer place."

"Oh, Father . . ." His kindness was the hardest thing of all to cope with. "If I can't be divorced, then I'd like to learn to be independent."

"I think you're turning away from your mother and me."

She felt a great pain in her breast. "I'm not. I'm very grateful to you and Mother."

Her father looked stricken, almost in tears, and she couldn't help him or her mother. She knew they thought she was committing suicide. And sometimes she thought so too.

"Go lunch with Walter," she said. "A divorce, a new husband, a family, a comfortable life, those are all my first choices. No matter what I do, those are the dreams I had—and lost."

"I'll try to see him tomorrow, Cornelia. I hope and pray you know what you're doing."

CHAPTER   45

Lorenzo Carthage threw another bash that November while waiting for the completion of the adit. He had to put most of the cost of his soirees on the cuff, because he was still earning only two hundred a month, but his suppliers were eager for his patronage. He paid those few who insisted on cash, and sweet-talked the rest.

He spared no expense. He imported pheasants for hunting and built a bird pen to hold them. He sent for a vaudeville troupe playing in Leadville, and a string orchestra. He introduced his elegant guests to a brass band in gaudy scarlet and gold livery brought up from Santa Fe. He completed his racetrack and invited every owner of Thoroughbred racing horses in the West to stage some races. Food arrived from all over the world: lobsters on ice from New England, truffles and fine wines from France, coconuts from the Pacific. Each guest received a twenty-dollar gold piece featuring a high-relief bust of Lorenzo on one side, and the words "Lucky Strike" on the obverse side. He continued the sleeping car arrangement, filling a whole siding with luxurious railroad cars.

Town people came and gawked and marveled. Off-shift miners came to the edge of his property, stared, and hulked off without saying a word. Lorenzo intended to ask them to stay away. They made the guests uneasy, especially since Telluride had become a hotbed of the Knights of Labor. The fame of Lorenzo the Magnificent's weekend parties spread through Colorado, and then through the West, and finally even into the grim gray newspapers of the East. The November party had cost him four thousand dollars, and he had paid very little of it. His monthly two hundred didn't even cover the cost of maintaining his growing estate.

But that would soon end. Each day, three face crews, working around the clock, bored deeper and deeper into the mountain. They passed the two thousand two hundred point—the theoretical junction of the adit and the Lucky Strike ore seam—without striking the ore, but Carthage kept them at it. Faults, compression, or displacement could alter the strike or dip of a seam.

At last, at twenty-two seventy-five, the second-shift crew blew into a seam, and the third shift mucked out ore. Carthage hurried into the adit, eyeing the water nervously, and examined the seam in the icy light of carbide lamps. The lustrous telluride ore glistened faintly, the seam broad but barely visible. The miners glared at him sullenly, all too aware of his opulent ways, and their own lives spun out at hard labor for three-fifty a day in the bowels of the earth.

"Ah, at last!" Carthage cried. He studied the seam, which appeared to be several feet thick there, and collected samples. He spent a while more in the adit, trying to decide where to start a rise to the mine far above, and what sort of water trouble he would have. High above, in the bowels of the Lucky Strike, the last two hundred feet driven down the ore seam had flooded. Well, he'd work that all out.

"Take this adit another ten feet or however much it takes to see what's on the other side of the pay rock," he said to the foreman. "My congratulations. You've all done a splendid job. We're all in the clover."

He headed out, feeling the gazes of the miners on his back. But he didn't mind. Let them make their own fortunes. Let them find the ingenuity to make a success of their lives, as he had. Some were born to succeed, others were born to fail. At the mouth of the adit he gazed proudly upon the mill and generating station below. Even now, drain water from the adit tumbled into the turbine and made direct current electricity for his mine. He was nearly done with development. Only the winze connecting the mine to the adit, and the endlessly delayed spur track, were keeping him from full production—and his thousand a month. He would start crews sinking the winze from above, and cutting a rise from below, at once.

He would have to wire Guggenheim, but he wanted assays completed first. He divided his samples and dropped off the ore at two independent assayers, asking for a rush job. By that night, he would have some solid data. The investors and directors had been getting itchy ever since the bore had reached twenty-two hundred feet. Costs had crawled well above even the most pessimistic estimates because of all the water trouble. The new capitalization of the Lucky Strike was going to run around six hundred thousand dollars, which the company was meeting by floating stock and securing loans. But now he would have good news for them. The Lucky Strike was a bonanza!

Late that December afternoon he picked up his two assay reports and studied them closely. The tenors had declined a little. This was lower-grade ore, with less silver and gold, and more base metals. And it was the same sulfide ore as above, hard to reduce. The two independent assays largely agreed with each other, ruling out error. That wasn't spectacular news, but not bad news either. The discovery of this ore radically increased the mine's reserves. What's more, the seam continued downward from the adit, its depth unknown, which meant still more reserves as yet unplumbed.

The Lucky Strike was proving to be a big, muscular mine, even if the ore wasn't as rich at this level. The looming problem now was the declining price of silver. Just a year earlier, in December of 1884, silver brought $1.75 an ounce. Now it was worth $1.25. The enormous production of silver from the Comstock Lode and thousands of western mines was pressuring the price of the precious metal downward, and no one knew how low it would get. All the more reason to have the United States Treasury mint silver money.

He envied Telluride's gold mines, which were largely immune to the shifting bullion prices that afflicted silver mines. The Lucky Strike did produce some gold as a by-product, and that gold would help insulate the mine if silver prices worsened. All in all, he thought, the mine looked good.

If he could find ways to drive down production costs, he might turn a good mine into a fabulous one. He knew of one way to save a great deal, and that was longer shifts. Even adding an hour to a shift would hike profits dramatically. He knew his miners wouldn't sit still for a pay cut, but probably would swallow a longer shift. And if they didn't like it, there were always more of them. He had just read that the skilled Cornish miners working the lead mines of Wisconsin were leaving that state now that the mines had declined.

Yes, that's what he would do. He would turn a good mine into a magnificent one, and he would be set for life. Cheerfully, he composed a lengthy telegram announcing that the adit had cut the ore seam, and all the rest. It would please the Guggenheims, and demonstrate that the Lucky Strike was no one-year wonder. This mine probably had a life of seven or eight years even if no new reserves were discovered, ample time to repay the capital investment and turn a large profit.

When he had drafted the lengthy report, he started for the railroad station, knowing that it would cause a sensation. His old friend Forest Zebulon Tucker, the night telegrapher, would soon gossip the news from one end of Telluride to the other, no doubt collecting all sorts of tips from hawk-eyed men eager to pay for just such news. There'd be a rush on the stock when the exchanges opened in the morning, and Lucky Strike shares would vault upward once again.

That got him to thinking: Why not delay the news slightly, and ask his broker to start buying every share in sight with the opening bell in the morning? He could send his news to Guggenheim first thing in the morning, and no one would suspect that he had withheld information from the owners and directors. His broker would need only a few minutes to make some purchases.

But he resisted it. He decided that this time, he would make no mistakes. If he were caught withholding crucial information from his employers while he made a quick killing he would never find a supervisory position in mining again. Thus stiffened with rectitude, or at least prudence, he laid his lengthy report on Tucker's desk. The telegrapher scanned it and smiled.

"That's mighty fine news, Mr. Carthage. Good for Telluride. Good for all the folks who've bought a few shares."

Lorenzo smiled, and agreed. "This is secret, Tucker. Absolutely confidential. I'm trusting you not to say a word. We'll announce the news when we're ready."

"You betcha, Mr. Carthage," the telegrapher said. "We keep confidences. Company policy. It'll take fifteen minutes to key this one. You want to wait for replies?"

"No, no, just send them out to my home."

That night, in certain privileged homes, residents of Telluride would celebrate. He headed home, knowing he had foregone the chance to make a quick killing, but knowing that he had been true to his employers. But tomorrow, he would still ask his brokers to buy some shares on margin.

But the next day brought an unexpected development. A delegation of Telluride's leading mining executives marched into his office at the Lucky Strike. He found himself in the company of Juan Hector of the Cimmaron Mine, Charles Goodfellow of the Liberty Bell, Allan Bark of the Smuggler-Union, Peter Stringer of the Tomboy, and Jules Adrian of the Gold King. Every major mine was represented by the delegation.

"Well, gentlemen, you've come to celebrate my good news," Carthage said.

"Yes, of course, we're pleased by that," said Bark, who seemed to be the spokesman for the group. "But we're here on another matter. As you know, we're the Telluride Mining Association."

"You'd like the Lucky Strike to join, I take it."

"Yes, but that's not why we're here, either. We've some thoughts about things that affect all the mines here."

"You want me to throw bigger parties. Did I fail to invite anyone?" He knew he hadn't. All of them had attended one or more, and thoroughly enjoyed themselves.

"No," said Bark, "we're hoping you'll stop them. That's why we're here. They're having a bad effect on this town."

Puzzled, Carthage waited for an explanation. But it took another five minutes of roundabout talk before Bark felt comfortable enough to broach the subject that had brought them here.

"You know, Lorenzo," Bark began, "Telluride's a town full of radicals and anarchists. The miners've organized into a chapter of the Knights of Labor. They've been pressuring us for wage hikes, which we absolutely refuse to give until economic conditions settle. We're mostly gold mine operators, but we rely on the silver too, and silver's dropping by the week. Now, so far, the talks haven't gone far. We've fired the hotheads, and let our workers know that they can expect the pink slip if they agitate. But it's still a touchy situation. And we can't afford strikes or stoppages. Too much invested in plant to let it stay idle. And that brings up your parties . . ."

Carthage was getting the drift of this now. "You think that my little gatherings are exciting envy in our laboring classes."

"More than envy, Carthage. Rage. These men go into the pits all day, do back-breaking work for three and a half dollars, and don't see much of the sun. That's a good wage, actually; a lot more than a clerk earns. But they don't see it that way. They see these big parties, or hear about them. They see those railroad palace cars, and the Thoroughbred horses arriving in boxcars fitted up more luxuriously than a miner's cabin, and they hear about the feasts, and the hunting, and the bird shoots, and all the rest. And they read about all this in the Denver papers, as well as our own. And you know what it does? They walk into our offices in a rage."

"I sympathize, to a point. But I started with nothing and made something of myself. They can too. Instead of grousing about a laboring man's wage, they are all free—every last one—to use their wits and skills and climb the ladder."

Bark remained silent a moment, absorbing that. "There's truth in it, Lorenzo. But the Telluride Mining Association is formally asking you to abandon these highly visible celebrations of wealth, especially during this time of tension between management and labor."

Carthage shook his head. "It's the way I live."

"We could form a club," Bark continued, "a membership society with a golf course and so on, they way they do in the cities. You could entertain all you want there without arousing the bitterness of our good and faithful miners. We've good men in our pits. The trouble is, you're risking labor trouble with these affairs of yours. Now, of course, we're not criticizing you, and we've each enjoyed your parties," Bark said. "But they're jeopardizing production and investment. Surely you'll heed that. At least for a year or two, we'd prefer some discretion among the . . . responsible people of Telluride."

Carthage smiled. "Sorry, gents. The miners themselves love to watch these big parties. Love the races, the bands, the fun. They get to see a lot of it. I'll tell you a secret. Working folks love the rich. Without the rich, their life'd be dull, and they'd never aspire to a higher station. I'm going to hold bigger and better parties. Wait until my New Year party. Then you'll really see something. You've only seen the beginning. I'm going to put Telluride on the map."

"I think you're more interested in putting Carthage on the map," Bark retorted.

CHAPTER 46

With the adit complete, Lorenzo Carthage began the next and most critical step, driving a winze, a vertical connecting shaft, from the upper works to the adit. When that was done, the Lucky Strike could resume production and achieve efficiencies never before seen.

He put three face crews on either end, one set of crews working up from the adit on scaffolding, and the other crews working down from the lowest gallery of the mine. He calculated that, with six crews and a little luck—water was always a threat—he might finish the expansion of the mine by the end of 1885. Early in 1886, it would pour a bonanza of silver ore laced with gold into the mill at the base of the mountain. Days later, the Lucky Strike would begin selling silver, gold, copper, arsenic, lead, and antimony on the market, and making money again. By mid-

1886, stockholders would see some dividends and the huge investment would be steadily amortized. By 1887 the shareholders would be rejoicing with every quarterly payment.

The beginning of production was an event so important that it was worthy of heralding to the whole world, and what better way to do it than hold a grand New Year's bash? The idea excited him. This three-day festival would outdo all his other parties. It would usher out the old, and usher in the new. And at the stroke of midnight, he would announce to his illustrious guests that the Lucky Strike was ready to produce: the winze had been completed, the mill and power plant and rail spur lay ready to bring the treasure to the world.

What a fabulous party it would be. There, before the assembled gentlemen in their swallowtails and black ties and starched white collars, and the begowned and bejeweled ladies, he would proclaim the news. Even as he thought of it, he could hear the happy exclamations, the surprise, the applause, the sheer joy, the orchestra swinging into Auld Lang Syne, the glittering ballroom awash in ecstasy. Yes, it would be the historical moment when skeptics no longer doubted Lorenzo the Magnificent.

It meant, of course, that he would probably have to keep his crews at work on Christmas Day. But perhaps he could give each man a basket of fruit. He wasn't unmindful of the desires of workingmen to share the feast day with their families. But they, too, would catch the excitement and work feverishly to complete the winze just ahead of the festival. He thought they might even finish two or three days ahead if all went well.

After the winze was finished, of course, he would have to reduce wages: a cut of fifty cents a day would hasten the amortization of that overhanging debt. No doubt there would be some grumbling—Telluride seethed with unhappy miners—but that could be dealt with through the time-honored carrot and stick. Grumblers would get their pink slips, and he himself would find little ways of rewarding the loyal men who faithfully remained at their stations.

All these dreams, plans, and hopes fused together, intoxicated him, and he worked feverishly, one moment on his great New Year's soiree, and the next on humdrum things, such as ordering Du Pont Hercules dynamite, blasting caps, tram rail from Pueblo, mercury for the stamp mill, copper wire, ceramic insulators and light bulbs for his mine lighting, new ore cars, a trestle to take slag to a waste pile next to the San Miguel River. Town people wouldn't like that waste pile next to their drinking water, but there wasn't any other place to put slag or country rock or tailings. When the rail spur was done, he might be able to ship out wastes, but not for a while.

He ached for some way of cutting expenses for his festival, but he couldn't find any. This party would cost four thousand, at the least. The champagne alone would come to seven hundred, but who could conceive of a New Year's Eve without ample supplies of Piper Heidseck? He would have to persuade the tradesmen to supply him on the cuff this one last time.

That first week of December, engraved invitations went out across the Centennial State to a hundred-fifty selected guests. He was mindful, this time, of his wish to begin a life of domestic felicity, and thus his carefully drawn guest list focused on couples who had eligible daughters. For Lorenzo Carthage, 1886 would be a time not only of triumph in business, but successful courtship of a lovely damsel, a grand wedding of a sort never before seen in Colorado, and the beginnings of blissful life as a husband and a father of several sons who would carry on his name, and several daughters whose marriage would ally the Carthage family with the elite of the world.

Trouble plagued him this time. Tradesmen insisted he settle old accounts before they would extend further credit. He itched to borrow funds from the company to tide him over, but sternly resisted. This time he would make no mistakes, do nothing that would raise an eyebrow. Quietly, he sold two Thoroughbreds—there would be no racing in winter anyway—and took other painful measures, such as selling his white trotters and three of his Purdy shotguns to pay the butchers and bakers and wine merchants a little something. But his best efforts didn't cover even ten percent of his eighteen-thousand-dollar debt, and he was reduced to confidences such as his little talk with the furniture man one mid-December day.

"Let me tell you, Cormaney, we're closing in on it now. Confidentially, of course, we're going into full production the first week of January. And at that point, of course, my contract with the company requires them to compensate me bountifully for services. I sacrificed only to get the Lucky Strike up and running—but thirty days from now, I'll be paying these accounts and keeping right up. Meanwhile, you know, the New Year's Eve party is going to be an announcement party, and when I do announce that we're back in business, the stock I hold should double or treble. You're covered, if you can just be patient awhile longer. If you're uneasy, I'll give you a note."

It worked with most of the suppliers, although he wasn't able to free his eight thousand shares from the State Bank of Telluride. In fact, the bank was threatening to foreclose his mortgage, all for the trifle of being three thousand dollars in arrears.

His other ploy was simply to turn to new suppliers. The world was full of eager purveyors, and as fast as he wired Denver merchants, they obliged him, all of course on thirty-day credit. It would be a scrape, but he would manage. This time, he was doing everything right. Even his confidential talks with his creditors turned to his advantage. Rumors of bonanza whirled around the Lucky Strike. The stock started another upward swing, much to the delight of his bankers. He heard that the Guggenheims, forever hedging, had sold more shares and taken a profit. That actually pleased Carthage. The less his employers worried, the freer he was to act.

Each day he met with his shift foremen and got a progress report. They gathered in his plush office at the end of each shift with news of the day's progress. Carthage knew immediately about each delay, each breakdown, and the conduct of each miner. The work had slowed slightly because of a need for shoring in the upper works, and a lack of air at the face that was tiring the men. As an expedient, Carthage rigged an electric motor to a pump with leather belts and ran an air duct to the work face. At this point, he would spare no expense to hurdle obstacles. If the men needed air, he would give them air.

"The men are planning on taking Christmas Day off, Mr. Carthage," reported the night shifter, Absalom Biggs. "And the same goes for the crews on Christmas Eve."

"I know they want to, but we can't afford that," Carthage replied.

"If you don't, sor, you'll have trouble on your hands. They won't stand for it. They'll have a few hours with their families, no matter what. You're not Scrooge, sor."

"No, Biggs, I'm not. It's just that this time, it's urgent. It's critical. I'll make it up to them next year. And after we get up and running in January, I'll give them some time off. They're each getting a basket of fruit and nuts with the compliments of the company. And anyway, not one miner in three has a family. They're mostly bachelors who won't mind a bit. Surely they understand. I've pressed it upon them over and over: the sooner we start production, the more secure we all are in our jobs."

Biggs shook his head. "That's not how they see it, sor. They earn three and a half dollars if they're experienced, three if they're just muckers. They work hard, in the dark, in bad air—"

"I know all that. They're a fine, manly lot and I admire them. But this one time—"

"They've organized, sor. Knights of Labor. Not strikes, at least not yet. The Knights try to avoid strikes. But they'll be organized and you can expect some sort of trouble. Maybe some brief walkouts to send you a message, slow things up."

"Who are they? Which ones?"

"All, sir. Every last man's become a Knight."

"Who's leading them?"

Biggs stared at the floor. "I don't rightly know, sor."

Carthage suspected the man was not being forthright. "I want loyalty, Biggs. Your task is to supervise, make this unprofitable mine become profitable as fast as possible. You search your memory. Tomorrow or the next day at the latest, you tell me the names of any ringleaders."

Biggs nodded.

"And Biggs. I'm going to have some painful news for them. As soon as we're in production, we're going to lengthen the shifts by an hour. That's only six hours a week. They'll get the same pay, have just as much to spend. It can't be helped. The Lucky Strike has stockholders, lenders, bankers watching it. We're extended to the limit. Interest is eating us up. I'll send a circular down there with the news, and I'll emphasize it's a temporary measure, to put the mine on a solid footing."

"Add an hour, sor?" Biggs looked shocked. "Keep 'em in the hole longer, after driving these men hard for months? Are you crazy?"

"Mr. Biggs, that sort of question is out of order. No, I don't like it any more than you. I'm sorry. But this mine is hanging on by a thread."

"You're begging for trouble, sor."

"I know, and I can't help that. I'm preparing for trouble as best I can. We'll have some security guards, and I'll be ready to hire replacements just as fast as I run into labor trouble. We'll get past it, but I'm holding you and all my foremen responsible for keeping peace in the pit."

"Security guards! Sor, I want to protest, formally and in writing."

"Mr. Biggs, you may want to spend this evening thinking through your allegiances and commitments. We're paying you well, and you've been a part of an exciting venture. You've contributed an excellent crew; your bunch is getting more done and overcoming more trouble than any of the others."

"A basket of fruit," Biggs said.

"What has that got to do with anything?"

"I'll tell you exactly, Mr. Carthage. You're throwing another one of those rich-men's bashes on New Year's, spending more thousands than my men in the pits see in a decade. You throw a party like that, you work them on Christmas, then you tell them they'll be in the hole eleven hours instead of ten next year, sixty-six hours a week in cold, miserable darkness, and you give them a basket of fruit."

"What's wrong with that? I worked twelve-hour shifts in a Denver smelter not long ago. Nothing compels them to be miners. We all make our choices. What I do is my business. I've earned the right to enjoy life. Each and every one of them has the privilege of making a new life—"

"Or killing you," Biggs snapped.

CHAPTER   47

The letter set Homer Peabody's heart to tumbling. It was addressed to Peabody and Peabody, Attorneys at Law, and was from Walter Kimbrough. In it he announced his recent purchase of the office building that housed the firm, and his intention to raise the rent to a thousand a month from its present hundred twenty-five.

Nor was that the end. Another letter from Kimbrough, addressed to Homer personally, announced Kimbrough's purchase of the apartment house where Homer lived, and Homer's eviction.

And that turned out not to be the whole story, either. Richard Peabody appeared in Homer's doorway, waving a letter.

"Read this," he said.

That letter came from the First National Bank, in which Kimbrough was a major shareholder. His closest business associates held the rest. It simply informed Richard that he was in default of his mortgage, and the bank was foreclosing.

"I pay quarterly, and I was late two days once—when Alice was having the baby," Richard said. "I'm current on my payments, but that's not enough for Walter Kimbrough's banking pals."

Again, Homer felt a burning pain in his chest, and leaned back heavily in his chair.

"It's because we hired Cornelia," he said.

"It's also Polly Pry," Richard said.

Homer agreed. The gossip columnist for the *Post* had swiftly gotten wind of Cornelia's new life as a secretary and receptionist for Peabody and Peabody, and had wittily described it in detail. She hadn't missed a trick, beginning with the divorce, Cornelia's allegations about her husband's absence from bed and board and house, her subsequent departure from the family home, her life at her parents' home, Kimbrough's public appearances without his wife, Kimbrough's vast indifference to domestic life, and more. Kimbrough had ended up looking like a cold fish but Cornelia hadn't fared any better, having been written off as one of Denver's haut monde.

The column had obviously triggered Kimbrough's violent retribution.

"I don't know what Alice and I'll do," Richard muttered. "We love that house. We've put a lot into it."

Homer felt a great heaviness settle over him. He wondered where he would find the strength to move to another flat, and whether the firm could find some safe harbor in Denver, a town largely owned and operated by Kimbrough.

Cornelia was standing at the door also, and she looked stricken. "I'm the cause of this," she said softly.

"No, no, only Walter Kimbrough's the cause of this," Homer said. In the month that Cornelia had been employed by the firm, he had come to love her all the more. Cornelia arrived early and stayed late and had a natural ability to deal with clients. She was delving into case law, mastering complex terms, taking the initiative, drafting letters for Homer's and Richard's approval even without dictation, bringing them coffee or sarsaparilla, making sure that her employers got to court on time and kept their appointments. And above all, Cornelia had brought a quiet cheer to the offices of Peabody and Peabody, somehow giving the place an aura of success and happiness.

"I should resign," she said. "Walter'd stop at nothing. If you move, he'll find ways of evicting you. He's a hater. Once he starts persecuting someone, he never stops. He's so ruthless—"

"Denver's a large city. He doesn't control all of it," Richard said.

"You don't know him. Don't forget, he owns the power company, the water company, the tram lines. He has more ways to hurt someone than you can imagine," she said.

"I don't quit," Richard said, showing some determination. "If I have to move, I'll move. If we can't find an office free from Kimbrough's grasp, maybe we can find a privately owned house and buy it with a contract for deed."

"I still think I should resign," she said.

"Cornelia, that won't help us. If Walter Kimbrough's going to ruin us, your departure won't change a thing."

She nodded, unhappily, and then brightened. "My father," she said.

They turned to her. "He owns real estate all over Denver, including some buildings on Sixteenth Street. They can't get at him through the banks, either, because they aren't mortgaged. Let me go talk to him. Right now." She turned to Richard. "He has some houses, too."

She vanished from Homer's doorway, and a moment later they heard their front door close.

Richard smiled. "When you took on Walter Kimbrough in court, you took on a boxcar full of tigers," he said.

"It was Polly Pry. I'd like to take that catty Mrs. O'Bryan to the woodshed."

"Gossip's a double-edged sword," Richard said. "I guess I'll call her and tell her about all this."

"Don't! It'll just make it worse."

Richard stared quietly. "Homer, the best way to fight back is to make it too painful for Walter Kimbrough to continue. I'm not inclined to walk to the tumbrels without a fight."

Homer's pain radiated through his whole body. He knew Richard was right: fight, and hard. He sighed and nodded, feeling a weariness he had scarcely known before. The lavatory beckoned; more and more, the slightest excitement had driven him to the water closet and long minutes of pain, frustration, and helplessness while he waited for the few drops his enlarged prostate gland allowed him.

"Homer, you look tired. Let me handle this. I'm itching for a fight," Richard said. "And Cornelia might have something there, if her father would rent to us."

"But your house—"

Richard smiled. "I'm going to keep that house. I guess I'll just go call Mrs. Leonel Ross O'Bryan and feed her the latest," he said, vanishing from sight.

Homer sat in his chair, feeling sick. He was having trouble breathing, and his heart was pattering. His swollen legs had been bothering him for weeks, and now they ached. How could he move again? He was having more and more trouble just walking to the office each day. And where would he find the money?

Ten minutes later he felt no better—worse in fact—and walked heavily to Richard's office. "I'm feeling a little under the weather, Richard. I'd better go home. Sorry to leave you here alone, especially with Cornelia gone."

"You look gray, Homer. It's the bad news. Get some rest."

Homer made his slow way down the stairs and to the street, feeling more and more dizzy. He decided not to go to his flat. His doctor, Jack Meek, had offices a block away. He trudged that direction, knowing he was ill. The two-flight climb to Meek's office all but did him in. Meek's receptionist, Elvira, took one look at him and hurried back to the doctor. Moments later Homer found himself sitting dizzily on an examination table while Meek listened to his heart with a stethoscopic trumpet and examined Homer's feet and ankles and legs.

"Swollen all to hell," Meek said. "You've got dropsy. Edema, cardiac dropsy some call it. Your heart's weakened."

"Is this an attack?"

"Yes."

Homer sighed. "Am I dying?"

"We're all dying," Meek said gruffly. "But yes, your heart's not pumping enough blood, and it's going to get worse fast. Congestive heart trouble. The prostate trouble complicates it. Renal disease. You having a worse time making water?"

"It's getting worse," Homer said. "I dread the day when I start the catheters and I fight infection."

Meek retreated to a table laden with vials and flasks and pasteboard cartons, all neatly labeled. From a pasteboard carton he extracted a pill and handed it to Homer, with some water.

"Digitalis," he said. "It'll help. It makes the heart muscle contract, and slows the pulse. You'll feel better. It's tricky stuff, so I'm starting you on half a dose, which may not do much. I'll give you some of these. If your pulse climbs or you're breathless, take another. I'll have Elvira take you home in a while. I want to watch you for a while, make sure the digitalis is working. I don't want you walking—not one extra step."

Homer nodded wearily.

"Now, the dropsy. The digitalis should reduce it. But lay off salt, all right? If it gets worse, if your legs swell and you have trouble walking, get back here fast—and don't walk.."

Heart trouble. "What am I going to die of?" Homer asked.

"Old age," Meek said.

"Which death is worst? Congestive heart disease, or prostate disease shutting off my water?"

"Dying of renal disease is hell. When the time comes, I'll make sure you've plenty of opium."

"Which'll happen first?"

Meek shrugged. "Digitalis should control your heart disease for years. It'd help if you lost a lot of weight. You could lose fifty pounds and be better off for it. Quit eating so much, quit salt, and your old ticker'll thank you for it. Oh, and take a glass of wine before dinner."

"Wine?"

"It'll help."

"I've teetotaled all my life, give or take a few glasses of sherry."

"Well, time to hoist a few, Homer. You're never too old to learn new tricks."

Later, Meek fed him the second half-dose, and Peabody felt his heart settle into a stronger, slower beat. He spent the rest of that day in bed, feeling that the worst of it was over. But the oppression that dogged him didn't lift. He dreaded moving to a new flat, especially now, feeling so sick and weak.

Maybe the end was coming now. It seemed to be rushing at him. It hadn't been much of a life until the last two years, beginning on the day that Cornelia walked into his shabby little office. That, and the younger Peabodys had given him joy. And now that Cornelia was brightening the office, he had found a sort of happiness. He loved to watch her at her daily tasks. It was too late for him to remake a life, but not too late to dream. Sometimes, languidly, he let himself dream of being young again, and finding a woman just like Cornelia, and marrying her, and raising a family, and practicing law successfully, and taking his family on picnics. Oh, to be young and full of dreams, and visions of a better future.

This past year, with the young people around him, had given him life. A vicarious life, of course, but a life. He could dream Richard and Alice's dreams, and dream Cornelia's dreams, and even in his mind turn back the clock and dream of a young Homer and a young Cornelia facing a young world together.

Meek had told him that a death from prostate disease would be hell. All he wanted now was a good death, that ultimate blessing. All right, then. He'd pour on the salt.

CHAPTER 48

. . . .

he digitalis took hold and Homer Peabody began to feel
better. The dropsy slowly subsided. But he stayed in bed,
too ill to return to the office. He needed, somehow, to
gather enough strength to move to a new flat at the end of
the month. That task loomed over him, infusing his bedridden days with
worry. The even more formidable task of moving the office to some
haven safe from Walter Kimbrough worried Homer even more, but at
least that much was in the hands of his young colleague.

Richard Peabody visited each day, always bringing the latest news.
He had acted immediately to thwart Kimbrough, seeking temporary in-
junctions based in equity. But Judge Plowman threw two of them out:
it was within Kimbrough's sovereign power as a property owner to
charge a rent that suited him, and select his tenants. If Kimbrough
wished to evict or charge a high rent, and no lease forbade it, that was
his prerogative. Homer would have to move, and the firm would either
pay the higher rent or move. But Richard did better with the mortgage.
Foreclosing a mortgage that was not in arrears, on the basis of a two-
day delay in one payment, was too much for Plowman, and he granted
a temporary restraining order, pending a hearing on the matter.

"So, it's not all bad," Richard said, sitting beside Homer's bed.
"The good news is that Davis Montfort can help. His office buildings
are fully rented, but he believes he could find a suitable home adjacent
to the business district, buy it, and put us in it. The firm would occupy
the ground floor. The upstairs would become your apartment. That'd
save you walking. In fact, he's itching to do it because of the way Walter's
treating us. I told him to go ahead; we're running out of time."

"How's Cornelia doing?"

"She's a pistol. She's out hunting for houses her father might buy.
She's already located two, both of them good locales for our office. One
would need some extensive remodeling, but the other—why, we could
set up shop the day we rent it."

Homer felt his spirits lift a little. "I suppose Kimbrough'll find some
other way to hurt us. All of this is going to cost me—I don't have any
reserves."

Richard grinned. "Nope. When that hearing comes up, I'm putting
Kimbrough on trial. I'm not going to argue the law of mortgage, or
even equity. I'm going to argue Kimbrough's malice."

That startled Homer. "But that won't win your case."

"Kimbrough may have law on his side, but I'm going to go for his vulnerable area—his reputation; the thing he shores up with so much effort. The law might give him a perfect right to be as malicious as he pleases, but I'm making sure that his malice is known to the world."

"Are you sure that's wise?"

"It's called trial by publicity," Richard said, a certain gleam in his eye. "Polly Pry's already published the first skirmish in the *Post*. But I've been a busy man, and the *Denver Republican* and *Rocky Mountain News* are covering the story. I gave both reporters a transcript of the divorce proceedings—at least certain parts of it. With some items underlined."

"But poor Cornelia—"

"She says she'll endure it. It's Walter who's not enjoying it. I think he'll call off the dogs. Of course Roderick and Hamilton are telling Judge Plowman that Kimbrough had nothing to do with the bank's foreclosure."

"How'd you respond to that?"

"I laughed. Then Plowman laughed."

Homer stared up at the young man. "You know, in my entire practice of law, I never used laughter as a response?"

"You get well, and then try laughing."

The next day, Richard brought Homer a copy of the *Republican*. Homer read it while sitting in his easy chair. Its second page featured a lengthy story about the Kimbrough divorce and the tribulations of the Peabody law firm. It dwelled at length on Cornelia's allegations that Walter Kimbrough had "failed to perform his marital obligations," dwelled briefly on Kimbrough's rebuttal, and swiftly recapped Cornelia's life since leaving Kimbrough's house, including her recent employment by the Peabody law firm.

"This doesn't improve Walter's standing in Denver," Richard said.

"But—" Homer was frightened. His heart tumbled in his chest. He saw the young man's grin and relaxed. Let the young do battle. If Richard Peabody wanted to take on the owner and operator of Denver, more power to him. Gently, Homer smiled at his young colleague. "You're a fine attorney, Richard. I never would have thought of doing that."

"You get well. Montfort's buying a brick house on Sherman for us. He'll do just fine, renting the downstairs to the firm, and the upstairs to you. Considers it good business, not charity. We'll have our shingle up in no time. I'm printing up notices to send to our clients. Don't you worry about moving. We'll have draymen over when the time comes."

Homer nodded. He felt superfluous. The world belonged to the young. But he felt happy, too. Richard and Cornelia were caring for him. It was the first time in his long lonely life that he was being cared for. He found something sweet and tender in that, a sort of rosy sunset for his life. He would go to his reward—if any—in peace, just one floor above his busy firm, the young people right there.

"Well," he said gruffly, "I'm taking you away from your work. Go sue 'em."

The following day Richard cheerfully dropped the latest editions of the *Post* and the *News* in Homer's lap. The *News* story was subdued, dwelling on the eviction, the extraordinary rent increase, and foreclosure, mentioning Cornelia's employment, but saying nothing about the divorce or Cornelia's subsequent life. The paper quoted Kimbrough as saying Cornelia was an unfortunate, confused, and wayward woman who was conspiring to damage his reputation.

"Looks like Kimbrough's got old Byers in his pocket," Richard said, alluding to the paper's editor.

"It's dignified coverage; no scandal. I approve," muttered Homer.

"Well, try the *Post* if you need something to disapprove of," Richard countered.

Polly Pry was at it again, this time with a truly wicked gossip column. She had, it seemed, wormed some things out of Cornelia, who probably wasn't very reluctant to talk anyway. Mrs. O'Bryan cheerfully recorded that Kimbrough kept a daily journal recording his hours at the manse, as evidence he was a dutiful husband.

"But," she wrote, "the wayward Mrs. Kimbrough reports that he kept to his rooms, and she scarcely saw him. He refused to let her live a separate life and won't hear of a divorce. She said she yearned for children but 'with Walter, that's impossible.' "

There was more in that vein. Whatever was left of Kimbrough's reputation had been buried in that column. Homer didn't approve, and frowned.

"I don't like it either," Richard said. "But Cornelia says it's time to put the truth before the public, as long as Walter's busy condemning her. I hear he's been saying plenty about her to all his friends in the Denver Club. She's determined and feisty. Figures she has nothing to lose."

The following evening, Richard stopped by with more news. The hearing, in which Judge Plowman would decide whether his temporary order restraining the bank from foreclosing should be made permanent, turned out just the way Richard wanted. He had spent little time dwelling on the obvious, that a two-day delay in one quarterly payment wasn't ground for the bank to act, and spent the rest of the time dwelling on Kimbrough's vendetta against the law firm that had handled his wife's divorce suit. Reporters from four Denver papers dutifully scribbled down everything he'd said. Kimbrough wasn't there, and neither were his attorneys, because this was theoretically a bank action. But no one, least of all Judge Plowman, doubted Richard's contention that Kimbrough's eviction notice, rent hike, and the bank's act were related.

Plowman had interrupted halfway through. "I've heard enough. I'm permanently restraining the bank from foreclosing, unless it brings new evidence of substantial delinquency," he had said.

"The evening editions'll have it, Homer," Richard concluded. "And if I know reporters, they won't spend much time on Plowman's decision; they'll write about Walter Kimbrough's malice."

Homer nodded. "Wish I could have been there to help you or represent you," he said. He was getting itchy at home, isolated and lonely. He hated the flat now that Walter Kimbrough owned the building. The whole place exuded Kimbrough's hostility.

"Well, that's not all my news. Cornelia's father's purchased the house on Sherman, and at the end of the month we're moving, and there's a place for you."

His next visitor was Cornelia, who entered his bachelor apartment shyly, no doubt wondering about the propriety of it.

"You're looking good, Homer," she said, settling in a chair opposite him.

"I've missed you, Cornelia. I'm better. The digitalis, you know."

"We'll be moving you in a few days. Is that all right? You know, neither Richard nor I asked your permission. We just made assumptions."

"You're my rescuers. I'm looking forward to it. And I'll be back in practice as soon as we're settled."

"It's a lovely house, Homer. You'll have the dining room for your office, and Richard'll have the parlor, and I'll have a foyer. It all works out. There's even a sunroom for a conference room."

"I shouldn't worry about you the way I do. I hope you're surviving. We can't thank you or your father enough—"

"My father's puzzled. I won't let him help me personally, but I came to him for help when the firm needed it. He doesn't understand that."

"I don't either."

She laughed. "I'm making my own life. I just want to make my way in the world. But helping the Peabody firm is something else. You've been victimized by my problems."

Homer eyed her solemnly. "There's no turning back, now."

"This isn't what I hoped life would bring me, but I'm making my way, and I'm happier than I've been for years. I'm a woman of independent means."

"Some means. Six a week. We should pay you much more."

She smiled. "I hope I get a raise when you and Richard can afford it."

"I promise you one, if it's the last thing I do," he said.

A few days later, Homer found himself ensconced in comfortable quarters, practicing half days, walking slowly up and down a stairway, and enjoying the largest, sunniest office of his legal career. But what he treasured most was being among those he loved.

CHAPTER 49

ose Edenderry awakened to the smell of hay. A gray light permeated wherever she was, somewhere uncomfortable and cold. She felt feverish and nauseous, so sick she couldn't even lift herself. She discovered only coarse burlap over her, and something else: a thin blond man, peering down upon her from bleached blue eyes.

"Well, no wonder Bob wouldn't eat. You're sleeping on his breakfast," he said.

She couldn't fathom that. She smelled horses and discerned that she was in a carriage barn. "Help me," she whispered from a throat so sore she could barely speak.

The blond man stared, paralyzed. "Himself's not here. Off to Central City. Pastoral visit."

"Himself?"

"The bishop."

"Get me a priest. I'm dying."

He looked doubtful. The horse nuzzled him roughly, and poked his nose into the manger. She felt its moist breath.

"Help me," she whispered.

"I'll get the sisters," he said. "You cold?"

"So cold . . ."

"Here." He lowered some horse blankets over her. "This'll warm you. I gotta move Bob, and I'll get the sisters."

She pulled thick blankets over her and trembled within them. She burned with fever but felt frozen solid. She watched him back the big black out of the stall, and heard the clatter of shod hooves on wood, and then silence.

Some time later—she couldn't tell how long—she stared up at a nun. This one was young, with the usual white wimple and black garb. She wore small gold-rimmed half glasses, and had soft brown eyes. The nun felt Rose's forehead and frowned.

"Help me," Rose whispered.

The nun turned to the blond man. "We need to move her."

"Forgive me, madam," he said to Rose. "I've got to carry you."

She felt his strong arms lift her out of the manger, and discovered not one nun but three. The man carried her across a lawn to a small house, through the door, to a small alcove where a cot stood. He lowered her onto it.

"I'll go fetch the doctor, Sister," he said.

Rose slid into a twilight world, swooning, aware of good things, warmth most of all. Hot tea laced with honey, a gentle scrubbing with soap and hot water, clean hair, the disappearance of her filthy clothes, a sweet-smelling cotton nightdress, a man hovering over her, taking her pulse, some talk about her illness, vague, cloudy, and then she didn't know where she was.

She heard prayers and felt soft hands hold her own.

She saw light and darkness and light again, a bishop standing over her, the collar of Rome, the episcopal shirt purple; the sisters in their white wimples and black habits, ministering to her. She tasted warm broth being spooned down her parched throat, felt her body howl with heat and fever.

"So sick," she muttered. "Bless me, Father, for I have sinned."

She slept again, while the world revolved.

Then she awakened. She didn't feel feverish. No one was present. She didn't know where she was, except the Holy Mother Church had rescued her, and she a poor colleen owed it her life. She guessed it was the middle of a winter afternoon. A low sun pierced the alcove. She felt desperately weak, and wild with thirst.

The first sister, the one with the glasses, hovered over her. "You're better," she said in a crisp voice that sounded English. "Our prayers were answered."

"Sister—"

"Sister St. George."

"I'm so thirsty."

The nun helped Rose to sit up, and handed her a glass of water. "Your fever broke. You'll want a bit to eat now," she said.

Rose sank back into her cot, unable to stop the tears that swelled from her eyes. "And me not in good grace, either, Sister," she mumbled.

"You're a blessing to us. A gift from God, arriving in a manger."

"I was so cold."

"You weren't wearing much. Would you like to eat now?"

She handed Rose a bowl of steaming porridge. Humble food it might be, but it tasted good.

"You'll get well fast now, I think," said Sister St. George. "We've been watching over you. Sister Grace worked with Florence Nightingale in the Crimean War, and knows nursing. Sister Florence loves to pray. She washed and mended your clothes."

"What order are you?" Rose asked.

"We're Holy Cross sisters."

"I never heard of those."

"We're an Anglican order."

"A what?"

"Church of England. Ever since the Oxford Movement, and the work of John Henry Newman, the Anglican Church has been recovering its Catholic roots. We have a dozen monastic orders now."

"What? What?" The only thing her rebel father hated more than the Crown was the Church of Ireland, a part of the Anglican communion. But on the other hand, her mother was an Anglican, and a pious one, too. Rose had heard a thousand bitter tales from him about the famine, the Protestant landlords who evicted the helpless potato farmers from their plots when they couldn't make the rent, the harsh courts and constables and spies, all of them the Crown's puppets, the rotten electoral system that disfranchised Catholics and the poor, the homeless people dying in the lanes, the potato blight that murdered several crops in a row and finally murdered a million Irish.

But here were Anglican nuns nursing her back to life, and she was grateful to them. They belonged to her mother's church.

"You're welcome here," Sister St. George said. "Would you like to tell me your name?"

Rose realized these sisters had cared for a woman whose name and background they did not know. "I'm Rose Edenderry," she said softly. "Born in County Offaly."

"Well, Miss Edenderry, we want you to stay with us for as long as you wish. It'll take a while before you have your health again. We haven't much, but if porridge and soup and stew are acceptable to you, we'll share."

Rose knew she was much too sick to leave this place. "Yes, I'll stay if you'll let me," she said.

Sister St. George smiled. "Our order does parish work, teaching, and whatever charity we can manage. We are poor. Whoever is sent to us is a gift from God, giving joy to us. If you'd like, I'll ask a Roman priest to come by for the comfort of the sacrament."

"No, please—"

The sister hesitated. "You've been through some painful times. One look at you tells the story. You had pneumonia, and it was a close call. Thank God, you were the child in our manger. We're here to listen if you need to talk, and help if we can, and no tales would be told to others."

"If you knew me, you wouldn't even let me in here."

"Miss Edenderry, there is nothing a woman can do that would shock us."

"Well, I'm not what you think."

"I don't think you're one thing or another. Are you hungry?"

"Thirsty."

"Yes, you would be after that fever. Here," she said, handing Rose a glass of water.

"I'd like to stay a few days. Then I'll do something to pay you back. Work, wash dishes, clean. All right?"

The sister smiled. "We've already been paid. You owe us nothing. But you're welcome to help if you wish. We would not turn away a gift."

"I wouldn't be able to live like this," Rose said. "I don't know how you do."

"We were called. We're here because we want this life more than any other. How do you live, Miss Edenderry?"

"Free. People are always saying no to me, and I ignore them."

"Is that a good life?"

Rose shook her head. "I'm a little wild, that's all. When someone says no, that's when I have to go do that. It's like waving a red cape at a bull. I've got to go do it. My father, I'm like him. He was with the O'Connors, and got hanged for sedition. My, ah, husbands, they always said no, and then I left them because I wouldn't put up with it."

"No to what?"

"Having a good time."

Sister St. George rose, swiftly, and gathered cups and bowls. "We're happy to have you here," she said. "You'll want to rest. If there's anything you want—"

"I'm all right."

The nun nodded and left the alcove. Rose felt miserable. These sisters had saved her life and were feeding her and caring for her and helping her to heal. She should have thanked them, but the words caught in her throat. It wasn't that they were just some Englishwomen playing at holy orders; it was that they would soon be saying no to her too, if she stayed. She pulled her thick blankets over her, relishing the warmth on a winter's day. On a plain pine dresser nearby her washed and folded clothing waited for her. She could get dressed and leave. But she knew she wouldn't. This cot, this warmth, this food, were ambrosial.

She wanted an ale. But they would say no to her. They wouldn't even give her just a little glass of wine. She drew her hands up and stared at them, and her arms. Her flesh looked gray. She was skeletal. She knew what she looked like: a raggedy female scarecrow. She regretted living so hard, like a wild creature, but she couldn't help it. She wouldn't bend to anyone, including English nuns. She would be free even if it killed her. Ruefully, she knew that death was the exact price she would pay if she continued the way she had. Only a miracle had led her to a manger, and the sisters, and life.

She ached to find fault with these Holy Cross sisters, but she couldn't. They hadn't judged her. She decided she would stay long enough to heal herself, offer to help them. Maybe she would stay a week. Then she would be fine. She was young and her body would spring back with a little food.

She'd have to be on her guard, though. These sisters would try to reform her, and she wasn't going to permit any of that. She had to be free to do whatever she pleased, whenever she wanted. That's how she would live and die.

. . . .

CHAPTER 50

The view of the Rocky Mountains from Yves Poulenc's window never failed to inspire him, especially early in the morning when the whole Front Range glowed gold and every canyon stood out in stark relief. Tentatively, he liked Denver, although he didn't wish to commit himself to loving it. He wanted no regrets, no sorrow, no entanglements when the relapse came, and therefore he would not permit himself to love place, woman, friend, or country any more than necessary. He was in remarkable health, the best he could remember, but that didn't mean that consumption wouldn't pounce again—probably soon.

He kept to Maria Theresa's regimen because he had given her his word of honor that he would, but he itched to modify it, simplify it. In time, he would. He resolved that for the next year or so, however, he would abide strictly by her instructions. It all amused him now: the gargles, the teas, the decoctions and tinctures and awful-tasting herbs. But he had to admit that he was enjoying his health. He still lacked wind, but he could walk, even run a little, and most blessed of all, the fever had departed. He had come to Colorado for his health, and had found health in the clean dry air, sunny climate, and mild temperatures. A third of the residents of Colorado had come for their health, and not a few were finding it.

This morning he gazed raptly as the sun shifted across the great range to the west, pouring silver and gold into its canyons. The mountains would inspire his poetry some day, but for the time being he was toiling at a larger project. He intended to write a great tragic poem about consumption and slow, agonizing death; an epic poem that would examine the helplessness of the dying; his lost loves, his loss of future, his loss of appetite, his loss of oxygen and hope and life. Maria Theresa would be in it, but not recognizably. His parents and family would be in it, though he wouldn't mention them by name. Every thwarted dream of his young life would be in it, along with every anxious thought about an early death. And it would end with a beautiful, soul-searching look at death and what lay beyond the grave, and the lonely horror of arriving at that awful gate. That profound poem would ensure him an honored place in the pantheon of the literary giants. He would be the American Keats.

The only trouble was, he could hardly manage to scrape a word onto paper. In Glenwood Springs, awaiting death, he had been inspired by dying, by fever, by the hopelessness and despair around him. There, he had churned out page after page of fatalistic verse, whenever his health permitted. Now he only stared bleakly at the blank pad of lined paper, desperately seeking an idea, an angle, an approach, an inspiration. It was as if health were strangling his muse.

He sat at his escritoire, pen in hand, ink bottle open, waiting for the sweet flow to begin. And like yesterday morning and a hundred mornings before this one, he faced a blank wall. It angered him. What sort of God would rescue a man from early death only to destroy his life?

At last, knowing he had experienced another bitter defeat, he set the pen down, corked the ink bottle, wrapped a woolen scarf around his throat, shrugged on his green lodencloth coat and black beret, and headed into the wind for the Swallow Café on Cherry Creek where they let him, and other important young literary figures, sip powerful black coffee, nibble pastries, talk poetry and literature, idolize the wild Paul Verlaine, the dream-deviled Arthur Rimbaud, the Symbolists, *Les Poètes maudits*, Victor Hugo, Mallarmé, Anatole France, and anything European and therefore superior to the American.

He had especially come to despise American belles lettres, and the Transcendentalists in particular, although in Glenwood Springs he had been a devotee of Emerson, a worshiper of Thoreau, and a somewhat cynical observer of Longfellow and Whittier. At the Swallow, he had learned from his astute friends that all his former idols were mere puritans and rationalists, and what the nation needed was a poetry of the West, unburdened by any rules whatsoever.

All this he absorbed, enjoying the company of other young literary lights who dressed very like himself, and often sponged coffee and a breakfast roll from Yves because he had a small competence. Yes, he thought, at the Swallow he could sit in the company of more literary genius than existed anywhere this side of the Atlantic Ocean. And he was a part of it all.

All of this formed a new life, but he didn't suppose it was much of one. Everything made sense when he was dying. He had reached heroic stature when he was dying. He had extirpated fear, envy, greed, love, hope, and joy from his life, and faced death resolutely, jut-jawed and strong. But now? He didn't even know who he was, or what to do with his miserable prolonged life. He couldn't really befriend these vagabonds because they had no idea what death was, and thus were shallow.

Months passed without any sign of relapse, and he grew stronger, if not happier. Maria Theresa's regimen won his grudging respect, even though he distrusted it.

Then, one day, the letter arrived that darkened his life. He opened the envelope from his father, and found a note and a draft for a hundred dollars.

"My dear son," said the note. "Your mother and I rejoice in your newfound health, which you have possessed for most of a year now. You are twenty-nine, and it is high time that you become self-sufficient and make your own way in the world. That is the wondrous thing about America. Almost all of its citizens can fulfill their destinies.

"While we could afford to provide for you, we have decided that it is time for you to become an independent man. The draft will provide another month's support while you find employment, but that will be all. Your brothers have gone into the family business and are self-sufficient. You will find life richer and more rewarding when you become independent. What we have elected to do is simply best for you. Our esteem and love are with you as you begin your new life. Your loving father, Guy Ste M. Poulenc."

Yves coughed violently, needing to bring up blood, but nothing stained his handkerchief. He took his pulse and found it fast; yes, that was a sign, surely. He raced to his looking glass, needing to see dark circles under his eyes, and fever on his face. But he found nothing. He would relapse, and then what? They had abandoned him to die. He was a poet, and they should respect his artistic bent, and not require dreary wage-slavery of him. Didn't his father know of his sensitive nature and still-delicate health?

He raged at his unfeeling parents. How could they do this to their least fortunate son, who had endured a fever from his eleventh year, who had never tasted life and love and blossoming hopes? Who had faced death with valor? Who had been dutiful toward his parents? Bitterness stole through him. Heartless! They had turned their backs on their youngest and frailest child!

He paced madly around his sunny Cherry Creek apartment, knowing he couldn't keep it. The apartment cost fifty dollars a month, and now he had no means. They had condemned him to wander the alleys like a tramp. They were denying him the herbs and medicines he needed. They were snuffing out the beginnings of a great poet. Never mind that he hadn't written in months; it was all in him, aching for release, but now in one cruel, thoughtless moment they had murdered his muse.

How would he live? Working at common labor, shoveling slag at a smelter? Breathing those obnoxious fumes until his fragile lungs surrendered? What was he fit to do? His body, weakened by years of fever, lacked hardness. Would he clerk in some dreary store for fifty a month, bored and humiliated? He had come from a prominent family. The least they could do for him was send him to college.

Ah! That was it.

Feverishly he composed a telegram. "Beloved father. I would like to go to college and acquire the education that would make me a professor of literature. Surely, if I apply myself, I could complete the course in five or six years. I am not suited for common labor because of my condition. Say the word, and I will apply at Yale or Harvard for the fall term. I will repay you once I am employed. You have launched my brothers in successful careers. I am grateful for your help during my illness, and now I want to prepare for a good life. Your son, Yves."

He rushed to the Western Union office and sent it. He felt certain that his father would relent, and that he soon would be traveling east on the railroads. He would be a little older than the other students, but after all, he had spent almost twenty years dying. He knew that this had made him a man, and he would bring a profound wisdom to his classroom work, and would win the admiration of his professors.

He returned to his apartment consoled. A career in literature awaited him. Anxiously, he waited that day and the next, wondering what delayed his father's assent. Perhaps his father was making the necessary arrangements with one or another university. Yes, that was it.

Days rose and fell. Then at last he received a letter from his father:

"My dear Yves, Your mother and I have weighed your request carefully, and have decided against it for your own sake. Nothing prevents you from becoming a professor of literature if you wish to become one.

"We sense in you a reluctance to assume the hard duties of self-support, and we fear that a lengthy stay in college at your age, dependent upon us the whole time, would harm you more than help you. I emphasize that it is for your own sake that we must refuse. With love, Guy Ste M. Poulenc."

Yves stared at the perfidious letter, this missive cloaked in love that condemned him to a mendicant life. Fear gripped him. His rent was due in three weeks. He would have to find some means to live. He wished desperately he could be sick again. The responsibility of caring for himself seemed heavier than he could manage. He paced his sunny apartment, storming at his father and mother, waving the letter. Then he collapsed upon his sofa, filled with morbid despair. He would die of starvation. They had abandoned him.

Sullenly, he spent the next days traipsing Denver's business district, looking for help-wanted placards in windows. He perused the *Post* and

Rocky Mountain News looking for employment ads and found few, and those only for skilled workers. He studied the ads, looking for anyone who wanted a trainee. He occasionally found a sign in a café window seeking a waitress, and one hotel wanted a waiter to serve dinner guests in the evenings. But he rebelled at such menial service. He, an established if unpublished poet with a fine reputation, would not demean himself in such a fashion.

He finally managed an interview or two, and had to fight back his contempt for the squalid, grubbing businesses that might employ him. He answered queries brusquely, dwelled at length on his frail constitution and his years recovering from disease, and found himself being shown the door. The fat, bald, mustachioed slave drivers who bought and sold human beings simply said they would let him know.

By the end of a fortnight, he had conducted eleven interviews, written a dozen other firms, most of which were outside of Denver, discovered that a man with no trade was not a desirable commodity, and discovered also that no one wanted a man with an infirmity.

He was a poet and a litterateur. It dawned on him that perhaps he could go whoring and work for a daily newspaper. He could string words together elegantly. The work would be far beneath him, but at least it wouldn't be the same as shoveling slag in a smelter. It would be a contemptible use of his talents, but perhaps it would put food in his mouth—a necessity that had assumed alarming importance, now that he was down to his last few dollars.

The next day, he visited the offices of the *Post,* the *Republican,* the *Herald,* and the *Rocky Mountain News,* filling out an application at each establishment. Then he returned to his sunny apartment and waited for the bidding to begin.

C H A P T E R   5 1

ixie Ball didn't much like working for Hod Tabor, but fighting dust in a mansion sure beat sewing in a sweatshop. And she sure got an eyeful of some fancy people.

She had her own room in the rear of the Italianate villa, and board also, so the six dollars a week was hers to spend on anything she fancied. During her first year there, she saved most of it, and now had a three-hundred-dollar nest egg in the First National Bank. But recently, she was allowing herself an occasional frock, or a straw boater for summer outings.

Sometimes the sheer quiet of the place bothered her. The Tabors didn't entertain society because no one would come. But plenty of politicians and lawyers and businessmen happened by, and she often cleaned up the saloon after poker games. She liked to clean the saloon: it was redolent with the smell of cigars and males and leather and ale, and had an aura about it, as if large events—not just poker—were transacted there over high-stakes games.

Dixie would clean up more cigar butts left in one evening than she had seen before in all her life, along with dozens of glasses with the dregs of whiskey in them. She liked all that, but her happiest moments were wrapped around Lillie, the firstborn child that both Tabors doted on. Baby Doe left it to Dixie to wash and change the child, to air her in a perambulator, and comfort her when she was colicky. Baby loved Lillie when the infant was powdered and clean and wearing fresh, starchy clothing, but not when Lillie's diapers needed changing. Sometimes Baby stared resentfully at Dixie, not saying anything as Dixie cleaned or coddled the baby, but Baby's silence was thunderous. Dixie was always reminded in those moments that Lillie wasn't her child; Lillie was a Tabor.

She had to cope now with Baby's brother, Peter McCourt, who was sponging off the Tabors and pretending to be a man of affairs. He was a charming rascal whose gaze occasionally lingered too long on her. She didn't mind as long as she had to deal only with his gaze. She had worse problems, such as Baby's open distrust of her. After some months of Baby's odd distance and coolness, it had dawned on Dixie that Baby considered her a rival for Hod's affection. Ever since Hod had mentioned that Dixie once worked in the Clarendon Hotel in Leadville, Baby had studied her silently, looking for signs of something that wasn't there and never had been. Dixie was amused at first, but Baby had a way of making things painful, putting Dixie in her place, reminding her whose home it was.

And what a home! A hundred peacocks patrolled the three-acre lawn. Several nude statues, which scandalized neighbors much to the Tabors' delight, stood on the grounds. Every room in the villa had been lavishly decorated, which made cleaning a problem for Dixie. The Tabors had five gardeners and housemen, two coachmen and two footmen. Whenever Baby went out, she chose the gig that matched what she wore. One was black, another was dark blue enamel gilded with gold, and the other was brown with red trim. She usually chose the blue carriage, drawn by richly caparisoned white horses, the blue of its satin interior matching her eyes. The footmen, of course, had different livery to match each coach.

As time rolled by, Dixie began hanging about the evening poker sessions, swiftly pouring drinks even before anyone asked. She knew the tastes of every politician and tycoon who sat in at Hod Tabor's table. At first the gentlemen felt a little reserved around her, and she supposed they wondered what they could say in the presence of a woman. Some kidded her a little, and she gave as much as she took.

"You got 'em all buffaloed, Dixie," Hod said one evening.

"That's 'cause I grew up with a mess of brothers," she said. "I plumb enjoy men."

That, in fact, was something that Baby discerned also, and she tried to keep Dixie away from the evening poker.

"Miss Ball, let the men be alone; we shouldn't interfere when they do business," Baby told her one fall day. "They're talking with Hod about the elections, and that's not for anyone's ears."

"Yes, ma'am," Dixie said.

But no sooner had she retreated from the saloon than Hod Tabor's guests demanded that she return.

"You just serve up the whiskey and branch, and wipe the ashtrays, Dixie," Hod said. "Those gents wouldn't miss you for anything. I told them you'd ushered a few hundred piggies into the world and you were all prepared to help Baby. That did it. They all figger you've got the credentials to be a senator. You're plumb popular, especially with the Republicans."

"Baby sure didn't need me," Dixie said. "Lillie got herself born faster than your three docs could get here."

"Lillie's precocious," Tabor said.

But the defeat only hardened Baby toward her. Whenever Baby entered that male sanctuary, conversation stopped, and the gents paid effusive compliments. But whenever Dixie bustled around that masculine company, the jokes got thicker and happier, and this did not go unnoticed by the young Mrs. Tabor.

Dixie sensed that Baby Doe wasn't a happy woman. No matter how much Baby tried, she was barred from the homes of Denver's upper crust. No woman paid her a call or invited her anywhere, and Baby's own invitations were politely refused. But she didn't mope about it. If she could not be queen of Denver society, then she could be queen of a more raffish society. She and Horace lavishly entertained every performer who came to the Tabor Opera House, and Dixie found herself serving drinks or hors d'oeuvres to Lillie Langtry, Sarah Bernhardt, Madame Modjeska, John Drew, Maurice Barrymore, Ada Rehan, and a host of other glittering people. In this company, Baby played the queen, often sporting décolletage so breathtakingly low that Dixie figured Baby'd catch pneumonia. Baby was going to be noticed, one way or another.

Dixie even got to meet Henry Ward Beecher when the scandalous old lecher came over to the mansion after he had lectured a modest audience at the opera house. Of course, Dixie never attended the opera house events, but she certainly heard about them. The Tabors, popping bottles of Piper Heidseck up in Box A, were more of a show than the performers on the boards, and some performers, notably Edwin Booth, resented it and stopped the performance to rebuke Horace and Baby. Not that Baby minded: being rebuked by a great actor standing at the proscenium arch merely focused the gaze of the entire audience upon her awesome bosom and cornflower blue eyes and brassy blond hair.

But it was obvious to Dixie that her mistress was an insecure, unfulfilled woman, eaten alive by a conscience formed in her childhood in an Irish Catholic family in Oshkosh, Wisconsin. And more and more, Baby's insecurity vented itself upon big, blond Dixie, who had an easy way with men.

"Miss Ball, you're not to talk familiarly with Mr. Tabor," Baby told her. "My husband should be addressed formally. You must call him Mr. Tabor, not Hod."

"He was Hod when him and me were partners in a mine, ma'am."

Baby was stunned. "Partners? In a mine?"

"Yep, me and Lorenzo Carthage and old Hod, we had a rip-snorter going in Silverton until a pack of lawyers took it away."

"You and Magnificent? You know Magnificent?"

"Sure do. Him and me, we had a good operation but we needed a little capital to expand it, and roped Hod into it."

"Mr. Tabor, not Hod."

"As you wish, ma'am."

"I'm not sure you should be here. It doesn't seem right."

Dixie remained silent.

"And you worked in the Clarendon in Leadville—where I was staying?"

"Yes, ma'am. We never met, though I saw you a few times in the big hat you used to wear." Baby was the heavily veiled mistress of the silver tycoon when he was still married to Augusta Tabor. "You sure made a picture, ma'am, you and Hod."

Baby smiled. She could never resist a compliment. "Oh, I made a picture, all right. I always make a picture. But it's Mr. Tabor, Miss Ball."

"I'll be sure and call him Mr. Tabor, ma'am."

"Did you associate with Mr. Tabor much?"

"Never met him in Leadville. Knew who he was, though. Everyone in the Clarendon knew who Mr. Tabor was. Nope. Only time I met him was at that bash in Silverton that old Magnificent threw. We were partners in the mine then."

Baby eyed her unhappily. "I will talk to Hod," she said darkly.

Another month drifted by, and Dixie thought the episode had passed. She helped the Tabors decorate for Christmas, served tarts and tea during their numerous Christmas soirees—attended mostly by politicians, and never by Denver's elite—and kept her featherduster and carpetsweeper busy.

And then Hod approached her. "We're going out to Telluride in David Moffat's private car. Lorenzo Carthage's having a bash there to celebrate his new mine, the Lucky Strike. Pretty near everyone'll be there. Dixie, for some reason Baby's not happy with your service. She doesn't like it that you and me were once partnered up, and now this bash of Magnificent's reminding her of all that." Tabor looked uncomfortable. "Baby wants me to let you go. I tried to reason with her, but when Baby gets her teeth on the bit, there's no denying her. I'm gonna be in Dutch until I do it."

A rush of anger flooded through Dixie. "Have I failed you? Have I not performed my duties?"

Horace Tabor looked miserable. "It's not that. She's just not gonna be happy with you in here."

Dixie sighed. "Happy New Year," she said. "When do I pack?"

"New Year's Day. We're coming back on the second, and she wants you around keeping house for Peter until then."

"You know a nice place a lady can go?"

"I'll get you back in the Windsor."

"Well, I don't know. Maybe they won't want me around either."

"I can get you on. Can't promise you'll earn as much, though."

"Would you write me a recommendation, Mr. Tabor?"

"I'm not good old Hod anymore, eh?"

"Mrs. Tabor asked me to call you Mr. Tabor."

"I'm plumb unhappy about this, Dixie. Sure, let's go to the study. I guess old Hod owes you a thing or two."

"Yes, you do. I was a woman of independent means once."

Hod Tabor whickered, the flesh wrinkling around his calf eyes. Dixie didn't care. She waited patiently at the door while Tabor scratched his letter. Then he handed it to her, along with something else. She found herself staring at a double eagle in her palm.

"Well, thanks a heap, Hod," she said dryly.

"Oh, well, I just have to keep Baby happy. You ever need me, you just stop by and see good old Hod."

"I'll do that, Mr. Tabor."

CHAPTER 52

ixie's buoyant spirits sagged during that Christmas season. For years she had taken in stride all of life's hard blows, but this time she couldn't overcome her desolation. She completed her daily rounds in the Tabor mansion, scarcely participating in the holiday season except to give a little cotton bonnet to Lillie. She wondered where she would go and what she would do with her blasted old carcass.

She knew she ought to rejoice. She had been living a secondhand life in the service of the Tabors. She enjoyed the luxury but it wasn't her mansion. She loved Lillie, but Lillie wasn't her child. She enjoyed seeing all the theater people and politicians in person, but the illustrious guests she waited on didn't pay her the slightest heed. Had Sarah Bernhardt or Maurice Barrymore even noticed her when she handed them a drink or held a plate of hors d'oeuvres before them? Of course not. Could she say she had even met them? Certainly not. She was the anonymous servant girl in black.

She knew she should not feel any loss. And yet, her options were bleak. She probably would become a chambermaid again at seventy-five or eighty cents a day, and end up sharing a crowded room with two or three other poor women because none could afford a comfortable place. She wished she could meet another Armand Cotton, but she doubted that she would. Her big frame had obviously not attracted suitors, so one of her deepest yearnings, to find a husband and begin a family, was thwarted. She would be one of the world's anonymous women who cleaned and swept and washed for others.

After Christmas she simply began taking time off to hunt for work, informing Tabor she was doing it. He didn't object, and the less Baby saw of her the better. She didn't want to be a chambermaid again, and restlessly stalked the streets looking for help-wanted placards in windows. She hoped she might become a shop girl, clerking in a grand store like McNamara's or Daniels and Fisher's, or the Golden Eagle. But she had no luck there, or in lesser shops. She turned at last to the Windsor, feeling defeated. They would remember her.

She turned into the opulent hotel and was directed to a Mr. Maxcy, the new manager.

"So you see, Mr. Maxcy, I've experience here, and I can start right in if you've an opening," she said to the young man.

The fellow examined her letter of recommendation and smiled. "My name is actually Maxcy Tabor," he said. "I'm the son of Horace and Augusta."

Augusta's son. Of course. And a letter of recommendation from Horace could doom Dixie. Augusta and her son despised Baby Doe.

"I guess I'll go, Mr. Tabor," she said.

"No, wait. I'm curious. Why did you leave Horace and Baby?"

"I don't think it's for me to say."

"Did my father discharge you?"

She nodded.

"For not doing your duties well?"

"I did them very well."

Maxcy laughed, perhaps maliciously. "Baby didn't want another young woman around. She'll replace you with a gray-haired widow lady."

She nodded again, afraid to speak.

"You have to know my father," he said. "Baby'll never be secure. She knows Horace. She knows herself." He grinned crookedly. "You seem to know more about my family than I do. I'll be interested in your impressions of life among the peacocks. My mother bought an interest in this hotel, and I'm managing it. Your records tell me you did well here. I've been wanting to replace a woman who's not working out. You can start January second."

"I don't want to take a job away from someone—"

"You're not. She's going to leave us, regardless. I was just waiting for a good replacement. You'll work six days, and we pay five dollars a week now."

He introduced her to several other women on the staff, and Dixie swiftly negotiated a place to live, rooming with two others northeast of the business district. The little flat was too close to the Market Street sporting district, but Dixie thought that was worth a good laugh. She was such a big, boxy woman no one would take her for a sporting lady, although she sort of wished someone would.

Her last hours before the Tabors left for Telluride seemed strained, though nothing on the surface confirmed it. Horace explained, simply, that Mrs. Tabor would like for Dixie to depart on New Year's Day.

"You have new help coming then?" Dixie asked him.

"Why, yes, an older woman, a spinster from Ohio who came to teach and gave it up, saying Colorado children lacked manners." Horace beamed. "Nice, gray-haired lady with beautiful manners and perfect diction. A little on the plain side. Baby hired her. Said she was very dignified. She'll start the first."

This time Dixie smiled.

So that was how it went. No good-byes after nearly two years of intimacy with the family. On New Year's Day she packed up and left, walking into an overcast world that hid the mountains and the future from her. Draymen carried her trunk to the crowded flat and she settled in. Both her roommates were working that day, and she felt oddly alone and melancholic. What a way to start a new year, she thought.

She began her familiar routine on the fourth floor of the Windsor, wrestling sheets off beds, polishing the plumbing, carpetsweeping the rugs, and once in a long while collecting a nickel or dime tip. It wasn't much of a life, and she tried hard to wash away her bleak spirits. She vowed that as soon as the mean weather passed, she would go on outings every Tuesday, her day off. She would join a theater group and sell tickets, or she would hook up with some female improvement society. Something, *anything*, to relieve the dreariness of this life. Her unhappiness bit at her, made her cross sometimes, and angry at Baby Doe Tabor.

She made friends with her two roommates, heavyset Clara, and simpleminded Sissy, and the threesome sometimes managed a phosphate at the ice cream parlor, or even a variety show on paydays. One night they purchased one-dollar tickets and watched Gilbert and Sullivan's *The Mikado* at the Tabor Opera House, and talked about it for days afterward. In the spring they would watch baseball or take strolls. But all that was time stolen from their sleep after working ten-hour days. For Dixie, it was a period of questioning. Was she better off after leaving the farm and the demands of her father and brothers? Yes. About that she was certain. But not much better off.

She needed more from life, or she might just as well go to her grave. She figured marriage was out unless some galoot came along who didn't mind hitching up with an amazon. No babies. No hugs. She didn't know enough to become a teacher. That required a degree from a normal school these days.

An answer, and a dream, arrived one pensive moment when she was eating scraps in the hotel kitchen, the aromas of good foods whirling around her. She would go into business. One thing she could do was run an eatery. Not a fancy place like this hotel restaurant, but some café that served workingmen, the kind of fellows she'd been with all her life. She knew what they wanted, potatoes and gravy and beef, and lots of it, to fill stomachs emptied by hard work in smelters or mines or fields. They wanted fresh yeasty bread and a crock of butter, harsh black coffee, and something sweet at the end of their meal.

She wouldn't have to become some fancy French chef like those in this hotel kitchen, or learn any more than she already knew about boiling vegetables or building an apple pie. She could do it. And she'd enjoy doing it. She'd enjoy bantering with the galoots, dropping tips into her pocket, coming up with new plates and specials now and then, and giving all her regulars a square meal for a good price. And most of all, she'd enjoy her triumph over the sort of wage slavery she had endured most of her adult life.

Could she do it? Ruefully, she considered her slender resources: three hundred fifty-seven dollars in the First National Bank, salted away during her years with the Tabors. She didn't know what it would take to start a beanery, but she knew she didn't have half enough to buy furniture, table service, pots and pans, a mountain of equipment, lay in the food, and keep enough cash in reserve to see her through the first weeks when business would be slow. But it sure held promise for a gal off the farm. Denver had more men than women, and men hardly ever cooked for themselves.

Somehow, she would find a way.

She went back to work full of dreams that afternoon. The idea animated her, and inspired a lot of thinking as she tucked in sheets and fluffed up goosefeather pillows. She could save a dollar a week out of her salary if she tried. In a year she'd have fifty more dollars. She could save her tips, too. Maybe she could find someone to back her. Maybe Lorenzo Carthage would lend her five hundred. He was doing well in Telluride, so she'd heard.

Maybe her roommates could come up with something. Maybe they could become partners in the restaurant, the three of them cooking, waiting tables, washing dishes, and sharing the proceeds. Maybe they both had something squirreled away. But she doubted it. Clara might have something put back, but Sissy was slow-witted and spent everything the day she got it. They didn't seem to be likely partners.

That night, instead of trudging back to her flat, she hiked north toward the districts where smelter workers lived, determined to see the hash houses and beaneries where they ate before and after their shifts. She found very few, and wondered about it. Maybe smeltermen couldn't afford even a fifty-cent dinner. Or maybe no one had thought to start up a café in their neighborhoods.

Then she remembered the saloons. One stood on almost every corner: The Mint, The Denver, The Good Times, The Silver Ore. Men drifted in and out of all of them, even as she watched. She couldn't go into those male provinces to see what they offered, but she knew that many of them served sandwiches and pickles and hard-boiled eggs along with a mug of lager beer, and not a few offered a free feed, pretzels or popcorn, along with a glass of beer. At first that competition discouraged her, but the more she thought about it, the more she thought her restaurant might be just the ticket. She'd serve real food, hot plates, not just something to fill up on. Where did these men get their breakfast? And how many would prefer to eat in a café rather than a saloon? The more she strolled that district, so devoid of ordinary comforts, the more she was persuaded that it would support a restaurant handsomely.

All she had to do was find the means.

CHAPTER 53

alter Kimbrough lashed back. It was all Cornelia could manage to read the new Polly Pry gossip column in the *Post*. "The poor demented woman should be put in an asylum," Walter was quoted as saying. "She's lost all sense of reality and is to be pitied. She scarcely knows truth from fiction, and is obviously no longer competent. Why, she's even moved to a boardinghouse of dubious repute and is earning a living at common labor. What rational woman would abandon a life of comfort for that?"

But that was only the beginning.

"I've suffered attacks on my reputation from this deranged woman. Of course, the whole world discounts every word she says, and I have numerous friends who will attest that she's gone over the cliff and there is nothing to any of it. But I keep hoping she will come to her senses and return to the comforts of my home. I'm quite ready to forgive her lunacies as soon as she retracts them."

All this and much more in that vein was quoted with relish by that doyenne of the gossips, Mrs. O'Bryan, whose bold column was one reason the *Post* prospered.

Cornelia's veins ran icewater. His defense of his precious reputation had reached the point of declaring his wife insane. Frightened, she read and reread the Polly Pry material. Walter had certainly turned the tables on her, using the gossip columnist ruthlessly. She knew that he had scored. A cloud would hang over her evermore.

She wanted to visit Mrs. O'Bryan and argue the case, but she knew the catty woman would love every moment of it and turn it into another malicious attack.

She turned to Richard Peabody, who had given her the copy of the *Post*. "It's awful," she said.

"It's libel, Cornelia. Walter's libeling you and threatening you. You've got to fight back, and I'm here to help. It's Walter who's got to be put on trial, not you."

"I don't want to fight anymore, Richard. This just gets worse and worse."

"He's saying you're crazy. You can't let that stand unrebutted. I've never seen better grounds for a suit. You want him to get away with that?"

"What I want is my private life, Richard. I have a good life now."

"Well, let me handle it. I'm itching to go after him and all his influential friends. Your reputation's been damaged. We can go to court and collect. And I'm going to put him through the wringer."

That disturbed Cornelia. "I don't want to fight Walter. I can't afford a lawsuit. I don't want to go through an ordeal like that. I just want to continue as I am."

Richard shook his head. "He won't let you. He's got you in his crosshairs now. He thinks his good reputation depends on proving you mad as a hatter."

"Well, it does."

"Then leave it to me. I'll file a libel action for starters. We'll go to court and blow this thing open."

She was horrified. "Please, please don't do anything. I want to think it over. I'm not going to rush into anything."

Richard grinned. "I'll be waiting," he said.

She could barely work that morning. She loved her position, and had transformed it into something much larger than secretarial work. She had learned how to hunt precedents in Homer's thick, battered law books, and now she spent hours tracking down information, jotting citations, joyously noting something germaine. She loved this law clerking, and all its challenges. Her clerking proved to be a real time-saver for both of the Peabodys, and they encouraged her. If she missed something, they took time to explain what was wrong. She learned to find parallels, and discover germaine material in cases that had no apparent relevance. If Richard or Homer needed to examine all cases that dealt with such things as trespass or accidental death or injury on the job, she could deliver. With each hour she spent in the law books, her horizons expanded. She had plunged into an exciting new world and loved it.

That afternoon, when Homer was at last free, she entered his office and closed the door behind her. He looked bad, his face gray and blotched.

"I've been expecting you, Cornelia. Richard showed me the story and told me what he wishes to do. How do you feel about it?"

"Oh, Homer, I don't know. I don't want to get into a fight with Walter. He's so powerful . . . I just want to be left alone. If I can't have my divorce, then I just want to live out my life, a little mouse in a corner ignored by all those people around Walter. I love it here, doing research for you and my other work. What do you think?"

Homer smiled. "I'm afraid this is one time when the partners in the Peabody firm are in sharp disagreement," he said gently. "As far as a libel suit goes, forget it. It's very costly, for one thing. And there's the question of a wife suing a husband." He grinned. "The courts are well aware that warring spouses say naughty things about each other. Forget the libel suit, wife against husband. Any competent judge would instantly dismiss it. My advice, dear Cornelia, is not to get into a spitting contest with Walter. The deck's stacked against you."

"Richard disagrees with you. He thinks of toppling the giant, and you're concerned about my privacy and serenity."

Homer sighed. "He's a fighter. That's a good instinct in a lawyer, but not always the best one for the client. Is your goal fighting Walter, or simply rebuilding your life?"

"What do you think I should do?"

"Duck Polly Pry, for one. She'll call you and want to keep this going. She'll try to worm something out of you. But you can refuse to comment. Now, in fact, you do have some options in this. Quite interesting ones. I could write Walter. My letter would say that madness is a ground for divorce, many precedents for it in common law."

"I don't know, I don't know."

Homer nodded. "The other option, and maybe the best, is to do nothing, say nothing, work quietly here. There's one thing Richard and I can do. We can boost you to fifty a month now. We're certainly getting new business, with all this unfortunate publicity. I've already talked to Richard about it and we were going to tell you at the end of the month. You've become more a law clerk than secretary anyway. You can move to a comfortable place."

"Oh, Homer!"

"The sooner the better, Cornelia. How about today? Take the afternoon off, find a respectable place, and we'll send draymen to move you. I feel there's some urgency in it, with Walter huffing and puffing. If Mrs. O'Bryan rings you up, turn her over to me. I'll tell her you're in perfectly respectable quarters at such and such an address. Take a little wind out of Walter's sails."

She clasped the hand of the sick old man whose wisdom, learned through a lifetime, she trusted a lot more than Richard's just now. The look of pain and love in his puffy face shocked her.

She did find sunny rooms in a better neighborhood, and by evening she had packed her few possessions and completed the move. Now, at least, she had a defense against one of Walter's insinuations. His assault on her respectability had troubled her even more than his questioning of her sanity. The miserable boardinghouse where she was staying wasn't disreputable, but neither was it above reproach. She'd seen and heard all too much. But now she was out of it.

What a pass.

That evening, Cornelia enjoyed a hot soak in her bathtub, a luxury she hadn't experienced in a long time. Then she put on her robe, made tea over the gas flame in her new kitchen, and settled in her only chair to contemplate a hard, exhausting day. Earlier she had had to fend off her alarmed parents, who wanted to move her to their house instantly. She had gently refused, determined to pursue her independence as long as she could. She also had to discourage her father's threats to sue Walter Kimbrough.

Life had actually become better in some respects. The more she had mastered legal clerking, the more she was enjoying life. For weeks she had entertained the idea in the back of her mind that remarriage and children weren't so important after all. She had dreamed of them because those were the traditional employments for a woman. She had never dreamed of entering a different world, such as the one that delighted and challenged her so much now. The law clerking broadened her mind and made her feel more useful than she ever had before. At the same time, divorcing Walter seemed less urgent. What did it matter? If she could pursue this new vocation, and if she no longer yearned for remarriage, then her marital status made little difference. Of course she would still prefer her freedom, but the hunger for it no longer gnawed at her. She had a new life, a life of a sort that rarely opened to a woman. All of this came to her in a luminous burst of knowing during that thoughtful evening, and helped her decide what to do.

She would turn down Homer's offer to write Walter. It would only cause more trouble. She simply wanted to work quietly in her marvelous new vocation, and live in this respectable new flat that was beyond criticism, and slip out of Walter's long shadow. She wanted him to forget her. That would be her safety and her liberty.

Richard had not accepted her reluctance to start a libel suit as gracefully as he should have. He wanted to fight, topple a giant, make war, and he took her refusal to bait Walter as timidity. It was the first real conflict in an otherwise happy working relationship, and it troubled her.

Homer, shy but wise Homer, had been the stabilizing force that day. But Homer looked sicker and sicker each week, and she wondered when the day would come when Homer could no longer practice and she would be working only for Richard, or perhaps Richard and a new partner.

Comforted, she wandered her rooms, teacup in hand, thinking of how they would be furnished when she could afford to furnish them, delighted that this harrowing day had wrought a sweet change in her life. She had things to be grateful for. She had weathered a public assault. She had won a raise, curbed the impetuous young lawyer, listened to an old man's wisdom, and best of all, learned who she was and what she wanted to do with her life. Not a bad day, she thought, welcoming the bed covers at last.

On this day, she had won her independence. She had a new vision of her life, a new dream, and a new perception of herself.

CHAPTER 54

An apparition from Cornelia's past walked through the door of the Peabody law firm one noon.

"Why, Keenan Clark," she exclaimed, upon seeing one of her old beaux. He looked just as he always had, not a bit handsome with his oversized beak and big ears, and the amusement had never left his green eyes. "What are you doing here?"

"I came to see if you're crazy," he said.

She smiled wryly. "And what's your verdict?"

"I won't know until after lunch. Would you join me at the Roof Garden?"

"The Windsor?" She hadn't been to the Windsor, or any posh place, for over a year. "Why, Keenan, let me see. I'm usually on duty during the lunch period."

She hastened to Homer's office and swiftly arranged to be free.

"Let's go. This is a treat."

They walked the half mile without saying much. There probably was some purpose in all this. Maybe just curiosity. He was going to see if she was as demented as Walter was saying in print. But it would be a nice outing. She grew more and more nervous as they approached the hotel, and she hoped she would not encounter anyone from her past, or set tongues to wagging once again. Keenan eyed her speculatively now and then, but seemed content to keep silent for the nonce. His winsomeness affected her once again. He had always been a little bashful, full of private thoughts one could only guess at. Now, a decade after they were schoolmates, he operated a large coal and ice business.

She saw no one she knew in the restaurant, and felt grateful. He negotiated a window table. The sight of Denver at her feet, and the great blue wall of the mountains, exhilarated her.

They ordered, and he opened a conversation at last. "How are you doing, Cornelia? Are you happy?"

"Fine. Life's not perfect. I wish I could be single. But as long as the courts say no, and Walter resists, I can't do a thing about it. I'm his prisoner."

"Not entirely."

"That's the good side of it. I've plunged into a world I never dreamed of, a man's world. I'm reading law, clerking, digging up precedents, and even drafting arguments with citations. It's rewarding, and I'm being paid well now, even though it was a struggle at first."

"So I gather from Polly Pry. Are you still living—"

"No! I'm in a nice flat in a good neighborhood, quite content."

He smiled. "You've excited a lot of gossip. I wish someone who knew you could see you now."

"I'm glad there's not a soul I know here. Keenan, that's the past. I like what I'm doing. I don't really care what they think. If they believe a woman's common if she works or has a profession, I don't care."

"You sound a little vehement about it."

She shrugged. "I care some. But I'm enjoying a good new life." She felt restless under all this scrutiny. "And what about you? You're still single?"

He nodded. "It's these big ears or something. But the business is going well. I have thirty-seven ice routes and twenty-four coal routes. My drivers just look for the card in the window. If it's blue, they pull in and run coal down the chute and bill the homeowner. On the ice routes, my men look for the white card, get out the tongs and haul a block of ice in. They pour the meltwater out of the icebox and put in fresh ice, and collect if they can. All I do is sit back and watch the cash pour in and buy coal or lake ice now and then."

"Oh, it must be more complicated than that."

"Not much. I have to store the ice and keep several grades of coal around, and deal with special needs. I may expand to fuel oil. Some boilers are designed for it, and more will be."

They ate crab soufflé and a salad while reminiscing about dear and bygone years. She sensed he wanted to learn a lot more about her, and she debated what to tell him, and what his purposes might be. Surely he did a lot of business with Walter, whose many buildings needed coal for their boilers. He pushed away his plate and sipped coffee for a while, his green eyes surveying the distant white-clad mountains.

"Well, what's the verdict?" she asked.

"Walter's a liar."

The bluntness shocked her.

"He's trapped you, cornered you, refused to give you your freedom, and he's obviously sensitive about certain things—one only had to follow the divorce in the papers to understand what you've put up with. Or let me phrase it another way: what he's failed to bring to the marriage."

She reddened slightly.

"All his witnesses attesting to his splendid character didn't make a dent in your case. If he weren't so powerful, you'd be a free woman, Cornelia.''

She nodded.

"Ever since your divorce case, I've had you on my mind.''

"I think of all my old friends often,'' she said, tautly.

"I wish I'd contacted you sooner, when you had returned to your parents. That wasn't a good time for you. So many of our set are afraid of Walter, or do business with him—ah, that includes me. I sell more coal to him than anyone else in town, and I'm always mindful of his ability to hurt others. But I knew that you weren't invited out much— we're all married now, except me. They have dinner parties, but it's all couples, except when they invite the homely bachelor and find someone's sister to make a table.''

"You have a lot to offer a woman, Keenan. You always did.''

"I was a little slow. All of us young blades were too busy having fun, and then serious Walter came along, adult, determined, different—and he won the belle.''

"I'm flattered, but I don't think I want to pursue this.''

"I want to, if you'll bear with me.''

She sipped her tea.

"Have you given much thought to getting out of this trap you're in?'' he asked.

"I thought of nothing else until I finally pitched it all overboard and went to work—as they say, doing wage labor. Now I know that I'm not in a trap at all. I enjoy what I do.''

He grinned infectiously. "They all think you were balmy. I've heard that you should be sent off to an asylum. Especially the old biddies. They're the worst. They measure their own worth on one scale: how little drudgery they have to do.''

She nodded. "What I do isn't drudgery, Keenan. It's challenging and rewarding. I've had two raises in two months. I earn sixty a month now. That's as much as skilled male labor. Only miners earn more. And I don't have a family to support, either.''

"I bet you wish you had one.''

"I'm getting too old for that.''

"Ever think of going back to Walter—and starting a family?'' She discovered a pixie malice all over his face, and laughed. He laughed.

"That's what I thought,'' he said. "I have a question for you. We've talked for only an hour or so, but everything that's happened here confirms something for me. Would you accept me as an escort? Go to dances with me? Set a few tongues to wagging?''

"Oh, Keenan." She felt a cramping of her stomach. She finally reached across the linen tablecloth and touched his hand. "I'm a married woman."

"No, you're not. You haven't been married for what? Eight or nine years?"

She had no response to that, and stared at him mutely.

"I'm going to be nosey, and forgive me if I am. Has any other male—any of your old beaux—contacted you since your effort to free yourself from Walter?"

"No."

"They're afraid to. I'm afraid to. But maybe I take more risks. I love to climb mountains. I've climbed Long's Peak, and I plan to climb every fourteen-thousand-foot peak in Colorado. I like a little risk in my life. You're a lovely, special woman, Cornelia. You're worth any risk. I'll cope with Walter and all his power and lawyers and ability to crush a business. I'll risk the gossips, and the arbiters and banishers. I'll risk all of that if you will."

"This is too soon. I'm touched, so touched, but Keenan—well, where is this leading? What've you in mind?"

This time he didn't reply quickly. "I think we'd have to decide all that after a while," he said.

"But it can't lead anywhere!"

He simply gazed at her, as if her words weren't the whole of it. And her words weren't.

"Oh, I'm so late. They'll wonder what happened to me," she said.

On their way out of the Roof Garden, they encountered the one person Cornelia least wanted to see, Mrs. Leonel Ross O'Bryan, Polly Pry herself. Cornelia froze as the formidable gossip columnist huffed toward them like a galleon under full canvas.

"Let me handle this, Cornelia," Keenan said.

"You two! You two!" said Polly Pry.

"Walter's right, Mrs. O'Bryan. She's crazy as a loon," he said cheerfully. "Come along, Cornelia." He herded her toward the waiting Otis elevator.

"Wait, you two!"

But the operator levered the door of the cage shut. Keenan bellowed his joy, and she found it so infectious she began laughing too, even though she felt shaky and giddy and taut.

"It'll be in print," she said ruefully.

"Yes, Walter'll enjoy reading it," Keenan said.

The thought of him reading that set her to worrying again. Homer had been right with his advice not to bait her husband, but to lay low and live her new life quietly. Three months had gone by peacefully. But now, she feared, it would all flare up again.

Keenan escorted her back to her office an hour late. She sighed, unsettled by these sudden things.

"May I take you to lunch tomorrow? If not the Roof Garden, then somewhere quieter?"

"Oh, thank you, but I'd rather—"

"Of course. Later then? In a week?"

She nodded.

"You have things to think over. Cornelia, this was a joyous day for me. You're so lovely, your company is so . . . well, treasured."

"Thank you for lunch. What a treat! I haven't been out for so long."

"I'll be in touch," he said, leaving her at the door.

He was right, she thought, watching his back as he strode cheerfully into town. She had a lot to think over, new yearnings and old, new fears and new joys. And beyond that, the rightness or wrongness of things.

CHAPTER 55

 orenzo Carthage coolly prepared to make his New Year's party the most memorable of the times. That was going to be quite a trick, given his modest wage while the mine was under construction, but that didn't faze him. Not for nothing had he been called the Magnificent. He invited President Grover Cleveland and assorted senators and governors and lesser fry. For every reluctant tradesman who would extend no more credit, he found two more, usually in faraway Denver, who would cheerfully ship him anything he wanted, from Chinese green tea to sandalwood incense.

The party planning went smoothly enough, but his mine didn't. Several times in recent days he had to stop work on the festival, have his carriage brought around, and ride up to the Lucky Strike to deal with his miners. He never failed, on these journeys, to bring along a little treat for all the men—chocolates, or pastries, or on one occasion, a bottle of lager apiece, which he would allow them to enjoy during their lunch.

But the real purpose was to instill his crews with a proper passion to complete the winze and to install the last of the equipment before the new year. He managed to get past Christmas while keeping his crews on the job, and during that holiday they drove the two faces of the winze twelve feet closer to each other.

"I'm proud of you, men," he said during one shift turnover. "We're going to surprise the world. The Lucky Strike'll go down in history as one of the richest mines. You'll have work here for a decade, maybe two, as we expand into untapped reserves. We're going to have an announcement New Year's Day. I'm going to tell the world that my faithful men have completed the development work, and now we're back in the mining business."

These men listened impassively, the concluding shift looking tired and eager to go home, and the new shift looking itchy and impatient.

One big man, Bill Rawls, interrupted. "Yeah, and what's in it for us?" he yelled.

"Job security," Carthage shot back.

"Some job. You're going to spend tens of thousands on your party, and we go into that hole and break our backs for three and a half a day."

"You're all good men," he said. "You'll be climbing the ladder. Shift foreman, timber boss, manager. A lot more cash goes with each step up." Carthage made note of the complainer. After the new year started, he would weed out Rawls and a few others like him. His purpose for now was to pacify these malcontents, especially when he desperately wanted the last fifty feet of the winze blasted out.

Still, the men were waiting for a better answer.

"The festival's simply a business event. It's a way of acquiring capital to develop the mine. We invite the men who are able to invest. Capital investment means better working conditions for you. Better air, better timbering, less trouble with water."

"And you'll have a fine old time, on our backs, all you rich men," Rawls shot back.

"I hope the day comes when each of you can have your own parties, your own entertainments. That's what this country's about. Getting ahead in the world."

He heard some short, unappreciative laughter, and abandoned that tack. "There are only fifty feet left. Let's complete the winze in two days. You know what it means to you? Much more air. Once you break through, you'll have natural circulation from the adit into the upper works. Much more safety. Two exits."

"And three-fifty a day," Rawls said. "Go ahead and fire me, Carthage. I'm speaking for all of us. We're hearing rumors that we may be taking a cut. We're telling you straight off, we're not taking a cut in pay. You can't have it both ways—a party so fancy that folks like us can hardly imagine it, and a cut in our pay."

"I'm not going to cut your pay. You'll walk out each week with the same amount in your pay envelope. Count on it. Now, I'm not really having a party. It's a festival. Everyone in Telluride should be proud of the festival. It's a celebration of a business event, the completion of our development. You'll see things you've never seen in Telluride. You'll hear a band from Mexico City, and a string orchestra from Sioux City. I've arranged public performances just for your benefit."

"And a basket of fruit for working us on Christmas," Rawls said. "Thank you, Lorenzo the Magnificent. Thank you for the fruit and nuts."

Men around him laughed.

"Well, enough of this. I admire you gents. We're on the brink of success. Once the mine starts producing, I'll be promoting some of you to positions of responsibility."

"And the rest of us collect our three-fifty a day," Rawls said.

Over the next two days he completed his party preparations, but his shift foremen constantly interrupted him with bad news. Rebellion hung in the air. The miners toiled, but with every bucketful of rock hoisted out of the winze, there were troubles.

On December 27, the crew boring upward from the adit fired its shot, dismantled its scaffolding and retreated, and then the crew sinking the shaft from above fired a well-planned charge that broke through, and the rock thundered eerily downward to the adit. A lot of water came with it. The new winze would function as a drain. The two bores were offset only six inches, a tribute to the engineers and foremen whose measurements had kept the crews driving straight toward each other. A great whoosh of fresh air swept the upper works, cool and delicious air that lifted the spirits of the miners as they whooped and danced. Carthage received the news jubilantly and hastened to the Lucky Strike to see for himself.

He felt something akin to ecstasy flood through him. He had done it! As his men cleaned up rubble, he peered up the dripping winze, noting the speck of light high above. A blast of air harried his clothing.

Now, all that remained was to install equipment and see to a raft of details. Swiftly he gave orders to his foremen: run electricity to the upper works, erect the hoist over the winze, clean up a few rough corners of rock and rectify the slight digression of the two bores, install the iron drainpipe in the winze and begin draining the upper mine through the adit, and then dismantle the pumping operation above, take assay samples every ten feet up and down the winze, install an iron ladder the entire length of the winze, check for rotted rock and shore up any likely trouble spots—and urge the men on. All this could not be completed by year's end, but the details wouldn't matter. He would have plenty to show his New Year's guests, and a few days' delay wouldn't make any difference.

His foremen eyed him skeptically. The one who troubled him the most, Absalom Biggs, had something on his face that looked like disdain. Well, when the mine was running smoothly in January, Carthage would review all his personnel, and there would be some changes. He had inspired his crews to heroic development, and soon he would inspire his crews to heroic mining.

"It's a great day, and I thank you all," he said to his foremen. "I'll be remembering you when it comes time to parcel out some bonuses."

He returned to his party-planning, confident that the last details would be worked out by his foremen. Now he had more important things to do, such as leaking the news, unofficially of course, to a few insiders. He wanted the share prices to rise another few notches before the party just for the sake of mood. Quietly, using coded messages that irritated the telegraph men at the railroad station, he let the Guggenheims and other backers know. Of course word would get out. All those miners off-shift would boast from one end of Telluride to the other, and even that suited Carthage just fine. Everything was perfect: his guests were going to step off their trains in a perfect glow, and that glow was going to increase when they were feted by Lorenzo the Magnificent, and increase still more at New Year's midnight, the first moments of 1886, when he would halt the celebration and announce that the Lucky Strike would begin to ship silver and gold concentrate to the Denver refinery in a day or two.

That would be a high point in his life. Proudly, he reviewed his ups and downs, thinking about the weaknesses that had defeated him twice previously, but also the strengths that had enabled him to climb up the ladder, sometimes from nowhere, with no assets except his own drive and genius. And now it would be time to celebrate the greatest triumph. He loved being a host, enjoyed bringing people across his threshold, welcoming them to his handsome home, seeing to their comforts, enjoying their exclamations as he paraded his drawing rooms and furnishings, his groaning board, his liquors, his stables and carriages, his sporting facilities, his library and card rooms, his billiards table and his vast dining room. Yes, indeed, let them see Magnificent, and know Magnificent was a man who had made his mark.

There remained one delicate task. He had to announce the longer shifts in a way that would be most acceptable to his men. He didn't doubt he would lose a few, but where could they go? Other mines? Most in the area were well staffed, and there were unemployed miners waiting for day work as muckers, going wherever they were needed in the Telluride district.

He decided that a printed notice in the pay envelopes he would distribute on the thirty-first of December would be best. The notice would simply inform his men that their shifts would run eleven hours temporarily until some of the mine's huge overhanging debt could be reduced, and that in six months they could expect to be back on ten-hour shifts once again. And of course he would express regret that he had been forced to it by circumstance, and thank them for their patience and loyalty.

This he wrote out and had printed by the local newspaper in deepest secrecy. If it did leak out, though, it wouldn't be a calamity; the news would simply drive the Lucky Strike stock higher. His own shares had trebled in value in recent months, growing almost as fast as his debt, and might treble again for all he knew. He hung about the printing office until the circulars were printed. Then he stuffed the still-wet notices into his briefcase, returned to the mine, and told his pay clerk, Soapy Evans, to insert a copy into each brown pay envelope for distribution on the thirty-first. The clerk nodded. He and other managerial personnel had been exempted from longer shifts.

"They won't be happy," Evans said. "You'll get a few rocks through your windows."

"And they'll be out of a job," Magnificent replied. "Now, Evans, you be my eyes and ears. I'll be busy with my social affairs and won't be around for a day or two. But if you hear any unusual grumbling, you come for me. No matter what's happening at my place, you come for me. I can handle the troublemakers."

Evans grinned. "With a shotgun and the sheriff, maybe."

"No, just with rational argument, quietly and plainly stated. They should be reminded that it's in their best interest to repay capital first, because capital is what gives them their jobs in the first place. Laboring men are best served by patience, and then they will share in the wealth by and by."

"Sure, Mr. Carthage," said Evans, with a leer.

CHAPTER 56

. . . .

L orenzo the Magnificent's first guests arrived on December 30 and were greeted at the railroad siding by the Mexican mariachi band, gauded out in fine charro uniforms and huge white sombreros. Carriages awaited the visitors, ready to take them to the estate two miles away. A crowd had gathered to watch the trains steam in, hear the brass band play its merry airs, and see the gorgeously attired people.

Carthage had thoughtfully provided a copy of the invitation list to the *Telluride Weekly Miner,* which the editor had dutifully printed. And now the crowd studied the fashionable people, wondering whether any among them was President Cleveland. He hadn't come, of course, but Carthage let the world think he might. Meanwhile, the crowd did discover Senator Teller, a few ex-governors, the Evanses, Cheesmans, Horace and Baby Doe Tabor, the Guggenheims, and many other eminent Coloradans.

Most of these guests would stay right there in the sleeping cars, but a few had opted for Telluride's hotels and the elect would stay in Carthage's home. He had agonized about that select list, wishing he had a dozen more bedrooms than he had. Politics and prudence won out: the Tabors had a room, along with Senator Teller, and the Guggenheims, who were, actually, his employers. But he had reserved rooms for two families with striking daughters. This grand soiree would be more than just a party; it would be an examination of suitable young ladies, because he intended to marry just as swiftly as the mining venture would permit.

Even the weather cooperated, staying mild and sunny, inviting people to stroll his grounds, peer into his stables, hike into the mountains, or do some trap shooting. He met each arrival at his door, lavished a red rose upon each of the women and a fine Havana cigar upon each gent. He steered them toward his long trestle table groaning under its burden of dainties, too numerous and exotic for him to enumerate, with everything from the meat of ostrich to chocolate-dipped cherries. And at his bar white-jacketed mixologists awaited the pleasures of his guests. The partygoers could not come up with a request that his barkeeps could not fill. He regretted only that he had not enough cash to put them into livery, and he hoped no one would notice.

He had wisely scheduled no events that day or the next, knowing that what his glittering company really wanted was to socialize, meander, put down their roots for the extended celebration. But the orchestra played softly in the ballroom, and a wire-haired New Orleans concert pianist performed periodically, relieved by a fat harpist from Argentina who happened to be on tour.

The Guggenheims surveyed the establishment, their faces full of questions, but they refrained from comment. Business would come later. Carthage intended that his closeting with his employers would occur after the grand announcement of the completion of the Lucky Strike New Year's night. He laughed softly, knowing that they were no doubt disapproving, and probably a little shocked by what they were witnessing.

He sighed, banishing worry. His soirees had put him twenty thousand in arrears, on top of his debts for this mansion, his equipage, and his little luxuries. His ten thousand Lucky Strike shares, now worth four-fifty each, would cover much of it and he intended to drive the share prices higher if he could with some little tidbits judiciously served to the assorted financiers.

More guests arrived on the thirty-first, some of them on specials that drew one or two cars. They meandered his grounds, exclaimed at the beauty of Telluride, and were having a grand time, as was he. At last, he was where he wanted to be. He counted. His genius was evident. His boundless largesse, his legendary hospitality, all these things would never be forgotten.

"Some shindig, Carthage," said Senator Teller.

"The first of many."

"You're sitting on a bonanza, that's plain."

"Every cloud has a silver lining, Senator. I'll tell you something: not even declining silver bullion prices can harm the Lucky Strike. There's gold in that ore, among other things."

"Is that so? What about the refining problem?"

"It's licked."

"Well, I'll have a lick at the shares," Teller said.

"I'm taking us out there tomorrow, and you'll see some exciting things, Senator."

"Looking forward to it."

Carthage smiled.

Around noon, Soapy Evans showed up like a cloud over the sun, and drew Carthage into his saloon.

"The men want to talk with you, and right now. It's the Knights of Labor wanting a word."

"They got their pay envelopes, Evans?"

"They took that like a dose of cod liver oil, sir."

"You tell 'em I'll talk with them on the second, when we start up mining."

Evans shook his head. "No, that won't work. You've got to go there now. They're in a mood to tear the place apart."

"A strike? I'm not worried about that."

"A strike's the least of it, I think. This is worse, sir. They're silent, not noisy. They said for me to get you, and they're going to ask you just one question. That's what they say."

"I can't go now, I'm busy. What's the question? Do you know?"

"The question is, Do you mean it?"

"That's the question? Of course I mean it."

"They want to hear it from you personally."

"Well that's crazy. You tell them that of course I mean it. The extra hour's necessary. It's needed to launch production. It's temporary. Emphasize that. They'll get just as much in their pay envelopes as ever. I'm sorry, but that's business."

"You'd better come with me and tell 'em. They're sitting out there at the mine, expecting you. I'm telling you this is serious, Mr. Carthage. I think if you tell 'em personally, they'll swallow it. But if you send 'em messages, who knows what'll happen?"

"I'm not going to be intimidated, Evans. They mean to embarrass me, right now when I'm occupied. I can't surrender to that."

"Absalom Biggs wants you to go out there. He's telling them you'll come and talk. He's keeping the lid on for you."

"Then Biggs is speaking out of turn. Tell 'em we'll have a meeting day after tomorrow, and I'll listen to them, and do what I can. Maybe I can change things a bit. I'll know better after this party. Every one of the company's financiers is here, and we'll be having a few meetings. Tell 'em that. Tell 'em I'll have news after this is over. Maybe good news; lower interest, or roll over the debt, something that might change things. I'll listen to them, and I'm flexible."

Evans shook his head and left, reluctantly. Irritably, Carthage returned to his company, pausing amiably to visit with each guest. Worry nagged him, and kept him from enjoying his own party. But driving clear out to the mine five miles away just for a palaver with miners was unthinkable at this zenith of his life.

Late that afternoon his guests all vanished to their rooms or sleeping cars, and then they drifted back in the evening, this time in formal attire, the women in glittering gowns and tiaras and necklaces that glinted under the chandeliers, the men in black-tie attire. Carthage, got up in a new dinner jacket with black silk lapels, sewn just for this occasion, corralled Margaretta Fairmont, the lovely, warm-eyed daughter of Augustus and Helena Fairmont, the Denver banker and his wife, and whirled her into a trot blared noisily by the Mexican brass. Her eyes danced as he expertly whirled her around his parqueted dance floor.

"Why, Mr. Magnificent, how you do dance!" she said.

"You inspire me, my lovely Margaretta," he replied. "You're the Salome of my life."

"Salome who danced to have John the Baptist executed?"

"Ah, no less, my beautiful Margaretta," he replied.

That went swimmingly. He had a fine repertoire of dance steps and little jokes and self-deprecating humor, and soon she was laughing. He checked the party from time to time, and knew from the buzz and hum that people were having a glorious time. He had an instinct about that. Let something go wrong and he felt it in his bones. If a guest felt left out, or ill, or something wasn't right, Carthage had his ways of mending matters. But now, as he spun this delectable young lady about, he felt only cheer emanating from this crowd.

But then his man, Gardner, summoned him. "Your foreman's here," he whispered. "Insists on talking to you."

Irritably, Magnificent excused himself from the punch bowl crowd and found Absalom Biggs outside the front door.

"Yes, Biggs?"

"Sorry to interrupt, sor. There's trouble. I've been hearing some things a foreman isn't supposed to hear. You'd better get to the mine and cool off some hotheads there."

"What sort of trouble?"

"Sabotage. They're seething, sor. Seething. The longer shift. This party—"

"This party's a private affair and couldn't have anything to do with it. As for the shift, I've already told them I'll listen and maybe work something out later."

Biggs's eyes changed somehow. "I've let you know," he said, and stalked into the night.

"Thanks, Biggs. I'll deal with it," Carthage said.

He found Margaretta and asked if he might have the midnight dance. She handed him her dance card with a cheerful grin, and he signed his name. The brass band and the orchestra alternated, one playing bright and brassy tunes, and the other smooth sweet music. He danced with her several times, fighting off a few young bucks, finding her supple and warm in his arms. He wanted to learn everything about her, but the music and his responsibilities as host prevented it. But he did ask her if she'd join him in a stroll the next morning, and she accepted with a nod. There were things to learn, not least of which was how she felt about a beau who was much older than she.

The compliments came thick and warm that night. "Magnificent, you've outdone yourself," they said. "Who'll ever forget this one? You've wrought a miracle!" He absorbed all that joyously.

Midnight approached, and the string orchestra surrendered to the brass band, which launched into a wild stomp. He whirled Margaretta around, they laughed, the moment came, they cheered the new year, 1886, and he hugged her. She hugged back. The moment lingered on within him. Then, at last, when the merrymakers had quieted and a few older people were preparing to quit for the night, he clambered up on the bandstand, and with some ruffles and flourishes commanded silence.

"My dear friends and distinguished guests, I've a little announcement to start the new year on its way."

That certainly quieted the whole crowd, even the matrons who were busily gossiping about Baby Doe Tabor's awesome décolletage.

"This week or next, the Lucky Strike will start mining, milling, and shipping ore," he said. "We've completed the expansion of the mine, more or less. The winze bored from the adit to the upper works is done and being fitted out. It is already draining water and supplying air. We've harnessed gravity. Ore and water will be lowered rather than lifted. That water will run our mill and power our electrical power plant. Gravity will carry ore through our mill and ultimately drop the concentrate into hopper cars below the mill. The mine's reserves have been greatly improved in the process, and we can look forward to ten to fifteen years of profitable mining, maybe even bonanza mining. Even though the ore is refractory, we've made this mine so efficient that those of you who've invested in it can look forward to years and years of comfortable returns. Tomorrow, starting at one, I'll escort those who wish to see the Lucky Strike through the mine and the new mill. And may your new year be as joyous as mine."

The applause drifted over him in waves, affirmation, respect, congratulations at every hand. He heard something much better than cheers in this quiet drumbeat; he heard respect for the mining magnate he had become, admiration, relief perhaps, and a great sigh of pleasure. And no one clapped harder than the investment bankers, the Guggenheims, his principal stockholders, and others of his backers and creditors. The clapping didn't stop, but continued on and on, minute after minute, an affirmation of Lorenzo the Magnificent that would not stop.

And because of it he barely heard the great rumble that echoed down the San Miguel Valley like thunder, frightening Telluride with its eerie roar.

CHAPTER 57

iamond tiaras scattered the first sunlight of the new year, making the crowd at the foot of the Lucky Strike Mine glitter and flash. Many of Carthage's guests had gathered there, dazzling the rest of the crowd with their black opera capes, jeweled hands and necks, patent leather shoes, and silk stovepipe hats.

The mountain hummed quietly, occasionally belching smoke out of the mine collar far above. Between the moments of violence, a thin column of gray smoke lifted upward in the quiet morning air. Down in the bowels of the mine, the timbers were burning, sometimes slowly when oxygen was scarce, sometimes violently when fresh air worked its way upward from the adit.

The adit itself was largely blocked by enormous heaps of rubble that started about fifty feet in. A little water still trickled from under that awesome heap, mostly between the tram rails, but the rock had dammed the drainage and the adit behind it was flooding.

Carthage and several others had gingerly walked a little way into the adit, fearing that any movement would dislodge loosened rock. The acrid smell of dynamite hung in the air, missed by no one of those seasoned mine investors and managers, and not missed by Sheriff Feeney either. The timbers in the works above might smolder for weeks, depending on how much air reached them. The heat would loosen rock all through the galleries, causing landslides, twisting rails, destroying the mine. The Lucky Strike could not safely be repaired or reopened. Those grim men surveying the angry mountain were watching a fortune go up in smoke, and many more millions in potential profit die in that New Year's morning. They stared bleakly at Lorenzo the Magnificent.

Down below, along the road and the spur track, humbler people from Telluride watched silently, their attention not only upon the dying mine, but upon the glittering crowd of gorgeously dressed magnates and financiers and politicians gathered in a tight, taut group.

No one had died. This had been sabotage. Feeney questioned the sole witness, Absalom Biggs, who lived on the premises and served as watchman as well as a shift foreman.

"The crew walked out at nine," Biggs reported to the sheriff. "I was the only man here. At least I thought I was. They said they were on strike, and left."

"What was a crew doing here on a holiday?"

"Rushing to get the mine ready for production, sor."

"Is that why they struck?"

"Oh, that and other reasons . . ." Biggs sounded uncomfortable. His every word was being audited by the most powerful and wealthy men in Colorado.

"What reasons, Biggs?"

"The longer shifts, sor."

"Longer shifts?"

"The, ah, management added an hour to their shifts, beginning today."

Ben Guggenheim squinted at Carthage.

"Who did that? Carthage?"

"Yes, Carthage, sor. He said the company debt had to be reduced."

Carthage intervened. "Just temporarily, Sheriff. I promised them this extra hour would last only a few months. I want you to find the perpetrators, and bring them to justice. It must have been that last crew."

Feeney stared at him, and at the bejeweled crowd around him.

Biggs disagreed. "Why would men destroy their own jobs? This mine's done for. Someone did a lot of drilling to collapse that adit. I don't know who did it. They were bitter men."

"But you heard a lot of discontent?" Feeney asked.

"Discontent is a mild word for it, sor. Rage. Hatred. Bitterness. They'd worked Christmas Eve and Christmas Day, and got no time off. And then they got the notice yesterday."

"Notice?"

"The extra hour. Mr. Carthage's new shifts—"

"That's when the trouble started?"

Biggs nodded. "I warned Carthage, sor. Before and after. So did Soapy Evans—he's the pay clerk and bookkeeper. I sent Evans to Mr. Carthage's house around nine."

The sheriff's bright black eyes bored into Carthage. "You were warned?"

"Oh, yes. I told them I'd deal with it tomorrow," Carthage replied. "I said I was flexible. I don't think my message reached my men."

"It reached them," Biggs said.

Old Meyer Guggenheim and his sons glared.

"I want these criminals brought to justice," Lorenzo said.

Feeney grunted.

"It was the party that did it," Biggs continued, a certain malice blooming in his words.

"I'm not done with this," Feeney said, closing his notebook.

A great sadness swelled in Carthage. His new mill stood idle and useless. His modern power plant stood forlorn and silent. The railroad spur, where they were standing, ran to nowhere. His brilliantly engineered mine, which employed gravity to operate efficiently, smoked and groaned and thundered high above. Now he couldn't even conduct his triumphal tour of the mine. What would all these splendid people think?

Whatever they thought, they kept it to themselves. Silently they stepped into waiting carriages and wrapped buffalo robes about them to ward off the chill during the long ride to Telluride. Miners and their families gaped at the ermine, mink, satin lapels, velvet capes, and kid gloves, as the elite of Colorado drove off in their lacquered carriages.

The rest of that strange, silent New Year's Day, his guests packed and headed for their palace cars, along with the band and orchestra. No one said a word to him; neither a thank-you nor a good-bye. He stood at the door, smiling, but they walked right past, as if he didn't exist. The bankers and merchants of Telluride eyed him coldly, surveyed the great house with a creditor's eye, and stalked away. Margaretta Fairmont managed a winsome and apologetic smile, and hurried out with her parents. His hired temporaries manning the bar and the kitchen abandoned him and his mountains of food and drink and hastened to their cottages. The whole contingent of Guggenheims silently exited, carrying the mine's books and papers.

"Delighted to have you, glad you came," Carthage said to them all, but no one replied.

He heard the two specials chuffing down the valley, and then he was alone. It had been a grand party. He meandered through the rooms, remembering the sound of the Mexican brass and the string orchestra, seeing the whirl of ballgowns on his parqueted floor. He saw in his mind's eye the well-coiffed women. The rich had ways of making themselves beautiful. He, Lorenzo the Magnificent, had never hosted so many gorgeous people. He saw again the diamond tiaras, the emerald necklaces, the sapphire rings and ruby tie pins. Ah, they were grand, these people, these favored few who had dared the world and built a new state. And he had become one of them, building a great mine out of a failed one, his genius flowering here and blessing all these people who had invested in it and trusted him with it. Ah, indeed, this had been the party of parties. He remembered the compliments, the melting gazes of the young women, the respect. Especially the respect. This time, for certain, he had made his mark upon the world. No one would ever forget Lorenzo the Magnificent.

It had been the greatest party ever thrown in Colorado, one for the books. Sometime, when influential men wrote their memoirs, they would tell the world about this party.

A blizzard of papers arrived over the next days: summonses, notices, claims. And with them, bankers and lawyers, one after another, walking in pairs or threesomes to his majestic front door and even letting themselves in. The bankers wanted the estate, and immediately. Merchants and other creditors wanted everything else.

"Just sign right here, Carthage," said his banker, Willard Coombs. "This gives you three days to vacate, and avoids litigation."

The lengthy document looked too long and too dreary to read, so Lorenzo simply took pen in hand and scrawled his signature on the agreement.

"What's this? Your name's Carthage, not Magnificent," said Coombs.

"I'm Lorenzo the Magnificent," he replied tartly.

Two lawyers arrived, men Lorenzo didn't know. "We represent thirty-seven of your creditors," said one, Olaf Berg. "We've a few papers for you here, and we'd like to ask some questions. We're seizing all your assets except your real estate. The bank is senior on that. Now here's a list. We've been going over everything . . ."

Lorenzo listened patiently. Somehow or other these gents had acquired a complete list of his assets, ranging from horses and carriages to pocket watches and his ivory chess set. He learned that he would save himself a trip to court if he simply signed on the line at the end of the document. He signed.

"What's this, 'Lorenzo the Magnificent'?" bellowed Berg. "That's not your name. Sign again, Carthage, and no nonsense this time."

Lorenzo stood up and gathered his dignity. "You are addressing

Lorenzo the Magnificent," he said. "Take the paper or leave it; I've signed."

They took it.

Still others arrived with instruments of debt and laid them on his desk. These acknowledged Lorenzo's indebtedness to one or another creditor and arranged a schedule of payments and a rate of interest and a default penalty.

"Just sign right there, Carthage. It'll save you litigation. It'll also save you some criminal complaints we'd file with Sheriff Feeney."

He signed.

"What's this, Carthage? You trying to dodge an obligation? Your name isn't and never has been Magnificent."

"I don't know what you mean," Lorenzo said.

"Never mind. All three of us witnessed it. It'll hold up."

Then the flow of visitors slowed and draymen arrived with wagons. Somehow, everything vanished. The horses disappeared along with the ebony carriages. The furniture went. The fabled collection of wines and spirits vanished into crates, each bottle resting in a straw nest. The draperies and bedclothes disappeared. The last of the Purdy and Greener shotguns went, along with the shooting paraphernalia. Someone collected the game birds. Lorenzo the Magnificent watched it all, wondering why they were doing all this.

Another set of attorneys arrived with papers involving the Lucky Strike Mine. These dapper gents from Denver represented the board, the principal stockholders, the Guggenheims, and the mine's various creditors.

"Just sign here, Carthage. The first one is a debt instrument, obligating you to repay your creditors and employers over a five-year period. The second acknowledges your mismanagement of the mine and holds my clients harmless to all future claims or obligations. The third . . ."

Lorenzo didn't listen. He dipped his pen and signed.

"Is this a joke, Carthage? 'The Magnificent'?"

"I don't know what you mean," Lorenzo replied.

The next day his Telluride banker returned. "You gotta get out of here today. We're showing it," said.

Lorenzo the Magnificent nodded. Odd how they treated him with disrespect these days. Even his old friend Coombs. It was time to leave Telluride. He had slept on the floor the previous night anyway. They had even taken his clothing, except for his New Year's Eve garb and cape. He had that, anyway, and some currency in his wallet.

That day, Magnificent donned his black opera cape, purchased a first-class parlor car seat to Denver, the best cigar he could find at the tobacconists', brushed dust from his boiled shirt and satin-lapel dinner jacket, had his black ballroom shoes shined, and boarded the train.

CHAPTER 58

 omer Peabody felt an overwhelming need to dress and descend the stairs to his office and sit at his desk. It would take his last strength, but that was where he wished to be found. He struggled out of bed, feeling dizzy and nauseous. The chest pain had awakened him, this time different and darker than before. There had been many such episodes, and Jack Meek had told him frankly his heart was giving out and the digitalis and various diuretics weren't going to help him much anymore. His renal disease was accelerating the process. He sensed that his time had come. The digitalis had given him an extra year, and that year had been the best of his life.

He breathed in small swift gulps, and felt the flutter of pain in his breast. Yes, he intended to be dressed in his best starched shirt with a fresh collar and a bow tie about his neck. He dreaded being discovered in bed, undignified, his privacy invaded. Dignity was never more important than at death. He had lived in dignity. He was dignified in court, dignified in the company of women, dignified among men, dignified when interviewing a client, dignified in public. He had always worn dignified clothing, a white shirt and tie, a suit and hightop shoes, wire-rimmed spectacles, nothing gaudy. Now he would arrange a dignified death. He would will himself through this last small drama in the wee hours of the night.

He lit the lamp, rolled slowly out of bed, found his bottle of digitalis, and swallowed one of the compressed foxglove-leaf pills. He waited for it to take effect, and then gave up when it didn't settle his tumbling pulse. Little by little he managed the business of dressing, pausing when his unruly heart tripped wildly or not at all. Fear ran wild in him, but it was mixed with other things, especially relief that he didn't have to suffer death from having his water stopped up by his murderous prostate. In that sense he had gotten his wish. What could be better than a good death?

He completed his labors a little at a time, regretting that he could not stand up and shave. He couldn't even hold up his hands long enough to tie his bow tie. He dreaded slipping into blackness before he was finished. He thought he was just being an old fool, wanting to die properly attired at his desk downstairs, but dying there had become terribly important. He couldn't tie his shoes; bending over was simply too much for him, and sent his heart into paroxysms. He felt heavy with his edema, which bloated his legs and belly. He breathed heavily, sucking air in and out, hoping to find time. Fear rose and ebbed in him. The blackness terrified him, and yet it didn't. More powerful than fear was sorrow. It hadn't been much of a life.

Little by little, he completed his self-imposed task, and then he crawled to the stairs and descended, a step at a time, sitting on each step until he could lower himself to the next. In a quarter hour he completed the journey and settled into his desk chair. The room felt chilly, but moonlight flooded through the gauzy curtains giving him light. He needed light more than warmth now. He had been chilly for months, the poor circulation numbing his extremities. But his mind remained clear, and for that he was grateful. He could devote his last minutes to a summing up. He had tried to sum up his life for months now, as the little heart episodes increased.

He sank heavily into his wooden office chair, glad to be there, knowing it symbolized his life. His swivel chair had been his humble throne. He had spent over three decades in a chair very like this one, surrounded by papers very like those about him, wearing the same sort of dignified clothing that wrapped him now. He felt bewildered, and tried to clear his mind because this last chance at reflection was crucial to him. There seemed to be two things to go over if he was to come to terms with this ending: his past and his future. He would take them in order.

Had these past three years, when things got better, somehow made a wretched life worth living? He couldn't say. His thoughts floated untethered, his mind adrift. He felt disappointed. At the moment of his demise, he expected great granitic truths to emerge. Instead, he slumped in his leather seat, feeling the pain and desperation in his chest, and scarcely had a thought worthy of the name.

But images drifted by, tintypes of those he knew. The images were of Cornelia, and Richard and his family. Cornelia the prominent young matron seeking divorce years before; Cornelia at work now, in subdued clothing, looking happy. Richard, young and bold, but listening to Homer's counsel. Images, one after another, and sometimes none, when all he knew was the coldness of his limbs, his desperate need for breath, the heavy edema that bloated his torso as well as his legs, and sheer nausea. He had wanted desperately to know whether his life had merit, and whether he had counted, but instead he knew only that very late in his days he had come to love two young people who had miraculously drifted into his orbit.

And then he knew. His life counted, simply because he had loved. Loved shyly, awkwardly, pompously, timidly, and blindly. But he had loved two young people. It wasn't what he had achieved or not achieved that counted, but only that he had loved.

He needed air, but his breath came hard and shallow, as if there were no space in his lungs to receive it. He wasn't sure where he was at times; his brain wasn't working well, and that troubled him. He needed clarity. The questions begged for answers. Had his presence on earth served any purpose? Had he been fated from birth to live out his obscure, frustrated, lonely life? And why? Could he have done things differently, found the will and courage to burst free of his own nature? His mind was awhirl with great questions, but all he could summon was more questions. No answers drifted through his consciousness.

His respiration was increasing rapidly, his lungs pumping faster and faster, and then he found himself breathing slower and slower, as if his lungs didn't want to breathe at all. There came a point when he didn't breathe at all for several seconds, and then the whole process started up again.

He loved Cornelia.

Richard had become a son.

They would inherit what little he had, but he doubted that if would come to anything. Burial would consume the few dollars he had put by since business had improved. He ached to leave them something other than a failed divorce case and a brief partnership. And yet he had given them something. Richard had learned patience and courtesy from him, and a little prudence. Cornelia had shared her troubles with him. His only gift to her had been to listen. But listening was not a bad gift in an uncaring world.

So it had come to three good years in his fifty-eight. And yet, that wasn't the way to look at it. His childhood hadn't been unhappy. And all those years practicing in Crawfordsville hadn't been lost. He had acquired wisdom, and in the end had found the courage to come to Denver and try a new life in the golden West.

And yet . . . Homer Peabody would be on no one's roll of honor, and Homer Peabody would leave no children and grandchildren behind him, and Homer Peabody would die a virgin bachelor, unknown to woman. No one would remember him. He would leave no contributions to law. Few clients would honor his efforts. Those were the truths. But there were other truths. He had lived as honorably as he could. He could be trusted. His overstuffed conscience had, at least, kept him from inflicting pain upon others. He had often worked for free, giving his time and expertise to the desperate. Maybe those for whom he had secured a pension, or fended off piratical predators, or drafted a solid contract, or drawn a thoughtful will, might find value in the life of Homer Peabody. He hoped so. He hoped that even an obscure, failed mortal like himself had scattered some good here and there.

His odd breathing spiraled upward to panting, and then slowly retreated until it bottomed once again in a long pause when life lay suspended. He watched himself die, helplessly, slumped in his chair. He needed to sit up and be dignified, but couldn't. His mind spun away and near, through clouds, and into memory.

He had never married. That saddened him the most. What would she have been like? Dignified, like himself.

He grew aware of the cold moonlight shifting across his desk. For a while he saw his fine new office clearly: the shelved casebooks, the great desk, the golden oak file cabinets, the accoutrements of a life. He felt cold, more cold than he ever had, cold from within his center. He couldn't move his limbs very well.

Then his world passed from sight, and he thought about the future. But the future frightened him. He had been bland in his religion, as he had been bland in everything else, and he knew God had no use for lukewarm believers.

He wanted to see his parents, but doubted that he would. Images of his father and mother drifted past: his mother at a young age, when he was a child, vigorously making ice cream. His father, a handsome man, hunched over his ledgers turning a workday into columns of numbers. The pictures drifted by, so many he could not fathom them all. Picnics, sitting in a white pew, learning the violin, walking along the river, examining a dead rabbit, playing with his garter snake.

What lay ahead? Something or nothing? It didn't matter, but he was curious. It didn't matter because he was helpless to change anything. If he had lived badly and would be doomed by God to perdition, he couldn't change it. If he would be admitted to some distant dark corner of paradise—he couldn't imagine more for himself—he couldn't change it. If nothing but terrifying nothingness lay ahead, he couldn't change that, either.

Cornelia, please put a blanket over me, I'm cold.

Ah, Cornelia, you walked into my office and made my days warm. If I could have married as a young man, I would have married the likes of you. Ah, Cornelia, come and help me lie down. It is hard to sit this way. Cornelia, take what little you get from the estate and buy some roses, and let them decorate your rooms until the petals fall one by one. Cornelia, I've never felt so cold and weak. You glow with goodness. I never told you that I loved you from the moment you walked into my office.

His breathing slowed, and slowed again, and then it stopped. He found himself walking through a tunnel, wondering whether there would be light at the other end.

CHAPTER 59

omer's burial made Cornelia heartsick. The death notices in the various papers had not elicited a single card or bouquet or wreath from other attorneys or law firms or the Denver bar association. The morning of the service she saw how it would be, and spent an extravagant sum on bouquets and a black wreath. Something, anything, to compensate for an uncaring world.

The undertakers, Alston and Fryer, had supplied a young Bible-thumper, the Reverend Mr. Gable, because Homer had not made any known connection with a Denver church. But that afternoon only three people came: Cornelia, Richard, and Alice. All those attorneys Homer had dealt with professionally found reasons not to come. Neither had any of Homer's clients shown up. Neither had any of Homer's distant relatives in Indiana, who had been wired the news. She sat there embarrassed for Mr. Gable, mourning Homer, and wishing someone else had cared as much as she did.

Before it started, the dominie addressed his congregation. "Would, ah, you like this abbreviated?" he asked.

"He's very much treasured," Cornelia replied.

"That pleases me deeply. Would you offer a eulogy?" the minister asked.

Richard responded. "I'd be glad to talk, even if it's only for us. Homer Peabody wasn't well known here, but believe me, sir, he was loved and admired."

"I am glad of it," Gable replied. He began with a prayer of thanksgiving for a life well lived, and then invited Richard to speak.

"The world is full of people we rarely notice, humble people wrestling with their painful private lives. Homer Peabody was such a man," Richard began. "One could easily miss him in a crowd, and if one did meet him, one would never imagine what a fierce struggle he had waged to make something of his life. Homer carried a lot of baggage, burdens that the rest of us don't have to lug around. That made everything ten times as hard for him. I can meet strangers easily; for Homer it was an ordeal. I can stand up before a court and feel at ease. For Homer, addressing a judge and jury and opposing counsel was an act that required every ounce of courage he possessed. I can express love to my sweetheart; for Homer, that was difficult and frightening.

"What we should remember about Homer Peabody is his courage. He had to cope with his inhibitions every hour of every day, and he did it with a bravery the world never witnessed. Behind his courtly conduct and measured words was his vision of the good, and a commitment to live by his lights. And yet the very burdens that inhibited him were blessings he bestowed on others. It was as if he had been born to be a counselor, in the sweetest sense of that word. . . ."

Thus did it go. Cornelia listened raptly. Homer's spirit would be pleased with Richard's gracious remembrance, she decided. But it all seemed so forlorn, three people celebrating a human life.

They buried Homer out at Mount Olivet. The undertakers supplied the manpower to lift the casket into their ornate black hearse and drive the black-tasseled horses to the trolley barn next to Union Station, where the economical pine coffin was placed in the Denver Tramway Company's closed black funeral tram for its trip to the cemetery.

It all desolated Cornelia, who believed that Homer Peabody deserved hundreds of friends and clients at his funeral, a tribute from the community, long obituaries in the papers, and a district judge or two to pronounce a benediction. Not even Polly Pry seemed to care, even though Homer had conducted the most notorious divorce case in Denver.

The minister hurried through a prayer commending Homer's old body to the earth and his soul to God, and then it was over. She and Richard and Alice rode the black curtained funeral tram back to the car barn and Richard paid Walter's traction company, which rented the black tram by the hour.

She wondered whether she would stay with Richard, or whether Richard could afford to pay her, or whether there would be a new partner soon, or whether Richard would stay in the offices her father rented to the firm, and what would happen next.

Homer's will had left the estate to Cornelia and Richard, but there would be no estate. The burial costs exceeded Homer's assets by almost a hundred dollars, although some uncollected debts might even things out if the money ever came in from half a dozen clients. Richard had shouldered the cost, and would handle the meager estate.

Poor, wonderful Homer. She had found him dead in his oversized swivel chair. He had somehow managed to dress and die where he wanted to die, decorously dead in his suit and even in his bow tie. It must have meant a lot to him to die that way. The signs of struggle abounded upstairs. Underdrawers lay on the floor. Three bowties on the bed. His digitalis bottle was opened. That, truly, was Homer. Dying in bed in his nightshirt would have been undignified, and so he had somehow arranged the final dignity, his portly old body properly suited for the most formal of all occasions.

She had walked into the office that morning and knew instantly he was gone. Morning sunlight struck his inert, slumped form, making his pasty white jowls even whiter. She had taken a hand and found it cold, and then summoned his doctor, Jack Meek, who had just arrived at his own office two blocks away.

When Richard walked in a little later, she had led him to Homer's office, where Meek was writing a report. Homer still slumped in his chair, but Meek had opened his shirt. Richard's response surprised her. He knelt beside the old man and wept. There had been something paternal and protective in the courtly old gentleman, something that had taught Richard a great deal about the practice of law: that it was much more than a great joust. That all came home to her now, as she beheld Richard, his face buried in his hands.

"I've lost a father," Richard said after absorbing the death. "I came here a young hotshot, and he quietly showed me that some things are more important than a victory at any cost. I'll owe him the rest of my life."

He closed the firm that day.

After those bleak ten minutes in Olivet Cemetery, Cornelia and

Richard and Alice silently repaired to the offices of Peabody and Peabody and gathered in Homer's office, needing the ghostly presence of the old man and his ancient file cases and ratty folders. Everything looked so tattered and worn and reused compared to the new equipment in Richard's office, and yet those humble tools of the profession radiated something warm and gentle and tender.

"I suppose we should talk about the future," Richard said. "But not if you don't want to."

"I do. I've been wondering."

"I've been so full of loss I haven't been very thoughtful," Richard said. "But we face some things. I can carry on here awhile, but the rent would be pretty heavy for one attorney. Actually, I earned most of the firm's revenue, so it's possible to go on here. I can handle some of Homer's work, but not all of it. Maybe we should move. The upstairs suite is the problem, not Homer's office. This is really a house, not an office building, and there's no separate stairway. In other words, we'll probably move. Unless you want to rent it from your father."

She didn't. She wanted her own flat, and her own life. She wanted to entertain without bringing guests through the law offices to reach her rooms, and she didn't want to be disturbed when Richard worked late hours. Beyond that, she didn't want to pay rent to her father, now that she had achieved independence.

"I guess you'd better plan on moving, Richard. I'd rather not live up there. The upstairs, it's really all part of the office."

He nodded. "That makes sense. I think I'd like to practice alone, anyway."

"With or without me?"

"With you, of course."

"Is this what you really want, Richard?"

"I certainly want you present in any firm of mine. I'm not sure about going alone, though. I'll have to let this settle awhile and see whether there's anyone in Denver who'd be a good partner."

"Well, it's all up in the air," she said, feeling as uncertain as he did.

"Let's go home, Richard," said Alice.

Nothing had been settled.

So uncertainty would be her lot for a while. Homer's death could have a profound effect on her life after all. Wearily, that somber day, she walked to her flat, her thoughts on the man who had helped her through painful times and given her new ideals.

She had come to her own crossroads, and hoped that she could think her way through. For several months she had been enjoying the society of Keenan Clark. He took her to lunch, and sometimes dinner, and once or twice to the Tabor Opera House for a play, and the gossips of Denver had been wagging their tongues. Everyone in Denver knew that Walter Kimbrough's crazy wife was frequently seen with the coal and ice merchant. Poor Walter. What a cross to bear, being married to a demented woman.

None of this had escaped the attention of her husband, who no doubt assumed the worst even though she and Keenan had scarcely even shaken hands and had never crossed a certain line. Some day, some way, he would strike out at her for these new embarrassments to his reputation.

That part of it she hated, but Keenan's company she adored. He brought her news of her old friends, loved to quip about Walter, and boldly said things about him that made her blush. He had been telling all those haughty women in their mansions on Capitol Hill that Cornelia Montfort Kimbrough was in fine fettle and enjoying the challenge of professional work. He made her laugh, describing all his encounters with the haut monde. The homely fellow had brightened her life, but at what cost? She knew that his own invitations were drying up, and he was no longer welcome in certain homes where Walter Kimbrough exerted influence. He didn't seem to mind, and it struck her that he was courting the ostracism—for her sake.

He was also pressing toward something they both understood even though it had not been voiced. He was unfailingly tender and sensitive, and didn't even mention the prospect that loomed larger and larger between them. Yet it was there in the tug of her body, sliding into her pillow-thoughts, tormenting her whenever she saw the beginnings of age in her face. He wanted her and she wanted him, with or without marriage.

She had tried to think all this through, but she couldn't. Words and ideas didn't help at all. She could just do it, move in, take up with Keenan Clark, and the consequences be damned. Let them banish her; they already had. If Walter had cheated her of life's most intimate pleasures and warmth, why shouldn't she seek it elsewhere?

Sometimes, when Keenan sat across from her at dinner, she just wanted to reach to him, touch him, and ask him to come home with her. Why not? What did it matter if it violated some moral law or propriety or civil law? What was her marriage anyway, if not a cold fraud? Ashes! Let them challenge her. She'd tell the world what marriage to Walter was and wasn't.

At other times, she quaked. There would be consequences. No matter how discreet she and Keenan might be, it wouldn't stay hidden. Polly Pry would pry, if only because Cornelia was a Kimbrough. Richard Peabody might cool toward her, be much less inclined to employ her. Keenan, who now was a part of Denver's society, would be shunned by all those powerful dowagers, and he might not like it, might even come to resent it.

But what did it matter? As long as she had her law career, she would have a good life.

CHAPTER 60

Yves Poulenc waited impatiently, certain that a man of his qualifications would be snatched up by one of the Denver newspapers. Journalism would be a snap. He could be an editor, although he supposed politics would enter into that, and some favored old fool would be ahead of him. But he could certainly dash out the opinion pieces and benefit Colorado with his insights. Or they could give him a bylined column. His brush with death had made him deep and sensitive, and he had no doubt that he could fascinate his wide audience with profound insights into life.

A week passed and he heard nothing. Another week edged by, and he was nearing the last of his hundred dollars. Panic gripped him. But then, mercifully, a bicycle messenger arrived at his door with an envelope from the *Post*. Would Mr. Poulenc drop by at once?

Hastily, he parked his beret on his head, got into his lodencloth coat, and tied his floppy green bow tie. He looked dashing, he thought, just the way a newspaper columnist should look. That was what he would insist on. Nothing less. A half-hour interview would persuade them of his erudition and worldliness. He hastened down Cherry Creek, feeling his damaged lungs pump hard, and arrived at the *Post* an hour later. He didn't think much of Bonfils and Tammen's yellow rag, the scarletink scandal sheet of Denver, but he knew he could breathe dignity into it if they gave him the chance. He felt elated. He would show that gaudy P. T. Barnum of a newspaper what a serious man could do.

Breathlessly, he made his way through the grubby double doors and asked to see Angus McQuaid, who was an editor of some sort. A receptionist escorted him through rank, odorous halls to a grimy bullpen jammed with men in shirtsleeves, green eyeshades, and sleeve garters. The smoke of dozens of cigars hung thick. The room was brightly lit with naked electric lights. Many of the gents worked with typing machines, while others scribbled on pads made of newsprint.

Mr. McQuaid occupied a glassed-in cage at one end of this dreary place. Yves' escort pointed, and then left him to his own devices. He made his way toward the cage, past sweaty reporters who worked on stained and burn-scarred old desks, and seemed to be surrounded by a mountain of moldering paper. It was a wonder the whole place didn't go up in flames. Yves coughed gently. The vile smoke would upset his delicate lungs. But of course he wouldn't be a part of this sweaty herd; they would have something better for him.

McQuaid did not inspire him. The man bulged out of his chair, grossly fat and odorous, his neck swelling out of a worn shirt enclosed by a soup-stained cravat. He stared at Yves with lidded gray eyes, as if surveying a hanging beef carcass.

"I'm Yves Poulenc. You sent for me. I'm applying for a managerial position."

McQuaid motioned him in, and offered him a straight-backed wooden chair. "McQuaid. Managing editor. All you'd be managing here is copy and galleys, Poulenc. I need a copyboy."

"What's that?"

"Fellow to run copy. Bring copy from reporters to me or other editors. Take edited copy over to the composing room. Bring back galleys from the composing room for the proofreaders and editors. Return corrected galleys. Run errands for reporters. Get sandwiches and coffee. Stuff like that. You want it?"

A wild indignation flooded through him. "I'd set my sights on something higher," he said stiffly.

McQuaid shrugged. "Your decision. We pay forty a month. If you can proofread, we can divide your job, give you a few hours a week doing that. Don't need a full-time copyboy, but do need some proofreading. I'd go fifty a month if you're a good proofreader. It's not an easy job, and you'd better know your spelling, grammar, and punctuation."

That didn't appeal to Yves much. "How about just hiring me as a proofreader for now, and then when a position opens, putting me into something more suitable?"

McQuaid grunted like a hog. "Nope, that's it. If you want to proofread, I'll have you do a little test."

Bitterly, Poulenc weighed his options. He was almost out of money. In fact, he wasn't sure he could survive until his first paycheck. But of course this would be temporary. He raged at his fate, but bit it back and smiled. "Try me. I'm an accomplished poet."

McQuaid grunted. "Don't tell anyone. You'll be on probation. See if you work out. I can let you go for any reason for a month. All right, here's a few galleys. Proof them. Find an empty desk out there. You know the proofing marks?"

"Ah—"

"You don't. Here's a chart. When you want to delete, you do the delete sign, the loop like that. Get it?" He handed Yves a second chart. "This is a style sheet. Make everything conform to our style. Like the numbers. Spell out below a hundred, numerals for everything above that, and spell out casual numbers."

"What are casual numbers?"

"Read the sheet."

Yves nodded. He hated to admit ignorance.

"I want speed and I'll clock you. You got six galleys there. Show me what you can do. It's eleven-twenty." McQuaid nodded dismissively, and Yves slithered into the ugly newsroom. The place appalled him.

He found a battered oak desk reeking of rotted food, and settled down with the galley proofs. He swiftly discovered that the sticky ink crawled over his hands and shirtsleeves. Worse, the proofs were blurry and hard to read. But he toiled valiantly at the proofing, consulting his chart to find out what marks to employ when a letter was missing, or a capital was needed, or punctuation erred. He came to words whose spelling he questioned, and looked frantically for a Webster's, not seeing one. He realized that had been deliberate: surely a proofreading staff would have all sorts of dictionaries. He toiled away in panic. It amazed him that so many words didn't look right, and he lacked the means to check spellings. Worse, there were words he had never heard of, not even after all his reading. Worse still, he didn't know spellings of Denver street names and buildings and companies.

The whole business agonized him. Sometimes a period was inside quotation marks, sometimes outside. The same with commas. Which was right? He consulted the style sheet. Periods and commas should be inside the quotation marks. Did *Arapahoe* have an *e* on the end? Shouldn't *Cheesman* be spelled with another *e*?

The lunch hour came, but McQuaid didn't budge. A boy—Yves assumed it was a copy runner—brought the fat man two sandwiches in white butcher paper, some giant dill pickles, and a foaming mug of beer.

So they drank beer on the job. It was all true, what he had heard about this boozy fraternity. McQuaid munched his lunch without paying the slightest attention to it. He was reading typing machine copy, making marks on it, sometimes crossing things out.

By the time Yves finished he was flooded with doubts. He had caught a few errors but something told him he had missed many more. In the space of an hour his cockiness had diminished to sullen helplessness. Well, what did they expect from a man who'd been mortally ill all his life? He rose, hating his ink-grimed hands, and took the long galley sheets to McQuaid.

"Ah, ten to one. Not bad," McQuaid said. "Now, let's see."

He pulled out another set of the galley proofs, this one covered with proofing marks, and began a comparison, circling dozens of spellings and other errors that Yves had missed. Yves watched, appalled, as McQuaid's pencil drew more and more circles. Well, he didn't want this vile job in this vile place anyway.

McQuaid finally sat back, eyeing Yves. "Not bad, Poulenc. You're literate. You don't know Denver names, though. I take it you haven't lived here long. You missed, let's see, seventy-three corrections my staff made. That's not as bad as it may seem to you. Proofreading is an art, and requires training and skills, like anything else. I'll give you a try. For a month, you'll be strictly a copyboy. Maybe it's humble, but you'll soon know how a newspaper works. After that, I'll put you on the proofing desk for a while each day. If you're good at it, you can make proofreader. Maybe six months, maybe sooner if you show a flare."

Yves itched to tell this bloated windbag where to take his job, but he swallowed back his bile and nodded.

"All right. Be here at six."

"Six? You mean in the morning?"

"No, at night. You'll get off at four."

"There aren't any day jobs?"

"No, everyone wants a day job except a few night owls. We have openings at night. That's when we put the paper together. You want it or not?"

He didn't, but he nodded. He needed sleep. Didn't McQuaid know how to treat a man just back from the grave? "I'll take it," he said.

McQuaid said, "Don't mess around. The harder you work, the faster you'll go up the ladder. Don't write poetry on company time." He stared steadily at Yves from those hooded eyes. "Don't think this job's beneath you. You barely qualify."

"Yes sir, I understand. Do I start next Monday?"

"Tonight."

"But I'll need sleep—"

"See you at six."

"When do I get paid? I may need an advance."

"Every other Friday." Suddenly McQuaid smiled. "Tough time, eh? If you can't make it, come to me. We can come up with a few bucks if you need 'em. This is a newspaper, not a damned bank."

That grin eased Yves' fears. Everything had been a terror up to that moment. McQuaid wasn't an ogre after all—at least not much of one.

He hastened to his flat, wanting to rest before the ordeal began. He couldn't keep the flat, not even by sharing it with a roommate. He would have to find something near the paper, perhaps one of those dollar-a-day boardinghouses near Union Station. Who could live on forty dollars a month? He had been born to better things, but now his life was a ruin. It would have been better if he had died at Glenwood Springs, if he had never met Maria Theresa Haas with all her nonsensical remedies. Better to be lying peacefully in Riverside Cemetery, an honored poet cut off from the living in his tender years, than to be reminded every minute of his low estate in life. He took no comfort in knowing he would be fed and sheltered because of the miserable little job.

He entered his flat, took all his potions and herbs bitterly, and then lay down to rest and prepare for the humiliating ordeal.

CHAPTER 61

Yves Poulenc discovered a brutal truth within minutes of the time he began his first shift. He was nothing but an errand boy. His task was to run edited copy to the composing room and hand it to the foreman there. And in turn, he was to race galley proofs or page proofs up one story to the proofreaders and editors. Or take reporters' stories to editors. What value was his erudition and his poetry in all this? The work could have been done by an ape. Why did they hire someone with a command of English? He didn't even need to read to perform this task.

He showed up promptly at six and found himself under the thumb of a goateed city editor named Larkin, who called him "boy" and neglected to learn his name or inquire about him.

"Boy, take these to the composing room," Larkin barked. "And any time you see copy on that spindle, you run it down there. Don't wait to be told."

So Poulenc had grabbed the sheets off the spindle and hurried down a flight of grimy stairs to a smoky room where three clattering machines made a racket. He found a likely-looking boss in a bib apron and handed him the copy. The man grunted.

"Boy, don't run off," the man said. So Yves had a chance to examine the new Linotype machines, which could set type much faster than even the fastest hand compositor. Acrid smoke drifted up from hotpots containing molten typemetal that would be cast into slugs, or lines of type, by these rattling monsters. The smoke seared Yves' delicate throat and lungs, and he desperately wanted to get out of there. Eventually that foreman handed him a sheaf of galley proofs, long thin sheets of newsprint containing a column of type printed with sticky black ink.

"All right. You're new. One set to the proofreading room, the other to Larkin."

Thus did Yves hurry back to the newsroom and deposit one set with the editor, and then wandered through various burrows until he found a room where several people sat on high stools under a glaring bulb and read galley proofs that were laid on a slanting surface. Grimy dictionaries, a city directory, and other reference works lay about.

"Boy," said one of them. "Take these downstairs."

So Yves returned to the composing room with the proofed galleys. And then he brought a big page proof up to the editor. This was an image of an entire page, with ruler lines between columns, headlines, woodcuts, and filler material. It amazed Yves that this plant could create a whole paper in a few hours, break it all down, and create an entirely different product the next day. This was no factory producing the same items by the thousands, but a place where each day's product was a custom job, and only a few items, such as nameplates, mastheads, and other standing material, remained the same issue after issue.

"Boy," said a tough-looking reporter. "Fetch me a ham and cheese sandwich at Ma's."

"Ah, where's that?"

"You got brains. You find it," the reporter said wickedly.

Yves hurried into the night, found no restaurant of any sort, but did discover an unnamed saloon on the far corner. He ran in and recognized several newsmen who had been in that big bullpen. Some were eating, but most were downing shots of whiskey raw. A bibulous crowd, he realized.

He ordered the sandwich from an elderly matron, wondering how it would be paid for. She produced it swiftly, wrapped it in butcher paper, and waited.

"It's for—" He couldn't remember the man's name.

"Ten cents," she said, waiting.

"Don't they run a tab?"

She laughed. He decided to pay, and collect from the reporter. Then he scurried back, enjoying the clean air after hours swamped in cigar smoke and acrid fumes, and delivered the sandwich.

"That's ten cents," he said.

"Beat it, punk," the reporter said, enjoying the moment.

"It cost ten cents. I paid."

"Put it on my tab," the reporter said.

Coldly, Yves learned he had been taken, and that this bully had probably taken a lot of new copyboys. Ten cents was a lot out of the dollar and a half he was earning that night. It had been a painful lesson but one well learned. After that, he demanded cash whenever anyone, including the editors, wanted him to run for food or drink or smokes. He revised his low opinion of newsmen down a few more notches. They were a cynical, dishonest, motley bunch.

By the end of that terrible shift at four in the morning, his whole body ached; his lungs hurt more than they had since his illness, and his spirits had dropped as low as they ever got. And yet, as he walked through the darkness out Cherry Creek, he felt a certain pride. He had weathered it. He had earned the first wage money of his life. He walked a little taller knowing that he could do it. Of course he wouldn't stay long, but he could see the value of a few weeks of this sort of thing. In a month he would be a man of the world, a sophisticate about the harsh ways the world worked.

At home, he lit a coal oil lamp and swallowed heavy doses of all those herbal medicines and powders he still took. Then he crawled into bed, wondering whether the oncoming dawn would awaken him. Turning his life around would be exhausting, but he would manage. He'd show his parents a thing or two.

The job grew no easier the next few days. He ran and ran, rarely had a moment to rest, found utterly no future in it, knew he was not mastering any skill, and discovered that unless he took a lunch to work, he would squander much of his precious pay on eating at Ma's. After a week he managed to find a dollar-a-day boardinghouse on the north side and moved into a dark, cramped room that scarcely held his possessions. Hateful as this life was, he at least was afloat. He had room and board, and nine or ten dollars a month to spare.

But what sort of life was this? An errand boy. Was this what his parents intended? Newspapers were loathsome places, seething with hatred, populated by rascals and fakes and power-mad fools. His life consisted of coping with one abrasive wretch after another. They all vented their spleen on the copyboys. If the editors were slow to return a page to the composing room, the copy runners heard about it, usually in blistering terms. And if an edition was late because the composing room had bungled, the copyboys took the heat. Yves seethed, itching to snap back at these petty tyrants and self-important satraps who always blamed others and never admitted they or their shop had failed. But he held himself in check. The prospect of starvation did that, he discovered.

Shortly after four each morning, he threw himself into his bed, too tired to eat. The golden sun sailed by each day, but he was scarcely aware of it. He had entered a world of blackness, a Hades of the living. And yet, even copy running had its moments. Sometimes he shared the excitement of a big breaking story, when almost every reporter on the staff worked feverishly to pull it together before deadline. He discovered he was privy to news before the public heard of it; he knew about fires and robberies and indictments, police raids, scandals, all the steamiest gossip, who was seen with whom, and what the bosses did. Newspapers were whirlpools of secrets and inside knowledge.

He also discovered, as the weeks slipped past, that he had acquired a grasp of newspaper operations. All that running gave him a sense of patterns and flow. He knew how the stories and advertisements were transmuted into print, knew how the lead stories were selected, knew why some advertisers wanted outside pages and other advertisers wanted their ads to be near local news or national news or sports news.

He had even made a few friends, not among the other copyboys, who struck him as cretins, but among the old, savvy reporters and some of the pressmen and compositors. He didn't try to befriend the lofty editors, most of whom regarded him as a worm. He rarely saw Mr. McQuaid, who worked days. But he had good moments at Ma's Saloon with Dan Hope and Mike Lawrence, two veteran newshawks. They talked about the business, and he blotted it up. Little by little, his contempt turned into grudging respect. These men and others like them worked for peanuts, were dedicated to their task, loved to scoop their rivals, loved to needle the other papers, and had an innate sympathy for the down and out, the persecuted, and the humble. Some of them, like Eugene Field over at the *Herald,* won a large and affectionate readership.

His health held up, even though he was stressing his fragile constitution. He forced himself to continue on his herbs and essences and vegetables and fruits, just as he had promised Maria Theresa long before. But he wondered how long he could survive in those smoky confines, how long before the acrid fumes from the Linotypes and stereotyping equipment, along with the thick haze of cigar smoke in the newsroom, destroyed his lungs.

The *Post* had no women employees except in the front office and the proofing room, where two heavyset old empresses with thick spectacles ruled the roost. He eyed them cautiously, knowing that he might be under their thumb soon.

A month came and went with no word from McQuaid, so Yves finally went to work early enough to catch the managing editor and ask about the proofing job.

"How's it goin', boy?" McQuaid asked.

"Yves Poulenc, sir. I'd like to talk a moment."

"Sure, boy. I was just folding up anyway."

"I've been here over a month, and I'd like to start the proofreading you said I could do."

"Did I say that? Guess I did. We get copyboys through here about two or three a month, I think. Yeah, sure. You want to try it?"

"Yes, sir. If that's the route to becoming a reporter."

McQuaid studied him through those hooded eyes. "You got bit. Lots of fellows get bit. It's a helluva profession."

"I didn't know there was so much to it. But I'm eager to learn, sir."

"Who've you been talking to? Lawrence, I bet. He makes chasing around the city looking for court papers and suckers to interview seem like being a silver king. I think he thinks he's the Horace Tabor of the newsroom."

"More like Maurice Barrymore, sir."

McQuaid laughed. "All right, kid. Tonight, report to the proofing room. We'll see whether you know the mother tongue before we turn you loose on a story. I got a dozen copyboys around, and I'll make the switch."

"Thank you, sir. And does this put me at fifty a month?"

"Try me in a coupla days. If Mrs. Hergesheimer doesn't throw you out on your ear, I'll put you at fifty."

Yves Poulenc walked away almost dizzy with gratitude and joy. He hastened to the proofreading warren, where the formidable Mrs. Hergesheimer ruled with an iron hand. She radiated something hard, bitter, iron, and sour. Maybe proofreaders were all frustrated reporters who hadn't made the grade. Or maybe she was simply scornful of this male world.

He explained that Mr. McQuaid had posted him to the proofing desk. She paused, as if reluctant to pull her gaze away from the columns of print before her, and surveyed him acidly.

"Why do you think you can do this?" she asked.

"I'm well educated, madam."

She snorted. "The more bookish they are, the worse they spell. And if you want a disaster in a newsroom, hire a professor. What do you do?"

He was about to say he was a poet, but something stayed him. He realized, in a rush, that he was embarrassed to proclaim himself a poet. He had stopped wearing his black beret soon after starting at the *Post,* because everyone mocked him, and it. And now, suddenly, he knew he would never again mention his poetry.

"After a long illness, I'm starting at the bottom, Mrs. Hergesheimer. I've been a copyboy. Now I'm ready for the next step."

"You're saying proofreading is one step above being a copyboy, is that it?"

Yves panicked. "Oh, no, it's just that—"

"You want to be a reporter. They all do. Well, without proofreaders, reporters and editors look like fools. I've rescued every fancypants reporter and editor on this paper a thousand times from gross mistakes, libels, slanders, obscenities, embarrassments you wouldn't believe. We're the most valuable people on the paper. A good proofreader is priceless, irreplaceable. You got that? Don't let me catch you scorning the most important function on this paper. Now sit down over there and start in. I'll have to redo everything you do, and you'll double my work."

"I hope I can prove myself, madam."

"Well, we'll see," she said.

CHAPTER 62

Rose Edenderry stayed. The Anglican sisters nursed her back to health, and never pressured her to join them or abandon her own religion. Her supply of clothing grew mysteriously. One day she discovered a worn but usable coat. Another day a gray dress appeared. Then a nightgown. Castoffs, maybe, but treasures for Rose, who had nothing. One day a small white missal appeared at her bedside. She opened it and discovered it was a Roman one. It mattered to the Holy Cross sisters that Rose recover her faith, but it didn't matter to them whether it was the Roman or Anglican sort.

She found herself living in a chapter house, not a convent. This was an ordinary home, occupied by four of the sisters, most of whom were gone each day doing parish work. But Rose was rarely alone in the house. Lay women came each day, sometimes to be taught, other times to sew and repair castoff clothing, other times to prepare for holy days and feasts. Rose decided she would not lift a finger to help the heretics worship, but she could repay other ways. She gravitated to the kitchen and quietly scrubbed pots, boiled potatoes, and lightened the load of whoever was there. Other times she scrubbed laundry over a washboard and hung up the clothing. This was purely female society, and she didn't mind it.

She could leave at any time, and they had even given her the clothing she might need to tackle the Denver winter. She certainly was tempted. The place was dull. She made no friends and dreamed of going back to a more exciting world. She ached for some hop, ached for a good shot of whiskey or three, ached to be serving in a saloon full of cheerful men, uproars, and sly pats on her behind as she brought a tray of drinks. Some nights she lay in her cot craving the wild life again. But always, the remembrance of her cold and fever and nausea and filth stayed her. She ached for that wild world, but it was poison. If she went back, it would kill her.

But what was life for, anyway? Restlessly, she wandered about the house, exchanging politenesses with the sisters or their lay colleagues, talking about weather or snow on the mountains or the bishop's plans, or the failure of Denver to provide for its homeless and destitute. Rose sighed, not exactly hating it, but almost. Boredom laced each hour of each day. She took to hiking around Denver, sometimes even walking past the sporting district on Market and Blake streets just to see a lot of men having a high time. The acrid smell of stale beer hit her at every door, and she ached to go in and kid with the men and maybe cadge a beer. She didn't have a cent. But in the end, she always returned to the chapter house. She didn't think her weakened body could stand wild times again.

Nights were the bad time. What was she doing in this pallid place, full of pasty women? Her several lovers paraded through her mind, and she remembered their passions and her own desires, which rose unbanked in her. She loved the jokes, and being in the middle of everything, and the raw power that pulsated in the saloons each night. She remembered the peace of the opium pipe, and the heightened sensations she got from the cocaine, and the bawdy humor, and the sense of being utterly aglow with living. She remembered the delicious feeling of being a rebel, bound to nothing, subservient to no man, embracing no ideal. She was her father's daughter, a wild creature who couldn't be tamed.

Ah, God, if only she could have some sort of life again, instead of this—porridge.

The sisters were praying for her. They had converted a parlor into a chapel and often gathered there, either just themselves or with a minister. Or was he a priest? Heaven only knew. He was a minister dressed like a priest, maybe. Praying for her! She laughed, knowing that all the king's priests and all the king's nuns couldn't put Rose Edenderry together again. Still, in tender moments, she loved them, especially Sister St. George, who simply smiled, offered something cheerful in passing, and left Rose to her own devices.

Life dragged. She needed a man.

That spring day, when nature was bursting with new life and her own needs flowed like a river through her, she hiked one evening back to the district and meandered through saloons. It didn't take long before some galoot bought her a mug of draft beer. Oh, that tasted good. She laughed and told jokes and got a few more mugs, feeling better and better. Some rotten little voice warned her to go back to the chapter house, but she resisted. To hell with all those prunes. This was better. She was alive again. She liked the galoot, a red-haired brute from the smelters named Roman somebody or other. He eyed her with lust in his hooded eyes, and that tickled her. She would have a whale of a time tonight.

Three mugs later he took her to his rooming house, and she was out of her clothes before he even had his shirt unbuttoned. Oh, that was good. She had a grand time with the big oaf.

"Hey, Rosie, you want to move in with me?" he asked.

She nodded.

"I can't afford to take care of you. Mind if I share you with another bucko? We could keep you and you could stay here."

"Sure, Roman. I'd like that. Only I want more stuff than that. I want some good booze and some treats, and some nice clothes instead of these rags. I want to turn every head in a club when we walk in, all right?"

"Yeah, Rosie, but we'd have to share you a little. Is that all right?"

Rose pondered that. She had never been an easy girl before. That would be pretty much like being on Market Street. "Maybe three," she said, doubtfully. "Come on, Roman, you falling asleep on me?"

She didn't return to the sisters.

In the morning he gave her a whole dollar and went off to the smelter. He said he'd bring the other jockos around that evening.

He sure had a crummy room. Colorless dark walls, a tiny window, a miserable lumpy little bed, a wash stand with a pitcher and basin, no kitchen, and the little toilet at the end of the hall. She should get out and go back to the sisters. That was a nicer place even if they were all poor, too. But a dollar would buy her ten beers, or five beers and lunch and supper if she stopped at a grocery for some bread or something.

She yawned, catlike, her body satiated for once. This wasn't so bad. She was on her own. These dudes would take care of her and she had a warm place and food and lots to drink. Sister St. George faded from mind, and she pushed aside the brush with death that had taken her there. But it didn't quite seem right. These knuckleheads could get tired of her and boot her out, and then what would she do? Or she could get sick again and die, and who would care? The sisters cared. They would weep if she died. She hadn't ever had a friend who would weep if she died. She sighed, unable to make sense of anything, and slept through the gorgeous spring day.

That evening she met Janos and Nils, both of them serious, burly men like Roman. Each had a room near Roman, one across the dim hall, the other down the hall. Janos spoke no English, but Nils had managed to master the tongue and usually spoke for Janos. They were all millmen with the Argo smelter. And they wanted her. She thought about that uneasily as the evening progressed. This was new, and a step downward. She didn't fool herself about that. It was one thing to be a tinhorn's girl and make a living of her own serving drinks; quite another to become a slut.

Roman watched carefully, as she sipped the beer they had brought her. "You don't like this, eh?" he said.

"I don't know."

"We ain't wild. We're three workingmen. We're not gonna do wild stuff or nothing. No parties. We just want a good woman, and we can't afford much. But we'll take care of you."

She nodded, suddenly too disturbed to say what was on her mind. She didn't want three lovers each night. "I just want you, Roman," she said, warily.

He smiled, something hard and male and powerful in the expression. "I just want you, Rose," he said. "But I got no money. They don't pay nothing to a millman. How about, you live with me one day, live with Janos the next day, like that?"

"I don't know . . ."

He grinned again, like a warm sun. "Okay, you go live where you want, and we come visit you. Just us three, no one else."

She shook her head. "I just want a good time." She smiled at him intimately. They were sharing memories.

He shrugged. "Room empty down there. Five dollars a week, cheap, not bad. You have your own room, and we come visit you."

"I gotta get going," she said. "I got my own home."

Roman shook his head, knowingly. He was a sophisticated devil, she thought. He saw right through her.

He got up. "Wait here," he said. "I'll go rent that room."

"I don't do it for money. I just like you, Roman."

He patted her hair and left, motioning two friends to come with him. When they returned, they had the skeleton key to the room down the hall, and had worked something out between them.

"Here, this here's your key. You gotta room now, and we'll come visit."

"Roman, I can't, I'm a proper lady."

He grinned. "You go get a job on Blake Street serving drinks. Then you got food and stuff. We'll pay for your room, okay?"

"I don't know that they'll hire me. I got—" She clammed up. Word had gotten around that she was a drunk and unreliable. But oh! It would be grand to be making tips and having a good time again. She smiled. "I'll get a job," she said.

And that was how her new life began. Memories were short on Blake Street, and she found ready employment in the Empress of Denver Saloon, and she had a free place to live, and three millmen who came to her whenever they felt like it. It was all right. She didn't drink a whole lot—it scared her. She stayed away from hop, too, at least at first. But once in a while she got something to sniff when things were crummy.

Her three men sure were different, and one of them, Janos, seemed angry all the time. She was glad no one else knew about her arrangement. Funny, she didn't recognize anyone. In the four months she had been in the chapter house, a whole crowd of Blake Street sports had come and gone.

It went well enough for a couple of months, until one day she had some sort of sore right where it hurt when she made love.

CHAPTER 63

he doctor, Anna Berger, was a matronly dark-haired woman who seemed to know everything there was to know about Rose, and to disapprove. Rose dreaded this examination and fought back waves of shame, desperation, guilt, and despair. She knew what Dr. Berger was going to find.

"All right, then, Mrs. Edenderry, you may disrobe behind that screen. There's a sheet you may use if you wish."

Moments later, Rose found herself on an examining table, clutching the sheet, feeling hot embarrassment crawl over her while the doctor pulled thick yellow India rubber gloves over her hands. The silent doctor hovered over her while Rose fought back tears.

When at last the doctor withdrew, Rose clutched the sheet about her violated body. The woman pulled off the thick rubber gloves and washed her hands in a bowl.

"You have first-stage syphilis, Mrs. Edenderry," the woman said matter-of-factly. "That's a classic chancre, eroded in the middle with a sharp border. There's another higher up. There may be more at the cervix."

Rose felt a new rush of shame.

The doctor smiled suddenly, an unexpected blessing that lit the little gray examining room. "There's a good chance we can cure you," she said.

"Oh, please God yes," Rose replied, this time unable to stop the tears. "I'll do anything you say."

"We'll talk about that later. Let me tell you a little about this disease. These chancres will heal over in a few weeks even if we do nothing, and you'll think everything is fine. But it won't be fine. You'll be carrying the disease in its latent stage. Then one day you'll find it has spread to various places in your body. It will start doing a lot of damage."

Rose wept. What was a wee lass born in an innocent thatched cottage in County Offaly doing here, with this shameful disease? How had she betrayed herself, her blessed mother, the church, and God?

"In the secondary stage there are various types of skin lesions, especially around the shoulders and upper arms. Another type develops on the face and palms and soles of your feet. Sores can develop around your eyes and ears. The ear infections may destroy your hearing. Others may develop upon your bones. Other sores can develop in your spine and nervous system. You may suffer malaise and headaches. If the infection reaches your brain you may suffer confusion, or seizures. The disease can weaken your arteries and heart. It will attack your mouth, throat, tonsils, genitals, anus . . . It can cause anemia. It can enlarge your spleen."

Rose wept.

"Mrs. Edenderry, we can stop this, I think. I did want you to know what happens if you don't act. There are often spontaneous cures. The body throws off the disease or keeps it in a latent stage. But there is a third stage, and it can be terrible."

Rose felt shattered.

The doctor reached over and took Rose's hand. "I know how you feel, Mrs. Edenderry," she said, holding the hand firmly. "It's good to feel that way. Now we'll do what we can. I want you to go urinate first."

Rose did that, and when she returned Dr. Berger had a douche ready. Rose endured that, clenching her fists, aching, weeping with the shame of it. All she knew was that the doctor was washing her, cleansing her thoroughly, swabbing something around her private parts. "This is a solution of a silver chemical I'm applying," the doctor said.

Rose swallowed back her despair. Maybe the doctor could help her after all.

"All right, Mrs. Edenderry, I want you to put on this rubber glove. I'm going to inject a solution of mercury bichloride, a lot of it, and when I'm done I want you to hold it in with your hand for five minutes. Press hard. The solution must stay in long enough to kill the syphilitic organisms."

Rose endured that, but she wished she were dead. She lay there mortified, desolated and helpless.

"This is going well," the doctor said. "You're doing just fine. Now we have one or two more steps. It's not so bad, is it? I'm going to douche away the mercury solution with ordinary water, and then I'm going to apply a calomel ointment to your parts and leave it there for about ten minutes. While we're waiting, I want to talk to you about the future."

The doctor proceeded through the rest of the treatment, and then settled into her swivel chair.

"Now then, I think you'll recover quite nicely. You were wise to come early. I know it took courage. I admire courage." She paused. "What are we going to do about your husband?"

"Oh—"

"He's no doubt infected you, and unless he obtains treatment, he'll infect you again. Over and over. Can you talk to him about this? Would you like me to talk to him? Can you bring him here? Or if he prefers a male doctor, I can arrange it."

"Oh, ah, I'll ask."

"Mrs. Edenderry, do you think you can resist him when he comes to you? Will he come to an understanding? Some men are very forceful, and if he's like that, why . . . you'll be back where you started, maybe worse off."

Rose began weeping again, unable to reply.

"Do you need to be away from your home for a while? I can arrange for a refuge, I think."

"Oh, Dr. Berger . . . I'll figure it out. I'll do something."

"The best thing you can do is talk him into treatment. That's hard. Some men are very proud. I tell you what. I'll write a note and you can give it to him."

"Oh, no, I'll—I'll tell him."

"You must. This disease is a public plague." The doctor eyed the pocket watch dangling from a necklace. "All right. You can get dressed now. I don't want you to wash or urinate for five hours, though. And I want to see you again in two weeks."

Numbly, Rose dressed and paid Dr. Berger out of the tips she had accumulated.

"We may have to do this again. But I think it's licked." The doctor sent Rose on her way with one of her rare smiles.

Rose stood in the sun, blinking, wounded by all the light. It was as if the harsh sunlight were the flame of God, exposing her and her disease. Surely the whole world knew.

She hastened back to her rooming house, knowing a phase of her life had ended that morning. The men were all at the smelter. She hadn't the faintest idea whether the sickness had come from Roman, Nils, or Janos, or all three. Shakily she packed her few belongings into a carpetbag, and walked away from that life and those men. She wondered whether to leave a note telling them they were diseased, but something told her just to flee, flee, and never be seen in that quarter again.

She stood in the harsh light, in a harsh city, and hadn't the faintest idea where to go. Something in her rebelled at going back to the Anglican nuns. She felt shamed; she felt covered with filth, like a hog in muck. She couldn't face them, no matter how gentle and forgiving and kind they might be. Her secret would torment her there. Don't touch me, Sister St. George! I'm a syphilitic!

Where could a diseased woman go? Ah, God, why was she alive? Why had she ever strayed? Why had she surrendered to every lust and vice? What had become of the innocent girl of long ago? What awful future awaited her now? She might drive this sin-disease from her body, but what of the syphilis of her soul? Ah, God, what a mess.

She drifted south, away from the district where millmen resided, away from the sporting district along Blake, driven by a terror in her. She passed Eleventh, and discovered St. Elizabeth's there. She knew it had a German congregation, but many Irish belonged in the parish too. She wandered in, found no one in the quiet nave, and settled upon a hard pew to decide her fate. She had passed beyond tears. Light played through stained-glass windows.

How could she return to grace? She wasn't sure she wanted to. She had often raged at the church, just as her father had raged at it. Soon someone would discover her and make her go away. Or worse, listen to her spill her troubles through a grille in a sacramental act. Did God exist? How could she know? She couldn't pray. What would God do to a woman with a vile disease in her belly? Still, she ached to pray, even if she couldn't. She ached to pray and shake her fist at Him at the same time.

She sat in the hard pew until she had rested, and then wandered into an administrative area, looking for someone. If only someone would tell her what to do.

She didn't hear the priest.

"You've come for the job, have ye?" asked the voice behind her. She whirled, finding herself facing a young, red-faced broth of a dominie.

"A job? I didn't know there was one, I didn't—"

"Well, what county do I hear, madam?"

"Oh—none. I'm not from anywhere."

"Well, that's a novelty. Is it a need you have that you're here?"

"No—no, I just needed to rest. I'll be going now."

"Going where? Forgive my curiosity."

"Nowhere."

"Ah, a lady from nowhere, returning to nowhere. Ye look like ye might need to set a spell. Would ye like a cup of good tea? Mind you, I'm a poor man to make talk. When it came to giving me a gift of blarney, I was left at the doorstep."

"Yes, oh yes. Perhaps you could tell me about this job. Maybe I'd be interested."

"Well, of course. It's not here. Not for the church. But one of our wealthy parishioners needs a maid, and he wants someone from the parish."

"That lets me out."

"Ah, maybe not. You could always join. He's the flour miller, John Mullen, and one of his servants is leaving him to get married, and he's looking to replace her. He's a good man, a leader in the temperance movement. Won't abide a drop of liquor in his house."

"Oh, one of those."

"I'm Terence O'Boyle, and who are you, eh?"

"Oh, I'm not anybody. I'm not qualified. I shouldn't even walk into the house of such a man."

He paused, something tender and gentle in his red face.

Then she was crying and couldn't stop, and the tears rolled hotly down her cheeks. She wanted to flee, but she wanted to stay, too.

"Let's go in here and have us some tea, Miss Nobody from Nowhere, and I've got a few handkerchiefs on hand for a lovely lady who needs one."

"I shouldn't even be here!" she cried.

"Everyone should be here," he said, steering her gently into a quiet study.

CHAPTER 64

orenzo the Magnificent was feeling testy. He deplored this fault in himself, but the whole world had gone mad and needed correcting. People were pretending not to know who he was. Just that morning, feeling the need of a shave, he had entered a tonsorial parlor and had himself shaved and shorn. But the barber refused to let him sign the tab.

"It's thirty-five cents, bub, or off you go to the stationhouse. I'll not be took."

"Don't be absurd. Send it to my office," Lorenzo said. "I'll sign it and be done with it."

"Stiffing me, are you? Well, I'll get a copper."

"My dear fellow, I'll make sure that your bank hears about this rudeness," Lorenzo said. "I'm Lorenzo the Magnificent."

"I don't care if you're Jesus Christ," the barber retorted, and began to drag Lorenzo toward the constabulary. But he yanked free, dusted off his dinner jacket, and huffed away amidst the curses of the oafish barber.

Irksome. This sort of barbarism had been happening more and more. People pretended they had never heard of him. Hadn't he been in all the papers, day after day, his glory and genius made known to all of Colorado? Just yesterday he had discovered that his boiled white shirt had become grimy about the collar and ragged at the cuffs. That was unthinkable. So he had found a tailor on Wyncoop Street and engaged the man to sew up three more shirts, and do some black ties while he was at it. But the tailor wanted a deposit.

"Yes, of course, send the invoice to my office," he said. "I'm Lorenzo."

"I'm afraid, sir, I don't know who you are."

"Lorenzo the Magnificent, of Leadville, Silverton, Telluride, and Denver. I'll take my custom elsewhere."

"Perhaps you should," the spindly old tailor said.

Of course not everyone was so rude. He had discovered a certain restaurant, and had favored it with his patronage for several weeks. They knew him there, and gladly let him sign his name to the dinner checks. Last night had been typical. He had wandered in around eight. He usually wouldn't patronize a place so plebeian, but they relished his favors, and so there had been mutual esteem.

"Howdy, Magnificent," said the proprietor, Mr. Worcester. "Be right with you."

In short order, Worcester delivered a fine, steaming mug of coffee and the plate du jour, which is what Lorenzo always ordered. He was tempted to suggest little improvements, such as a pinch of thyme, or a dash of rosemary, or a bit of sage, but he refrained. He enjoyed his stays at the Marlinespike Restaurant, because his presence there always excited a crowd of gawkers. Whenever Lorenzo the Magnificent showed up, a dozen people followed him in, just to watch him eat, which he did daintily and with great dignity. These people all ate too, while watching him and whispering, and enjoying the sight of the most famous entrepreneur and genius and partygiver and social lion in Colorado. Thus did he eat in public, sometimes annoyed by all the attention. At the conclusion of each repast, he thanked Professor Worcester, as the man fashioned himself, and signed the check, writing "Lorenzo" with a great flourish. Such was the fame of that name that Mr. Worcester swiftly auctioned it off, often for more than the tab was worth.

Sad to say, sleeping had been rather another matter, and some obnoxious fools had pretended not to know his bona fides, and wouldn't accept his signature. So crass was Denver that it had sometimes compelled him to sleep on park benches. But even when the knaves at the front desks refused to acknowledge the presence of Lorenzo the Magnificent in their hotels, he found that his fame was well known to maids and bellboys, who led him down corridors and into empty rooms, all unseen by the managers and clerks. He always blessed them with his signature on a piece of blank paper. Such was his fame that people all over Denver strove to collect his signature, and some even had four or five of them. One maid at the American House had acquired five before a dense manager discharged her.

Odd how his own class scorned him, while humble people everywhere celebrated his triumphant life. How often he was stopped on the street by people who wished to converse with him, or discover his wisdom about some mining stock or another. He dealt kindly with these people. It was all noblesse oblige, his desire to do whatever favors he could for the world's less fortunate people. So whenever they accosted him, he would listen carefully, allude now and then to this or that fortune he had acquired, and explain how he did it. He delighted in the joy in their eyes when they learned of his feats, and many of them promised him they would seek their own fortunes in the same manner, inspired by his awesome story.

He loved to wander Denver, wearing his black velvet opera cape, his dinner jacket, boiled white shirt, black silk top hat, and black trousers. Wherever he went, people nudged one another, or pointed, or whispered. What could be better proof of his reputation? He encouraged them all, sometimes with a sweeping bow. One day someone even showed him a piece by that *Post* gossip woman Polly Pry, describing Magnificent's magnificence on the boulevards of Denver. He was a legend at last.

Whenever his clothes grew tattered, he headed for the most elegant clothiers in town, most of them in the Tabor Opera House, and serenely ordered whatever he needed.

"Yes, sir, Magnificent," the obsequious clerks would say, and produce a new dinner jacket, or a bow tie, or a fresh silk topper.

"I'll just sign it, and you send it to my office, and they'll take care of you," he said, upon picking up a shirt or a new pair of shoes or a walking stick.

"Of course, of course, your signature's good as gold," they would reply.

All that was fine, but the occasional rudeness he encountered among hack drivers and others of that ilk continued to plague him. His most abysmal defeats came from barbers, operators of Turkish baths, and the proprietors of the Windsor Hotel, who chased him into the streets whenever he set foot in their establishment. It was an indignity, but he knew that one in his position had to be patient with lesser people. He had been poor once, and knew the sting and frustration of it.

One of his favorite recourses was the Denver Mining Exchange, where he repaired most every weekday afternoon to build his fortunes. He usually swept in around one, pulled off his opera cloak, set aside his silk stovepipe hat, and studied the day's action as prices were chalked onto boards and scrubbed away.

His favored broker these days was a new man, Arnold von Trapp, a gentleman with a spiked mustache who hastened over to Magnificent and waited to take the order.

"Von Trapp, buy ten thousand shares of Colorado Milling and Mining, on my account. Don't pay more than thirteen and an eighth for it. Got that?"

"Yes, sir," von Trapp said, and hurried away.

Then, some while later, von Trapp would return. "I got your ten thousand for an even thirteen," he might say. "Now, sign here. It comes to a hundred thirty thousand plus my commission."

"Why, yes, certainly. Send it to my office."

This was such a pleasant ceremony, this signing, that half the exchange gathered around to watch. Such was Lorenzo's great stature that even the most senior traders paused to witness this ceremony. Of course, this was most flattering, and he smiled at them all as he signed "Magnificent" with a flourish of the nib, and handed the accounting back to von Trapp.

"Where am I now, von Trapp?" he usually asked.

"Why, sir, I believe you are eleven million one hundred and forty-eight thousand ahead."

"Yes, yes, send it all to my office," he would reply. "They're very good with the ledgers."

"Got any tips for us?" asked a young man.

"Oh, let me think awhile. Some days I'd just as soon not put a young fellow like you at risk."

The miracle was that he never lost. Whatever he purchased simply made money. It was such a heady feeling to have that touch, and that is why the brokers always crowded about each day. Eleven million dollars made him one of the richest men in the country, and he found great peace and comfort in it. He intended to will it all to charity.

Eighteen eighty-six sailed by splendidly, and he enjoyed life as never before. His routine rarely varied, although with the coming of autumn he began to feel the chill. Sometimes an obnoxious constable chased him out of a park. Once he was accosted by hooligans, who wanted his purse.

"I'm Lorenzo the Magnificent," he retorted, and they skulked away, defeated by his very name. That, too, had been a heady experience.

With the advancing cold he began to think it was time to rent a suite at the Windsor, perhaps the one the Tabors had lived in. Yes, he would do that. One icy day he walked along the boulevards to the great hostelry, swept through the familiar lobby, boarded the elevator, announced his destination on the seventh floor, and was duly deposited there. Ah, yes, a fine floor, reserved just for people like himself. Gilded cornices lined the walls, doors with golden knobs lined the lushly carpeted hallway.

Of course the door to his suite was open. Sun poured into the hallway. He entered the suite, peered about, and settled on the Louis Quinze sofa. He waited for whoever was in the other room to emerge. When, eventually, a lady did appear, she was perfectly familiar to him.

"Magnificent!" cried Dixie.

"Why, my dear, I was just going to invite you to dinner. But here you are," he replied. "I'm glad you could come."

"Come?"

"To my suite. I suppose you've one across the hall. How's the Cotton enterprise coming?"

She studied him a moment. "Just fine. Actually, I don't live here. I have my own place about nine blocks away."

"Well, you should be here. Did you just drop by to see me?"

She seemed slow-witted this afternoon, and he wondered why.

"I heard you were in town. I'm working here in the hotel. If you'll wait here about an hour, we'll go to my place for dinner. All right? I want to hear all about what you're doing."

"I never turn down the invitation of a beautiful woman, Dixie," he replied.

"I'll be with you soon, Magnificent. I have a little more work to do."

Much to his astonishment, she began running a carpetsweeper over the rug. "Have they no help, Dixie?" he asked. "Help's so unreliable these days."

"Oh, I don't mind doing it."

"Well, you should hire it done," he said.

An hour later she escorted him into the hall, locked the door to the suite, and led him across town to her little flat.

"Why, Dixie, with your fortune you could afford better," he said, after she let him in.

She smiled. "I share it with two friends, Clara and Sissy," she said. "They'll be along in a minute. We all work at the Windsor."

"You're set for life. You must work just because it pleasures you."

"No, Magnificent. I don't have a cent."

"Well, my dear, let me write you a draft for a hundred thousand. I've more than I know what to do with."

"That's mighty fine of you, but I'm getting along all right. I'm going to have my own restaurant some day. I think that'd be fun."

"A restaurant? A fine, blue-chip chophouse?"

"No, just a beanery for working stiffs."

"We'll start a chophouse. Best steaks in Denver. Truffles and beaujolais and asparagus."

"It's a dream, isn't it. Meanwhile, you just park yourself there, and let me fix up some potatoes."

"Send it to my office," he said. "They'll take care of it."

All that afternoon, Dixie's understanding of Lorenzo the Magnificent had advanced in small, tender shocks. As she prepared the simple supper of Polish sausage, cabbage, and potatoes, she eyed him quietly. He looked somehow grand, even though a week of beard stubbled his face and his unkempt hair lay matted on his head. Something larger than life, something noble radiated from him, even though his tuxedo was smudged and his boiled white shirt had yellowed around the collar and the French cuffs were grimy. A magical dignity radiated from him as he surveyed this world, seeing and yet not seeing her and her humble flat and the tawdriness of her life.

Clara and Sissy walked in, and instantly turned shy in the presence of this apparition in their humble world.

"I want you to meet Lorenzo the Magnificent," Dixie said. "These are my roommates, Clara and Sissy," she explained. "Lorenzo has made many fortunes. He's a mining genius. But he's best known for his hospitality. He's entertained almost everyone in the world at his estate, and his parties are famous."

"Gee," said Clara, unable to say more. They studied him as if he were an alien, seeing his unkempt attire, yet seeing also that bright, magical glory in him.

"Well, uh, welcome," simpered Sissy.

"Delighted, my dears. How exquisitely you've prepared this repast, and how I rejoice in your distinguished company," Magnificent replied, gravely shaking the hand of each.

Clara and Sissy fled to the kitchen, unable to cope, and in a few minutes they had set the battered table with Clara's chipped and cracked service, hotel castoffs mostly, and extracted a spare chair from the rear bedroom. Then, shyly, they invited him to his place at the end of the table.

He took his place graciously, and when they had settled he grasped the glass of water before him and arose.

"A little toast," he said, surveying them with bright burning eyes. "Mr. President, senators, governors, distinguished guests, ladies and gentlemen. It is my profound pleasure this memorable evening to toast the most admirable of all women, the mining entrepreneur, legendary beauty, wondrous philosopher, and princess of all she surveys, Madame Dixie Cotton.''

"Ball, Lorenzo. I never married that son of a gun.''

"Ah, a faux pas, forgive me. Distinguished guests, Miss Ball is the queen of all womanhood, the Aphrodite of mental accomplishment, the Venus of beauty, a triumphant rival of all the greatest women in history, Cleopatra, Saint Mary, Helen of Troy, Queen Elizabeth, Florence Nightingale, Joan of Arc, Juliet—why, I could go on and on, but Mr. President, members of the Cabinet, it is time for us to enjoy this splendid repast, the feast that will be forever remembered by gourmands such as yourselves, and this rare company gathered here this remarkable autumn day of eighteen and eighty-six.'' Lorenzo bowed graciously, hearing something unknown to Dixie, Clara, and Sissy, smiled radiantly, and sat down.

"Gee,'' said Clara.

They ate in silence, marked only by furtive glances at the exotic creature who supped delicately at their table. At the conclusion, Magnificent stood, smiled, donned his black velvet opera cape, and announced his departure.

"But where will you go?'' Dixie asked.

"I have the Tabor Suite at the Windsor,'' he said. "But sometimes they forget to give me the key.''

"If they forget to give you the key, you come back here.''

Clara looked horrified, but Dixie ignored her.

"Oh, they always come around. So many ignorant people these days,'' he said testily.

"How can I get ahold of you?''

"My dear Miss Ball, every weekday afternoon I can be found at the Denver Mining Exchange, trading. I'm up to eleven million eight hundred thousand, you know. Arnold von Trapp—my broker—is a genius, but I do the selecting.''

On that note he vanished into the night. Dixie wondered if a man dressed like that would make it through her tough neighborhood without getting into trouble. God help old Magnificent.

During the next weeks he showed up at odd moments, always unexpectedly, sometimes when she was cleaning a room at the Windsor, other times at her doorstep, once in a while when she and other maids were resting in an alcove next to the hotel laundry, relishing a few minutes off their feet. Sometimes he looked numb with the deepening cold, but other times he seemed warm and comfortable. Occasionally he showed up shaved and clean and immaculately groomed. More often he appeared begrimed and odorous. He had become the wonder of the chambermaid staff. At first he frightened the women, but in time they came to love him, and helped him edge in and out of the great old hotel without being collared by managers.

It was down there, in that basement alcove, that he heard more about Dixie's dream of owning a restaurant.

"Why, Miss Ball, my dear, you must have the grandest place in Colorado, French cuisine, truffles, fine red wines, a gypsy violinist . . . Call it the Champs Élysées Cotton Club. We'll bring in a maître d' from France. I'll make sure it's known to everyone in Colorado."

"But all I want is a beanery up in Globeville for working stiffs. Steak and eggs. I just love to be around good, strong men. I slung a lot of hash for my brothers and pa, and I'd love to lay a good plate of potatoes and gravy and beef before these hungry men. But I can't."

"What do you mean, you can't?"

"It'd cost me maybe five hundred for a barebones place—you know, all the service, food, some used dining tables. A thousand would be better. I just can't. I spend every cent I earn."

"I don't understand it," he said. "You've a fortune from the Cotton mine."

"No, Lorenzo."

"Oh, yes, you've mentioned that. My dear Dixie, you just let me have a talk with my broker. He keeps telling me that any day now I'll be able to draw on my fortune. Those people in the office keep mishandling the paper."

She smiled. "That'd be nice."

The next day, a bitter one in December, he materialized in the Windsor basement again.

"Here now, Dixie, you can start up the Champs Élysées," he said, and pressed ten hundred-dollar federal bank notes into her hand.

She was frightened. "Where did this come from?"

"Trust old Magnificent," he said.

"Lorenzo, I don't want this money."

"Tut tut, my dear. I was at the exchange yesterday, bidding on some Denver Traction shares—that's Kimbrough's company, you know, and they're going electric soon. I tried to get von Trapp to give me a thousand from my account, but he said he couldn't just then. But there was Horace Tabor himself, listening to all this, so I told him about his very own partner in the Tall Cotton in need of a temporary infusion, and next thing I knew, Hod was peeling hundreds off a roll he kept in his pocket. And here you are.''

"Hod Tabor?''

"Himself.''

"Are you sure? When does he want it back?''

"It's all yours, Miss Ball.''

Impulsively she thrust a hundred at him. "You take this. You can use it. Nine hundred'll buy me a wonderful restaurant. It's a dream come true,'' she said.

He stared at the greenback in her hand. "What would I do with that miserable thing? I've eleven million. I never carry cash. I just sign, and my office takes care of it.''

"Please take it. You could buy a new tuxedo and a winter coat.''

"Trifles,'' he retorted.

She sighed. Mad as he was, Lorenzo Carthage was magnificent in his own way, and she adored him. What a grand, brave spirit still flourished within that bosom. "You're going to be my first customer, Lorenzo,'' she said.

But even as she examined those amazing ten bills, her vision grew. She knew she would immediately look for her own flat, and there would be a room for Lorenzo in it. She would take him in, no matter how distant the shores of his life.

"Ah, God, Magnificent, we'll have a partnership,'' she said.

"Why yes, Dixie. I envision a great restaurant in every capital of the world, patronized by princes of the blood and rich men's mistresses and their poodles.''

She laughed. Her dear Lorenzo.

During the next days she scoured the humble, crowded neighborhoods two miles north of central Denver where she wanted to start her café, and finally discovered an empty store that would work perfectly. She leased it, rented a flat nearby, purchased a used stove and other kitchen equipment from a supplier, employed a carpenter to build booths and counters and all the rest. She decided to call the place "Dixie's'' and hired a painter to put the name on the front above the door. She found time to buy some used hotel service, assorted chairs, a giant icebox, and all the rest. Between her maid's rounds at the Windsor she found moments to talk to the suppliers and drummers who came to the hotel, and arranged for regular deliveries of groceries.

Then one day she gave the Windsor a week's notice, which surprised Maxcy Tabor.

"I'm sorry you're leaving, Miss Ball. I had hopes you'd become our chief of services some day."

"Gonna work for myself, Mr. Tabor," she said.

One January day she said good-bye to Clara and Sissy and moved to the new flat near the smelters, a tiny place but one with a little room for Lorenzo. She took him there the next time he showed up.

He peered about the humble place, his eyes bright.

"This is your room. It's no suite at the Windsor, but it's all yours. You can keep it as long as you want. It sounds to me like you're having a little trouble getting cash out of your stockbroker, so I thought I'd just fix you up."

"Why, my dear Dixie, look at this place. It's a Taj Mahal. It surpasses the Tabor suite. See the walnut wainscoting. Ah, the crystal chandelier! Oh, my, observe that wash stand with the Sèvres china. Yes, this is most acceptable. Now if you'll just let me sign, they'll take care of it."

"Sure," she said. She thrust a paper and a battered old pencil at him, and he signed in a great flourish.

"You just send this to my office," he said.

"All right, Lorenzo. Here's a key. Now come with me. I'm gonna try a trial run tonight, and you're going to be my first customer."

She took him down the street to Dixie's, and led him into the gleaming, unadorned workingmen's beanery, which was poised to open the next day.

"Oh, a chophouse to end all chophouses, with Escoffier himself cooking," he said. "Decorated like a French bistro. Why, we're in Paris. A veritable trencherman's paradise, a solace for the lovelorn, a cornucopia of spices, a place where great men will gather to do deals."

"I don't know who Escoffier is, but it's just me in the apron. And you're getting beef and noodles and an apple pie for dessert. See what you think of 'em. And be honest. I want my stuff to please the smelter crowd."

She started some coffee and began the first of her daily menus while he sat and rubbed his hands.

He devoured her food, his face a field of dreams.

"Ah, Dixie, you've outdone yourself. This elegant repast tops Antoine's in New Orleans. This little feast beats Maxim's in Paris. Word of your genius will spread from one end of the world to the other."

"You really think so?"

"I do. Just send the tab to my office," he said.

CHAPTER 66

. . . .

ichard Peabody looked acutely uncomfortable sitting on the other side of the desk, and Cornelia wondered what the bad news was going to be. She had never seen him like this.

"I've found some suitable partners," he said.

"More than one, Richard?"

"Driscoll and Bates, a firm that's been around quite a while. Evan Driscoll and Irwin Bates, plus a new man named Garwood, a law clerk named William Bolles. They've been looking for better quarters, and this big house next to the business district is ideal. We've formed a new firm, Driscoll, Bates, and Peabody."

"That's a lot of people," she said.

"It'll fill both floors. We'll be putting Bolles upstairs along with one of the secretaries, plus a law library and conference room."

"And myself?"

"Ah, I've negotiated an alcove upstairs."

She was beginning to see why he was discomforted. "Not with the secretaries?"

"Both of them are male. One will serve as receptionist." He reddened and twitched. "Look, Cornelia, Evan Driscoll and Irwin Bates are old-fashioned. They're part of the old Denver law establishment. They don't think women should be in law firms, at least not visibly. I insisted on a place for you, but they weren't happy about it."

"What would my new duties be?"

He reddened. "Secretarial work for me. Bolles is a law school graduate and he'll be doing the law research for all of us. The firm has a great library. Neither Driscoll nor Bates would hear of letting you do it, even though I insisted that you had done it brilliantly for Homer and me. Because I can't share you, or employ you in your full capacity, I can't afford to pay more than thirty a month, but if that's all right with you—"

"No," she said.

He looked relieved. It wasn't hard to see how this was going. He wanted her out. He would have the two male secretaries and a law clerk.

"Cornelia—"

"It's all right. I must be the only woman in Denver employed in a law firm for anything more than stenography."

317

"If you need time to hunt a job, and if you need recommendations, I'll supply them."

"I'd like both. A recommendation and a little time."

He brightened. "I'll do that. You plan on a couple of weeks. They aren't moving in until the first of the month anyway. And I'll draft a recommendation for you to type up on your Remington. And if there's anything else, please call on me."

She smiled tightly. "It's a man's world," she said.

"I feel terrible about it."

"I know you do."

That's how the interview ended. Another of her worlds had come to an end. Cornelia slipped outside, just to walk around the block, needing to settle her feelings. She missed Homer, that courtly old lawyer who had given her a chance to enter a challenging and absorbing world. He had thought of himself as a failure, but little did he know how he had touched her life when she needed help.

There weren't many things a woman could do except raise a family and be a mate. But for her, at least, even that door was closed. She would have to move into something cheap, and become a shop clerk or something like that. Maybe she could teach somewhere. But whatever she did, she would earn half what a skilled male would earn, and she would be forced to find a tiny cubicle somewhere in the poorest quarters of Denver. She wouldn't go back to her parents' home. That wasn't a life.

There was always Keenan Clark, her affectionate escort two or three times a week these days. But that posed problems too. The unspoken question loomed larger and larger every time they met. She couldn't marry, and she refused to cheapen herself with some sort of liaison. Respectable women didn't do that. She couldn't explain her feelings. It wasn't just religion or the opinion of others, or the scorn the dowagers of Denver heaped on someone like Baby Doe Tabor. It involved her own dignity and her sense of decency, and her innate respectability. As tempting as Keenan was—and she adored him—she knew that this delightful whirl would not lead to his bedroom.

She sighed, knowing a sadness so ineffable she couldn't even describe it. She lived amidst loss: loss of stillborn children, loss of intimacy in her marriage, loss of love, loss of Homer, loss of her old friends, and now more losses. A fascinating legal career, a comfortable flat she had lovingly furnished, a good income—ah, God, was she doomed to lose everything she had striven for?

She had a dinner engagement with Keenan that evening, and decided it was time to put things on the table. She returned to the office,
put in the day digging up precedents on a mining apex law case for
Richard, taking special care to do a thorough job even though her heart
wasn't in it anymore, and then retreated a little early to her flat, where
she steeped some tea and sipped unhappily, trying to make sense of her
burdens. She roused herself only minutes before Keenan was due, managed to wash up and change into a black dinner dress, and then he was
there. He took her to the Roof Garden that night.

"You're very subdued this evening, Cornelia," he said as they rode
in the hack to the Windsor.

"A lot's happened," she said.

"Things work out for the best," he said. "I'm an optimist. Just consider a problem to be an opportunity. That's how I live. Whenever something frustrates me, or makes me mad, I see potential in it. Let some
merchant sell me shoddy goods and I see a chance to make money with
better goods or better services. I really got started in the coal and ice
business because other outfits were lazy, or wouldn't deliver coal on
Sundays even in winter."

She smiled. "You always cheer me, Keenan," she said, but it was
half-hearted.

At the Windsor she fortified herself with a second glass of red wine,
and then a third. She had never done anything like that before. But
this would be a difficult dinner. She looked for people she knew, and
saw several of the old crowd. No doubt their tongues were wagging, and
no doubt Walter would hear of this night out, just as he had heard about
all the rest. The thought of him soured her mood, and she knew she
would have to struggle to make a pleasant companion for Keenan that
night.

He loved to order for them both, and she enjoyed his tasteful se-
lections, so she sat silently while he dickered with the skinny waiter.
Another glass of bloodred wine materialized before her, and it dawned
on her that Keenan was going to ply her with wine with a certain end
in mind. She giggled suddenly, a small private jot of humor in her bleak
mood. The wine made her slightly giddy, but no less sharp. She didn't
want fuzziness, not this important evening. She sipped while he gossiped
about her old friends, some of whom sat on the other side of the Roof
Garden.

She hardly knew how to open the subjects she wished to discuss, or
when to do it, but she favored a moment after they had eaten. She

listened attentively, and yet her mind was adrift, and after the waiter materialized with a dinner under burnished pewter covers, she ate her gorgeous beef medallions, black on the outside and pink within.

"You're very quiet tonight," Keenan said.

"I am suddenly unemployed," she said.

He cocked his head and waited, but she didn't respond until she had taken her fill.

"Richard Peabody's going into a partnership with Driscoll and Bates," she said. "They don't need me. No, I'll amend that. They don't want a woman around."

He grinned. "I'll never understand all those gents who beat homely old Keenan to the altar—then turn their backs on women," he said.

That wasn't what she was talking about, but it gave her the entrée she needed. "Keenan, what have you in mind? For us?"

Delight filtered through his face. "Just to let this go where it's obviously going."

"A liaison."

He didn't reply, but neither did he object.

"It's very tempting," she said. "I'm so fond of you, dear Keenan. And—there are things I miss." She would not pretend that she didn't want the passion, the love, the touching, the sharing of lives and intimacies.

He seemed uncertain, and dabbed his face with a snowy linen napkin. "If you're out of work, Cornelia, I could help you."

"Yes, but I wouldn't accept it, Keenan. That's what I want you to know." She reached across to him and pressed his hand. "You're a treasure, and you've brought so much to me, and made my life so pleasant. But I wouldn't want to mislead you. Some things are just unthinkable to me. It's not the gossips or the queens of society I'm thinking about; it's my own understanding of myself. You're terribly attractive to me, dear Keenan, but there can never be a liaison of any sort. I think you've always known that."

He looked crestfallen, and nodded.

She felt a rush of relief flood through her, and realized she had been so taut that her body had been rigid. "You deserve a real wife, Keenan. You're an attractive man, even if you don't think so. I'm not available, but dozens of lovely women are, and you'll find one if you look."

"But I love you, Cornelia."

She hardly knew what to say. He did love her; she knew that. But she wasn't available.

"In a way, I love you too, Keenan."

He grinned bitterly. "In a way, eh? In a way, we're having a nice evening."

"I'm sorry. I've hurt you and ruined this lovely evening. Please, let's make this a happy occasion."

He sighed, and dabbed his face with his napkin. It didn't escape her that what he was dabbing was not his lips, but the corners of his eyes. "I'm proud of you," he said, his voice half-broken. "You're a lady, Cornelia. You're my dream. I've loved you ever since we were young. And one of the reasons was because you're a thoroughbred. Here you are, suddenly out of a job, and in my shabby way I thought maybe this would—change things. But you're much too magnificent to surrender your ideals in a bad moment."

She cried, too, and blamed the perfidious wine.

CHAPTER 67

ves endured, mostly by keeping his mouth shut. Mrs. Hergesheimer was a woman on the prod, looking for the faintest hints of rebellion or dissent in her crew, and never failing to find some. Her arrogance was insufferable, but Yves figured he preferred to endure that than an empty stomach. He had gotten his raise, and found he could live on fifty a month, and even had a few coins left over for a mug of beer now and then.

There were other consolations. This position didn't threaten his health or invite a relapse. The air in the proofreading room didn't ravage his weakened lungs. He reported at six in the evening and toiled under a glaring electric bulb until four in the morning, which was soft living compared to the twelve-hour shifts smeltermen worked. He was the youngest of the six proofreaders, and the rest made the most of it. He had never met such a dismal lot. They were capable of wrangling violently over the spelling of an obscure word or street name, sometimes growing so angry they stomped out of the little warren.

At first he tried to please Mrs. Hergesheimer, but he soon gave that up. Nothing he did ever won her approval. When he thought he had done a splendid job, discovering odd errors in some text, she only sniffed that he shouldn't waste time on such nonsense. But if he missed some rare spelling, she was swift to condemn him for carelessness.

They all damned the whole news staff, whom they regarded as a pack of semiliterate ignoramuses. And they reserved their most withering contempt for the paper's biggest hotshots, Mike Lawrence and Dan Hope. Beside Yves sat a malodorous old gentleman, one of those learned idiots who could spot a grammatical error a mile away but couldn't find his way across the street to Ma's for a sandwich. On the stool across from him sat a whiner, who obviously felt he belonged behind an editor's desk and not in this backwater. Two stools down sat a young man as solemn as a divinity student, but truly gifted when it came to picking up errors. He rarely talked, almost as if he dreaded human company. He was the only one Mrs. Hergesheimer treated with some diffidence.

Occasionally they had nothing to do. No galleys arrived. Then they took to bickering. Not a one of them brought a book to read. They were all sick of reading, so they bickered until they were rescued by a new load of galleys or a few page proofs. These moments depressed Yves.

He had Tuesdays off, and on several of these precious days he repaired to his old haunts on Cherry Creek, sucking beer with the riffraff he had befriended long before. He alone among them held a job, and now he looked down upon them from some Olympian heights. They were all poseurs, trashy poets and artistes, parasites and fools. He shuddered to think that he had been one of them, posing as an American Keats, a tragic artistic giant.

And yet . . . he still enjoyed their humor, their self-important opinions, their raffish rejection of the whole business world. Among these failures he was a lordly poet; at the *Post* he was an obscure toiler with no future. If he had had the good sense to die a tragic death, he might now be revered as a great figure in American literature. He sighed. When he was dying, he was courageous, realistic, coldly truthful, and strong. He was noble in death and extremity. But Maria Theresa Haas had robbed him of all that. Now he didn't count. She had started it, and his miserable parents had finished it. And now he was an obscure wage-slave. It galled him.

But the thought of her reminded him of her courage and optimism, and her determination to heal herself by whatever means lay at hand. She had been the angel of Glenwood Springs. He hoped she was doing well now.

He remembered her tenderly that Tuesday afternoon. She had transformed a stuffy narcissistic poet into a man, though she didn't know it. The more he thought of her, the more he wanted to write about her. He grew excited at the idea. He would pen the story of the angel of Glenwood Springs and give it to Angus McQuaid. Maybe it would be the first step toward a satisfying career as a newspaper writer. Maybe he could even be another Eugene Field, whose columns enchanted Denver.

He uncorked the ink bottle, found his notepad, dipped his nib— and stared at the forbidding blank page before him. Catching Maria Theresa in words was going to be the hardest thing he had ever done. He thought of various opening ploys, and discarded them savagely. Why was this so hard? He thought to make her a metaphor of charity. He thought to portray her as a symbol of optimism. He thought to plumb her character, or compare her to Florence Nightingale.

He scribbled a few things along these lines, and then crumpled the sheets. Why couldn't he write? Her image filled his mind; her smiles, her hours concocting herbal medicines, her sheer determination to heal herself—and those around her.

It came to him at last that he was being much too erudite and pompous. All he had to do was tell the story in simple terms, record his impressions, even his hostility. And avoid all the high and mighty claptrap he had intended to insert in the piece.

After that, the writing went better. He wrote of her arrival in Glenwood Springs, fever-ridden, gaunt, but with smiles and herbs and a vision of hope and healing. He wrote of his own disdain and disbelief and even his determination to die. He wrote of her radiance, her affectionate regard for her suffering neighbors, her sharing. He remembered to include some of her recipes and formulae, her dietary advice, her tenderness that gave him, and others around her, a rage to live. He filled a half-dozen pages with this, always keeping it simple. He scorned literary devices and graces, used adjectives sparingly, avoided arty, affected metaphors and figures of speech, and tried to keep his prose as plain and journalistic as he could.

When he read over his work at last, he realized it wasn't a pretentious essay; it was a story, with a beginning, middle, and ending. He scratched out a few phrases and worked on the ending.

"Hers was the triumph of faith, courage, hope and love over disease," he concluded. "In the end, it was her spirit more than her herbs and concoctions that pierced the self-obsessed soul of the young man and transformed it, bestowing life."

The next afternoon he came early, to catch McQuaid before he quit for the day. He approached the editor's cage with knots in his belly, wondering whether his first effort at a newspaper feature would be dismissed out of hand, or worse, scathingly criticized.

"Well, Poulenc, haven't seen you in weeks," McQuaid said affably.

"I've got something I want to submit, sir," Yves said.

McQuaid eyed him cynically. "Everyone wants to be a hotshot reporter," he said.

"No, sir. I wouldn't make a good reporter. But I do want to write features now and then, and maybe even become a newsroom feature writer."

"A feature, eh?" McQuaid seemed more interested now. "Sure, Poulenc, let me take a gander."

"It's very important to me, sir. Even if it's not something you could take, I hope you'll give me a critique."

McQuaid belched and nodded. "I'll get it back to you," he said.

That didn't sound good. Yves fretted his way through a cruelly long shift, slept scarcely at all, returned to the *Post* the next afternoon, and found a message awaiting him when he arrived at the proofreading room: "Good stuff, Poulenc. I'm using it in the Sunday edition. McQuaid."

Joyously he hurried to McQuaid's cage, but the editor had left for the day. That night he was offensively happy, and had the whole sour proofreading crew snarling at him just because he was cheerful.

Saturday night, Mrs. Hergesheimer herself proofed his piece, and sneered at him.

"Everyone wants to be a hotshot," she said. "Look at this. Our hero here's writing purple prose." The proofreaders crowded around the galley.

"You got a byline," said one.

"Too good for us, eh?"

"No, it was just a story I had in me about a lovely young woman who healed herself—and me."

"Ha! You probably aren't telling all the story," snarled Mrs. Hergesheimer.

In spite of the savagery of the proofing staff, he sensed that his position had somehow improved. Most of the *Post*'s proofreaders were also skilled writers, and suddenly they had been confronted by some good writing by one of their own. They hated and admired him at the same time.

When the Sunday edition rolled off the press in the wee hours of the morning, Yves was on hand to snatch a copy from one of the pressmen. There it was, in the lower lefthand corner of the front page, the place often reserved for features. It even had the headline he wanted: ANGEL AT GLENWOOD SPRINGS. A quarter of the feature was there, and the rest had been jumped to the rear page. His story. His byline. Dizzily he read every word, and then grabbed a spare copy. He would send this story to his parents and show them a thing or two. He would send another to Maria Theresa, too. It was her story, and she might find pleasure in it even though he had never used her real name, alluding to her as the angel, or the woman from the East.

When his shift was over, he pocketed several copies he had clipped from papers lying about the newsroom, and slipped into the quiet night. Denver slept. A great peace lay upon the city, and upon his soul. He didn't feel like going to his room. He wanted to celebrate.

This was his first professional writing, and he knew there would be more. That night, as he trudged the quiet streets in mild air, he felt thankful for what had come to pass. He had passed through youthful vainglory and conceit into an adult world where he was making his own way and mastering all the skills he had once scorned. He had triumphed over disease, almost against his will, but had become a parasite, feasting on his father's cash. For the first time, he understood why his father and mother had cut off the funds. It was for his own good, not theirs.

He no longer saw himself in grandiose terms, as a great tragic poet. He saw himself as a young man who had weathered disease, who needed to catch up to others in the working world, who found reasons to like himself now that he was opening a pay envelope every two weeks. He had a future. The death he once had yearned for had been delayed, perhaps for a long lifetime. Now he was among the living, and he had a future.

CHAPTER 68

Father O'Boyle was in no hurry. He sat quietly, saying nothing, letting Rose sip the delicious tea. Kindness and curiosity lit his face.

"A first name would be a gift to me," he said. "Even an invented one."

"It's Rose."

"Ah, my Irish Rose," he said. "You don't have to say a word if you don't want, but forgive me if I ask a few questions. Have ye a place to stay?"

She shook her head.

"And be ye hungry?"

She hadn't eaten for a long time, but she had no appetite. "I don't need anything."

"Ah, the body doesn't need much. That's not what's starving in most of us. But are ye ill, Rose?"

She didn't reply.

"I see," he said. "Sickness is a mystery. I never know whether it's a visitation of God to heal our souls, or a punishment to straighten our paths. Or just happenstance."

He didn't talk for a while, and she didn't encourage him to. She wasn't certain she wanted to be there in a priest's office.

"Well, Rose, there isn't a thing that shocks our Lord, and not a thing that can't be forgiven, and not a life that can't be reborn and made new."

"Father, I know you'd like me to pour out my troubles, but I can't. I'll never tell them to anyone. If God exists, he knows all about them anyway. It's between Him and me."

The priest lifted his hands and subsided with a smile. He gestured toward the teapot with a questioning eyebrow.

"Maybe ye'd like to think about it. I'll be here. Take it a bit at a time, a wee bit here, a wee bit the next day. Life's hard to live, and not a soul escapes tribulation."

"Thank you," she said.

"Ah, Rose," he replied softly. "I feel you're about to fly away like some frigate bird in the middle of the sea. Sit on the spar awhile. It's a big ocean we're crossing . . . Do we come from the same county?"

"Offaly."

"Ah, no, it's Cork I'm from. Are your pa and ma alive?"

"My pa was hanged during the troubles," she said. "I take after him. Four things he despised. The English, the Catholic Church, the lords and ladies, and the Protestants."

Father O'Boyle smiled. "I'd fancied this might be a homecoming for you, but I suppose not. It never was your faith. How about your mother?"

"She was an Englishwoman. She died a few years ago. We weren't in touch."

The priest gazed out the window, and Rose was glad he wasn't pushing too hard. She knew he was yearning to help, yearning to rescue her. He affected a lazy indifference but in truth his mind was whirling.

"That job," he said suddenly. "John Mullen's a rich miller, and he needs a servant, and he wants a good woman of the parish to keep house for his family. I can send you to him, Rose."

"Me, Father? Ha! I will not set foot in his house. I won't touch a good clean child with my dirty hands. I won't eat off his plates or soil his linens. I won't join your parish." Her vehemence surprised her as much as it surprised the priest.

Father O'Boyle nodded. "Life's a mystery," he said. "We struggle to find happiness, and never do. Or we can surrender our lives, stop struggling, and live for something larger. And then happiness comes, unbidden, when we least expect it. Are you happy, Rose?"

She was damned if she would reply, and sat stony-faced before him.

He stood, suddenly, and paced behind his desk. "Would ye like absolution?"

"No."

"I'll be here tomorrow at this time, Rose. And the next day, if ye wish to visit. And I'll be here the day after that and the week after that."

"Thank you for the tea."

He nodded. She retreated into a cold, glaring afternoon and hastened north. The visit had at least clarified some things for her. This had been a momentous day. Dr. Berger in the morning, then packing up and throwing herself out upon the world, and Father O'Boyle now. There wasn't any place on earth for a rebel soul. If she joined the parish and lived that life she would slowly wither away and die. If she returned to her old life she would destroy herself fast. Her life would be short, wild, funny, bitter, but never dull. She really had no choices.

She was a wild Rose, and she'd die if she were caged. She would live wild, and die wild. A hard, stubborn lump of feeling coalesced in her as she walked. She felt flinty inside. No one would ever tell her what to do. Not John Holliday or William Masterson. Not Dr. Berger or Father O'Boyle. Not Sister St. George or God himself. Fiercely she stomped toward Blake Street in the thickening evening. There she would live and die, do whatever she damned well felt like, and not a soul would stop her.

In the last light of that fateful day she traipsed the street, examining the gin mills. A new one, The Mint, caught her eye. She plowed through double doors and discovered a ritzy place, with glass chandeliers and some big nudes hung on the walls. She spotted the usual faro layouts, poker tables, and a couple of roulette wheels, too. This place had a gorgeous mahogany bar and back bar, and three barkeeps in clean white aprons. She saw no serving girls, and wondered about that.

"Who runs this outfit?" she asked a barman.

"Apollo Bandig—over in the corner."

She beheld a swarthy gent with slicked-down black hair against the wall in back. "Does he hire serving girls?"

"Yeah, if they're nice and pretty."

That didn't encourage her, but she hiked to the rear, past a sparse crowd. It was too early for the evening rush, and it was only a weekday.

Bandig straightened out of a slouch as she approached.

"You hiring?"

He studied her as if she were hanging beef. She felt shopworn, and wished she had found a way to paint up.

"You look fifty but aren't," he said. "Probably thirty-something, but you've been around the block a few times."

"You bet I have, and I know how to push the drinks."

"I like younger women around the place. This is for young sports."

"Try me."

He shrugged. "I might. Until you mess up. What did it, booze? Hop? Living with a few woman-beaters?"

"What do you pay?" she asked.

"You get tips."

"I want food, too. And if you got a room in back, I want that, too."

"No rooms. This isn't a girly house."

"I don't mean that. I'm not like that. I need a place to stay."

"You have it tough, don'tcha?"

"Make up your mind. There's a dozen other joints on the block, and plenty would be glad to have me."

He grinned suddenly. "Help yourself," he said. "Which is it? Booze? Hop? Men?"

"All three," she replied.

"You gonna get me in trouble? The city's looking over our shoulders here more and more."

"Probably."

"I got an apartment. I deal faro. All the tables are mine. You want to deal?"

"I can learn."

"You know roulette? Can you keep track of the odds and chips?"

"I never did it, but I know what pays what. I know all the bets. God, I've played it enough for ten lifetimes."

"I've always wanted to try a woman dealer. I'll put you on the roulette and we'll work together tonight and tomorrow night. Then it's Saturday and you'll be on your own. You'll need an outfit."

"What's my pay?"

"Tips and my rooms upstairs. The buffet over there."

"Okay, your rooms and the rest. But you gotta wait a few days." She figured she owed him that. Dr. Berger had said the treatment would heal her in a few days.

He grinned slowly. "Whatever you say." He dug around in his pocket and handed her a key. "My last girl left some stuff behind. Go in there and pick something out and put it on. Lock the door again when you leave."

"Sure," she said. She hiked into a gloomy corridor at the rear, found the door, unlocked it, hunted around for an electric light switch, and finally found one. She meandered through a spare suite, the sort of place inhabited by birds of passage. In an armoire she found some frilly stuff. She knew what he wanted, and put on a scarlet silk blouse that would probably give her pneumonia. She didn't look very good in it; her flesh was turning crepey. But so what? She'd draw the plungers to her table. She studied herself in a looking glass. Shopworn, still half-pretty, and in need of a good washing. She liked this image a lot better than the one she had of herself that morning on Dr. Berger's table.

She'd been promoted. Now she would deal instead of serving booze. She'd smile at sports, let 'em admire her assets, spin the wheel, fire the ivory ball, watch it drop on a number, and rake the chips. This wouldn't last long, though. She'd down too much of his whiskey some night, mess up the play, and Bandig would kick her out. But what difference did it make? She was a wild Irish Rose, and nothing on earth would tame her except death.

CHAPTER 69

uch to Dixie's joy, her café flourished in that Globeville neighborhood. She hired another cook and a waitress to handle the crowds of hungry smeltermen who flocked in after both shifts. The first crowd arrived after six in the morning, wanting full dinners, not breakfasts, and the second shift arrived after six in the evening. They all gladly paid fifty cents for a hearty meal, including all the seconds they wanted. She closed only on Sundays and holidays, and was clearing anywhere from two hundred fifty to three hundred a month.

She loved her work, loved the galoots who piled in after each shift, learned their preferences, and gradually refined her simple menu to please most of them most of the time. Some ate silently and departed; others befriended her, or kidded her, or left tips.

Bit by bit, she had domesticated that wild bird, Lorenzo the Magnificent, and now he was comfortable and no longer a vagrant. Each night he stayed in his cot in her little flat. He arose mid-morning, drifted into the café, sat himself in his regular spot beside the window where the sunlight poured over him. She served him breakfast there, which he ate with gusto. He always insisted on signing the check, so she always brought him one. "Magnificent," he wrote on the back of each one.

"Send it to my office," he said ritually.

She delighted in keeping him attired. Now that she was practically rich, she could afford his upkeep. Quietly, she put cleaned shirts in his armoire, a new dinner jacket, new shoes, a white summer suit, and assorted bow ties. Little by little she added to his wardrobe. Good kid gloves, stockings, fresh drawers, a robe, a nightshirt, a gold-plated pocket watch, handkerchiefs, not to mention some witch hazel, English lavender soap, and other toiletries. Lorenzo looked magnificent again, natty and polished, his clothing always clean.

He was an astonishing figure in that smeltermen's café, and at first the customers eyed him distrustfully and sometimes angrily. He wasn't one of them, not of their toiling class, and a dampening presence on their own camaraderie.

But one by one, she had introduced her customers to him.

"This here's Lorenzo the Magnificent," she would say to one or another smelterman. "Lorenzo's a mining genius, a millionaire, and a famous host and a legend known clear around the world."

"Why, sir," said Lorenzo, offering his pale white hand, "I am honored by your illustrious company, and I hope you will advise me about your enterprises. I'm always looking for good stocks. Come, let me buy you a cup of java, or a glass of some of the finest burgundy known to France."

"Well, ah—"

"Lorenzo has thirteen million dollars," Dixie explained. "And he adds a couple hundred thousand a week at the Denver Mining

Exchange. If he keeps it up, he'll be the richest man in the world.''

She always wondered whether to humor him, or whether it ultimately hurt him to encourage his delusions. She had fallen into the pattern of keeping to reality when the subject was herself, but nurturing his own beliefs otherwise. He was living in a happy world at last, and she didn't want to destroy something as precious as that.

Most of her customers enjoyed Lorenzo, and those who didn't went elsewhere, but she didn't mind. She had all the business she could handle in that small place, and she didn't need soreheads around. One or two of them remembered how hard Lorenzo had been on his miners at Telluride, and wanted nothing to do with him. But most of her smeltermen not only forgave, but came to adopt him as one of their own, passing time with him and asking his advice about buying shares.

Sometime early each afternoon, he donned his black opera cape, which he wore in all seasons and climates, and walked the two miles into central Denver to spend the afternoon at the stock exchange, where his fortune leapt upward day by day.

"Von Trapp tells me I'll soon be the richest man in the United States," he told Dixie one day. "I've topped fourteen million, made a killing in Chicago Traction common shares."

"Oh, that's grand," she said.

She usually found time to sit with him in that delicious sunlight midmorning, after the night-shift smeltermen had eaten and left. That's when she told him about her own fortunes.

"I never dreamed I'd end up so lucky, Magnificent. Look at this. It's a gold mine. All these men were desperate for a beanery."

"It's your hobby," he said. "You don't need a cent of it."

"Yes I do, Lorenzo. I don't have the Tall Cotton anymore. This is my living."

"Oh, pshaw, I'm sure you have a million or two salted away."

"No, this is all I have. This little café. And I owe it all to you—and Hod."

"I think you should add an omelette to the menu. Nothing like an omelette. The French are mad geniuses with eggs. Add a little bacon, a few spices, ah, paradise."

"Well, Lorenzo, my customers wouldn't go for that."

He cocked his head and grinned. "Part of being a good host is offering your guests treats they've never sampled. Why, I scour the four corners of the world for little delights. You know, I should be having one of my parties one of these days."

"That'd be nice."

"Yes, I'll talk to the Windsor. They've been so impossible about my signature lately. But yes, I'll have a party to end all parties, and I'll invite Victoria Regina and the Prince of Wales."

"Oh, some royals would sure give it tone."

"Yes, one grows weary of presidents. I think Victoria would love to see Denver."

Dixie discovered that Lorenzo was even becoming a draw. People came clear up from central Denver just to see him holding court at his window seat. Sometimes they followed him from the stock exchange up to the café, or wanted his signature on a menu or a slip of paper. He signed with a flourish and a smile.

Tidbits about him began to appear regularly in the Denver papers. Eugene Field regularly covered Lorenzo, and Polly Pry ran items every week or so. Now that he was always clean and well dressed, the Windsor relented and let him wander through the hotel. He could often be found at one of the saloons in the hotel, signing his tab with a great flourish each time a drink arrived. Polly Pry said that the presence of Lorenzo the Magnificent had increased the saloon traffic by 10 or 20 percent whenever he wandered in, and the managers had swiftly discovered the profit in it.

He had also become highly quotable, which is why the journalists flocked to him, especially on off days when no news was breaking.

"Mr. Magnificent, what do you like about Denver?" one had asked one day.

"The fact that I own it," he had replied.

If he owned Denver, then perhaps Denver owned him. The apparition in the opera clothes found himself welcomed by hack drivers, who took him where he wanted and let him sign a chit. Likewise, he could enjoy a coffee and pastry most anywhere. And sometimes he even showed up at the Tabor Opera House in a prime front-center orchestra seat, signing every scrap of paper thrust at him by gowned and bejeweled ladies.

"I'm glad Arnold von Trapp finally got the funds straightened out," he told Dixie one day. "It certainly was an ordeal. But right now, my dear, I could buy or sell Alaska for small change."

"Why don't you buy Hawaii, Magnificent?"

"Who'd want to own Hawaii?" he retorted.

Then one day, over coffee in the dazzling sunlight, Lorenzo slipped into a very quiet mood, and eyed Dixie, while wave after wave of feeling slid across his face. She watched, fascinated, knowing something very large and important was coming up.

He took her hand. "My dear Miss Ball, my exquisite Dixie," he said softly.

"It's just me, the old hash slinger."

"Oh, how you joke. My dear, there's only one thing lacking in my life. Here I am, almost the richest man in America, but something's missing. You are the fairest of women, the most enchanting and gracious and tender and sweet lady in all of Colorado, nay, all the United States. My dear, would you favor old Lorenzo, your business partner, with your hand in marriage?"

It came so unexpectedly it stunned her. She hardly knew what to say or what to think.

"Lorenzo, let me think this over a few days, all right?"

"Why of course. These things shouldn't be rushed into lightly," he replied. "You do me an honor, weighing this seriously. Here I am, still young, with countless assets, and they're all yours. All yours, for ever and ever," he said softly, his eyes alight with love.

"You're a dear, Magnificent, and your proposal's very sweet," she said. "I gotta start some potatoes now."

She slipped back to the kitchen, her mind troubled. She couldn't marry a madman, not even a gentle, delightful, sweet madman. Or could she? And would she enjoy it?

He was happy, no doubt of it. His new world had magically filled a need in him. He might be crazy in one sense, but the rest of him was kind, loving, aware, and always tender. What sort of marriage could she have with a man who was daft? And would the officials let her marry him at all?

As time flew by, she mulled his proposal. But the more she thought about it, the more she believed she just might do it. She adored him. She loved caring for him. She had nursed him back into a good life, pulled him off the cold streets, shared her life with him. Maybe it wasn't the sort of passion a woman might feel for a man, but she knew love, and she knew he was grand company, and that somehow he gave her own life meaning and joy. Whatever it was she felt, she grew certain it would be a good match.

One sunny spring day she sat down across from him while he whiled away the morning, sipping coffee and reading stock market news.

"Magnificent, are you still up to marrying me?"

He paused in his reading, and smiled. "You would be the diadem in my crown," he said.

"Well, let her rip," she said.

"Let her rip! Never has fair maiden replied to a marriage proposal in such eloquent terms. Let her rip!'' He laughed softly. "All right, I'll make the arrangements. We'll just take over the Windsor, and invite half the world.''

Oh, oh, she thought. There goes my savings. But who cares?

"Let her rip," she said, and they both laughed.

CHAPTER 70

That fine June morning, Lorenzo the Magnificent adjusted his black tie, picked up his black umbrella, donned his black silk top hat and opera cape, and marched into the sunlight. He decided he would walk to the Windsor; some hack drivers had become insolent lately, and were demanding cash even though he never carried any. Why, anyone in Denver knew that his signature was good as gold.

Up in the humble neighborhoods around the smelters, he seemed an odd figure, but as he wended his way south through a balmy day, he became by degrees a jaunty boulevardier, a feast to the eye, a gentleman who delighted all he encountered with a bow, or a doff of his silk hat, or a cheerful nod.

More than once he stopped to scribble a signature for someone or other.

He arrived at last at the ornate, elegant hotel, the heart and soul of Denver. There, in its gorgeous confines, everything noteworthy happened. There he would stage the most magnificent wedding known to the world. Whatever else they remembered him for, they would not forget his nuptial day.

He made his way through the lush lobby, past the potted palms to the manager's office, and walked in.

"I've come to rent the Windsor," he said to a stern matron. "Show me to the manager, my beautiful lady.''

She eyed him up and down. "Why, yes, Mr. Carthage.''

"It's Magnificent to all my friends, and you're a charming friend.''

She rose, vanished through a door, and a moment later ushered him in. A young man with his dark hair oiled down stood behind a beeswaxed desk.

"Ah, Carthage, Maxcy Tabor here."

"Tabor is it? Hod's boy."

"Let's say I'm Augusta's son. You're here about the wedding. Congratulations."

"How did you know?"

"Your lovely fiancée was here not long ago. Quite early, in fact. She and I had a most pleasant discussion. I've known Dixie for years, you know."

"Oh, yes. A lovely woman, the diadem of my life, the tiara of womanhood."

"Have a seat, Mr. Carthage. We'll just do some planning."

"Ah, it's Magnificent. I don't know why people call me Carthage."

Young Maxcy nodded. "Of course. Magnificent. I'd have it no other way."

"Good. Now, this is going to be the wedding of the century. I'll spare no expense, mind you. Just send it all to my office, and they'll take care of it. Arnold von Trapp—my broker—says I'm almost the richest man in the universe."

"We'll take care of it. Don't worry about that, Magnificent."

"Good! Now, first off, I'll want the ballroom. Bank it with the best flowers that money can buy. Hire two orchestras. I'll want a half a dozen bartenders and a long table full of treats. Spare no expense. Don't save me a dime. Just send it all to my office."

Tabor was busy scribbling, nodding, smiling.

"Now, find me a divine. If I were Catholic, I'd have the pope do it. Or half a dozen cardinals. Say, that's not a bad idea. I wonder if I could convert and invite him. No, I guess not. No time. I want this in a fortnight, the last Saturday of June. No way to sail him here from Rome."

"How about a Colorado Supreme Court justice?"

"Ah, there's the ticket. Brilliant. Anything supreme I'll go for. Get the fellow. Bribe him. Whatever it takes. I never carry cash, but just hand me the tab and I'll sign. My office takes care of all these petty details."

"Yes, a justice."

"Now, young Tabor—you're a fine, intelligent fellow—I'll leave the details to you. Engraved invitations. All of Denver. The governor and senators, of course, but I draw the line at representatives. We won't have room for everybody. Send some to Mr. and Mrs. Cleveland, the White House. Include the press. This event should be written up."

Young Tabor nodded, and scribbled. "Very good. Now who'll be in your wedding party?"

"Why, my old partner Hod—your dear, kind, cherished father. I'll make him best man, and Baby can be the matron of honor."

Maxcy Tabor smiled peculiarly. "We love carnivals," he said.

"Now, we'll want the Tabor Suite, my bride and I."

"She already arranged it."

"She did? Amazing woman, Tabor, absolutely a gem. Now, there ought to be a parade. Is there a circus coming to town? I want a string of elephants from here to the South Platte. Get me marching bands, volunteer fire companies with their engines and dalmatians, fraternal orders, a hundred cowboys, drum and bugle corps, circus wagons, tigers and lions, ostriches and emus. Get them all up in silk, with my monogram, eh? And fireworks. Get me General Sherman and President Grant, and invite Phil Sheridan. Get me the Grand Army of the Republic, and don't forget the cavalry. You buy enough skyrockets to blow the stars out of the sky, and my sweetheart and I'll watch from our window."

Tabor nodded and scribbled.

"Now, I've always believed in sharing all that God's given me. I want a medallion struck—one ounce gold, with my bust on one side, and Dixie on the obverse—strike a thousand of those, and I'll hand them out. Talk the mint into it. Just send the tab to my office. I want every chambermaid and bellboy to have one. Let them know that old Magnificent was thinking about them on his wedding day."

Tabor nodded and scribbled.

"Now, upon the conclusion of my little ceremony, I want every church bell in Denver to ring. I want the Protestants and Catholics, Mormons and Seventh-Day Adventists, to ring bells. I want the fire department to ring bells. I don't care how you do it; use the telephone, or put a man on the roof of the hotel with a heliograph. Dixie'd be thrilled to hear a thousand bells."

Tabor scribbled.

"Now, after the ceremony, I'll want to show off Dixie. I'll want the finest ebony lacquered carriage in town, with matched white horses, and get up a man in livery. I'm going to pop her into that carriage and drive from the Windsor around and about for an hour, and then we'll have our reception. Now, when we receive people, I'll want a dozen flunkies to keep the lines orderly and steer people to the punch and treats. Got that?"

"Truly magnificent, Magnificent," said young Tabor.

"And get me a dozen photographers. I'll want a hundred tintypes made. And print up ten thousand mementos, the sort of thing I can sign. Hand 'em out, got that?"

He had dozens of other ideas, which he described to the hotel manager over the next half hour: orchids for the ladies, incense, candy for children, a twenty-foot-high wedding cake—the ideas kept bubbling up.

"I guess that does it," he said at last, "but feel free to add your own fine touch." Magnificent stood and shook hands with the manager. "Just send it to my office," he said.

"I'll get right on it."

"See that you do. All this requires genius! Genius!"

He plowed into a heady June day, enjoying the glow, and walked to the Denver Mining Exchange for a little talk with von Trapp. He always spent his afternoons there, amidst the hurly-burly of the trading pit, the quotations chalked on blackboards, the debris on the floor, and the rank smell of sweat and armpits. He found his broker at the man's usual post away from the trading floor.

"Ah, there you are, von Trapp. How'm I doing today?"

"Oh, let me see." The skinny man in shirtsleeves consulted his ledger. "Your Pullman Company advanced seven-eighths. You had a hundred thousand shares, so that's up nicely. Ah, yes, you're pushing fourteen million, I see."

"Good. Sell Pullman and buy a hundred thousand Diamond Match. I've been watching it. The whole world needs to start fires."

"You bet, Magnificent. Let's see, it's trading at forty-two and a quarter. That's an expensive stock."

"I can afford it."

"You can afford anything."

As usual, whenever Lorenzo appeared in the exchange, strangers gathered about. That was good. He wanted them to hear the next.

"You know, von Trapp, I'm getting married in a fortnight. Now, I've been thinking about a little wedding gift for my sweetheart, Dixie Ball, and I've decided to share my account with her—half of everything I possess. How do I arrange that?"

"Half of all you possess? Why, that's truly a majestic gesture. She'll be thrilled. It happens to be the simplest thing in the world. Just change your account. Add her name."

"I never thought it'd be so simple."

"For you, Magnificent, all things are possible."

"Do it, von Trapp. Write it up, and I'll take it to her this afternoon. Seven million dollars for a wedding gift. Do you think that's a record? I want it to be a record, one for the books."

"If it's not a record, it should be. Give me a few minutes to scribble some things, and then you take this new account sheet to her."

Magnificent basked in the glow. Traders darted away to tell the world about the greatest wedding gift the world had ever seen. It would make Polly Pry's column in the morning. He waited patiently while the broker scribbled something or other. It didn't matter. He was too rich to worry about anything. He had Dixie, millions of dollars, and all of Denver. Eventually the broker completed his paperwork and handed him a ledger. He read it carefully.

"On account with von Trapp and Billings," it said. "Securities and other equities in the name of Lorenzo the Magnificent and Dixie Ball Magnificent, née Dixie Ball. Effective, June 13, 1887."

"That do it?" the broker asked. "You have her stop by; we need her signature on a card."

"I'll do that. And von Trapp. Come to the wedding. Tell them all to come." His gesture included all the traders on the floor below.

"That's some gift," said a stranger.

"Yes, fellow. Make it and give it away, that's the law of life. Come to my party."

All aglow, he made his way back to Dixie's Café, basking in the sun, twirling his umbrella, scaring pigeons and exciting children. He had never been so happy. Dixie would be delirious.

He settled at his regular table in the glow of the sun and waited for Dixie, who was busy preparing for the six o'clock rush. But she knew he was there, and when she could, she brought him coffee and sat down across from him, a smile illuminating her lovely face.

"Well, my dear Dixie, it's all arranged. We'll have the grandest wedding ever seen on earth," he said.

"Oh, Magnificent. I can hardly wait. Did you talk to Maxcy Tabor? He used to be my boss, you know."

"I can't imagine that. Yes, of course. He'll make the arrangements."

"Is he giving us the Tabor Suite?"

"Yes, indeed."

"Good. It costs ten dollars a night, imagine it! And a little reception room plus some punch and hors d'oeuvres was thirty-five. And fifty for other stuff."

"Peanuts, peanuts."

She smiled. "A lot of money," she said, "but it was worth it."

"Dixie, my beloved, my crown jewel, you're a millionaire seven times over."

"Yes I am, Magnificent."

"How would you know? I just did it."

"Did what?"

"Here!" He thrust his new account at her. "It's my wedding gift to you."

She read it, delight illumining her face. "You did that for me? You make me very happy. I've never received seven million dollars' worth of securities before. You give me more than you'll ever know."

CHAPTER 71

hen Cornelia answered the knock on her door, she discovered the one person she least desired to see.

"May I come in and talk?" asked Walter.

"You own the rest of Denver; you may as well own my apartment, too," she said.

"I won't come in unless I'm welcome," he said. He stood patiently on her stoop, his black derby in hand, looking as severe as usual.

"Oh, all right." She let him walk in. His quick glance revealed utter disinterest in her flat. He settled himself on her sofa and she sat in a stuffed chair opposite.

"I just wanted to talk a little. You seem to be at an impasse," he said.

"And you always seem to know all there is to know about me. You have good spies."

"No, Cornelia, I don't spy on you. People tell me things. They think they can curry my favor by telling me any scrap of news about you. I don't welcome it."

"Why did you come here?"

"You're out of work. I can help, if you wish. And also, I was curious about you."

"It's the first time in your life you've been curious about me."

He stared through the gauze of the window curtain, not answering at first. Then, surprisingly, he agreed. "That's a fault in me," he said.

"I don't really need your help. It will come with strings attached."

"No, no strings. There's a position in the medical school library at the University of Denver and Colorado Seminary. You could fill it very well. You have a good command of Latin, and know your way around law libraries. You'd be the librarian there, and help the medical faculty with research.''

"That's kind of you, but what's the hitch? And why is it suddenly all right for the wife of Walter Kimbrough to hold a position? And for that matter, why are you here? Never mind, I'll answer that. This has to do with your reputation. You want your wife in a respectable position, if she must work.''

"Cornelia—''

"No, I'm not dealing. I still want a divorce. You offer me nothing— nothing,'' she continued, relentlessly.

"I know that. Maybe I'd better go.''

She felt a rush of remorse. "No, stay and talk. I'll put on some tea if you wish.''

"That would be fine, Cornelia.''

She banged around her kitchen, terrorizing pots and pans, and finally got her tea things together. Why had he come? What did he want? Why was he being so civil? The more she puzzled it, the more curious she got. She started water heating on her gas stove and returned to Walter, who sat stock-still, his black derby resting gently on his skinny legs.

"Why did you come here? Not to tell me about that position, I'm sure.''

"To talk. To tell you I've been too absorbed in business to be a good husband.''

She registered that slowly, looking for wild cards, and then trumped him. "I'm glad you've reached that point in your thinking. But I still want a divorce.''

"The courts have spoken, Cornelia.''

"Maybe they'll listen to new evidence.''

"What? You and Keenan?''

"There, I knew this would all come out. Just for your information, there was no—what's the sophisticated word these days?—liaison. I have my standards.''

"I know that. You've made my point for me.''

"I still want a divorce. Let's keep that right on the table.''

"There's no way the courts would permit it. The public perception is that rich people can get what they want from the courts, but it's quite the opposite. If we were anonymous and poor instead of socially prominent, a divorce would slip right through. But not for us. Colorado is blessed with a singularly honest judiciary, and they make no bones about holding us to the law."

"What are you saying, Walter?"

"Simply that a divorce is beyond my power or yours, unless there's new evidence for one."

"If I try, you wouldn't fight it?"

"Not now. But being a poor husband doesn't constitute grounds in Colorado. I just wanted you to know that I recognize my failing."

She softened toward him a little. This was as close as Walter Kimbrough could ever get to an apology, and she accepted it. "I'm glad. You've come some distance yourself."

"I've been helped along by Polly Pry."

She laughed, and amazingly, he smiled. She could count his smiles on the fingers of her hands.

"I have a request," he continued, mysteriously.

"Strings."

He shrugged. "I don't really know you, Cornelia. I've reached my middle years without knowing my own wife. I'd like to listen to you. Maybe even achieve some level of—if not friendship, then at least a truce. So we can talk."

"I can't think of a thing to say to you."

His gaze darted away, and she knew she had stung him.

"I shouldn't have come," he said.

"The teapot's whistling. Just hang on, and I'll pour some, unless your business is pressing." She waited, her head cocked.

"Tea would be perfect."

She poured some into battered cups, her mind as unruly as her hands. He gripped the saucer and let the cup cool, obviously working toward something.

"I can't repair a marriage. It's too late now. I was thinking the other day I wish I had children. I wish I had what other men have, a companion at home."

She waited suspiciously, damned if she'd cave in to him. She itched to tell him he had had his chance and threw it away, but she bit her tongue.

"I owe you something for some lost years. I'll maintain you in a nice place of your own. I wouldn't set foot in it if you don't want me to. If you take the librarian job, you'll want to live closer in."

"What does it pay?"

"Seventy-five a month."

"I can manage on that."

"I admire you for managing on that."

That hit her hard. She couldn't remember a compliment, or an expression of esteem from him, at least not in private. Years before, he said kind things about her—to others, in social circumstances. "Oh, Walter," she said, and faded away into silence.

"I think you'll enjoy the position. Students are cheerful company. You'll learn medicine by osmosis, and find it a challenge."

"How did this come up? Why are you steering me there? I thought you were dead set against my working."

"I'm a director of the college."

"You'd be my boss—"

"No, no, Cornelia. I thought it might be a way for you to enjoy the rest of your life. Doing something productive. Working with interesting people. Maybe even solving a medical mystery or two."

"But why? Why are you offering me a position?"

He shrugged. "In the small hours of the morning, a man faces truths. Mine is that I'm a cold fish. Before the divorce, it didn't matter. Now, in my middle years, it does."

That was all he would say. She studied him, realizing that half a dozen years apart had changed him—a little.

"I haven't thanked you, and I should. It's a nice offer, and I may take it."

Something changed in his face. "I know you won't come home to live, and I can't change that. But I've spotted a little brick house in Auraria, a short walk from the medical library, and I'd like to buy it for you. They're going to move the university south to a new campus in a few years, but for now, this'll do."

"And what do you want in return?"

He sat silently a long time. "Cornelia, just let me do something for you without hunting for rattlesnakes in the chocolate box. I want to do it."

"Oh. I—I'm not used to this. I apologize."

He extracted a slip of paper from his shirt pocket. "If you want this position, talk to Dr. Silas Adams. He's the medical school dean. I've already recommended you. I think he'll hire you. Here's his address."

She took the slip. "I need to think about all of this."

He stood. "May I have the honor of taking you to lunch? The Roof Garden perhaps? Or any other place?"

"Yes."

"Day after tomorrow? Noon up there?"

"Yes."

"Thank you." He turned almost apologetically, offered his hand, which she took, and then slipped out the door.

She watched him head down the street, her mind crawling with suspicions, curiosity, dread, and also possibility. She would have to sort this out.

She filled her teacup and sat down again, wanting to go through it all. Her mind was awhirl, and she couldn't think rationally. But after she had sipped a minute or two, she did know where to begin. He wouldn't fight if she tried again. That was progress. But was his warning true? Would the Colorado courts throw out a new petition for divorce? The young state was more relaxed about such things than most eastern states, where divorce was all but impossible. She would have to ask Richard Peabody about that.

But did divorce matter so much now? Would it alter her life, now that she had discovered her gifts as a researcher? The youthful dream of love and family wasn't as important as she had thought. Maybe she could make another sort of life at the college, as rewarding as the one she had yearned for. Maybe some day she and Walter could be divorced in some other state.

Well, she'd see. She set down her teacup and changed into a smart frock, and headed out the door. Her first step, plainly, was to see what Dr. Adams had to say, and whether she thought she would enjoy the position. It could be a good life; not what she had dreamed of, but rich and rewarding in its own way, a happy second life.

CHAPTER 72

ornelia had to wait until Dr. Adams finished teaching an anatomy course, but she didn't mind. His office was fascinating, a chaos of books, papers, charts, lithographs of skeletons, and other paraphernalia. He appeared suddenly, in a white smock, grave and graybearded, looking to be just what he was, an academic and physician.

"Ah, yes, they told me you'd be here, Mrs. Kimbrough. Now, about the library position. Your work would consist of everything from manual labor, shelving books, to the highest level of intellect you can command. We're flooded with papers and tracts, medical journals and texts. All these need to be organized. Our previous librarian, Himmelfarb, began an extensive file card index, with cross-references. If a medical journal comes in with articles about toxicology, brain tumors, renal disease, and pathology, you'd want to supply cross-references in all our files. Let's say a student comes in wanting to read every known case and all the literature about ovarian cancer. Your task is to supply him with the references. Can you do it?''

"Yes, but I confess it sounds a bit formidable."

"It is formidable. You have Latin, Mr. Kimbrough tells me. That'd help a great deal. German would help. Koch, over there, is a great man. The Germans are leading the way."

"I don't have German."

"Maybe you could learn it. That'd help. You'll be dealing with material that'll be difficult to cope with sometimes. Are you squeamish?"

"I guess I'll find out," she said.

"Medicine can be horrifying. I like to warn women about that. Medicine deals with topics that you won't find in polite society. Some of these things are so sensitive that they're published in Latin. Why, just the other day we got a book by Krafft-Ebing, written in Latin, and for good reason. *Psychopathia Sexualis.* You get my drift? Are you up to it?"

"I understand. I'm sure I can cope. And if you and the others will teach me your categories, I believe I can index the material helpfully."

"Good. Himmelfarb's not leaving for a fortnight. By then you'll have the system down. Now, are you seeking a serious career position, Mrs. Kimbrough? Surely a person of your background doesn't lack other diversions."

"I discovered I have a knack for this sort of thing—only it was in law—and now I'd like to tackle this. Yes, Doctor, I would consider this a career. It fascinates me."

"We pay rather well, seventy-five a month, because of the responsibility and skills involved."

"Yes. I'd like to try it. Will I be the only woman here?"

He smiled. "Oh, no, we have three female students, and our first will graduate next June. And one of our faculty is a woman, Dr. Bird. She teaches obstetrics and female disease. After you've been here a few years, you'll be almost a physician in your own right."

"Really?"

"Every day, you're going to absorb more medical knowledge than our students. Of course, they'll be doing and acting and dealing with the human body, while you'll be here, reading and organizing, but even so, you'll master the profession."

They talked awhile more, and he showed her the library, which struck her as ruthlessly organized, not chaotic at all. He probed again about her motivation and desire to work, and then, satisfied, offered her the position.

"I accept," she said. "I can start on Monday. I believe I can be an asset to you."

"Ah, grand, grand. A lovely woman like you, why, you'll be therapy for the whole faculty."

She walked down to Auraria and looked at the little brick house Walter offered her, and decided she would take that, too. She felt almost dizzy with change and challenge, but gladdened by it all.

When she met Walter at the Roof Garden, she knew they were generating gossip. But she didn't care. She had been the victim of gossip for years. He welcomed her gravely, and escorted her to a choice table with a view. She studied him while they ordered, still uncertain and bewildered by him. He was not a lovable man, nor would she ever love him. But neither was he the man she had tried to shed years earlier. There could be a truce, and maybe even a tentative friendship. But somehow, that wasn't important. Her new position had swiftly dominated her every thought.

"I have the position, Walter, and I thank you for arranging the meeting. I think I want this more than anything else that's ever happened to me."

"You'll do well. The grand dames of Capitol Hill will secretly admire you, even if they won't admit it."

"That's not my world anymore, if it ever was."

"Would you like the house?"

"If you'd give me that house, Walter, I'd be very pleased and grateful."

He dug into his breastpocket and extracted a folded paper.

"The deed," he said.

"Thank you. When I'm in and it's furnished, I'll have you for tea."

That was how it was going to be. Tea with Walter now and then. He fell into his usual silences, but she had the impulse to talk, so she described her work with the Peabodys, her skill at looking up case law and marking texts, and she even talked about old Homer, that tender old man with too many manners and inhibitions, wondering what Walter thought.

"He was a gifted lawyer," he said neutrally.

And so the lunch ended amiably.

That evening, after packing most of her scanty possessions, she paused to ponder her life. The story of it was clear now, though she didn't know how it all would end. Maybe they could manage a divorce somewhere else, sometime. Maybe she would outlive Walter and remarry in her middle years after all. But she doubted it. She had found a different sort of happy ending. Everything she had dreamed of had gone aglimmering, forever lost to her. She would soon be past childbearing age, and probably would never have dear children or grandchildren. She might never know the joy of a husband's whispers beside her in the night. That dream had withered, but not her life and not her happiness.

She intuited what the future would bring. Hard, fascinating, challenging work. Contact with keen intellects. Swift expansion of her own knowledge and skills. A new profession as a librarian, and a new mastery of the ancient art of healing. She knew she would come to enjoy the young students, the faculty, the delights of academia. She knew she would enjoy herself. All this might not have been her first choice, but some intuition told her that this new life would be better than the one denied her. She felt a pang of loss—what woman wouldn't feel loss at the prospect of a life lived unshared with a loving husband? But that was how life always was and always would be: gain and loss. In this case, though, her story would have a happy ending.

AUTHOR'S NOTES

. . . .

Ever since reading Graham Greene's great novel *The Power and the Glory* a few years ago, I have wanted to write about ordinary people whose interior strengths and courage are not readily apparent to the world. The hero of Greene's novel is a weak and doubting priest who is fleeing for his life during an anticlerical period in Mexico. When at last he is caught and executed, his humble parishioners realize that the despised priest was a man of courage and faith. Greene had shown what singular strength can exist deep in the souls of the most unlikely people, and by showing us how miraculously ordinary people live out their painful lives, he gave us a vision of what we mortals are capable of doing and being; a vision of a divine presence within us.

Second Lives is largely about that vision. For years I've nursed the dream of weaving a novel around that perception, and this is the result. Each of this novel's central characters is a frustrated person with little hope of triumph. Each nurses a shattered dream that is beyond repair, and must turn an undesired life into some sort of worthwhile existence. Each must find the strength to carry on, even when life is dreary.

With that as my goal, I created my characters: Cornelia Kimbrough, bound by Victorian law and circumstance to remain in a marriage that torments her; Homer Peabody, a failing old man who has wrestled all his days with one of those terrible oversized consciences that paralyze people; Lorenzo Carthage, a man enraptured by the Gilded Age vision of opulence, but whose judgment is fatally flawed; Rose Edenderry, a woman who could not govern herself even to save her life; Yves Poulenc, who yearns for death and artistic immortality but is forced to live an

347

ordinary life; and Dixie Ball, who simply has everything taken away from her. These people are frustrated in their primary quest; they never achieve their heart's desire. Each must settle for a lesser life, and find peace, happiness, and a sense of worth in the ruins.

This obviously is a risky theme, and as I write I am not sure whether readers will sit still for it. How much safer it would be to let each of these characters triumph one way or another. And yet, storytelling is more than that. And real life is not so orderly. Such things as disease, or impairment of the senses, or a lifelong bad habit, or a brutal upbringing demolish our hopes, and then our bright dreams fade as the years slide by.

I set the story in Gilded Age Denver precisely because that was a period and place of unbridled pursuit of wealth and ostentation and self-aggrandizement. In that milieu, my characters' dilemmas are all the more sharply etched. I hoped, in the end, to show that all but one of these struggling people weren't defeated at all, and all but one found rewarding ways to spin out their lives, perhaps not the way they hoped, but in the only way they could. Sometimes second lives turn out to be inexpressibly beautiful, sweeter than the original goal, a gift from God.

I have depicted historical characters, such as the Tabors and Guggenheims, Bat Masterson and Doc Holliday, entirely fictionally. This novel re-creates a giddy historical period in Denver and the surrounding hinterlands where the city's great wealth was gathered. But I have not depicted actual historical events. Where I have not been able to unearth certain details about places or buildings—for example the restaurants in the Windsor Hotel—I have invented them.

—Richard S. Wheeler
March, 1996